D

HOW THE
WEST WAS WON

HOW THE WEST WAS WON

LOUIS L'AMOUR

BANTAM BOOKS
TORONTO · NEW YORK · LONDON · SYDNEY

HOW THE WEST WAS WON
A Bantam Book
Bantam rack-size edition / March 1962
Louis L'Amour Hardcover Collection / April 1982

If you would be interested in receiving bookends for The
Louis L'Amour Collection, please write to this address for
information:

The Louis L'Amour Collection
Bantam Books
P.O. Box 956
Hicksville, New York 11802

ISBN 0-553-06215-8

Published simultaneously in the United States and Canada

Bantam Books are published by Bantam Books, Inc. Its
trademark, consisting of the words "Bantam Books" and
the portrayal of a rooster, is Registered in U.S. Patent
and Trademark Office and in other countries. Marca
Registrada. Bantam Books, Inc., 666 Fifth Avenue, New
York, New York 10103.

PRINTED IN THE UNITED STATES OF AMERICA

0 9 8 7 6 5 4 3 2

HOW THE
WEST WAS WON

PART 1

THE RIVERS

The shining land lay open—ready for conquest, and the ways into it were the rivers. Slow and mighty, turbulent and frothing, the rivers were the roads the first settlers took, building rafts, and flatboats, floating down water that was green, brown, black, flecked with foam, but that led ever onward into the heart of that dangerous but unawakened land where riches waited for the bold and the strong.

ONE

The sun was not an hour high when Linus Rawlings came upon the trail of the Ute war party. The high walls of the narrowing valley of the Rio Grande barred all escape, and Linus knew he was in trouble.

A man of infinite patience, he was patient now, sitting his line-backed buckskin in the dappling shadow of the aspens. Behind him trailed three pack horses carrying his winter's catch of furs, while before him the mountain slope lay bright with the first shy green of spring.

Nothing moved along that slope, nor in the valley below . . . only the trembling leaves of the aspen. Linus, never one to accept the appearance of things in Indian country, remained where he was.

Against the background of the aspens he was invisible as long as he remained still, for his clothing, the horses, and their packs were all of a neutral color, blending well with their surroundings. Methodically, his eyes searched the slope, sweeping from side to side, taking in every clump of brush or aspen, every outcropping of rock, each color change in the grass.

It had been a long time since Linus Rawlings had sky-lined himself on the top of a ridge, or slept beside a campfire. He had known men who did both things . . . they were dead now.

3

It was no accident that he always stopped with a background against which his shape could offer no outline.

When in Indian country you never took a risk, whether you suspected an enemy to be near or not. You learned also to make a fire that was small, on which to prepare your meal, and after eating to shift your camp a few miles and sleep in darkness, without a fire.

Such things as these were the simple rules of survival in the Indian country; and besides these, there were others—never to take a step without a weapon, as well as to observe the movements of birds and animals as indications of danger. Linus no longer even thought about the necessity of doing such things, for they had become as natural as breathing.

He saw that the Ute war party comprised a dozen Indians; and if they were headed for a raid on the Spanish settlements to the south, they might well plan a rendezvous with other Indians along the trail. They were only minutes ahead of him, and the question was . . . did they know he was behind them?

He studied the slope with a skeptical eye. Behind his lazy, easy-going façade, Linus Rawlings' mind had been sharpened and his senses honed by thirty-two years of frontier living. Born in the dark forests of western Pennsylvania, where his family had been among the first to settle, Linus had moved west with his father to Illinois when only fifteen, and shortly after his father's death he had taken up with a keelboat outfit and had gone west to trap fur.

In the sixteen years that followed he ranged from the Kootenai River in Montana to the Gila in Arizona, from the shores of the Pacific to the eastern slopes of the Black Hills. He trapped in company with Jim Bridger, Uncle Dick Wootton, Bill Williams, Joe Walker, Osborne Russell, and Jedediah Smith. In those years he left the mountains only twice, aside from a brief visit to the Pueblo of Los Angeles. Those two trips away from the mountains were to St. Louis and New Orleans.

Now Linus searched out the probable line of travel of the war party and studied it with care, but he could see no movement, nothing. But he recalled what Kit Carson had told him many years before: *When you see Indians, be careful. When you do not see them, be twice as careful.*

Linus had great respect for the Indian. He knew him, not as

a poor heathen of whom the white man took advantage, but as a fierce fighting man who lived for war and horse-stealing. The Indian knew the wilderness, and how to live with it. No cat could move more quietly, no hawk had a keener eye; for the Indian lived by and with his senses, and a man could survive in Indian country only by being a better Indian.

Time lagged . . . the morning sun touched the ridges behind him with gold. The grass was still; only the aspens trembled. A pack horse stamped impatiently, a bee buzzed lazily in the low-growing brush.

His rifle lay in front of him across the saddle, the muzzle pointing down slope, his right hand grasping it around the action, thumb resting on the hammer.

Below him and to the right was another, somewhat larger clump of aspen. He gauged its height and his own position. To reach it he need be visible for no more than a minute.

A slight breeze moved behind him dancing the aspen leaves and stirring the grass, and when the breeze and its movement reached him, he moved with its movement, keeping the first clump of aspen behind him. He paused again when he had rounded the second clump, then started down the slope on the opposite angle to that he had been using.

A short distance ahead the narrow valley narrowed still more; then it widened out until it finally opened upon the plains. If the war party knew of him and planned an ambush, that would be the place. Not in the narrows, but just before they were reached or just after leaving them.

When approaching a dangerous place a traveler's attention is directed ahead, toward the likely spot for an ambush, and he overlooks the seemingly innocent ground he is just about to cross. After passing a dangerous place, there is a tendency to let down.

Linus was in no hurry. The fleshpots of the East could wait a few hours or a few days longer. Using infinite care and holding well to the side of the valley, he worked his way along the bottom of the valley, following the river and keeping close to the trees or under them.

When he reached the place where the Utes had crossed, he drew up and allowed his horses to drink, and when they had drunk their fill he dismounted and drank himself, choosing a spot upstream from the horses. He was rising from the ground when he heard the shot.

He remained where he was, without changing position, listening.

How far off? A half mile? A mile?

The second shot barked hoarsely, followed by three more shots fired in rapid succession, one of them overlapping a previous shot.

Stepping into the saddle, he crossed the stream and pushed on, keeping in the shadow of the trees. When he approached a rise in the ground where the stream dipped through a cut, he left the stream and mounted the rise until his eyes could look over the top.

Before him lay a grassy meadow of some three hundred acres or more. On his left the waters of the stream pooled—perhaps behind a beaver dam—and they caught the sunlight and sparkled with the ruffling wind. Beyond the meadow the stream again crossed the valley to flow through the narrows along the opposite side.

At this point the walls of the mountain towered over a thousand feet above the meadow, sloping steeply up to the crests of the ridges. A man on foot might have climbed those walls at almost any point, but at no point could a horse scale them.

A puff of blue smoke hung above the dew-silvered grass, and some fifty yards this side of that smoke a horse was down in the grass, threshing out its life in bitter, protesting kicks.

At first Linus saw nothing else. The morning held still, as if waiting . . . a slight coolness remained in the air despite the bright sun on the ridges. The Indian pony gave one last, despairing kick and died. The blood on its shoulder was bright crimson where it caught the sun. . . . And then an Indian moved.

When the Ute moved, Linus immediately saw two others, their presence revealed by his suddenly focused attention. All were facing down the meadow, their backs toward him.

Obviously the war party had ridden into an ambush. Linus thought they must have been following a party of either Arapahoes or trappers without being aware of it. Rising in his stirrups, he looked beyond the dead horse, and from the vantage point of the knoll he could see them clearly . . . five trappers lying in a buffalo wallow. Undoubtedly their horses were hidden in the trees where the stream again crossed the meadow, with a man or two on guard.

Near the body of the horse lay a dead Indian. If there were any wounded they had been hidden. It was not much of a score against the Indians, and the white men were still outnumbered two to one.

Searching the terrain before him, he picked out several other Indians. The others in the party must be hidden somewhere among the trees along the stream.

There was nothing he could do. To advance was to lay himself open to attack by the Utes, and perhaps by the ambushing party, who might not recognize him as a white man. All he could do was wait . . . a chance might come for him to make a run for it across the open meadow.

Where he was the trees were scattered, but close on his left was the thicker forest along the stream, which meandered back and forth across the narrow valley. Shadows fell about him and he was in a good position to remain unseen. He stayed in the saddle, ready to fight or run, as the developing situation might demand.

The smoke disappeared. The echoes of gunfire lost themselves down the canyon, and the sun crept further down the slope. Here and there the clefts in the mountain allowed shafts of sunlight to reach the meadow and the river.

Birds chirped and twittered in the brush nearby, and Linus relied on them for a warning if an Indian started to move in his direction. His eyes continued to search the meadow.

And then he saw what he had half suspected. Two Indians were creeping through the grass toward the buffalo wallow. When the others fled, these two must have deliberately fallen from their horses in simulated death, for the sole purpose of this attack.

Lifting his rifle, he estimated the distance. The target was poor, the range too great. He was hesitating whether to chance a warning shot when someone fired from the trees where he believed the horses were hidden.

One of the Utes screamed hoarsely and leaped to his feet. Two buffalo guns boomed from the hollow and the Indian was slammed back to the grass, where he struggled an instant, then relaxed and lay still.

The other Ute did not move, and three searching shots sent into the grass near him drew no response from him.

Linus chewed thoughtfully on a stem of grass and considered how rarely combat was as you expected it to be. Moments of smashing, thundering struggle were few; so often it was like this . . . a few lazy-sounding shots in the still air, and then endless minutes of waiting, when nothing happened.

Dew sparkled on the grass, and the birds were twittering again among the willows. His horse stamped a restless hoof against the turf and flicked his tail. The pack horses cropped indifferently at the grass, or stood three-legged, heads down, dozing in the morning warmth.

The position of the trappers was well chosen. Such an ambush in the open was an Indian trick, but obviously the Utes had been surprised by the use of their own tactics. Counterattack on the part of the Indians was difficult, because of the ones in the willows near the stream.

Yet if the stalemate continued until dark, the excellent position of the trappers would be worthless, for the superior numbers of the Indians could close in quickly. The trappers had laid their ambush, but now they had a bear by the tail. When they had failed to destroy the larger part of the party, they left themselves in a bad way.

For some time Linus had realized that his own position was increasingly perilous. Other Indians might come to rendezvous with these, or some Ute might move back far enough to discover him. Once seen, cut off as he was from the other white men, he would be surrounded and killed.

But a sudden attack by him now, from an unexpected quarter, might work in his favor. At that moment, when the Utes were likely to be confused and uncertain, Linus chose to act.

Three Utes were exposed to his rifle. One was some distance away, two were relatively close by. Lifting his rifle, he settled his sights on the spine of the nearest Indian. He took a deep breath, let it out easily, then squeezed off his shot.

The gun boomed in the narrow valley, and the Indian at whom he had fired stiffened sharply, then rolled over, face to the sky. Instantly Linus fired again, then swinging his rifle far left, he squeezed off the third shot, each booming report slamming into the echo of the one before it.

The first shot was a clean hit, the second a miss, the third a hit. Linus slapped his heels into the ribs of his buckskin and fled across the meadow, whooping and yelling.

He counted on the sudden attack, which he had tried to make appear as coming from several men, to surprise the Utes into giving him a running start.

Astonished by the attack, the Utes fled for the brush, and as Linus dashed by the buffalo wallow, he saw the trappers on their feet, firing at the retreating Indians. Drawing up among the trees, Linus saw a lean, powerful man with slightly stooped shoulders drop from a tree.

"Waal, Linus," the man said as he came toward him with a broad grin, "you showed up when the squeeze was tight. Where you come from?"

"Over on the Green."

The other trappers had come in, and they began to mount up. Their pack horses were heavily loaded.

"You took a sight of fur," Linus added.

"Bad year," Williams said, "and then a few weeks back we found us a mountain branch an' took more fur'n we'd took all year."

Williams swung his leg over the saddle. "We're followin' the Rio Grande down to Taos."

Linus moved alongside him. "I'm for the East. Down the Platte and the Missouri, then up the Ohio. I've taken urge to see the ocean water."

"Fancy gals, more'n likely."

"Sure enough. It's a coon's age since I've seen a woman all frilled out an' fussed up. And I aim to. But that there ocean water's been on my mind. I got to thinkin'—a man as old as I am, and I ain't seen nothin' but Indians, mountains, an' fur."

"You'll see water . . . a sight of it. Raised up in North Carolina myself. Never did see the ocean back thataway, but I seen the Pacific. Ain't like mountains, though. You seen it once, you seen it all."

"Most water I ever saw was Salt Lake."

"Folks do say that country back yonder is fillin' up. No time at all, folks say, until they are comin' thisaway. I hear talk of steam cars and a railroad clean to Californy."

"Fool talk," Linus commented. "Who would be fool enough to bring his womenfolk into Injun country? Besides, what's to bring 'em? Fur's gettin' scarce, and there ain't nothing else. Not to speak of."

"Land . . . folks want land."

"The Sioux will have something to say about that, the Sioux an' the Cheyenne, and the Arapahoe."

"You step light back east," Williams warned, "or you'll lose your hair. More devilment back east than in all these mountains. I hear tell the women folk really lay for a man back there . . . ain't like Injun country where you swap a buck a couple of blankets and two, three ponies for a squaw."

Linus traveled with the trappers for two days. The wind blew cold when he parted from them, but the flush of green was on the hills and the trees were leafing out. Here and there were dark patches where the earth was still damp from the melted snow.

Linus Rawlings rode with care. After all, this was Ute country.

If all the Indians were like the Shoshones, Nez Perce or the Flatheads, it would have been different. A man could get to know them; to know them was to like them. The Nez Perce made the boast that no warrior of their tribe had ever killed a white man, and Linus was ready to believe it.

But this was Ute country and next to the Blackfeet no tribe was more trouble to the white man, and beyond the Utes were the Arapahoe.

TWO

E ve Prescott stood alone, a few feet back from her family, watching the boats that thronged the Hudson River and the Erie Canal. The shore was piled high with bales, barrels, and crates, merchandise and household goods, all awaiting shipment to the West. Nothing on the farm where she had lived until then, or in the tiny village nearby, had prepared her for this.

Big, roughly dressed men pushed back and forth, shouting, wrangling good-naturedly, loading or unloading boats and wagons. Huge drays rumbled past, drawn by the largest horses she had ever seen, big Percherons or Clydesdales. On the river there was the shrill piping of whistles, the clang of bells, and the sound of steam exhausts.

Bunched about the Prescotts were other emigrants like themselves, huddled about their goods and clothing, waiting for the call that would take them aboard a canal boat. They, too, were cutting all their ties, leaving all that was familiar behind, venturing into a new and frightening country.

Looking about her, she saw other men like her father, men who talked loudly of the Ohio country, of taking up new land, of opportunity, the black earth, rainfall, and the wild game to be had for the hunting. They talked loudly to cover their own

11

dismay; for it is one thing to talk of and plan a venture—there is room for excitement, enthusiasm, and conjecture—but it is quite another thing to actually begin a new life, to take one's family and step off into the nothingness of the unknown as these men were doing.

They had been bold before, and Eve, knowing such men, knew they would be bold again, but now they were frightened, as she was.

Now she felt her heart pounding, and she seemed to have difficulty in breathing. All this activity was so impersonal. These bold-eyed men shoving past her, shouting at their work— what could they care about her, about her family? Yet here and there her eyes intercepted a bold, appreciative glance that warned her these men *could* care . . . on one level, at least.

She was surprised to find that she was excited and pleased by such glances rather than repelled. Back home every man had been catalogued; she knew the ones who were married, and therefore ineligible, and those who were single. She knew exactly how to gauge each man's interest in her, and what it meant or could mean—and she had not been interested in any of them.

Also, they knew *her*. They knew she was not to be lightly had by any man, and they found her stand-offish when they came courting with marriage in mind. She felt no real regret for what she was leaving behind, other than the fact that she was leaving all that was familiar, all that she had known.

She was leaving the familiar fields and trees, the school where she had learned to read, write, and work sums, the house where she knew every board that creaked, and could tell how the fireplace would act on clear or cloudy days, or when the wind was strong.

Inwardly she shrank from the dust, the coal smoke, and the confusion of Albany. The green fields of her upstate home had been fresh and cool. They had been home—but they were home no longer.

The farm had been sold. Other feet trod the boards of the house now, and it was just as well. She felt that there was nothing for her.

"You dream too much!" Her father often told her that in his half-irritated yet affectionate way, and it was true. Now her dreams lay westward, somewhere down the Ohio.

She knew only vaguely where the Ohio River lay, or the lands to which they were going, those uncertain lands, theirs for the taking, which no one had seen. Her father had not even seen a map, if any existed. All they had seen was some scratchings in the dirt near the back stoop as a drifter traced with a stick the course of the Ohio River and pointed out the lands that lay open to taking.

The Ohio country was the wild west, the wilderness. And that was where they were going.

For several years now she had been hearing that name . . . the Ohio . . . until it was burned into her consciousness. Men talked of it as they talked of the Promised Land.

Nearby a bearded man talked knowingly of the Missouri and the Platte, of keelboating and the fur trade. He was talking to two drunken Canalers about the Indians in the wild lands along those rivers. She had never heard of either of those distant rivers—the Ohio was far enough west for her.

A self-contained girl, she quietly watched the movement about her, but her thoughts were far away in that yet unknown Ohio country. If she had met no one here, how could she expect to find anyone out there where there were even fewer people? More than one of her friends had settled for less than they wanted. When a girl passed eighteen she began to feel a little desperate. Her face, though, showed none of the thoughts that were held tightly within her.

Her sister Lilith, slender, pretty, and sixteen, turned swiftly and came to her side. "Oh, isn't it *exciting*, Eve? But I don't understand why we have to go *west*. Why can't we stay *here*?"

"Pa's a farmer. He's got to go where there's land to be taken. Besides, you'd soon find this very dull. Things are only exciting until you get used to them, until you know their pattern, and then it all becomes humdrum."

"But don't you ever want to do anything *different*? Eve, I just don't understand you at all!"

"Why should you? Sometimes I think you don't even understand yourself."

Lilith glanced quickly at her sister. "But you do, don't you? I mean, you know what you want, and everything. I wish I did." Her brow furrowed. "Eve, I don't know what's the matter with me. All I know is that I don't—I just don't want any of this . . .

of the farm, either." She looked out over the crowded river. "Am I bad? Or just a fool? I mean, I dream about so many things . . . impossible things."

"Are they impossible, Lil? If you can dream of them, maybe they are possible. And in the meantime they help you to be happy. It helps . . . I know it helps."

"It's easier for you. You know what you want. You want a man, and you even know the kind of man . . . and you want a home. That . . . that isn't what I want at all. Not for a while, at least."

"I know."

"Eve . . . what if you never find him? After all, you're twenty and an—"

"And an old maid?" Eve smiled. "Don't be afraid to say it, Lil. But I know I'll find him. I just know I shall."

A shrill, piping whistle came from a boat on the river, and then a blast from the horn of a canal boat. The boat reversed its wheels and the water flew.

"It isn't a place that makes you happy or unhappy, Lil, it's the people you love, and who love you."

"Ma says I'm flighty. Do you think I am, Eve?"

"No." Eve paused. "You're different from us, Lil, but in your own way you're just as steady. I never did see anybody catch on to the accordion the way you did. . . . Pa says you take after Aunt Mae."

"The one who ran off with a gambler? Pa has never said any such thing to me! Why, he would never even mention her name in front of us! Whatever happened to her, Eve? Was she awfully unhappy?"

Just then their brother Sam, a lean, husky young man of nineteen, with a quick, easy smile, came strolling up from the river and paused alongside of Zeke, who was lying on their rolled-up bedding. "It will be soon now," he said. "How are you, Zeke?"

Zeke opened his eyes abruptly. "I ain't half as poorly as ma makes out. If she'd stop spooning that medicine into me, I think I'd get well."

Eve's eyes went from her brother to her parents. Zebulon and Rebecca Prescott looked every inch of what they were— sturdy, independent farmer folk . . . and pioneers. At first her mother had objected to leaving a home that was becoming more comfortable year by year; but once their decision had been made, the excitement had taken hold of her too.

Zebulon's best argument was a good one. They were not getting rich where they were, which was not important, for they lived well, but there was no land for the boys—not for more than one of them, at least.

Suddenly there was a surge in the crowd about them and over the confusion they heard a voice proclaiming: "The *Pride of Utica*, now loading! All a-boarrrd for the *Pride of Utica*! The Ramsey family . . . the Peter Smiths . . . John and Jacob Voorhies . . . L. P. Baker . . . the Stoeger family, all eight of them . . . all a-boarrrd for the *Pride of Utica!*"

"We're next, pa," Sam said, stooping to lift a trunk to his shoulder. "We'd best move down to the shore."

A gaunt Scotsman in a faded homespun shirt let his glance fall to Zeke, who was struggling up from his temporary couch. "The boy's health your reason for goin' west, Prescott?"

"Partly . . . only partly. Mostly," Zebulon said gravely, "our trouble was rocks. Why, there'd be years when we'd crop a hundred bushels of rocks to the acre."

"Now, Zebulon, you shouldn't lie to the man like that. Ours was good land."

"Lie? Now, Rebecca, you know I'm a God-fearing man, and I'd not lie. I tell the truth as I see it. Why, in that country where we lived a man never used a plow. He just blasted out the furrows with gun powder.

"Time came it was too much for me. When I hauled the bucket out of the well, even that was full of rocks, and I says to myself, 'Zeb, here you be with an ailin' son an' a twenty-year-old daughter who won't take to herself a husband—' "

"Pa! How you do go on!"

" '—and another daughter who acts like she ain't just right in the head,' so I just made myself a vow. If I could find a man who had five hundred dollars there'd be another fool ownin' that farm. Well, sir, the Good Lord provided such a man and here we are!"

"Mr. Harvey," Rebecca protested, "don't you believe a word of it. We had the best farm in the county. It was pa's itching foot that brought us to this, and heaven knows where we'll end up."

"I'm headed for Illinois," Harvey replied, "and folks say there are grown men out there who have never seen a rock."

He gestured toward the three hulking young men who lurked nearby, staring hungrily at the girls. "These are my boys, Angus, Brutus, and Colin. I think they want to become acquainted with your daughters."

"Single, I take it."

Harvey nodded. "So far . . . but they're girlin'."

"That Illinois country sounds good to me. Lilith, take up your accordion an' strike up a tune for the lads."

"I ain't in the mood, pa."

"Lilith," her father said sternly, "there's a time for coaxin', but this here ain't it. You play something."

She shrugged, and picking up the accordion with a disgusted glance at Eve, she started to play and sing "Miss Bailey's Ghost." It became apparent at once that she both played and sang with an uncommon flair.

"Now, you see here, Lilith! You know better than to play that one! Play something the boys can sing."

She glanced at the three boys. "What songs do you know?"

"I can sing 'Yankee Doodle,' " Colin suggested.

" 'Yankee Doodle'!" Lilith stared at them scornfully. "Who wants to sing *that*?"

"Their ma's dead," Harvey explained apologetically. "They ain't had much schoolin' in the social graces, but they are good boys, an' strong."

"Go ahead, Lilith. Give them 'A Home in the Meadow.' "

Lilith looked at Eve again and shrugged, indicating her distaste for the whole idea, but she began to play and sing.

Prescott turned to his older daughter. "Eve!"

Reluctantly, Eve joined in, no more impressed with the three hulking, hovering Harvey boys than Lilith was. Coming closer, the boys began to follow the words of the song and, caught by the spirit of the thing, Zebulon himself started to sing in a deep, strong voice.

"Zeb!" Rebecca warned. "Mind you don't drown them out!"

Several people from nearby groups drifted over to join in. As the group grew in number, Lilith lost her reluctance and, stepping out from the others, began to lead the singing with zest.

They sang for pleasure, without self-consciousness, or even

awareness that most of them sang badly, and their singing seemed to brighten the whole shore. Men straightened from their work to listen, and from a distance a deck hand on one of the river boats joined in. A half-drunken Irishman cut a few quick steps in time to the music, and for a brief time that somber shore echoed to the sound of their voices.

As the song ended, Lilith, captured by the mood of her own playing, swung into "The E-ri-e Canal," and everyone within hearing joined in. But they had scarcely completed the first chorus when the despatcher's voice boomed out, "Loadin' for the *Flyin' Arrow*! All a-boarrrd for the *Flyin' Arrow*!"

Zebulon picked up a heavy sack. "That's us! Pick up an' let's go!"

As they had moved closer on Sam's suggestion, they were only a few steps from the gangway, and Lilith, waving a response to the shouted good-byes of several of the singers, struck up a lively march and led the passengers aboard the waiting canal boat.

The deck was crowded and Eve was pushed to the rail, where she turned her back on the boat and looked back at Albany. Her throat was tight, for the very act of boarding the boat seemed to have finally committed them to a course from which there could be no retreat.

From Albany, a person could walk home if need be, and in Albany they were still among their own kind of folks, but the mere act of stepping aboard had put an end to all that. It was an act so different from any she had ever taken, and it indicated how deeply they were now involved. Now they no longer had roots. They were adrift.

All around strangers crowded, easy-going, boisterous strangers, but at that moment even her own family looked strange. Eve had stepped into another world, and she was frightened.

Under lowering gray skies, the clouds swollen with impending rain, the *Flying Arrow* started to move. Out upon the canal bank, a man in a checked shirt drove the team along the towpath, hauling the boat.

Slowly, as the passengers found places for their boxes and bundles, the stir upon the decks settled down. From behind her, Eve could hear the mutter of voices and occasional laughter.

From the Hudson River at Albany to Lake Erie at Buffalo, a ditch four hundred and twenty-five miles long had been dug. The digging had been done by several thousand wild, bog-trotting Irishmen fresh from the old country, and they had been eight years in the digging.

Governor DeWitt Clinton had opened the canal in the fall of 1825, and it was a major step in opening the West to settlement. Within twenty years, Ohio leaped from thirteenth state in population to third, and the population of Michigan increased by sixty times. Four thousand boats plied the waters of the canal, and more than twenty thousand people lived upon its waters.

The Irish had built the canal, and they set the pattern for much that followed. Life along the waterway was a continual brawl and a struggle. Men fought over drinks, over women, over space at the docks, over horses, over anything they could think of . . . often enough they fought for the sheer joy of fighting.

Some of the Irish stayed with the canal, others moved west to build the railroads or to join the Indian-fighting army. Many an old-time army roster reads like a voter's list from Belfast or Dublin. A time came when their sons and grandsons were no longer despised as "shanty" Irish, becoming political, social, and industrial leaders in fifty cities—respected, honored, and wealthy men.

A canalboat had a crew of three to four persons. A boy or man, working for seven to ten dollars a month, drove the team along the towpath to haul the boat. The steersman might earn as much as thirty dollars a month, which was good pay for the time. The captain often did his own steering; otherwise, he sat on deck smoking his pipe and shouting insults at the other boats. Sometimes the cook was the captain's wife; more often she was one of the thousands of women who followed the canal, taking up with this boater or that, as jealous of her independence as any man on the ditch.

Of all shapes and sizes, and of every color, the boats moved up or down the canal, fighting or racing for cargo, all their actions accompanied by the shouting of men and the long-drawn-out sound of the horns—the horns of the boats along the Erie Canal.

The westward movement of which they were a part was more than a hundred years old, but only now had it gained the impetus that was to make it unique in the world's history.

There had always been men who went west, who probed the wilderness; there had been trappers of fur and traders with the Indians who each season went a little further into the wilderness. Like the mountain men who went to the ultimate West, they were adventurers and hunters, and they were single men. They filtered through the mountains and down the Ohio, and finally to the Mississippi. Daniel Boone was such a man.

Then in 1803 Jefferson made the Louisiana Purchase, and overnight the young nation became a land of far-reaching boundaries. And with this change came a change in the national psychology.

The Lewis and Clark expedition went west, exploring a route across the distant mountains and down to the Pacific; and when they returned, a few, like John Coulter, elected to remain in the West. After them came Kit Carson, Jim Bridger, Bill Williams, Joe Walker . . . and Linus Rawlings.

Boys from the farms walked away from their plows and headed west. St. Louis or Independence was the jumping-off place. Standing on the streets, the farm boys watched the keelboats and canoes come down the Missouri from the Platte and the Yellowstone, and they watched the buckskin-clad men with the cool eyes come ashore, their leggings and breechclouts leaving their bottoms exposed and brown as the buckskins they wore. Around the river-front taverns they consorted with river-front women, drank and shouted and told great yarns of the far-off mountains, the rushing streams of white water, and the fair Indian maidens. The farm boys listened and envied.

Some said it was fur that took them west, and some said it was gold or land; but in the last analysis it was simply the West that took them west. All the other things were easy excuses, obvious explanations for obvious questions. They went west for the wild, free life, the love of high adventure among the lonely peaks, and for the call of the open prairie where the long winds blew down a thousand miles of grassland.

They went by the Erie Canal, by the Wilderness Road, by

the Natchez Trace, and strange names came back to awaken strange longings in the ears of listening men, names that made them restless and eager-eyed.

Men went west along the Overland Trail, the Santa Fe Trail, the Oregon Trail, the Hastings Cut-Off, the Applegate Road. And many of them left their blood upon the land, but where they died others followed and lived.

Upon the plains they met the Indian, the greatest light cavalryman who ever lived and rode. The Indian lived for warfare and battle. He swept down upon the camps of the white men, and where he defeated them he looted and burned and tortured, returning to his villages laden with plunder. But still the white men came.

But now there was a difference in their coming, for they brought their women along. They came to stay.

The young, the old, the middle-aged—none were immune to the dream that drew men to the West. The weak fell by the way, or gave up and went back to their villages and safe streets to huddle frightened with others of their kind, but the strong survived or went down fighting, and those who survived grew even stronger.

It was a time of exploration, of struggle, of titanic men walking a titanic land. It was an age akin to the Homeric or the Elizabethan, and a man bred to either age would have been at home in the West, and would have talked the language of the men about him.

Achilles and Jim Bowie had much in common; Sir Francis Drake and John Coulter or Kit Carson would each have understood the other.

They were men of violence all, strong men of strong emotions, men who lived with strength and skill. Ulysses could have marched beside Jedediah Smith, Crockett could have stormed the walls of Troy. Either would have been at home among the crews of Drake, Hawkins, or Frobisher.

Eve Prescott stood by the rail as the canalboat moved slowly along the dark waters; behind her the strange, musical, poetic names were spoken and their sound stirred her blood.

They were wonderful, exciting names, each one the symbol

of some wild romance. Santa Fe and Taos, Ash Hollow and the
Cross Timbers, the Arkansas, Boggy Depot, the Washita . . .
Cottonwood Creek and the South Fork of the Cimarron . . .
there was a magic in their sound.

The canal banks slid by, sunlight reflected from the staring
windows of houses, and then the sudden call would ring out:
"Bridge! Bridge! Duck your heads or lose your scalps!"

The great horns blared; from a voice nearby she caught the
strange word Arapahoes; beyond it, other voices, all in their
separate conversations, sent words that drifted to her ears in a
confused medley that nonetheless made music.

"I favor the North carbine. Nobody can make a carbine like
Simeon North" . . . "Cheyennes" . . . "lost his hair" . . .
"Spanish Fork" . . . "Hal's patent, by Simeon North" . . .
"percussion rifle? What if you run out of caps? I favor the
flintlock . . . pick up a flint anywheres" . . . "Comanches"
. . . "river pirates" . . . "Texas" . . . "live off the country"
. . . "fur so thick you wouldn't believe it" . . . "thieves everywhere" . . . "river pirates."

The horns sounded . . . "Bridge!" . . . a whip cracked like a
pistol from the towpath . . . "too far south for Sioux" . . .
"down the Ohio" . . . "never seen again" . . . "Bridge!" The
horns again, blaring, the sound echoing back from the hills.

Sam came up suddenly beside her. "Hey, ain't you excited,
Eve? I wondered where you'd got to. Think of it, Eve, we'll
build rafts and float down the Ohio. Ain't that something?"

"Yes, Sam. Yes, it is."

But her thoughts were asking: Would that man she had
never seen, that man of whom she dreamed, would he be out
there somewhere? In the Ohio country?

She looked up at Sam, so eager, so ready for the challenge.
Suddenly she felt a sharp pang of fear, so sharp she almost
cried out. "Be careful, Sam," she said, almost whispering it.
"Oh, be careful!"

He grinned at her, his eyes dancing. "Careful? What's there
to be careful about?"

THREE

E ve Prescott straightened up from the fire and brushed back a lock of her hair. Her face was hot from the flames and she stood back for a minute, listening to the bubbling of the pot.

The tall trees towered above them, blacker than the night itself, even this night without stars. They were ancient, massive trees . . . her father, Sam and Zeke could scarcely have reached around the smallest of them with hands joined.

The wind moved among the branches, and the fire sputtered briefly . . . out by the riverbank, not twenty yards away, the water rustled mysteriously.

The bright gaiety and easy talk of the Erie Canal lay far behind them. They had left the canal at its terminus in Buffalo and had paid a few dollars for a decrepit two-wheeled cart which would hold all their goods. Together they had pushed and hauled it nearly three hundred miles to the Ohio, and there rafts had been built—they had built one for themselves, and the Harveys, who were traveling with them, had built one.

Now the two rafts were tied to trees near the bank, and in the morning they would be gone again, floating the day long down the river that by now seemed endless. It was a strange life, this traveling. Each day was sufficient unto itself, and as long as they traveled there need scarcely be any thought except

for today. Everything else was suspended until their journey
was finished.

The fire was a comfort. Even here in this clearing by the
river's edge the distances seemed enormous. Sam and pa were
rigging a canvas shelter for the night, and ma was cutting slices
from a haunch of venison killed that morning by Sam.

Eve was beginning to realize what the wilderness could do to
a man. For the first time she became aware of a subtle alter-
ation in the attitudes of her parents toward each other. Ma had
always been strong, and had stood upon an equal footing with
Zebulon, and even at times superseded him in authority. Now
she deferred more to pa. Zebulon went about everything—
making camp, chopping wood, and all the other camp duties—
with a quiet assurance, a forcefulness she had never noticed
before. Never before had Eve realized what a tower of strength
he was.

In the wilderness a man grew important, for on his strength
others must depend. More than ever she could understand
why men loved the wilderness, for it made demands on their
strength, on their ingenuity; and they loved the feeling of
doing and of accomplishment that the wilderness provided.

Eve sat down and took up her book, leaning closer to the
flames to see the print better. Lilith came up to the fire, and
Eve looked up.

"Lilith . . . listen to this: 'Theirs was a poignant parting in
the forest. The handsome young backwoodsman carved two
hearts on a tree trunk, and then, from ten paces, hurled a knife
at the junction of the two hearts—' "

"Junction—what's that mean?"

"It's where the two hearts come together. Now be quiet and
listen: 'His marksmanship was uncanny. Three times he hurled
the knife. "That was for luck," he said the first time, and "that
was for love," after the second. "That was a prayer, a plea for
love undying—" ' " And then Eve added, dreamily, "Isn't that
beautiful?"

"I reckon. If anybody ever talks like that."

"It's the sentiment, not the talk."

"You don't make sense, Eve. You want to be a farmer's wife,
but you'll never find a farmer who's the kind of man you want.
You don't really want to marry a farmer."

"Neither do you."

"I don't want anything to do with farms." Lilith stared at the fire. "I want silk dresses and fine carriages like those we saw back in Albany."

She turned her head to look at Eve. "I want a man to smell good, and I want to go out to eat in fancy places. All I want seems to be back east, yet here we are, going further and further away. But you wait—I'll have those pretty dresses, and all."

"You're only sixteen, Lil. There's plenty of time. Besides, it's the man that counts, not where he lives."

"The man you want doesn't live, never has, and never will."

"I don't believe that, Lil. I just can't believe it. I know how I feel, and I can't be the only one who feels this way. I want a man who loves me, not just one who needs a wife to do for him. Somewhere there's a man who feels as I do."

"And you think you'll find him out west?" Lilith scoffed.

"Where else? A man who would think like that would be likely to go west, it seems to me. There'd be poetry in him, and that sort of man would incline toward mountains and forest. As far as farming goes, there's poetry in farming, too. Hard work, of course, but most things worth doing are hard, and a man who plows the earth, plants seed, and watches his crops grow—I think there's poetry in that. One time I heard a man say that all real strength comes from the earth, and I believe it."

"Eve!" Rebecca called. "Watch that stew! Time to put the onions in!"

Zebulon and Sam came up to the fire. "We must keep a sharp lookout tonight, Sam," Zebulon said. "There's talk of river pirates and folks murdered for their goods. With the womenfolks to think of, we'll have to watch special sharp."

"I'll set the first half of the night, pa. You can set the second half. Those Harveys," he added, "they sleep too sound for comfort." He glanced at the trees. "They say where they're goin' there's plains . . . folks say it's an altogether different way of livin'. Rich soil they say—deep as a man wants to dig, it's rich soil."

"A man wants to build close to fuel," Zebulon argued. "What's he going to burn, come wintertime? You boys never rustled for

wood like I done as a youngster. Not that I had far to go, but
any distance is too far, come wintertime."

He listened to the ring of an axe from the Harvey camp.
"Strong boys," he said. "I wish Eve would set her cap for one
of them."

"Now, pa," Sam protested mildly, "you don't wish nothing of
the kind. Those boys aren't for Eve . . . nor for Lilith. They're
good enough men, I expect, and good men to work beside, but
Eve and Lilith—they're different. They weren't cut out to
marry with men like those."

The two girls had moved away from the fire, and the men
could hear water splashing as they bathed near the lean-to.

"Don't see no reason why they should be so all-fired different. Your ma's a sensible woman."

"They get it from you," Sam replied reasonably. "Those
stories you're always a-telling . . . how you went off to Albany
to see those show-folk. I declare, pa, sometimes I think you
don't know your own mind. Take this trip, now. And don't get
me wrong—I was for it. So was ma, for that matter. But don't
you forget you cut loose from a good farm to go west. Now why
d'you suppose that was? You've got a feeling for different
things. You like change, and color, and folks singing, and I see
nothing wrong in it. But you marry one of our girls to a Harvey
and you'll break her heart."

"You're talking nonsense," Zebulon growled, but he was
pleased despite himself. "Still . . . did I ever really tell you
about those show-folk? Sam, there was a gal there in a red
spangled dress—you never seen the like."

Suddenly they heard a man running, and turned as Zeke
came up to them, his eyes wide and excited. "Pa . . . there's
something out on the river. Seemed like I heard a paddle
splash."

Brutus Harvey had started for the river with a bucket. Now
he turned and walked out on the raft to get a better view of the
river, away from the glare of the firelight.

"No honest man would travel the river at this hour of the
night," Zebulon said positively, and went to get his rifle.

"Can't see but one man," Brutus said, just loud enough for
them to hear.

Sam took his rifle and slipped away into the darkness. Already the wilderness had begun to weave its pattern around them, and the ancient instincts, so long dead, were coming back again—the instinct for darkness, to remain concealed until an enemy has revealed himself.

Harvey and his son Colin walked over from their fire, and there was an assuring competence about them that Sam was quick to appreciate.

"They tell me it's a trick of river pirates to lie out of sight in the bottom of a boat until close up," Harvey said, "and then they jump you."

Brutus put down his bucket and crouched down beside the raft's hut and drew a huge pistol from his belt.

The canoe came slowly from the darkness, a paddler seated in the stern. The rest of the canoe was covered with sewn deerskins, under it a bulky cargo.

"Rides low," Zebulon Prescott whispered to Harvey. "There could be men in her, all right." Stepping out into the light from the fire, which was some distance behind him, Prescott said, "Just come in slow and easy, stranger, and keep your hands where we can see 'em."

Linus Rawlings let the canoe glide under the last impetus of the paddle. In the background he could see women standing, and from the shadows near the trunk of the nearest tree he caught the gleam of a rifle barrel. Another man crouched, scarcely visible, on the nearer raft. They were the only two who acted as a man should.

Farmers, he thought. *If they go on west they'll lose their hair. Excepting maybe for two of them.*

"Hold your fire," he said casually. "Name's Linus Rawlings, hungrier'n sin and peaceful as your Aunt Alice."

Harvey walked down to the bank and peered suspiciously at the bundles under the deerhide. "What you got there?"

"Beaver peltry." As Harvey stepped closer for a better look, Linus Rawlings' voice lowered and chilled. "I said *beaver pelts.*"

Harvey hesitated, still suspicious, but aware of the implied threat in Rawlings' tone. "You're almighty touchy," he said irritably.

"Out west," Linus replied, "you don't question a man's word." Seeing the doubt in Harvey's eyes, and realizing he was a tenderfoot, he added in a more friendly tone, "We run short on lawyers and notaries west of here, so when a man gives you his word, you believe it. And when a man's word proves no good, he's finished . . . he'll be trusted by nobody, nor can he do business, anywhere.

"Result is—" Linus moved the canoe alongside the raft and stepped out of it as he talked—"you call a man a liar and it means shooting."

He tied up the canoe, and when he straightened up he saw the girl standing beside the other man. She was slender, but beautifully rounded, and she had a poised, proud way about her that he liked . . . like a young doe at the edge of a clearing.

"I never had a chance to look at a beaver pelt, Mr. Rawlings," Eve said. "Would you show me one of yours?"

"Well, ma'am, in that case—"

He knelt on the edge of the raft and loosened the rawhide thongs which bound the deerhide in place, and from beneath it he drew a beaver pelt. The fur was thick, brown and lustrous. When he stood up to hand it to her she realized for the first time how tall he was.

There was a kind of quizzical good humor in his face that she immediately liked, yet there was coolness and a quiet strength such as she had never seen in anyone before.

"It's soft," Eve said, "real soft."

"That's a prime pelt."

"We was afeared you might be a pirate," Harvey said. "We've heard tell of them."

"Come up to supper," Prescott added, "and get acquainted. We would admire to hear talk of the western lands."

Eve handed the pelt to Linus, but gently he pushed it back. "It's a present. You keep it, ma'am."

Too surprised to thank him, she held the pelt close against her cheek, watching his lean back as he walked to the fire with her father.

Lilith moved up beside Eve. "Well!" she whispered. "You wasted no time! Is that the backwoodsman you've set your cap for? Likely he's got a wife and six kids waiting for him back east."

Sam came from the shadows and walked to the fire, and Linus glanced at him. "You'll do. Pays to be careful."

Sam flushed with embarrassed pride. "Mister, that's a fine rifle you've got there. Have you been all the way to the shining mountains?"

"Lived in 'em. Been fourteen years from home."

He seated himself cross-legged a little back from the firelight and accepted a plate from Rebecca Prescott. The Harveys trooped over, bringing their pots and kettles and placing them around the Prescott fire.

"That land to the west," Harvey asked, "is it good farm land?"

"Hadn't farming in mind, but some of it is, I reckon. Maybe most of it. Trouble is that folks back east spent two hundred years learning how to pioneer in timber country, and when they first see the plains they call it a desert. It ain't nothing of the kind. Just a different way of living, that's all."

He cleaned his plate and accepted a refill. Lilith had begun playing "I Wish I was Single" on the accordion, playing softly to keep from disturbing the conversation.

"You're traveling late," Harvey commented.

"Anxious to reach Pittsburgh. It's been years since I've seen a city, and I aim to whoop it up a mite."

"Are those mountains out there as high as they say?" Sam asked.

"Now, about that—" Linus frowned thoughtfully, emptying his plate—"I can't rightly say. Jim Bridger and me, we started out one time to climb one of those itty bitty foothills. That was early June. About mid-July we were gettin' pretty well up toward the actual mountains when we seen a feller with nice white wings and a harp in his hands. 'Jim,' I says, 'I don't like the way that feller is lookin' at us.' Jim, he looked and he said, 'Neither do I.' So we skedaddled back down again, and to this day I can't rightly say how high those mountains are."

In the brief silence that followed, Zebulon cleared his throat, but before he could say anything, Rebecca spoke. "Now, Zebulon, you just stop. One liar's enough."

Linus passed his plate to Rebecca, who refilled it without comment, and Linus said, "Thanky, ma'am. That there's right tasty."

"Don't know how you could tell," she said shortly. "You've already had two plates."

"Doesn't pay to eat too much on an empty stomach, ma'am, but I can't say I ever et better."

Zebulon got to his feet. "Bedtime . . . we make an early start. You'll have breakfast with us, Mr. Rawlings?"

"Thanky, Mr. Prescott, but sometimes I wake up and take the urge to move. By sun-up I may be long gone. Good night."

Linus Rawlings took up his rifle and moved away from the fire, pausing to glance at the arrangement of the camp. Grudgingly, he admitted that for tenderfeet they had placed their camp wisely, and when he saw Sam Prescott settling down to stand watch, he turned his back and walked toward his canoe.

Movement under a tree near the shore drew his attention, and he saw Eve kneeling there, spreading blankets over a pile of neatly cut boughs. The distinctly Indian pattern of the blankets was obvious even in the dim light.

"Those look like my blankets."

"They are."

"Then I'm a mite confused. Whose bed would that be?"

"Yours."

"You cut all them boughs?"

"Is it enough?" she asked anxiously. "I never made a bough bed before."

"You did right well." He glanced at her warily. "Why? Why would you do a thing like this? You ain't thinkin' you've got to pay me for that beaver pelt?"

She got to her feet, as gracefully as any Indian girl. "It ain't . . . isn't polite to ask a girl why she does things."

"My manners ain't much, ma'am. Had no use for them for some time now." He placed his rifle carefully on the boughs where his hand could fall easily upon it. "Thanky, ma'am, an' good night."

She made no move. "Are those Indian girls pretty?"

"Some of them . . . some of the others—well, it depends on how long since you've seen a white girl. They get prettier an' prettier as time goes by, seems to me."

"How long since you have seen a white girl?"

Linus was cautious. He was too experienced a trapper not to be wary, and he sensed trouble. "I ain't quite sure where you're headed, ma'am, but it's gettin' right late. Your pa might—"

"How pretty do I look to you?"

"Ain't you bein' a bit forrard, ma'am? I mean . . . well, you'd be a mighty pretty girl if a man never went away at all. You'd be counted pretty wherever, but it seems to me this conversation is headed right into some mighty swampy country."

"You're headed upriver and I'm going down. There isn't much time to get questions answered."

"Are you sure—dead sure—you want 'em answered?"

She was proud, he thought suddenly, very proud. It was not like her to talk so to just any man . . . she had gumption, all right.

And she was lovely. He had scarcely dared look before, not being a forward man himself, and knowing from long experience that strangers had better be careful in their attentions to womenfolk. He shifted his feet uneasily. This thing had come upon him too fast, and he was not accustomed to judging such situations quickly. If it had been a buffalo, now, or a cougar . . . or any kind of a redskin . . . but this was a civilized white girl, and a very pretty one.

"Are you sure, ma'am?" he repeated.

"Yes."

"Bein' alone at nighttime . . . in the forest and all . . . it ain't exactly the safest place for a girl to be. There's something about the woods, ma'am—it stirs need in a man."

"In a woman, too."

He shifted his feet. This was getting out of hand. He was ready as the next man, but this here . . . she was a decent girl, with her folks hard by.

"I've come a far piece, ma'am, and I'm goin' on. You'll likely never see me again."

"There is a chance of that." She looked straight into his eyes. "I would be sorry if that happened."

He took her by the shoulders and drew her toward him. She came willingly, yet with a certain reserve that let him know this was something special, something different for her. He took her in his arms and held her close and kissed her. He kissed her thoroughly, becoming more interested as the seconds fled, but he kissed her no more thoroughly than she kissed him.

She stepped back, breathless. "Glory be!"

Linus was startled to find himself a bit breathless too, and the feeling worried him. "Ma'am . . . seems like you've not done much kissing before."

"I never been kissed permanent before."

Uneasily, he glanced toward the fire, almost wishing her father would come looking for her. Linus Rawlings had never cared for the word "permanent" and it aroused all his old-time wariness, which had been in danger of subsiding.

"There's something you shouldn't forget. I'm headed upriver and you're goin' down."

"Lovers have parted before, and they have come together again."

So it was lovers they were now? Linus hesitated, uncertain of what to say. He had a notion he should turn and run . . . run like a yellow-bellied coward. He should leave the bed, his blankets . . . even his rifle if need be.

"Ma'am—"

"Eve."

"Eve, I been a sinful character. Deep-down, black, rock-bottom sinning. I'm headed for Pittsburgh to sin again. Can't wait to get at it. Why, it's likely I'll be dead drunk for the first month and won't even remember the fancy gals I dally with or the men I carve up out of pure cussedness—any more than I'll remember you."

Deep within her, Eve was sure, as sure as a girl could be, that this was her man. She was fighting now, fighting for what she wanted, for what she had always wanted. She was not at all sure her weapons were adequate, and she had little experience to guide her, but she knew the battle must be won here and now.

She was acting shamelessly, she knew that, but she remembered something she had once heard a woman say: that men marry by accident, women by design, and that every man is by instinct a wanderer and will not willingly forfeit his freedom to wander.

Every woman wanted a home, protection for herself and the children she would bear . . . hence, whenever man and woman meet there must ever be this struggle, not so much to win the man, but to keep him after he was won. And she did not have weeks or days, not even hours . . . she had minutes only.

"Linus, I am asking you . . . can't you still feel that kiss? Or was it only me? Do you want to forget it? Do you want to walk away?"

"You make me feel like a man come face to face with a grizzly b'ar on a narrow trail. There just ain't no ignorin' the situation."

He stepped up to her again and she stood her ground, her face lifted, calm, secure, proud . . . but frightened, too.

FOUR

The hour before daybreak was still and cold. Zebulon Prescott eased from under the blankets so as not to wake Rebecca. He did it with the practiced skill of many years, for the habit of early rising was deeply ingrained in his being. And his wife would need rest . . . the travel would be hard on her, no matter how he tried to ease the way.

In trousers and undershirt, galluses hanging, he started toward the water's edge carrying the tin washpan. The two rafts were there, as they should be, but the canoe was gone. He walked out on the raft and started to dip up water to wash, then paused as an idea came to him.

"Eve!" He straightened up as he shouted the name. Fear and astonishment mingling in his voice. He looked toward the girls' lean-to. "Eve?"

Heads lifted from under blankets, and Harvey sat up, staring toward him. Sam swung his feet from under the blankets and started to pull on his boots.

Zebulon dropped the tin basin and started back toward the lean-to, fear gripping his insides. Suddenly Lilith pushed back the canvas that served as a curtain. "What is it, pa? Is anything wrong?"

"You can tell me where your sister is," he said, anger sounding in his voice.

The flap turned back again and Eve stepped out, tossing her hair back. "Pa? What's wrong?"

"Well, you're still here, anyway," he said testily. "I was afraid you'd gone off with that—that trapper."

"Gone?" The word had an empty sound. "He's gone?"

Her eyes went to the river. The space beside the raft was empty. The canoe was gone . . . Linus was gone.

"I knew you were settin' up with him, but I told myself you were at least lookin' at a man, even a wisp of smoke like that'n."

Tears welled into her eyes. Linus was gone. She had tried . . . what else could she have done? She had wished him to stay, she had tried to keep him with her.

"You cryin' for him? What's that mean?" Prescott's suspicions mounted. He grasped her shoulder. "Tell me," he almost shouted, "what's it mean?"

"Nothin', pa. Linus is gone, that's all."

"What time did you come to bed?"

"It was early," Lilith lied promptly. "I was still awake."

Eve's chin lifted. "No, it wasn't. It was late."

"Daughter"—Zebulon Prescott's voice was stern—"I'll only ask you once. Is there anything for your ma and pa to worry about?"

"No . . . no, there ain't, pa. There's not a thing."

Eve turned back to the lean-to and took up the washpan and, with Lilith beside her, started toward the river. Under the tree where she had made the bed of boughs there was only the mat of twisted branches now. The blankets were gone.

"Lilith . . . look!" Eve went around the tree and pointed. On the tree, cut deep into the bark, were two hearts, freshly cut, and cut deep. They were joined by a deep gash.

Lilith was amazed, and envious. "You mean . . . you mean you actually got a grown man to do that? Did you get him to say those crazy words, too?"

"I did . . . just like in the book. Seemed like he·enjoyed it."

"Eve Prescott, you're lyin' worse than pa! You cut those hearts yourself!"

"I won't say I didn't coax a little, but he did it. He said it was a mighty solemn occasion, like shootin' rapids without a paddle."

"Well, it sure didn't keep him by you. More'n likely he did it just so's he could get away. You know how driftin' men are . . . they never want to stay put. You're lucky he's gone. Do you want to live out your days like some squaw? Like an Indian squaw? More'n likely that's all he's used to."

"I'll see him again," she said confidently. "I know I will . . . and he hasn't got a wife and six kids, either. Not yet he hasn't!"

Evening brought coolness to the river. Behind Linus the setting sun painted fading colors upon the darkening waters. The bluffs were higher now, and the trunks of the forest trees were merging into one solid wall of blackness, although their tops still etched a jagged line against the sky.

It had been a slow day. The current seemed stronger than before, and perhaps he was not trying quite as hard. It irritated him that his thoughts kept reverting to the girl at last night's camp. His mind was usually crystal clear, open for impressions, warnings, dangers. His instincts were alive to every change of sunlight or shadow, to every hint of movement.

"That was quite a woman," he said aloud. "Now, if'n I was a marryin' man—"

He could see the white of the sign before he could make out the words. The sign was on the river bank, and behind it a path wound up the bluff to a cave where a feeble glow of light could still be seen.

With a sweep of his paddle he swung nearer to read the sign, feathering the blade as he swung alongside.

FINE OLD LIKKER SOLD HERE

The sign presented an invitation and a challenge. Besides, it was getting late. A few drinks would make him sleep good and sound, and it wasn't often he dared trust himself to let go and really sleep.

"Waal, now . . ." He turned the canoe deftly to the spot where two dugouts were moored.

From the cave above came a faint sound of music, harmonica

music, played with a dancing lilt. "Waal, now!" he repeated. "I don't mind if I do. This ain't Pittsburgh, but a man might as well try a hair of the dog that's goin' to bite him."

Tying the canoe, Linus took his rifle and mounted the trail. Off to the left, through the trees, he saw just the vestige of another trail. It was not dark, although the sun was down sometime since. That old trail was long out of use, but it indicated that somebody had probably lived here long before these folks had moved in. More than likely it had been an Indian trail, or one made by some early hunters.

Then from above he heard the music break and a voice called out, "Customer!" A bare-footed, yellow-haired girl, quite pretty despite the rags she wore, appeared at the mouth of the cave.

"Thirsty, mister?" she called. "This here's prime whiskey."

"Drier'n a grasshopper on a hot griddle." Linus wiped the back of his hand across his mouth and followed her into the cave. The harmonica player, he noticed—for he noticed most things—was a lean, scrawny youth who looked at him with a queer, taunting expression, as though he had just scored some victory over Rawlings.

The cave's interior was lighted by a fire that burned in a sort of natural fireplace, the smoke issuing through an opening in the cave roof. There was a bar composed of two planks laid across two barrels, and beyond the end of the bar Linus could see a high, narrow opening that gave into another room. A faint stir of breeze came through that opening.

Two haggard, hard-looking men played cards near the wall, using the bottom of a packing case for a table. Another man leaned on the bar in conversation with the white-haired patriarch who stood behind it.

The patriarch thrust out his hand. "Name is Hawkins, suh. Colonel Jeb Hawkins, late of Alabama. Where you bound, suh?"

"Pittsburgh."

"He looks like a mountain man, pa. I'll bet he's got a canoe full of furs."

"Ah? Now, suh, that I admire! A man bold enough to face westward, to dare the redskin of the plains, to challenge the distance and the mountains. Suh, the first drink is on me. Set *down*, suh!"

Linus leaned his rifle against the bar and watched the colonel take down a pewter cup and a brown earthenware jug.

"No pepper, no rattlesnake heads in this whiskey, suh. Just pure grain and the sweet kiss of malt, and water from the springs of Bourbon County, Kentucky. Finest spring water this side of heaven, suh. We call the whiskey bourbon, after the county."

Linus ignored the cup and reached for the jug, turning it easily over his bent elbow, and let the liquor flow down his throat. The men at the card table stopped their game to watch in open-mouthed admiration.

At last Linus paused for breath. "Yes, sir! You're right. That there's real sippin' whiskey."

"Springs of Bourbon County, m'boy! You can't make good whiskey without pure water, and this here's the best. Limestone water, she is. Limestone cuts all the impurities out, leaves nothing but the pure and sparkling. Drink *up*, suh!"

"Pa," the girl suggested tentatively, "him bein' a trapper and all, d'you suppose he'd know what that varmint is we've got?"

"Well, now, Dora, he might at that. Suh"—he watched Linus Rawlings' Adam's apple bob with the whiskey—"we cotched some kind of a cave-dwellin' critter like no man in these parts ever seen before. Be mighty interestin' if you could tell us what it be."

"Don't know much about cave-dwellin' varmints." The whiskey had reached his brain and Linus turned his head slowly. "Of course, I've seen a few varmints in my time, and I might—"

"It's just yonder"—Dora pointed toward the inner cave—"and you can bring the jug." She smiled invitingly, holding out a hand for his. "I'll show you."

There was just a hint of something more than a varmint to be found in that inner cave; and she was, Linus told himself, a likely filly.

Torchlight flickered from the walls. She passed her torch to him and, taking another from a small pile, lighted it. This cave was smaller, and Linus heard a distant roaring sound as of water running.

"Do you know any sweet-talkin' girls in Pittsburgh?"

"Nary a one—not yet, anyway."

"Pa an' me, we figure to winter here."

She was closer now, her hip touched his . . . was that an accident?

"I'll be at the Duquesne House if it ain't burned down." He held the torch to one side and looked down at her. She was mighty young, but she was rounded in all the right places, and there was nothing so young about that look in her eyes. "Are you *sure* you've got a varmint back here?"

"We keep him in the hole yonder."

She indicated what seemed to be a pit at the end of the cave, a hole perhaps six feet square. "You'll have to look mighty close, dark like it is."

She held his arm as if for protection, keeping her body close to him, hanging back just a little. He lifted his torch and bent forward. "Where—?"

In that instant of incredible realization he felt the girl's grip on his arm suddenly tighten, jerking downward and forward, and a leg was thrust sharply between his legs. Off-balance, he started to fall forward toward the blackness of the pit, gripping the torch in one hand, the jug in the other.

As she tripped him and he went forward, her hand jerked free. He did not see the knife, but he felt the bite of the blade; he was already falling, and the knife ripped only buckskin and a little hide . . . and then he was toppling into the awful blackness of the pit.

Even as he fell, he caught one glimpse of her, and saw the expression of ugly lust on her face. The torch struck the water an instant before he did, hissed sharply, and then he hit the water in utter blackness. It was incredibly cold . . . and he went down, down, down into roaring, abysmal night.

"He's seen the varmint, pa!"

Hawkins, who had been facing the passage with a double-barreled pistol in his hand, turned swiftly. "All right, lay into it! We've got other fish to fry. Down to the island!"

Instantly all of them turned to stripping the cave and carrying whatever was worth keeping down to the dugouts.

"That was nicely done, Dora," Hawkins said, putting a hand on her shoulder.

"I ain't so sure. He was hard-muscled and fallin' away from me."

"Practice, that's what it takes. Your ma had the knack, Lord rest her soul."

How far down he went, Linus never knew, but suddenly his senses came back with a rush, and he struck out, swimming up, trying to find the surface. The shocking immersion in cold water had sobered him . . . at least partly, and when he broke water his mind was working cold and clear.

Obviously, he was at the bottom of the pit, but there was no light above, and no sound but the roaring of the water. That roaring came from some underground stream joining the one into which he had fallen. Clutching the edge of the pit where it met the water, he gasped wildly for breath.

He had walked into a trap, suckered like any tenderfoot, but all that was important now was to get out of here . . . if he could.

Carefully, clinging with his hands to the rocky edge, he worked his way around the pit. The walls were wet and slippery and, although uneven, there was no hand-hold anywhere, no chance of climbing up there in the darkness.

The current into which he had fallen swept away toward the south . . . and to the south lay the Ohio.

How far away was the river? He had walked from his canoe . . . was it fifty yards? Perhaps less. He had walked uphill for part of that distance, so where he now clung to the edge of the pit couldn't be more than a few feet below the surface of the river.

Would the water's opening be large enough to let his body pass? Was there brush and debris that might choke up the passage? In the few seconds in which he clung, waiting, he thought of everything, but he was aware that none of his thinking could make any difference, for he had to chance it. . . . He could die where he was, or he could chance that dark, roaring, water-filled tunnel.

Immediately, he let go his hold and went into the opening head-first, letting the water take him. He was hurled brutally against a rock wall, the current pushed him off it, and he slid into a dark channel where he was rushed along at what seemed terrific speed. At one point, for a moment, both shoulders were touching . . . and then he shot through into warmer water, and he struck out, swimming up.

He bobbed out of the water, gasping for breath, with the fresh air around him and the bright stars overhead.

He was a fool. That was his first thought. He was several kinds of a damned fool to be chancing his life like this, when he could have stayed back there with that girl, that . . . what was her name? . . .

Eve. . . .

He swam to shore and struggled up the muddy bank and lay still, still gasping, his lungs aching with effort. He could feel the bite of pain where the knife had reached him, but he had been wounded before, and this could not amount to much.

He rolled over and sat up; then he stood up, to stagger a few steps before falling. When he sat up again he could see the river.

He was still seated there, slowly recovering his strength, when he saw the small flotilla go by—the two long dugouts and his own canoe.

If he only had his rifle . . . but all he had was his knife, still secure in its scabbard under its rawhide thong.

He got to his feet and tried to squeeze some of the water from his buckskin shirt and leggings. The fringe would help to drain the water off. Then he started up the hill to the cave. Something might have been left behind, something he could use.

He no longer considered Pittsburgh. Without his furs there was nothing for him there, but he did not mean to relinquish them so easily. He had risked too much, worked too hard. And when it came to that, they had cost him too much to let them go for a season of drinking.

How much did a man get out of life, anyway? What was it Bridger used to say? That every man in his life deserved one good dog and one good woman.

The thought made him grin. Now what would Eve say to that? She'd probably go out and get him a dog.

There he was thinking of Eve again. What was he, some fool

kid? And that nonsense about carving two hearts on a tree, and then throwing a knife into them from six paces. . . .

Six paces! That made him laugh. He'd carved the hearts, all right, and enjoyed it. But *six* paces? He'd backed off and thrown the knife to the mark at twenty paces, and in the dark. Well, there had been a little light from the fires.

But now, first things first. The thieves were headed downstream, and they must stop somewhere. Obviously, what they had done to him they had done to others, for it was too well planned to be the first time, it had worked too smoothly.

He would need a boat or a raft. Worst of it was, when he fell down that hole he lost the jug, and right now he could use a drink. Thief the man might be, and a murderer as well, but he sold good whiskey.

FIVE

The wooded island was narrow, its flanks worn and shaped by the flowing waters of the river. On the upriver point of the island, where it was instantly visible to all downstream traffic, a crude landing had been thrown together, a mere platform of peeled poles raised a couple of feet above the water of a tiny cove. Above the landing was a sign:

BEDLOE'S STORE—WHAT DO YOU LACK?
PITTSBURGH PRICES

Some distance back of the landing and at the end of a short trail up through the woods, was a tent house of logs and canvas. Marty, the harmonica player, paused and lowered the bale of furs to the ground to mop the sweat from his face.

Pa should be able to figure out an easier way of doing things, he told himself, but pa was almighty skittish. Maybe a narrow escape from a hanging did that to a man, but pa had it in mind to change places often . . . and fast.

Hawkins came down the trail as Marty shouldered the furs. "There'll be settlers an' folks comin'," he said, "so you act spry and talk kindly. We want to make a good impression on folks. And bust up that canoe."

"Pa," Marty protested, "that there's a good canoe. It seems a shame to bust—"

"You do what your pa tells you," Hawkins interrupted sharply. "No tellin' who all may have seen that canoe. We don't want folks askin' questions."

Marty lowered the bale to the ground again. "Pa, where be they goin'? All of them folks, I mean?"

"West . . . there's a mighty movement afoot, son. Greatest movement since the Children of Israel fled from bondage in the land of Egypt. The world has never seen the like, folks from all the lands of creation, streamin' west, flowin' like a great tide, some of them walkin', some drivin' wagons, and some a-horseback. You look upon this and remember it, son, for these folk are goin' west to populate a new land."

"Be we'uns goin' west, pa?"

"I reckon not, son. We are of the afflictions that beset these poor travelers, these wayfarers upon the earth. And, I might add, bein' an affliction is a sight more profitable than planting or plowing and tilling. It surely is . . . or digging gold, for that matter."

Colonel Jeb Hawkins canted his hat at a rakish angle. "Son, you listen to your old father. The world is made up of two kinds of folks, the spoiled and the spoilers . . . and to my way of thinking it's a whole sight better to be a spoiler. Now you look sharp. Folks will be comin'."

Hawkins turned back toward the log and canvas hut, but paused to add, "And mind you . . . destroy that canoe."

When he had deposited the last bale of furs at the shack, Marty returned to the landing to sink the canoe. He did so reluctantly, for he admired its fine, clean lines. When he turned it bottom up and dropped a rock upon it, he had to try several times before he cracked the bark. Then he shoved it off into the water and sank it, weighting it down with other rocks, just in case.

His thoughts returned to the mountain man's rifle. Pa should give him that rifle instead of selling it. Pa was always for selling everything, and meanwhile he'd let his own son be without a rifle-gun.

Movement on the water some distance off caught his eye. "Pa!" he called. "Rafts a-comin'!"

Another man stepped from the woods and shaded his eyes upstream. "Two," he said, speaking back over his shoulder. "Two big rafts."

Marty watched them coming, almost with regret. Pa knew what he was doing, he guessed. Anyway, things mostly turned out the way he said, only sometimes the folks on those rafts seemed like right nice people. Dora, she was like pa. She took right to it . . . like with that mountain man last night. . . . He scowled at the rafts, almost hoping they would not stop. There was a wistfulness in him, too. Why couldn't he and pa and Dora go west of their ownselves? Pa always made light of a man owning land, but a place of their own . . . he would fancy that.

The idea of cutting loose and leaving to be on his own had never occurred to him. They were a family, and they had always been together. He had never liked to think of what they were doing . . . actually, he had taken part in only one killing, and that had been a fight. It was mostly Dora and pa who did that, while he handled the outside work.

Marty scowled as he turned away from the river. Pa knew what he was doing. They almost always had money, and time to time they went to town to do some spending; but there was a time or two when he'd been on the land, when he'd smelled the earth freshly plowed, or hay freshly cut . . . it made a man want a place of his own.

Zebulon Prescott sighted the narrow island from well upstream, and he stood tall, holding the steering oar with one hand, shading his eyes toward the island. There was a sign of some kind . . . and what looked like a building.

Harvey's raft was not far off to the right, and Harvey called over: "Island! Do we stop?"

"Might's well," Prescott shouted. "Likely the last the folks will see of a store for some time." He was close enough to make out the sign now. "Might be news of the river."

There had been talk of the falls of the Ohio, and while some said it was not much of a falls, to a man with his family on a raft, any falls or rapids could mean trouble. Using his steering oar, he worked the big raft in toward the breakwater.

This was a natural barrier of rocks and debris that partly

sheltered an acre or so of shallow cove where the landing had been built. Unwieldy as the big rafts were, the cove was so situated that it required only a few moves of the big sweeps to get the rafts into the cove.

Such rafts varied considerably in size, owing to variation in materials available and the requirements of the builders. Prescott's raft was just over twenty feet in length and fifteen feet wide. In the center of the raft was the hut, which was merely a frame covered with tent canvas, seven feet long by six feet wide. Behind the hut was a mound of their goods, covered with another stretched canvas.

The Harvey raft was almost a duplicate of theirs, except that the hut was larger, built to shelter the boys and the family goods.

Colonel Hawkins himself was at the landing to greet them. He lifted his hat and gestured toward the store. "My name is Bedloe, gentlemen! An' this here is Bedloe's Landing! We have all manner of fixin's an' supplies, whether for man or beast."

Zebulon Prescott hesitated, his attention going from Bedloe to the store. He decided instantly that he did not like the man, but on the other hand, he had seen the eagerness in the faces of Rebecca and the girls and knew they were excited at the prospect of shopping in an actual store.

Bedloe was obviously a windbag, and Zebulon did not take to his kind, but the prospects of a store interested him too. There were a few things he wanted, and several he would get if the prices were right. After all, a man starting a place of his own could use tools, and there were a couple of items he had overlooked buying.

"Come up to the store, folks! Welcome to Bedloe's Landing! Do come up—all of you! My boys will see to your things!"

Excited at being ashore and at the chance to shop, they trooped up the path, laughing and talking.

The "store" was well stocked from loot taken from dozens of settlers and from an occasional peddler. Bullet molds, powder, flints, knives, hatchets, coils of rope, axes, saws, bolts of canvas, and a few used rifles, pistols, and shotguns were offered for sale.

On a board at the side were some bottles of toilet water, some cheap jewelry, and a dozen lithographed prints.

Lilith picked up a bottle of the toilet water. "Pa, can I have this toilet water? Genuine Parisian scent, it says."

Zebulon took the bottle in his fingers. "Fifteen cents? That's too dear."

"Right, suh!" Hawkins said. "Save the pennies and the dollars will grow. Likely a man of your judgment, suh, has made many a dollar grow."

"Well, Mr. Bedloe," Zebulon replied dryly, "my life long I been strivin' to avoid riches, and I think I've succeeded right well. And whatever I've got in the sock is goin' to stay there."

"My sentiments exactly, suh!" The colonel turned to Harvey. "And you, suh—a man of property if I ever saw one. Why, a man like you might be holdin' up to a thousand dollars!"

Harvey merely looked at him, then glanced down the counter at Sam, who had picked up a rifle, which he was slowly turning in his hands. Burned into the wood of the stock were the initials, L. R.

"Pa?"

Something in Sam's tone arrested his father's attention, and Zebulon turned and walked to where Sam stood, holding the rifle.

"Pa"—Sam lowered his voice—"did you ever see this rifle before?"

Hawkins glanced at them sharply, half-overhearing the words. Quickly he turned to Dora, who was talking to Eve.

"Have you any books?" Eve was asking.

"We got an almanac, I think. I'll look around." From the corner of her eye Dora caught the frantic signal from her father, and hurried from the door.

"It's his rifle," Sam whispered. "Now, how does it come to be down here when he was headed upstream? And he would never, under no circumstances, sell his rifle."

Zebulon Prescott was struck with sudden panic. *Get out,* his instincts warned him. *Get out fast.*

"Son, I think—"

The canvas walls of the tent store suddenly fell to reveal four rifles lying across the top of the log wall, four hard-eyed men standing behind them. Rebecca cried out sharply and gathered Zeke to her. Zebulon turned his head carefully. Three more rifles were aimed at their backs.

"Now, now!" the colonel cautioned. "Nobody needs to be scared. There's womenfolks an' children here, an' it seems likely you folks wouldn't want no shootin' to start."

Zebulon Prescott hesitated, fury mounting within him, and Sam glanced uneasily at his father. He well knew his father's temper, for easy-going and friendly as he was, Zebulon was hot-headed and bull-strong when pushed.

"We'll stand," Sam said quietly.

Almost as if by agreement the men of their party turned to face the river pirates. Zeke pulled away from his mother and stood with them.

Briskly, Hawkins, Marty, and Dora began frisking their prisoners for what valuables might be carried on their persons, carefully avoiding the line of fire in the process.

"Be of good cheer, folks!" Hawkins said genially. " 'Tis in the noble tradition to fare forth and conquer the wilderness with bare hands and stout hearts. We will leave you upon this island, and if you stand quiet, perhaps even an axe might be left behind so you can build new rafts and sally forth in the spirit of your forefathers. Americans just can't be whupped!"

"I'll see you hang, Bedloe!" Zebulon declared furiously. "I'll see you hang if it's the last thing I do!"

Linus Rawlings, guiding an ancient canoe, sighted the island in midstream. Dipping his paddle deep, he shot the canoe toward the brushy shore. There had been no sign on the island when he had passed it going upstream, yet the painted letters had a familiar look. Accustomed to interpreting the tracks left by all manner of varmints, he found something in the shaping of the letters that he thought he recognized. If he was mistaken, it would take but minutes to find out.

Back there at the cave, when he had recovered sufficiently to examine the place where he had been tricked and robbed, he had found the cave abandoned. At the landing there was nothing of which to make a float—everything was gone.

It was then he recalled the abandoned trail he had seen on first approaching the cave; and returning, he followed the ancient trail to a hidden, tiny cove. Concealed in the brush he found a battered canoe with a hole stove in the side. He

repaired the hole with birch bark peeled from a nearby tree, a
patching job that had taken him less than an hour to do. The
canoe had been long abandoned, and it was unlikely that the
thieves had known of its existence. The paddle he found by the
simple expedient of looking in several places where he might
himself have hidden one had the canoe been his.

Now, having moored his canoe close under the overhang of a
tree, he worked his way through the brush toward the landing.
Wily as any Indian, carrying only the knife for a weapon, he
drew closer.

Men were coming down the trail carrying furs . . . his furs.

"We pullin' out?" he heard one of them ask.

"Kit an' caboodle," Marty said. "Pa wants to be shet of this
place before others come along. Powerful lot of folks on the
Ohio these days, an' you know pa . . . he likes to keep movin'.
Maybe six months, maybe a year from now, he'll be back along
here, workin' the same stands."

Marty glanced at the rafts. "Turn them loose when you're
finished. We'll let 'em go into the rapids an' bust up."

The men who had carried the furs returned along the trail
for another load, and Marty went to a dugout and began
stowing rifles.

Wraithlike, Linus eased back into the brush and then into
the water. Swimming under water, he made for the landing.
Only a minute or two later he came up soundlessly in the
shadowed space beneath it. For an instant he remained still,
catching his breath. Dust and fragments of bark fell from the
log landing as Marty worked above him. The stern of a dugout
drifted out from the landing and Marty reached out to draw it
near.

Coming along the trail with a load of furs, one of the men
saw Marty reach for the dugout . . . and vanish.

The man stopped, staring and trying to make sense of what
he had seen. Marty had been there, now he was gone. A
widening circle of ripples showed on the water.

Suddenly Marty lunged up from the water, gasping and
crying out in a panic of fear. Blood streamed from a wound in
his side. Then he fell back into the water.

With a frightened yell the man dropped his bundle and fled
back up the trail . . . but not quickly enough.

Linus lunged from under the landing, and grabbing a rifle from the dugout, he flipped it to his shoulder and fired just as the fleeing man was disappearing from sight. But Linus was too old a hand to miss such a shot, leading his target just enough.

The man threw up his hands and fell face forward, out of sight.

Instantly Linus leaped for the brush and, once out of sight, was instantly still. He had neither powder nor shot, and his weapon was now empty, useful only as a club.

Moving swiftly through the brush, he reached the clearing where the store was. Colonel Hawkins stood outside the store, clutching a double-barreled pistol. He was obviously listening, trying to figure out what had happened at the landing.

A quick sizing-up of the situation at the store told Linus his best chance for quick action would come from Zebulon or Sam. Drawing back his knife, he threw it into the back of the man guarding them.

Then all hell broke loose. Zebulon grabbed the falling man's rifle by the barrel and drove it hard at the face of the guard close to the wall of the store. The thief leaped back and Zebulon reversed the rifle, and the two men fired as one. The thief's bullet was a clean miss, and it smashed into the wall on the far side, scattering chips of bark. Zebulon's shot killed the guard.

Hawkins wheeled and fired simultaneously. His first bullet struck Sam and knocked him to his knees; the second bullet killed Colin Harvey. Hawkins ducked and ran, coattails flying, into the brush. Dora followed him out of the clearing.

Swinging his rifle like a club, Linus had followed his knife into the fight. It was by no means his first experience in such a melee, and he floored the last of Hawkins' men.

Eve, retreating toward the brush with her mother and Lilith, recognized Linus. Her eyes caught his lean, swiftly moving figure even as he left the brush to plunge into the fight. "Oh, it's him!" she cried out. "It's *him!*"

As always in such situations, the action ended as abruptly as it had begun. At one instant there had been cries, shots, wild blows, and running men; then there was sunlight and shadow falling over the clearing's edges . . . some gasping for breath . . . a muffled groan.

Rebecca for once had forgotten Zeke, and was kneeling above Sam. The Harvey boys had gone into the brush, pursuing Hawkins and Dora, while Eve ran to Linus. "You're hurt! There's blood on your back!"

"It's all right," he said. "I've got to round up my furs and get goin'."

She drew back, dropping her arms stiffly; her eyes searched his face. "Then you didn't come back to—?" The excitement was gone from her face. "No, I see you didn't. Somehow they got your furs and it was them you came after. I might have known."

He avoided her eyes, embarrassed by his own sense of guilt and by the hurt in her eyes. This was quite a woman, he told himself, a woman with the kind of courage he had always admired. He knew what it must have cost her in pride to have come to him that first time. Trouble was, he was no marryin' man. If he was, this would be the girl—she surely would be.

The Harveys came plodding back through the brush. "Got away," Harvey said tiredly. "Had them a dugout hid on the other side of the island."

"I fired," Brutus said. "I think I put lead into him. Can't be sure."

"Let them go," Prescott said. "Their sins will catch up with them."

He avoided even looking at Sam. Rebecca, assisted by Lilith, was doing all anybody could. The thought of losing Sam shook him deeply, and he could not stand knowing how serious his wounds might be. Sam had changed since the trip began, becoming a man almost at once, making his own decisions and moving with a certainty Zebulon had never seen in him before.

Perhaps the very act of leaving the farm, Zebulon's farm, had been responsible for that. Now they were just two men together, each standing on his own feet, doing his own share of the work.

For the first time, looking at Sam and at the body of Colin Harvey, Zebulon Prescott began to realize what the cost of this western venture might be. No new land is gained without blood and suffering, and they had been bold to leave all behind to go into the Ohio River country. They might yet pay a high price for their boldness.

They had scarcely begun . . . how many would die before the West was won? How many by river, by disease, by blizzard and tornado and flood? How many by starvation and exhaustion? It was a long way to the shining mountains. He was glad they were not going that far . . . nor many miles farther, when it came to that.

Turning away, he began to go through what was left within the store. There was a little they could add to their own supplies—some food, some ammunition, extra bullet molds, and weapons. With Zeke to help, he began slowly sorting things out. All, or most of it, had been stolen. The owners might now be dead—dead or gone on west. Sometimes it amounted to the same thing.

Linus Rawlings piled his own furs on the small landing. He had seen his canoe on the bottom of the cove, only a few feet under the water, and was hopeful it might be repaired. He recovered his rifle, and added to his store some of the stock of powder and lead.

Eve and her mother had made a bed for Sam that was shaded, and Linus helped Zebulon move the wounded man.

Only when all his furs were on the landing did he wade into the cove and remove the stones from the canoe. Brutus Harvey helped him beach it on the slanting shore, and Linus checked it for repairs. It needed only two sections of birch bark, for Marty's efforts to destroy the canoe had been halfhearted at best.

Linus swore softly as he went to work. It seemed all he was doing these days was patching canoes. This one was large, and other than the damaged areas it was in good shape and comparatively new. The beat-up old canoe he had found in the brush near the cave was too small for his load of furs, but it had been swift and easily handled.

Footsteps sounded on the path behind him . . . he cringed inwardly. Yet even as he did so he felt an odd warmth, a very real pleasure. It irritated him that he should be so confused about himself. After all, what *did* he want to do?

She walked up beside him and stopped, looking down at the damaged canoe. "It'll be a job," Linus said, "but I can patch her up as good as new."

"Linus . . . ?"

"Eve, let's talk no more about it."

"Linus, I'm telling you. You don't know your own mind."

"Maybe so, maybe not. I ain't denyin' you been in my thoughts, but I still went to see the varmint with that pirate gal. I'll always be goin' to see the varmint, Eve—I just ain't cut out to be either a farmer or a husband."

"Linus, I'm not going to bring the matter up again, whether I ever see you again or not."

"That's best, and I wish you Godspeed, Eve, and it's been a long time since I said the like to anybody."

Fighting tears, she turned swiftly away toward the path. Linus straightened up and for an instant he was about to call after her. Then, grimly, he closed his mouth.

To himself, he said, "You ain't no marryin' man. No sooner'd you squat on some land than you'd start to thinkin' how the wind blows over South Pass, or the way that water ripples on that lake at the foot of the Tetons.

"All the time you were plowing a furrow you'd be rememberin' the long winds in the pines atop the Mogollon Rim in Arizona, or the slap of a beaver's tail on the water of a pool some place up the Green. No, sir. You ain't no marryin' man, Linus, not by a long shot."

He cut a patch of bark from a birch tree and settled down to remove the damaged square and replace it with the fresh piece, but the girl's face remained in his mind, interfering with his work. He swore softly, scowling as he stitched the patch in its place.

It was time he set off for Pittsburgh . . . and the sooner the better. This was no time to be thinkin' soft about any chance pilgrim girl.

SIX

Although it was midday, darkness lay upon the river. The black, swollen waters ran swiftly, warned by lowering black clouds that hung low above. Thunder rumbled down far-off halls, and there was the sound of rain upon the water.

A quarter of a mile ahead the Harvey raft raced through the water, seen through the steel veil of the rain. That would be Brutus at the oar . . . he was the stalwart one, the stable one. Never excited, never disturbed, when trouble or danger came he simply bowed his head and pushed on, as his sort will always push on, to their last day.

When others panic or shout, when they wail and shed bitter tears, decrying the changing times, there are those like Brutus who simply go on. Changing times, anger, disappointment, defeat—all these they take in stride, living their lives with quiet persistence.

Eve thought of that as she looked from the shelter into the rain. Brutus was a good man, and it was too bad it was not he whom she wanted. Not that he had ever indicated any interest in her, more than a normal, friendly interest.

Zebulon squinted his eyes against the rain that hammered his cheeks, staring ahead, searching the river for snags. Lilith

53

was fighting a rope, trying to tie the tent more securely over the frame, for a fierce gust of wind had torn it loose.

"Watch yourself, Lil!" he shouted, striving to be heard above the rumble of thunder and the rush of rain and wind. "You be careful!"

He could no longer see the Harvey raft, for rain had blotted out everything. The river seemed to be rushing swifter . . . was it the rain and wind that made it seem so?

Anxiously, Zebulon peered ahead. One boy wounded and the other sickly . . . the girls trying hard to make up for Sam. He had never realized how much he had come to depend on Sam until now; suddenly, strangely, one half of his mind began to think of him, while the other half tried to estimate the river and fought with it.

Surprisingly, he actually had no idea what his son was like. A man has children and he takes them for granted; they are his, they have grown up in his home, and in many ways he knows them. And then he realizes of a sudden that they are people— individuals with thoughts, dreams, and ambitions perhaps far different from anything he had ever known.

He thought of Sam, comparing him to the girls—to Lilith, who did not know what she wanted . . . or hadn't found the words for it, at least; and to Eve, who pointed at what she wanted with quiet persistence. Sam had seen through him. He had commented upon him going off to see that show and those show-folk. Sam had seen that in him, read him for his dreams, and it had made Zebulon suddenly shy before his son. Sam had understood at least something of him; but what did he know of Sam?

Suddenly, from the front of the raft, Zeke turned and cupped his hand. "Pa!" he yelled against the wind. "It's the *falls! The falls of the Ohio!*"

Shocked, Zebulon strained to his full height, staring through the veil of rain. It could not be . . . it simply could not be. The falls were on the other channel.

Unless—unless they had missed it. Where were the Harveys? After all, they couldn't be that far ahead of him. Somehow he had missed the channel, and now the Harveys were gone, down the other side.

Fear rose within him. He fought it down, fought the ugly

táste of it in his throat. There was no white water in sight, but Zeke was right: he could feel the pull of the current, he could feel the power of it against the raft, against his oar.

Now there was a dark smoothness to the water, and the raft seemed to gather speed. He had been warned that he would see no white water, not until too late, and that the rapids would seem anything but alarming. Only one who had tried to navigate those waters could understand their danger . . . it all looked so easy, so smooth. . . .

Zeke shouted again, panic in his voice. Ahead Zebulon saw a huge rock, water boiling over it. Beyond it, he saw another.

Fear flooded over him like an icy wave. Desperately, Zebulon worked at the long sweep, but even as he fought the current, he knew how little he could do with the cumbersome raft in that strong current that was already sucking them toward the rocks.

The raft was no longer simply swept along by the current, it had become like a live thing, plunging and bounding upon the boiling water. Suddenly, as the bow of the raft lifted on a swell of rushing water, the wind caught the tent that had been tied over the framework to roof the house. The canvas billowed up like a great balloon, and Lilith caught wildly at the edge.

In the next instant she was jerked over the side and plunged into the racing water, the canvas ripping loose and going with her.

As she surfaced in the racing water, Eve thrust a pole toward her, but Lilith failed in a wild, futile grab at the end of the pole, and was swept away. At the last, before she vanished from sight, they saw she had turned and was swimming strongly, half riding the current, fighting her way toward shore.

"Pa!" It was Zeke. "The tent's draggin' us! Cut her loose! Cut it away!"

Dropping his useless steering oar, Zebulon caught up his axe and, staggering across the plunging raft, he struck wildly at the entangling ropes. The canvas tent, acting like a huge sea anchor, was turning the raft broadside.

He struck, and struck again. Wildly as he seemed to strike, he struck true; the ropes were slashed and the tent disappeared on the wind. An instant more and the whole raft might have been turned over, capsized in the wild water.

"Straighten her, pa! Straighten her!"

Zebulon started for the steering sweep and was thrown head-
long. He felt a wicked blow across the skull, and then he was
up and grasping the sweep just as the end of the raft struck a
rock. It was a crashing blow that shook the raft its entire
length, and then the current swung·the stern around and the
raft had turned end for end.

With mounting horror, Zebulon saw that the jolt of the blow
against the rock had snapped at least some of the binding
cords, and the logs were spreading. Water showed between
them. He shouted hoarsely, and dropped the useless oar to go
to his wife, who was beside Sam.

"Grab holt!" he shouted. "Grab holt of a log!"

Eve heard her father shout, but she never knew what he
said, for the next instant the logs parted beneath her and she
was plunged down into the icy water.

Logs smashed together above her. She struck out, fighting to
escape them. Dead ahead of her one log struck a rock and the
current lifted the butt end of it, turning it end over end.

She heard screams, a hoarse cry, and she saw her father had
an arm around Rebecca. Logs smashed together like the shot of
a gun, and Eve felt the sharp sting of a flying chip as it struck
her face. Then she struck out, swimming downstream and across.

Glancing back upstream, she saw a log plunging toward her,
and managed to avoid the charging butt end of it. As she
grasped wildly at the rough bark she felt it tear at her hand,
but somehow she got an arm over it and clung for dear life.

The falls itself was only a few feet high—from shore it might
have seemed like nothing at all. She went over, clinging to the
log, and was still hanging on when she came to the surface.
Suddenly the log was ceasing to plunge. Ahead there was a
wide eddy and beyond it a place close in to the shore where
the water was almost smooth.

Freeing one hand, she brushed the wet hair back from her
face. There was a low riverbank ahead, and on it lay something
dark and still. Her throat tight with fear, she began to paddle
with her free hand and kick with her feet to get the log closer
in.

When her feet touched bottom she let go of the log and,
straightening up, splashed ashore.

At the sound, the dark body quivered, and a head lifted. It was Sam . . . and he was alive.

She knelt beside him and he struggled to sit up. His body shook with a spasm of coughing, and he spat river water into the mud.

"Are you all right, Sam? Are you hurt?"

He shook his head, leaning it forward to his drawn-up knees. "I'm all right."

She turned her head, looking all about her, afraid of what she might see. Something—it was some distance off and might be a log—was caught in the brush along the shore. There was nothing else in sight. The hour was late and the sky was heavily overcast.

"Did they make it? Lil . . . have you seen Lil?"

"She'd be miles upriver." She shivered in the cold wind. "Sam, we've got to have a fire."

Helping each other, they staggered to the edge of the trees where Eve gathered broken branches and debris cast up by high water. Near the roots of a great tree, she put together the wood for a fire. Tearing bark from a tree, she got at the dry inner bark and shredded it; then with a little dry moss found high up on the side of a tree, she had tinder for the fire.

With flint and steel, Sam struck a good spark after several attempts; it caught, smoked, and then was fanned and blown into a tiny flame. This he fed carefully with shredded bark, then with twigs, until the fire was blazing brightly.

By the time the fire was going both were shivering with a chill. A cold wind had started to blow and in their soaked clothing they had no defense against the wind. But they worked together to build a lean-to, a windbreak to protect them from the night.

From a forked tree to a forked branch, its other end thrust deep into the sodden earth, Sam placed a long branch. With other branches slanting to the ground from this ridge-pole, he made a roof and back wall for the lean-to, and then they swiftly cut branches to weave into and place over this. When the shelter was finished they built a reflector of branches that would throw the heat back into the lean-to itself. Then they removed their outer garments and draped them near the fire to dry while they huddled close to keep warm.

The afternoon was gone. The rain continued to fall, but the heavy downpour had dwindled into a fine drizzle that promised to continue through the night. At intervals Sam got up and cut more branches to add to the roof, or dragged more sticks close for fuel.

Eve was frightened when she looked at him. His face was drawn and gray, and his wound had been bleeding again.

"Sam? Are you all right?"

He did not reply for a moment, and when he did he said: "All right . . . just almighty tired."

He dropped to the damp ground near her. "Eve . . . what do you think happened? To them, I mean? Do you think we're the only ones left?"

"I can't think. I saw pa catch hold of ma . . . she never did learn to swim."

"She was afraid of the water."

The wind blew chill from over the water. The flames flickered and jumped beneath the hand of the wind, and occasionally a drop of rain fell into the fire. The lean-to gave little shelter, but by keeping their fire small, they could huddle close to it. Once Sam went out into the woods after more fuel, and came back dragging a dead-fall, from which he broke the branches to add to the fuel.

Eve was afraid to think of Lilith and Zeke. Lilith was the best swimmer of the lot, better even than Sam, but Zeke was the weak one . . . or he seemed so. His boyhood illnesses had given their mother the idea that he was not strong, yet he had always seemed eager to be out and doing.

They talked no more, but huddled, wet, cold, and miserable over their small fire, moving only to add fuel. Eve tried not to let Sam see her fear. He needed rest, needed it desperately. . . . But what of her father and mother? Where were they?

The wind mounted . . . it was not yet fully dark. In the east there was a break in the somber clouds. The rain had ceased, but the trees dripped great, slow drops, except when a sudden gust of wind blew a small shower from their leaves.

Her clothing was dry, or as dry as it was likely to get, so she dressed and walked out along the riverbank. She was drawn toward that dark, inscrutable something she had seen entangled in the brush, but it was obscured by night and she could see nothing.

She did find a canvas-wrapped bundle of clothing that had floated ashore, secure in its water-proof tarpaulin. She also found a wooden bucket and a teakettle, both of which had somehow remained afloat.

Suddenly she heard a shout, and Zeke rushed from the forest . . . and Lilith was just behind him. They ran into each other's arms and clung tightly, saying nothing. It was Zeke who spoke first. "Ma? Is she all right? And pa?"

"Sam's over by the fire," she said—it was all she could say.

Lilith was still soaking wet. "When I got to the bank," she said, "I knew there was nothing to do but follow the river down and hope to come up with you."

"You didn't see what happened?"

"Zeke told me. I've been walking since I got to shore . . . that was a mite after noontime." She huddled close to the fire. "I came up with Zeke about half a mile back."

"Sam's afraid they didn't get to shore," Eve said to them. "Ma couldn't swim, and pa was sure to try and save her. He wouldn't be likely to give up."

Here and there a star was visible now through the broken clouds. They gathered branches and worked to enlarge the lean-to. Zeke and Lilith had made it, so mightn't pa and ma?

"Supposin' they . . . supposin' we don't find them," Zeke said. "What are you figurin' to do?"

Lilith tossed her head defiantly. "I am not goin' west, that's for sure. I never did want to go, and now there'd be nothing out there for me, nor nobody."

Eve looked from one to the other, sitting very still and thinking that this was the end of something, the end of the family they had always been. First the farm had gone, and with it all they knew of home, of stability. And now their parents . . . for in her heart she was sure.

This was an end of all they had known, the beginning of all they had yet to learn.

And Lilith? Ma had worried about Lilith, with her fancy notions, but Sam had been closer to Lilith than any of them had been, and he was not worried. She was young, but there was in her a kind of steel he recognized. Lilith would make her own way, and in that way she was as much a pioneer as any of them, perhaps more than any of them, for her way would be different. In each generation there are some who break with tradition, and she was such a one.

Sam would continue to the West, Eve realized, for Sam had wanted to go, and had talked of it even before pa had become interested in the idea. He had said nothing to pa, but he had talked to Eve and Lilith about it . . . always thinking that it would be he alone who went, not the family.

Eve looked across the fire at Sam. "You'd better lie down, Sam. You looked tired."

He looked worse than tired, and for once he did not protest. He simply crawled deeper into the lean-to and curled into a ball. Eve opened the bundle of clothing they had found wrapped securely in the tarp and found a coat of pa's. With this she covered Sam, then spread an edge of the tarp it had been wrapped in over him, too. They all would have to share that tarp.

The wind picked up, whispering in the leaves. Zeke turned and crawled in beside Sam, and she sat alone with Lilith.

"You think they're gone, don't you?" Lilith asked.

"Yes."

"I do, too. Even if they were carried downstream pa would have found us by now from the fire's light."

"Lilith . . . what are you going to do?"

The younger girl huddled under the blanket that had been wrapped in the tarp, drawing it around her shoulders. "I don't know. All I can do is play that old accordion and sing a little, but I like people. I want to be where there are people . . . where things are happening. And I want nice things, pretty things."

Eve listened to the river. How many men, through how many ages, had sat by night listening to the sound of running water? How many had sat beside this very river? She remem-·bered some man telling pa about the strange mounds in the Ohio country, huge artificial hills made for what purpose nobody knew, by a people far and away stranger than any she could imagine. Those very people might have sat here beside this river—the Mound Builders might have sat here, or Indians, or explorers . . . no telling who.

She lifted her eyes to the trees. They were huge old trees, and it would be a task to clear land here. Then she recalled a glimpse of a meadow she had seen that lay behind them . . . only a glimpse, but a big meadow green with tall grass. Maybe no land would have to be cleared.

It was a thing to consider.

Miles away, Linus rose with the dawn and went to work on the canoe. It had taken more time than he had believed, for he had found another crack, at first unnoticed, and had gone back to the woods for another section of bark. By the time he found the exact piece of bark that satisfied him he had also forced himself to admit that he was stalling.

There was nothing about the island that pleased him, yet he was reluctant to leave. Once he started upriver, every dip of the paddle would take him away from Eve.

He wanted to see Pittsburgh, and then he wanted to go on east to New York or somewhere and see that ocean water he'd heard tell of. Must be a sight of water out there, it being bigger than Salt Lake, and some folks said it was wider than the Great Plains. He kept thinking of Pittsburgh and of that ocean sea, but in the background of all his thinking there was Eve.

Straightening up from pitching the seams of the canoe, he saw a dugout approaching, paddled by two men making slow work of it.·

"Howdy!" The man in the bow wore a faded red woolen shirt, and had a wide, friendly grin. "You goin' upriver or down?"

"Pittsburgh, when I get this canoe fixed."

They rested their paddles in the backwater near the landing, and the man in the red shirt offered a chew from a twist of black tobacco. Linus thanked him and refused.

"Met some folks name of Harvey down below the falls. Terrible accident down there, they say. Friends of theirs."

Something within Linus seemed to stop dead-still. He lifted his eyes. "Accident, you say?"

"Some folks travelin' with the Harveys took the wrong branch of the river in the storm, an' they went over the falls."

"You hear the name?"

"Prescott . . . an' good folks, Harvey said." They looked at him curiously. "Harvey said he lost a boy in a fight with river pirates hereabouts."

Linus indicated the island behind him with a jerk of his head. "He's buried right back there. How about the Prescotts? Was anybody saved?"

"Harvey didn't know. He was twenty mile downstream and hadn't seen any of them, so he figured they all were lost, the whole shootin' match."

The man in the stern of the canoe spoke up. "We'd better high-tail it." He grinned at Linus. "Way I feel, you better hurry or there won't be any whiskey left. I aim to drink it all."

Linus returned to his work, and finished in a matter of minutes. He lifted the canoe and shoved it into the water, then stood watching for the telltale seep of water, but there was none. While he stood there his mind was a blank . . . he thought of nothing, simply staring into the bottom of the canoe.

Finally, he began to load his furs, taking his time and thinking as he worked, and by the time the canoe was loaded he decided he did not wish to live in a world where there was no Eve.

Within him there was a vast emptiness, an emptiness of feeling, of resolution, of everything. The girls and the whiskey of Pittsburgh no longer drew him; even the sight of the ocean seemed somehow unnecessary and pointless.

She was gone . . . Eve was gone.

Until that moment he had not realized how much she meant to him. For years he had lived with no care but for himself. He had been free . . . but he had been lonely too.

Eve had come quietly into his life with her own kind of loneliness, and fearing that loneliness more than what might happen to her pride, she had come to him. Quietly and honestly she had tried to win him.

There had been no skill in her, no feminine artifice. She was frank, open, sincere . . . and terribly in need . . . as he was in need.

Bitterly, he considered the years so recently past, and knew that much of his restlessness had been inspired by his own loneliness, his need for somebody, for something to care about. At first his wandering had the love of the strange, wild lands—

that free, open country with its magnificent mountains, its rivers flowing from God knew where, its towering beauty . . . but after a while the strange lands had not been enough.

He knew that now, when Eve was gone.

Yet . . . suppose she still lived? Suppose even now she lay back there, somewhere on the banks of the river, alone and hurt?

He had lived too long in the wilderness not to know that the human body can survive all manner of hardship and torture. Every mountain man knew the terrible story of Hugh Glass, ripped and torn by a grizzly, left for dead by his traveling companions; yet he had crawled more than a hundred miles and walked more hundreds, fighting wolves for the carcass of a buffalo, and coming safely to civilization.

Every mountain man also knew the story of John Coulter, who was forced by Blackfeet to run the gauntlet, and how he broke through the line and, stark naked, raced off, pursued by the Blackfeet. He had killed his closest pursuer with his own spear and escaped, fleeing until his bare feet were mere ugly masses of blood and flesh . . . yet he had escaped, and he had survived.

At least two men Linus had known had survived scalping . . . there were many such tales.

He loaded the last bundle of furs and covered them with the buffalo hide and lashed it down. He was no longer thinking, he was acting swiftly, for he had to know. If she was dead, he must be sure. If she was lying back there injured and alone, he must go to her aid.

He shoved off, downstream. The falls were not bad for a man in a canoe who had run the rough water on the Yellowstone and the Snake. For a larger boat or a raft they were deceptively dangerous. He dipped his paddle deep and shot the canoe into the teeth of the rapids.

She might be, she had to be alive.

He glimpsed them standing on the riverbank before they saw him. He saw them, but could not quite make them out, for the canoe was shooting the chutes of the falls . . . then the falls themselves, and he dipped the paddle deep and shot the canoe off into space. It hit the water with a smack . . . a dip of the paddle, then another, and he was out of the churning pool.

"It's Linus," Eve said, and walked to meet him.

He drew the canoe up on the shore and turned to face them, and their faces told him all he needed to know—their faces and the few odds and ends they had saved from the water.

Sam looked thin and drawn, and had no business even being on his feet. It would be weeks, maybe months, before he was back to normal. Zeke looked all right, but the boy needed some age on him.

"Your folks? Were they—?"

"We buried them yonder," Eve said quietly. "They drowned together. Ma was no hand in the water, and pa wasn't the sort to leave her. We found them snagged in the brush, a mite downstream."

"If anybody had a straight ticket to heaven it would be them." His eyes looked into hers. "Eve, I ain't much on talkin', nor am I any hand to court a woman, but all the way down here I been tellin' myself that if I found you alive . . . Eve, will you go east with me?"

"No, Linus, I'm stayin' right here. I'm not movin' a foot, one way or the other. Ma and pa, they wanted a farm in the West, and this is as far as they got. Seems to me this is where the Lord intended them to be."

"Sam will need rest an' care, Eve, an' winter's comin' on. I mean there ain't but a couple of months of time—less'n that— before snow flies. Winters here are tol'able hard."

"I'm going to stay, Linus. I'm going to make my home right here."

"I don't like to say it, you being bereft an' all, but you ain't makin' much sense, Eve. I don't need to tell you that."

"Half the folks who come west don't make much sense, Linus. You know it as well as I do."

Linus looked at her for a long time, and then he looked up and studied his surroundings. Dense forest of huge trees stood about, and very little brush, for this was virgin forest that had never been cut off to give the brush a chance.

But the meadow drew his attention as it had drawn Eve's, and he stepped around her and strolled out through the trees to look at the meadow and the grassy bench that overlooked it. Yes, he decided reluctantly, it was a good place, a very good place.

That trickle of water running down from the bench meant there was a spring up there somewhere, and the stream in the meadow's bottom was three to four feet wide and half that in depth. The grass was good, and judging by the grass and other vegetation, he knew the soil was rich.

He had noticed already, his hunter's eye being quick to observe such things, the tracks and the droppings of deer. A bit earlier when coming downriver he had seen a black bear at the water's edge. Oh, it was a game country, no mistaking that!

The river offered good transportation. From here a man could easily go downstream to the Mississippi with whatever he had to sell—furs and the like—and he could grow most of what the forest did not provide.

A man could build a right nice house on that bench, using timber from the slope behind, and there was plenty of fuel for the winter in the dead-falls and such like that lay about. If a man looked spry he might even find stray cattle in the brush, for he had heard of westing pioneers losing their stock.

"Eve," he said when he again came back to her side, "you're a strong-minded woman. I reckon I've seen the varmint for the last time."

He turned to the others. "You're all welcome to stay on with us. This here will be your home as long as you want, and whenever you're of a mind to come back. Sam, I'm thinking you'll be wanting to go west, but you'd best stay on an' get your strength back. Zeke, you're welcome."

He turned to Lilith and she drew back. "I'm goin' east, Linus. I said it to them and I'll say it to you. I don't want to live on no farm."

"Why, that's what I figured," he replied mildly. "If you don't feel you ought, you oughtn't. But you'd best wait until I sell my furs.

"Fixin's . . . you'll be needin' some fixin's. If a woman is goin' east among proper folk, she'd best be dressed to meet it. Without folks knowin' you, they set store by the way you look. And then I figure you'll make out if you have one of those there accordions like you had."

He took out his pipe and filled it carefully. "When I sell my furs I'll see you're fixed up proper, with some money to bide you. After that, it will be up to you."

Lilith started to speak, then her eyes filled with tears and, turning, she fled toward the riverbank.

"Eve, if we're fixin' to stay, we'd best pick a site for a house. You boys come along. We'll be needin' advice, more'n likely."

Together, they walked up the slope to the bench where the house would stand. The meadows would lie before them, and on their right would be the river where they could watch the boats go by.

"I figured the kitchen about there," Linus suggested. "If a woman has something to watch, she doesn't feel so closed in, like. And there you can see the boats. Time goes on, they'll be plentiful."

He turned to Sam. "Even if you're not going to stay, you'd best stake out some land next to mine. I can farm it, and if you never come back, I'll have it. If you do, it will be yours. Always warms a man to feel he owns himself some land, somewheres."

He looked toward the river. They would have their own landing, of course.

PART 2

THE PLAINS

The distances were immeasurable, the difficulties un-countable, but hundreds of men and women with white-topped prairie schooners came in plodding, dogged streams. This was a land of peril, thundering herds of buffalo, savage red riders who struck and slew and fled to turn and strike mercilessly again. This was a land whose asking price was blood and raw, unbeatable courage . . .

SEVEN

C leve Van Valen paused on the corner and glanced distaste-
fully at the river of mud that separated him from the lush
confines of the Planters' Hotel and its boasted 215 rooms and
"the largest ballroom west of the Alleghenies."

He was not planning to dispute their claim. All he wanted
was to get across the street without ruining the polish on his
elegant Paris-made boots or spattering the fine broadcloth suit,
tailored in New Orleans.

The truth of the matter was that Cleve Van Valen was riding
a streak of bad luck at the tables and elsewhere, and he knew
enough of gambling to know any man was a loser who played
when he had to win.

The run of bad luck was no new thing, for it actually had
begun, he decided bitterly, almost fifteen years ago when his
father dropped dead of a heart attack while Cleve had been
taking the Grand Tour of Europe.

Rushing home as swiftly as the sea would permit, he found
he had been less swift than the vultures, for in the interim his
father's estate had mysteriously vanished. Scarcely twenty-one,
and without business experience, he listened to the glib explanations of his father's associates and knew they lied . . . but
they had covered their actions very well.

69

They showed him notes signed by his father that he knew were forgeries, but he had no evidence, and the men who had defrauded him were prominent in business and social circles. He had no evidence, and what little sympathy there was for him was lost when he called John Norman Black a liar and a thief.

Black challenged him, making a great show of regret at the necessity. A skilled duelist and a noted pistol shot, Black assured all who knew him that the duel had been forced on him, and the last thing he wanted was a duel with the son of his former partner.

Yet on the field of honor, when they stood briefly back to back and out of earshot of the others, Black spoke over his shoulder. "Had your father not dropped dead, I should have killed him, for I did rob him and he discovered it. I shall now kill you."

Perhaps he hoped to make Cleve angry enough to be careless. Perhaps he merely wished to twist the knife in the wound. John Norman Black was a dead shot, and unworried. He took the required paces and turned, bringing his pistol down on the target.

Cleve Van Valen had never fought a duel nor fired a pistol in anger, yet there was nothing wrong with his reflexes. Instead of bringing his pistol down in the usual way, taking careful aim, he had simply turned and fired. Black's pistol exploded harmlessly in the air, and he fell, shot through the heart.

Feeling was against Cleve. All believed he had made wild, unreasonable accusations against a reputable citizen, and that he had been a hot-headed fool to challenge him. All agreed he had been astonishingly lucky to kill such a man. Without friends, the estate now far removed from him, he had nothing to gain by remaining in Maryland. So he started west, following the Natchez Trace.

He had neither profession nor trade. The business education which his father planned to give him on the job had gone glimmering. The one thing at which he possessed a degree of skill was cards. He had a natural card sense, a good memory, and he played well.

He worked New Orleans, winning and losing, always able to live well, but making no progress. He was young, and he had a liking for money and the spending of it. Moreover, he was a man without a destination.

Natchez, St. Louis, and Cincinnati followed, the river boats, and then, riding a winning streak, Europe. He spent two years there, moving from London to Paris, to Weimar, to Vienna, Innsbruck, and Monte Carlo. He fought his second duel at Nîmes, with sabers, and won.

But the winning streaks became fewer, and of shorter duration. He lived well, but the margin with which he played grew narrower, and the feeling grew within him that he was headed for the discard.

He returned to the United States, played a little around New York and Saratoga, often in small, private games. He played honestly, as always, but he played with skill, and he won.

He was well ahead of the game when one night he was recognized as a professional gambler. By noon the following day the clubs were closed to him, and an invitation he had accepted to appear at a party was quietly withdrawn.

In Cincinnati he lost much of what he had won, and now in St. Louis he was doing scarcely better. He stared at the river of mud that was the street, and wondered if here, too, he might sink clean out of sight.

He was nothing if not honest with himself, and he knew the slight he had received in New York had hurt. Deeply sensitive, he had been proud of his playing, and had never considered playing a crooked game . . . although he knew how it was done.

He stared at the mud. He was no longer a gentleman—he was a gambler, a questionable character in any sort of society. He was a gambler, and he consorted with gamblers.

Suddenly someone moved up beside him; it was Allen Jones, known wherever men gamed. "Going across to the hotel?" he asked. He smiled and indicated the street. "You'll never cross that in those boots, Cleve."

"I'll bet you the best dinner in St. Louis that I can cross that street without getting a speck of mud on me!" Cleve said quickly.

"Done!" Jones replied. "I'll take that bet."

Cleve glanced around. A bulky, heavy-shouldered man of middle age was coming up the street toward them. "You, there!" Cleve said. "I'll give you five dollars if you'll take me on your back across to the hotel."

The man hesitated, looking from Cleve Van Valen to Allen Jones.

"I've a bet on," Cleve explained, "that I can cross the street without getting muddy."

The heavy-set man smiled grimly. "All right." He backed up to Cleve. "Get aboard."

Cleve stepped astride him from the walk's edge, and, carrying him piggy-back, the man started slopping through the mud.

"Hey!" Jones yelled. "Ten dollars if you drop him!"

The man spoke over his shoulder. "Want to raise the ante?"

"We made a deal," Cleve replied. "I stand on the terms."

"Twenty dollars!" Jones yelled.

Hunching Cleve higher, the man struggled on through the mud, then deposited Cleve on the steps of the hotel.

Taking out a thin packet of bills, Cleve peeled off the five dollars and handed them to his bearer. Coolly, the man reached in his own pocket and removed a sack bulging with bills and coins. He added the five dollars to the sack, then grinned at Van Valen. "A little here, a little there. One day I shall be a rich man."

"You refused a larger sum to dump me into the mud," Cleve said.

The man glanced at him. "You said it yourself. A deal is a deal. If a man's word is no good in this country he's nothing."

"Come inside," Cleve suggested, "and I'll buy you a drink. Are you new to St. Louis?"

The stocky man grinned. "Don't take me for a man to be plucked, my friend. I'm no gambler. That's not to say I wouldn't take a flyer in a business way, but business is my game. Never play another man's game, that's what I say."

He stamped the mud from his boots. "Yes, I'll drink with you. They tell me Professor Jerry Thomas has come up with a new one called the Tom and Jerry."

"He's the best bartender in the country," Cleve said. "Come on inside." In the bar, he looked at the man again. "Maybe I'm wrong, but you look familiar, now that I see you in the light."

"I doubt if you saw me more than once or twice. I worked for your father."

Cleve's expression grew cold. "Oh? I don't recall any friends back there."

The man was not disturbed. "I'm Gabe French. You didn't know me; your father did. A time or two when the going was rough he gave me a hand up." French tasted his drink. "A good man."

"They robbed him," Cleve said bitterly.

"That they did . . . and you as well. It was a good job you did—shooting Black. He'd had it coming for a long time." French gave a quick glance at Van Valen. "Ever done any shooting since then?"

"When necessary."

"You've the knack, my friend. I saw it, you know. You simply turned and fired . . . instantaneous reflexes, no aiming. You simply turned and fired . . . bull's-eye."

Allen Jones joined them. "I owe you a dinner. Want to collect?"

"Mr. Jones . . . Mr. French."

French thrust out his hand. "I know you, too, Mr. Jones. Knew you when you were a saddle-maker."

"I made good saddles." Allen Jones spoke a little proudly. "There's a great feeling in it," he added. "Nothing better than turning a nice bit of work with good leather. I'll come back to it some day."

"Join us for dinner?" Cleve said to French.

"No, thanks. Got to be moving. Selling mules to folks bound for California, and I've about decided to go myself." He turned to Cleve, putting his glass down on the bar. "Want to come along? You could do well out there."

"I know when I'm well off. I'll stay here."

When Gabe French was gone, Jones turned to Cleve, chuckling. "Do you know who he is—that man you hired to pack you across the street? He's the biggest stockdealer in this part of the country. He's the richest man in town, if you skip old Choteau."

"I can see why he's rich," Van Valen said. He put down his glass. "I'll take that dinner now, Allen."

"The food is better right here," Jones said, "but the best

show is down the street. There's a new girl down there, just out from the East. She's really lovely. Dances, sings like an angel, plays the accordion. Her name is Prescott, Lilith Prescott."

The theatre-restaurant was crowded, but the waiter guided them to a table near the stage, for he recognized Allen Jones at once, and Cleve Van Valen was obviously cut from the same cloth.

Cleve glanced around, thinking wryly that if his present bad luck held he soon would no longer be able to afford meals in such a place, or the gambling in the rooms at the Planters'. He would be forced to work the wolf traps or snap houses on the bluff over the river.

Anything but that. Discontentedly he watched the girls on the stage. The dancing was not particularly good, but the swirl of their petticoats was enticing, and his discontent turned to half-amused interest.

The food was excellent, and the Chateau Margaux was a vintage wine. He relaxed slowly. Dick Hargraves, already notorious on the river, joined them, ordering a second bottle of wine. "Wait until you see Lily," he said. "That girl's got something special."

Jones laughed. "Anybody can see that, but nobody seems able to find out how special it is." He gestured. "Here she comes."

Lilith moved with an easy, impudent grace. It was at once apparent that she had something the other girls did not have, for aside from her very real beauty and that impudence, she had style.

Her eyes swept the crowd, and she began to sing, leading the chorus in "Wait for the Wagon." Her dancing was far better than Cleve had expected. Certainly, wherever she had learned, her instruction had been good. He sat up abruptly, refilled his glass from the bottle, and watched.

Cleve Van Valen, who had seen dancing in Paris, Vienna, and Rome, could see that she knew a great deal more than her present routine demanded. Somewhere, at some time, she had worked very hard to learn.

Curious, he watched her face. She was lost to all but the

music . . . and then their eyes met. Hers held his just for an instant, then moved on, away from him.

Had she really seen him? The footlights were not overly bright, so she might have been able to see, and he was close to the stage. He had a feeling that she had seen him and had in that instant catalogued both himself and his friends—drifters, gamblers, ne'er-do-wells.

"I say three at most," Hargraves was saying.

"Three what?" Cleve asked.

"Petticoats . . . Jones thinks she is wearing at least four."

"Four? I am sorry, gentlemen. She is wearing six."

"Six!" Jones exclaimed. "You're crazy, Van. It's all that lace that fools you. She can't be wearing more than four."

Hargraves put down his glass. "You'd better not bet with him, Allen. From all I hear, Cleve's an expert on everything pertaining to the female of the species. Anyway, there's no way to prove it."

"Look." Cleve had scarcely taken his eyes from the girl on the stage. "I just stuck you for dinner, and don't mind doing you in a little more. I will lay you an even hundred she has not less than six petticoats on."

"How would you prove it?"

"Go backstage and find out. Is it a bet?"

"If I go with you to check."

"Fair enough." Cleve got up. "Let's go!"

It was crowded backstage. Girls were coming and going in various stages of undress. There were no proper dressing rooms, simply shoulder-high screens, and behind each of these a girl was disrobing or changing costume.

Cleve Van Valen worked his way through the group with the assurance of a man to whom no situation is entirely strange, and the two gamblers followed.

Lilith Prescott was easy enough to find. She was behind a screen, only her head and the very top of her shoulders visible, while over her head hung an elaborate dress suspended by wires and prepared to be lowered about her. A wardrobe mistress stood outside the screen ready to take her clothing as it was removed.

Cleve looked across the screen at the girl's pretty, somewhat flushed face and asked himself if he had really come backstage to satisfy a bet, or to see more of this girl? Was it because her glance seemed to have catalogued him and brushed him aside as of no importance? He smiled at the thought of his pride being injured by so slight a thing, but admitted that it nettled him. He was not, he believed, more than ordinarily vain, but he had been fortunate with the attentions of women, of all sorts and kinds . . . and after all, what sort of girl would be dancing in such a place?

As he hesitated, awaiting the proper moment to ask his question, he heard someone say. "Oh, I beg your pardon!"

Glancing around, he saw a middle-aged man moving somewhat diffidently through the backstage crowd. Obviously, he was both confused by the disorder and embarrassed by the visible extent of bare flesh and stockinged leg, but he persisted until he reached Lilith Prescott's screen. Hesitantly, he said, "Miss Prescott? Miss Prescott?"

She did not even look up. "Later."

"It's quite important, Miss Prescott. I—"

"It's always important. The older they are, the more important it becomes."

A petticoat flopped over the edge of the screen, and Cleve lifted a finger.

"Miss Prescott, you misunderstand. I am Hylan Seabury, attorney in the matter of Jonathan Brooks." Seabury paused. "Does he mean nothing to you?"

"That old goat?"

"Well," Seabury said testily, "you evidently meant something to him. He included you in his will."

She looked over the screen, startled. "He *what?*" Her eyes went past Seabury, meeting those of Van Valen. She looked away.

A second petticoat flipped over the screen, then a third. Cleve's fingers registered them as they appeared. "I'm going to win, gentlemen. Not less than six."

As he spoke there was a momentary lull in the noise backstage and his voice sounded loud in the partial silence.

"You will have to go to California, Miss Prescott, to take advantage of the bequest, but if I were you—"

"You're not me. And I wouldn't go to California if John Jacob Astor willed me all of San Francisco." As she spoke the fourth petticoat flopped over the screen and was taken up by the wardrobe mistress.

Cleve's fourth finger came up. "See? That makes four. And my bet was not less than six."

"Mr. Astor has no such holdings in San Francisco, Miss Prescott. However, you will discover the yield from Mr. Brooks's holdings is not to be scorned. Definitely not."

The fifth petticoat appeared atop the screen, and the men whose task it was to lower the ornate costume cleared their lines.

"That's all, Mary. All right, boys."

"All?"

"You heard me. *That's all!*" She lifted her arms into the dress as it descended around her, moving her shoulders to settle the dress into place.

"Yield, you said. Yield of what?"

"Gold, Miss Prescott. In fact, I am advised the property is considered quite a good one. Now, if you would like to sign these papers—"

"Did you say . . . *gold?*"

"Precisely. The claim yielded thirty-five hundred dollars during the first week."

Lilith glanced past Seabury at Cleve Van Valen, who was counting gold eagles into Jones's outstretched hand. "You win," Cleve said, "but damn it, I'd have sworn—"

"You did swear, but you lost. Not less than six, you said, and we all heard you."

Dropping the last coin into Jones's hand, Cleve heard Lilith saying, "For that much, I might even go to California."

Disgusted with his luck, Cleve turned away, and as he walked off, Lilith flopped the sixth petticoat over the screen, then stuck out her tongue at his retreating back.

EIGHT

Night, and a distant glow upon the sky . . . now, what would that be? Stars overhead, and somewhere, not too far off, a dog barking. No sound but the creak of his saddle and the *clop-clop-clop* of his horse's hoofs. The air was cool, and he thought he could smell the river.

Cleve Van Valen knew he was seven kinds of a fool, starting off after a girl who might not even have come this way. Had he not heard her say she would not go to California? Still, when the lawyer mentioned gold she was interested . . . and so was he.

Cleve took a long, slow look at himself and did not like what he saw—a grown man who had wasted fourteen or fifteen years of his life gambling, and who was now searching for a girl simply because she had inherited a gold mine. And why? Because he hoped to marry her and so gain possession of the mine and its income.

There was little in the past of which he was proud, yet nothing of which he was actually ashamed; but if he did what he had set out to do there would be reason for shame. If he could manage it at all . . . and that was the joker in his little deck of cards, for Lilith Prescott had manifested not the slightest interest in him at any time.

She had glanced his way, seen him and the company he kept, and had ignored him from then on. And that was what rankled.

Yet the thought aroused amused irritation. What kind of a child was he to be irritated because she ignored him? He had been loved by women, and he had been hated by them, and once a girl had even tried to kill him, but none had ever been indifferent to him.

Was it that which disturbed him? Or was it the thought of losing a chance at all that gold?

She had cost him a hundred dollars because of one petticoat, and he intended to have his own back. So he told himself—and he lied in his teeth. He was going to try to marry Lilith Prescott, not because he loved her or even liked her type, but simply because he had failed at everything else and was looking for a soft spot to light before he got too old. And when a man faced up to such a decision it was not a very nice thing.

But how in God's world could he find one girl in a place as wide as the open West? Even such a girl as Lilith Prescott?

Find her he must. In his pocket he carried three twenty-dollar gold pieces, and he owned the horse he rode. He had a pistol in his belt holster, and a few clothes wrapped in a blanket behind his saddle. He had no rifle, no experience with the frontier, and nothing to warrant his going west.

He had suddenly, on a mere whim, tied his future to this girl with her legacy; yet what else could he have done?

He was not even sure she had come this way—only that she had quit her job and disappeared into thin air. But coming on the heels of the legacy, it was a likely supposition. Around Independence and its neighboring area, gathered the people who were moving westward in their wagons and on horseback. There they gathered, arranged themselves into wagon trains, repaired equipment, and generally prepared for the long journey ahead of them.

Suddenly Van Valen topped out on a rise and drew up in amazement. Before him, the wide plain stretched toward the river, and in the center of that plain was a town with lights ablaze, although it was past midnight. But it was not the town that surprised him, nor even the fact that it was lighted at this late hour—it was the campfires around.

Even the low hills had their encampments, and it seemed as if there must be a campfire for every star in the sky. Wherever he looked, the night was sparkling with their lights, flickering, inviting.

Since he was a child he had heard tales of men who went west, and talk of others who planned to go, but never in his wildest imaginings had he dreamed of such an exodus as this appeared to be. They must have been gathering here for weeks. Undoubtedly a few venturesome souls had already headed out across the prairie that lay to the west, but still several days away.

It was an hour later when he rode up to Bob Weston's blacksmith shop. There were other smiths in town, but this was the largest and most active, and it was a focal point for travelers planning to go west. Both a place of rendezvous and the place for the organization of wagon trains, it was always crowded. Here he would begin his inquiries.

A dozen anvils were clanging under the blows of hammers, the forges glowed with their fire, and the soot-darkened faces of the smiths reflected the red of the fire on their faces and bodies. At least twenty smiths were working, hammering out shoes for horses, shoeing them, or doing bits of ironwork for wagons. And this was the middle of the night!

A wagon rolled by, a woman on the seat holding a crying child, a man walking beside the wagon carrying an ox goad. But they were going west.

Suddenly a hand grasped his stirrup. "You, is it? You're going west?" It was Gabe French.

"Thinking about it. How about you?"

"Pulling out tomorrow with the Roger Morgan Company, and I'll have four wagons. If you want to come along, see me before you join up. I could use an extra hand."

"I'll look around."

Gabe French lifted a hand and hurried away with his odd, bandy-legged walk. Cleve looked after him. "He's the one who will make it, boy," he said to his horse. "When you and I are still broke, he will own half of California."

Under a torchlight across the street a man was operating a three-card monte layout. Cleve looked closer. It was Canada Bill.

Riding on along the street, he watched wagons loading and pulling out on the prairie. Wherever he turned his attention there was activity, and there was talk. Never in his life had he seen so many men talking and using the identical words so often. It was talk of the trail, of the best wagons, of oxen, horses, or mules. There was speculation about Indians, about forts being established. They were rapt, excited . . . they were men involved in a colossal binge, a gigantic migration, and West was the magic word. It was the "Open Sesame" to fantastic futures.

Turning his mount, he started back. He was dead-tired and had best find a place to bed down, and Colonel Noland's inn was just up the street.

Then, just as he was again nearing the clangor of Bob Weston's blacksmith shop, he saw her.

She was deep in conversation with a tall, powerfully built man who was examining some whips laid out for sale on a table just outside the door of the blacksmith shop.

Drawing rein in the deep shadow near a building, he listened. The man was speaking. "You got a wagon, I suppose?"

"I can get one," Lilith replied.

"And a team?"

"Whatever I need, I'll get."

"You're married?"

"I am single, Mr. Morgan."

"Travelin' alone?"

"Yes."

"Not on my wagon train. A woman alone an' single, that puts deviltry into men. Gets 'em all worked up, an' believe me, on these trains they're wild enough already."

"I shall keep to myself, Mr. Morgan, and I can take care of myself. After all," she added dryly, "any problem that is likely to arise will be one I have handled before."

"No doubt. But a woman of your sort? One day you'd find yourself in trouble and there'd be hell to pay just figurin' out who."

Lilith's face went white. She caught up one of the whips and, taking a quick step back, she unfurled the whip in a business-like manner. "Now," she said icily, "you repeat that, Mr. Morgan, and you'll get the horse-whipping you deserve."

Morgan laughed, but there was respect in his eyes. "Well, now. I like a woman with spirit, and I'd no right to speak as I did. I have an idea you'll do to take along." He took the whip from her hand. "This is the whip I'll want," he said, and tossed a coin on the counter.

Then he turned to Lilith again. "There's a woman named Clegg—Aggie Clegg. You might try getting her to join you, or vice versa. I'd be glad to take the two of you."

Cleve waited in the shadows until Lilith started away, then followed at a discreet distance. She walked with a purpose that indicated she knew where the Clegg woman could be found.

At the end of the street she turned toward several wagons standing on the prairie's edge. By torchlight a woman was loading a heavy crate into the back of a wagon.

When Cleve came within earshot he heard the woman saying, "Well, I don't know. I'd been hoping to make the trip with a husband, and almost caught me one last week."

"They tell me there are forty men to every woman in California. Look, Miss Clegg, I'd be willing to pay you."

"I don't want money, I want a man." Looking at Lil, she added, "You'll need one, too, before this trip's over."

Gently, Cleve touched a heel to his horse and walked him forward. They looked up at the sound.

"Good evening, ladies, a very good evening to you. Miss Prescott? Cleve Van Valen, at your service. At your command, if you will, from here to California."

"Thanks," Lilith replied brusquely. "Whatever it is you're offering, we don't need."

Agatha Clegg wiped her hands on the front of her apron. "Speak for yourself, honey. Like I said, before this trip is over—"

Cleve interrupted. "Perhaps you do not understand, Miss Prescott. I—"

"I understand, all right. And I know a tinhorn when I see one."

"I'm offering an honest day's work for an honest day's pay."

"Good-bye, Mr. Van Valen."

Cleve turned to the older woman. "It has been a pleasure to meet you, Miss Clegg. And I've never seen a woman with more beautiful hair . . . naturally, I worry, because what a

prize it would be, hanging from the mane of an Indian pony."
Glancing at Lilith, he said seriously, "I hope you realize what
you are doing, Miss Prescott. Two lovely ladies, alone in the
wilderness, and who will protect you? When Indians attack,
each man is busy protecting his own, and they can't be blamed
for thinking of their families first." He lifted his hat. "Good
evening, ma'am. Or should I say good morning?"

Turning his horse, he rode away between the wagons, and
Lilith looked after him, half irritated, half amused.

"Gosh!" said Aggie. "Nobody ever said that to me before."

"What?"

"That I had beautiful hair." Self-consciously, she put a hand
to her hair, then she said to Lilith, "You know, I've a hunch
you'll draw men like fish to bait. Maybe I can catch one as he
swims by." She thrust out a hand. "All right, Miss Whatever-
Your-Name-Is, you've got a partner."

"The name is Lilith Prescott," she said, "and don't think I
won't carry my weight. I grew up on a farm in northern New
York state."

"I'd never have guessed it." Agatha looked at her thoughtfully. "It's a wonder a fine-looking girl like you isn't married."

"I haven't been looking," Lilith replied stiffly. "When I find
the right man, I'll marry, but I'm in no hurry."

Cleve rode back toward town, not at all displeased with the
situation. He had a feeling that he had sowed seed on fertile
ground.

From time to time he drew up to listen to some of the
conversations about him, worried for the first time about his
own inadequacy for the venture that lay before him. He had
handled teams, and there had been a time or two when he had
done some physical work, but those times had been few.

These men about him were all manner of men, from all
professions and trades, and of every nationality. There were
Germans, Swiss, French, Poles, Swedes, Norwegians, and
Spaniards. In short, there was every conceivable kind of man,
with all sorts and kinds of wagons.

A tall man in a stovepipe hat with mutton-chop whiskers
stopped him. "Sir, would you have a light? I've spent my last
match."

Cleve provided the light. "Are you among the pioneers?" he

asked, though he realized how foolish the question must seem at this place and time.

"Lawyer, sir. Attorney-at-law, and westward bound. Gold, sir. I am after gold, but I shall not mine for it. I shall wait for them to bring it to me."

"You're a gambler? Or are you planning to open a saloon?"

"Neither, sir. As I said, I am a lawyer, and where there are men and gold there will be litigation, and where there is litigation, lawyers will be needed. I have no doubt, sir, that I shall become rich."

Cleve rode on. Lawyer he might be, but with that nose he had without doubt seen the inside of many a saloon. Cleve rode to the Noland House and was fortunate enough to find an empty bed, although it was still warm from the body of the last man, who was undoubtedly now preparing to start west with a wagon train. Four trains were leaving that morning.

At breakfast the following morning in Noland's dining room he heard that the Morgan train had gone. The first day they would scarcely move more than eight to ten miles, just enough to break in the teams and get them used to the work. They might even stop short of that, for it was customary to make the first day or two easy, until the stock became broken to the trail.

Twice during the morning men came trying to buy Cleve's horse, but he refused to sell. Later, after he had sat around the hotel listening and keeping his eyes open for a small game which failed to materialize, he went out and laid in some modest supplies. He bought a coffee pot, some pemmican, and, from an old Missourian, some cold flour.

He had never heard of cold flour, but the Missourian merely chuckled. "Lots of folks hain't heard of it," he said. "Mexicans, they use it. You just take some corn and grind her up good after it's parched. Then you add a mite of sugar and cinnamon. Man can live a month on a half-bushel of it, and tasty, too. A feller just mixes a bit of it into water and drinks it down."

He bought a gutta-percha poncho, against possible rainstorms, a couple of blankets, and a ground sheet. He added a canteen, and a hundred cartridges for his pistol.

The provision stores were crowded with men buying, planning, asking advice of the storekeepers and of others—of anyone, in fact, who had time to listen.

"Butter?" Cleve overheard a man saying. "Why, butter's no problem at all. Boil it . . . boil it well, and skim it off until it's clear like oil, then you put it in tin canisters and solder it up. Even down Texas way where she gets mighty hot, that butter will keep.

"Vegetables? Sure, you can have them too. You get them desiccated vegetables like the army uses. They're pressed down and heated into cakes as solid as a rock. A chunk of it no bigger than a woman's fist will make a pot for four, five men. I et 'em with the army out Utah way when we went out to keep an eye on Brigham an' his Saints. Tasty, that's what they are, an' they stick to your ribs."

He found a supply of his cigars at Noland's and laid in a stock. It was the one luxury he was to permit himself. His was a small outfit, but he had little money, and wanted to keep a few dollars for a stake in case somebody started a game on the way west.

His horse had been ridden but little, and no great distance for some time, and would need breaking in to the trail. He mounted up and started west.

He had no plans to catch up to the wagons for a while. He wanted to be far enough away from the settlements so it would be impractical for Roger Morgan to order him to return.

Roger Morgan had a reputation. He was known as a fine wagonmaster, one of the few who organized such trains, for the usual procedure was to elect a captain from among the pioneers themselves, and to depose him if he failed to lead and command as he should. Morgan had been over the trail several times, and functioned both as a guide and as a wagonmaster. He was known as a hard man, who permitted no nonsense on his trains and was prepared to handle any difficulties that arose.

There were scattered settlements and ranch houses for some distance west of both Independence and Leavenworth, and they were pleased to welcome a visitor. People were hungry for news of the world, and they wanted to know what was happening in the outfitting towns like Independence.

An easy talker, polite but never forward, Cleve Van Valen found a ready audience for his accounts of what was happening in St. Louis and Cincinnati, and in Independence itself. He took his time, often riding only a few miles a day, stopping on the way at ranches to share the home cooking, and with it all, he asked questions.

He was too wise in the ways of gambling not to realize his handicap in going into an area where he must play the other fellow's game, something no gambler believed in doing. During long sessions over card tables and around frontier gambling houses and on the river boats he had heard much talk of Indian fighting, of life on the plains and in the mountains, and the result was that he understood what he was facing. Now he made further inquiries from the settlers along the frontier. He wanted to fit in when he caught up with the wagons, to prove valuable to Lilith Prescott and the wagon train.

A Cherokee he met west of Leavenworth was riding to join a party of hunters, and Cleve rode along with him. The Cherokee, who had once owned a plantation and slaves in Georgia before being forced to move west during the Indian removal, explained to him about the Kiowa, the Arapahoe, and the Cheyenne Indians he would meet further west. These, in contrast to the Cherokees, Choctaws, Chickasaws, Creeks, and Seminoles, were wild Indians, given to raiding, horse-thieving, and scalp-hunting.

"They will stampede your stock if they can," the Cherokee explained, "driving it off to round up later. And any man caught out away from the train will be killed—be sure of that."

After three days' riding together, they parted on the bank of a small stream, and the Cherokee pointed out the wagon road west. Turning his mount, Cleve Van Valen rode away. He crossed the stream, emerged from the brush on the far side, and started his horse up the long grassy slope.

The air was very clear . . . no clouds were in the sky. It was pleasant, not too warm, and his horse walked easily through the tall grass. On top of the hill, with the wagon road below him and some distance off, Cleve drew up.

As far as the eye could see, there rolled the endless grass. Far off, two dark objects grazing upon the grass would be buffalo. He drew the fresh air deep into his lungs, and it was like drinking a long draught of cold, clear water. Nothing moved out there, nothing but the wind and the low grass that bent before it. Yes . . . it was a man's country.

His gelding pricked its ears at the distance, stamping an impatient foot at the delay.

All through the day he rode across the miles of grass, and when he camped that night it was in the willows near a stream. At daybreak he was up, and for the first time he made coffee and mixed a little cold flour with water and drank it. Then he started on.

The wagons were drawn up for a "nooning" near a river when he came near to them. They were not far beyond Vermilion Creek and were headed for a camp on the upper crossing of the Big Blue.

Almost the first wagon he saw was that belonging to Agatha Clegg and Lilith Prescott. The big man sitting his mount alongside their fire could be none other than Roger Morgan, who turned his head to look as Cleve cantered up.

Cleve removed his hat with a graceful sweep. "Ladies," he began, "I—"

"I thought," Lilith interrupted dryly, "that we had seen the last of you."

"Frankly, I was worried. I couldn't bear to think of you making the trip alone and without help. If anything had happened to you I could never have forgiven myself."

"You rode a hundred miles alone?" Morgan asked.

"I'll take your word for the distance. I was so filled with anticipation that I scarcely noticed."

"You can anticipate another hundred on your way back. We'll have no gamblers on this train. When a wagon breaks down I want men who can fix it, not bet on how long it'll take."

"You mean you'd turn a man adrift? In Indian country?"

"We ain't into Indian country yet, and you got here by yourself, so I guess you can get back."

Lilith started to protest, but Aggie was already speaking. "Mr. Morgan, I talked to this man back at Independence. I told him if he got his affairs straightened out and caught up with us that we'd take him on. We're likely to need a man before this trip is over."

"I'm a good man on a horse, captain, and a dead shot," Cleve said.

Morgan turned to Lilith, his irritation obvious. "Is that right, Miss Prescott? Did you actually agree to hire this—this gambler?"

"Miss Clegg spoke of it," she replied, honestly enough, "and it seemed the thing to do. Besides, Mr. Van Valen has another friend on the train. Gabe French speaks very highly of him."

Morgan was surprised, and doubtful. "You know Gabe French?"

"Of course. As a matter of fact, we did a bit of business together once—transportation, it was. I will confess that Gabe carried most of the load, but our association was mutually satisfactory."

Somewhat reassured, Morgan nodded. "All right, then, if that's what you want." He rode off toward the head of the wagon train.

Lilith then turned sharply on Agatha. "Agatha! What's gotten into you? Are you crazy?"

"He said he'd do an honest day's work, and you an' me have come far enough to know this here is a lot too much for us. I don't mind rustlin' buffalo chips an' drivin' a team, but takin' them to water, stakin' them out, an' cuttin' what wood a body can find, that's too much."

"You are right, of course." Lilith measured Cleve with a cool eye. "One thing I promise you, Agatha. He will do his work. He'll do it, or I'll see that he starts riding alone—no matter where we are."

"Yes, ma'am," Cleve said politely. "As you say, ma'am."

Dismounting, he tied his horse to the tail-gate and got up on the seat. He picked up the reins and spoke to the mules.

"Hey, you ain't had nothing to eat!" Agatha protested.

"Another time, fair lady," Cleve replied, keeping a straight face. "My ruthless employer allows no time for such nonsense. Besides, it is time to pull out."

Cleve removed his coat and folded it carefully, and Lilith glanced at the immaculate white shirt. It would not be white for long.

Before them the plains stretched wide and lonely, and the wagons rolled on over the dusty grass. Soon the spring rains would come, and Morgan wanted to have them far enough along so they would be free of the worst of the mud.

Sitting behind a team of mules on a long day's march allows time for thinking, and Cleve Van Valen settled down to plan his course of action. Lilith had a gold mine and he wanted it, so the first thing he must do was to win Lilith.

Yet the last thing for him to do was to seem to want her. She was no fool, and was far too worldly-wise to be easily taken in. No doubt many men had flattered her and lied to her, and she was already suspicious of him. Therefore he must avoid her.

He must do his job well, but avoid all contact with her in doing it. He must never seem to wish to be close to her, never begin a conversation with her. Also, he must be efficient at what he had to do; if he was not, he might not last long enough with the train to work out his plan.

The few days of travel while the wagons were getting well out upon the prairie gave him a chance to break himself in to the life. The Cherokee had been of enormous help and, finding Cleve eager to learn, he had packed a lot of instruction into their few days together. Now, with time on his hands Cleve tried to recall everything he'd ever heard that might be useful.

In the course of his traveling about and being around the frontier towns he had listened to a lot of conversation and had retained much of it, for he had a retentive memory, and he had always been interested in concrete information and facts, and he had listened well.

Odd fragments of information began to return to him, things remembered from trappers or Indian fighters with whom he had spent long hours, gambling or talking. Fortunately, he had read a good bit, too—among other things, Washington Irving's *Tour on the Prairies* and Dr. Gregg's *Commerce of the Prairies*. Systematically, he began sifting his memory for whatever he could remember from those books.

The Big Blue was clear and cold when they made camp at the upper crossing. At that point the river was all of sixty yards wide. There was good grass and there was wood.

Cleve, who had planned every step he would take upon arriving at camp, swiftly unhitched the mules and stripped them of their harness; then, leaving them tied to the wagon, he got a fire going, using buffalo chips and what sticks lay at hand. Once the fire was ablaze he took the mules to water, then turned them into the rope corral with the other stock to be watched by the night guards. His own horse he picketed near the wagon.

Taking an axe, he went to the timber along the stream and cut wood for the night fire and for breakfast in the morning.

Unaccustomed as he was to such work, he found it hard. His hands blistered on the axe, and the blisters broke. During his boyhood he had often hunted or fished in the mountains of Virginia, and all through his early years he had lived an active life of riding, shooting, and fencing. But he had never done any such work as this.

When he returned to the fire with an armful of wood for morning, Agatha handed him his plate filled with food. His hands felt cramped and stiff, and she noticed the awkward way in which he accepted the plate from her. But he took the plate and walked a few yards away and sat down by himself. Lilith glanced at him curiously, but he appeared not to notice.

He had almost finished eating when he looked up, to see Roger Morgan beside him.

"Why'd you keep your horse up?"

"It seemed to me," Cleve replied, "that if Indians stampeded our stock I'd look mighty foolish hunting them on foot."

Morgan made no reply, but looked at him a moment, then walked over to the fire. Lighting a cigar, he stood there talking to Lilith and Agatha. After a few minutes Agatha came over to Cleve and refilled his cup. He refused another helping of food, although he could easily have eaten it.

The next morning, awakening early, Cleve rolled out as soon as his eyes were open, and went at once to water his gelding. When he returned, he saddled him and tied him to the wagon wheel. Then he knelt by the fire.

Stirring it up, he added fuel and put on a kettle with water. It was cold, and by the time he had the fire going he was shaking with chill. He went to the stream, bathed quickly in the cold water, dressed, and returned to the fire to add more fuel. Agatha was up, so he left the fire and went to the corral for the mules.

By the time the team was harnessed coffee was ready, and Cleve hunkered down near the fire, nursing his cup of coffee in his cold hands.

Today their position was near the end of the wagon train, for the positions were changed each day, working by rotation. As he finished harnessing the mules, Cleve turned to Lilith. "Would you like to ride my horse? I don't like him tied to the back of the wagon when we cross that river."

"Of course," she agreed.

Taking up the lines, he turned the heavy wagon into the column. When the wagon that preceded them was well into the stream, he followed. The mules, he was pleased to see, showed no hesitation at going into the water. It was not deep at the ford, coming scarcely to the wagon bed, but he took no chances and lined up carefully on the wagon ahead and followed with care.

Agatha, beside him on the seat, commented, "For a gambler, you handle a team right well."

"I never drove very much, actually. As a youngster I drove a coach and four a few times."

Just then from behind him there came a sharp exclamation, then a scream. He handed the reins to Agatha and, thinking of Lilith, jumped up on the seat to look around the canvas top. There was another scream, then a frantic splashing in the water, followed by a hoarse shout: "Sarah! My God, *Sarah!*"

Looking around, he saw that the wagon following them had gone off into the deeper water beside the ledge by which they were fording the river. A large snag had entangled itself in the wagon wheels and rolled over. Thrown clear, the woman was splashing in deep water, obviously unable to swim. Cleve peeled off his boots and dove from the seat into the water.

Coming up, he caught hold of a half-submerged tree and looked around quickly to locate the struggling woman. He was just in time to see Morgan extend the end of his whip to her and pull her to shore. Unnoticed by anyone, Cleve reached the bank and staggered up, dripping with water. Glancing back, he saw Roger Morgan watching him.

Nobody else seemed to have noticed his futile gesture. But as he started up the bank to rejoin the wagons he slipped and sprawled full length in the mud, and heard a ring of laughter. Looking up angrily, he saw Lilith laughing at him, and even Agatha had a smile on her face.

He got to his feet and stared down at his clothing. "Don't try to wipe it off," Agatha said. "If you wait until it dries, most of it will brush off."

He went to the wagon and climbed aboard, taking the reins from Agatha.

"Well," she said dryly, "you did more good by falling on your face in the mud than anything else you've done."

"I felt like a fool."

"No woman objects to a man looking the fool once in a while—makes 'em more human, somehow. Oh, I know what you've been doing! Don't think I'm altogether a fool, Cleve Van Valen! Thing is, you did it today. From now on she'll be on your side."

"I doubt it."

"You wait an' see," Agatha said, "and mind what I tell you."

NINE

Firelight played shadow games on the white wagon-covers, and the people of the camp moved through the ritual steps of the nightly pause as though through some strange, stately ballet performed only for the stars above. Nearby the waters of the Blue chuckled over the stones—this was the Little Blue— and the horses in their rope corral stamped and cropped grass against the demands of the coming day.

Cleve Van Valen glanced around at the tightly drawn circle of wagons. They were in Indian country now, and there were the usual rumors of war parties. These rumors drew the circle tighter as apprehension grew, and the men were more watchful, sensitive to the slightest noise or to a change in the nightly hum of insects.

There were those, of course, who scoffed at Indian attacks and who did not fear, who believed death was something that happened to others, and not to them. They had not yet discovered the impartiality of death.

Carefully, Cleve cleaned his pistol, removing all the dust, adding a drop of oil. Then he checked the loads in the three spare cylinders he carried. This was a wise precaution, he decided. It was not easy to load a cap-and-ball pistol in a hurry; it was much easier simply to switch cylinders, which a man could do on a horse and at a dead run. He was checking the last cylinder when he heard someone approaching.

It was Morgan. He indicated the pistol. "Gabe French tells me you can use that thing."

"When I have to," Cleve commented. "I've grown up with it."

"You may have to." Morgan lowered his voice. "We saw Cheyenne tracks today, and they're scouting us. No travois trails, so it's a war party." Morgan glanced toward the wagons, but Lilith was out of sight. "How are you with a rifle?" he asked.

"Good. But I don't have one."

"Gabe's got a Colt revolving rifle. Fires six shots. He said you could use it."

"All right." Cleve looked up. "How did you know they were Cheyennes?"

"Moccasins . . . every tribe's moccasins are different. Other things, too. Different ways of doing things."

Reluctantly, Morgan strolled on, making his nightly survey of the camp.

This was the fifth day since the Big Blue and the events at the crossing, and they had made good time to this point. Seventeen miles the first day, fifteen the next, and the last two days had each been nineteen-mile days. In fact, the last one had been slightly more than nineteen miles. And that, with a wagon train of this size, was good going.

The grass had been good and so far there had been plenty of water, but all knew that the worst travel lay ahead of them. Cleve, profiting by talk overheard before this trip began, had hung a canvas ground sheet under the wagon and into this he had heaped buffalo chips, chunks of wood, and odds and ends of fuel. There was no shortage of fuel now, but in the days ahead this would not be true, and he intended to be ready before they reached that stretch where most of what was available would already have been burned.

After a few minutes Lilith came from the wagon to the fire. She had offered to mend a pair of Cleve's pants and she carried them now. He stood over her for a minute or so, then dropped to a rock beside the fire.

"I'm overwhelmed at all this attention, Miss Prescott, but I am surprised too."

"Surprised?"

"I had no idea you were so domestic."

"My home was a farm in upper New York state. I have often mended trousers for my brothers."

"I never had a brother—or a sister."

"My sister lives on the Ohio. She married a mountain man—Linus Rawlings. And I have two brothers."

"No parents."

"They were lost at the falls of the Ohio. That was four, almost five years ago."

"I want to confess, Lil," he said suddenly. "I lied about why I wanted to work for you."

"Did you think I didn't know that?"

"The real reason is . . . I'm in love with you." He stopped her as she was about to speak. "It's the truth. Since the first time I saw you I've known I couldn't live without you."

"I'd not like to be the cause of your death, Mr. Van Valen," she said lightly.

"I'm serious. And I'm ready to assume the responsibilities of a faithful husband."

"And to assume the responsibilities for my property as well, Mr. Van Valen?"

"Really? What kind of property?"

"Gold, Mr. Van Valen. Gold by the ton, from what I understand. Bright, yellow, shiny gold."

"Why, I—I had no idea."

"Oh, I'm sure you didn't," she said mockingly. "It is simply a remarkable coincidence."

"Coincidence?"

"Oh, just the fact that when you were back stage settling your bet on how many petticoats I wore, I should receive word of my inheritance."

"You knew about the bet?"

"Of course. And if I could overhear what you were saying, I am sure you could overhear what Mr. Seabury told me. Or am I too suspicious?"

"I think you are."

"Here comes Agatha. Now, if you must propose to somebody, I suggest you get on your knees to her. She has such beautiful hair."

Lilith got to her feet, smiling sweetly. "And by the way, Mr. Van Valen—there were *six* petticoats!"

Agatha indicated the circle that had gathered about a neighboring fire where they were singing "Home, Sweet Home." "Listen to 'em. You'd think they was buryin' somebody."

Lilith broke her thread and handed the mended pants to Cleve, then she tossed back her hair and, gathering a fold of her skirt, moved toward the circle. She started to half-speak, half-sing the words of "Raise a Ruckus," emphasizing its humor and bounce.

As she reached the chorus in full voice, she moved back toward her own fire, and people drifted over to listen. As she sang she saw the sadness and weariness leaving their faces, and by the second chorus their voices began to join in. Roger Morgan paused outside the circle, watching them and observing the effect of her voice on the others. Over their heads his eyes met those of Cleve, and then he walked away.

The night was pleasantly cool, the sky clear. After watching the singers for a few minutes, Cleve slipped away to check his gelding, and then the stock that was encircled by the rope corral.

It was very still. Far off a coyote serenaded the night with plaintive music. Cleve's boots crunched in the grass as he walked up to the mules, and they flicked their long ears at his voice. He paused near them, liking the sound of their cropping of the grass. His ears had learned to sort the sounds, to hear only the strange, different ones while being aware of all the others.

That Lil . . . she had known all along why he had joined the wagon train. She had seen through him from the beginning, and it was no wonder that she wanted nothing to do with him.

Some night bird was moving in the bushes, the crickets were singing. He walked a little further, listening to the singing, unable to distinguish the words, but liking the music. Lil's voice reached out, clear and strong. There was more to her than he had suspected. She had intelligence, and she was shrewd as well—and the two are far from the same thing. Moreover, she had character.

He considered the future. It was not going to be easy—far from easy, in fact; but she was lovely, and he was not going to mind too much if it took a little longer. After all, what else was there to do on a wagon train?

Day had not yet come when he rolled out of his blankets and went for the mules. The night guard let him out of the corral with his six charges and he took them at once to water, then to the wagon to harness them. He was snapping a trace chain in place when he heard Morgan talking to Lilith. She had been carrying water from a spring near the river to fill the water barrels.

"Miss Prescott," Morgan said, "I've been thinking."

"Oh?"

"Wet or dry, you're the handsomest woman I ever did see. You've got spirit, and a fine, sturdy body—a noble combination. Why, to you child-bearin' would come easy as rollin' off a log."

"If you leave it to me, Mr. Morgan," she said dryly, "I'd rather roll off the log."

"Ma'am, I'm tellin' you. You got the build for it, and that's what I'm lookin' for. I want you for my wife. I've got a cattle outfit just below the Merced, an' I'll be settlin' down there, fit an' proper."

"I'm sure you'll be very fit and proper, Mr. Morgan."

"Then you just naturally couldn't do any better than to marry me. We could have ourselves a fine family in just no time at all."

"I believe it, but I can't accept your proposal, Mr. Morgan."

"Why not?"

"A woman likes to hear something more inviting in the way of a proposal, something to indicate she is valued for herself."

"Ain't that what I been doin'? Invitin' you? I'm invitin' you to share my life, Miss Prescott."

"I'm sorry, Mr. Morgan."

"It's something else, something naggin' at you. Well, I don't intend to let it stop me, you can count on that."

As quietly as he could, Cleve completed his job with the trace chains, and saddled his horse. He heard Agatha speak then.

"What did he want?"

"Children."

"Children? Well, I'll— Why don't he come shoppin' to the right store?"

They stood at the rear of the wagon, and the jangle of harness chains had helped to deaden the sound of his own soft movements. Lilith emptied the bucket of water she had brought from the spring and started toward the front of the wagon.

Guiltily, he started to worry with a stirrup strap, keeping his eyes averted.

"Mr. Van Valen?" He glanced around. Her eyes were cool. "How long have you been standing there?"

"I've been harnessing up, but if you mean did I hear the proposal, I did. In fact," he said seriously, "I think he made you a good offer, and he's a good man. Of course, I might have done it a little different."

"You already have—or had you forgotten?"

"How could I forget? Children . . . I guess every man worth his salt would like to have children—a son, anyway. But he would also like to think he's marrying a girl who loves him, somebody he can do things for."

"And what would you do for a girl, Mr. Van Valen?"

"Why, I don't rightly know," he said honestly enough. "A man thinks of this sort of thing, but when it actually comes— well, for one thing, I'd try not to ever let her forget she's young and beautiful."

He dropped the stirrup into place and gathered the reins. "If I didn't have the money for perfume or fine clothes, I could at least go into the fields and gather flowers."

She looked at him thoughtfully, as if measuring his sincerity. After a minute, she said, "You could teach Mr. Morgan a good deal about women, Mr. Van Valen, but his example could also teach you a few things."

Irritated, he demanded, "What, for example?"

"That a woman also likes stability, Mr. Van Valen. If she is to have children, she will want a home for them. Men may think only of today, but women must plan for the months, and for the years. It is not a light thing to have a child, Mr. Van Valen."

She paused, remembering something her father had said,

long ago, beside the Ohio. "A woman wants a man, not a wisp of smoke!"

But even as she spoke the words she recalled the man to whom her father had referred, for Linus Rawlings had made Eve a good husband; moreover, he had understood when Lilith wanted to go away and try her wings. It was he who had provided the money that gave her a start in the theatre.

It had not been much money, but it gave her respectable clothes, an accordion, and enough to live on while finding her opportunity. He had given her all but a small portion of the money obtained from the sale of his furs.

She remembered that morning out by the woodpile when he had handed her the money. "Eve an' me," he said, "we want you to have this." He looked into her eyes and he said seriously, "Lil, when a dream becomes so much a part of you that it shines out of your eyes, you'd best give it rein."

Linus had rested his hand on his axe handle. "I followed a dream into the West, and I seen the far-off places an' the shining mountains. I rode the rapids of streams no white man had ever seen, and trapped fur alongside of Carson an' Bridger. I fit the Indian an' I seen the varmint, an' this much I know: without a dream a man or woman is less than nothing; with it you can be anything.

"You doubt what you're of a mind to, Lilith, but never doubt your dream. No matter how hard it gets, you hold to that. That, an' your self-respect. Folks will judge you as you judge yourself."

She had looked down at the money in her hands . . . how much that money could mean to her! And yet, how much of struggle, danger, and hardship had been demanded to earn it.

"I can't take it," she had said, brokenly. "I simply can't. It's yours, and it's Eve's."

"What's the use of a dream unless it can help to build another dream atop of it? I had mine. I seen the things I said. I seen the buffalo running and heard the coyotes holler at the moon of a nighttime. I seen the grizzlies fishing salmon, and moonlight on the Teton snows. I made tracks where no man had been, and I left my print on the land. Now I'll raise a boy to follow where I went, a boy who'll blaze fresh trails himself.

"I know what you want, Lil, believe me I do. I know the

hollow ache of yearning inside you, I know how desperate you feel sometimes of a morning when a day has come again and finds you trapped in the same place. You go . . . you have your dream. And don't ever rate yourself cheap, or settle for anything less than all you want.

"You'll come on hard times, but when you do, you remember the tale I told you of Hugh Glass, wounded sore an' left for dead, an' how he crawled and dragged himself hundreds of miles through wild country to get to help.

"You think of John Coulter, naked, with his feet torn to bloody flesh, escapin' the murderin' Blackfeet. You think of them and try a mite harder."

She took the money; and now she recalled every instant of that time out there by the woodpile. Her eyes had been blind with tears, and she remembered how Linus patted her shoulder. "You go on now," he said, "somewhere out there things are waitin' for you. I seen it in you from the start."

Linus Rawlings had been like that, a drifter and a mountain man, but strong when strength was necessary, and with a vision in him.

She remembered another thing he had said: "A land needs heroes. Small men and small thoughts come from small dreams. A man is as big as his dreams are. There are always those who scoff and bicker and cower . . . but if you want to make big tracks on the land, you got to step out and start walking."

Was Cleve Van Valen like that? Or was he simply a gambler, a drifter, a fortune-hunter?

Gabe French liked him, and Gabe French was a canny man who wasted no time with the second run of things. In horses, dogs, and men, Gabe respected only quality.

When she had eaten and went to their wagon to sleep, her hand touched something on her pillow—rough stems, soft petals. The perfume was delicate, as that of prairie flowers is likely to be.

She gathered them up and held them close to her face, and tried to remember the last time a man had given her flowers. They had offered her clothes, money . . . even a carriage and horses. But none of them had ever picked flowers for her.

The coarse stems brushed her cheek, and when she put them carefully aside and settled down to sleep, she did not feel like a worldly-wise young woman, with the hard, direct mind she seemed to have. She felt like a girl who might swing on a garden gate, waiting for a boy. And it was a nice way to feel . . . a very nice way.

In the morning there was rain, a rain that came with a sly whisper on the canvas wagon cover just before daybreak. It settled the dust and lifted an odd smell into the air as rain will do when it first falls into the dust. The wagons rolled westward when the first light was yellow on the grass, but this morning there was no dust cloud.

Roger Morgan rode far out on the flank, and he was a worried man. Three times that morning he had cut the sign of unshod ponies . . . one band fairly large. They had been stalked for the past week by Indians, but now there were several bands, which meant a gathering . . . and Indians did not gather by accident.

He glanced back toward the wagons. They were strung out far too much. He must get them bunched up, not one long line today, but two lines driving parallel. He cantered back to the train and as he cut through between the wagons he heard a voice say, "I call . . ."

Another voice said, "All right . . . I'll stay."

Then Cleve Van Valen spoke. "Gentlemen, are we pikers? I'll raise it this fine pepper-box pistol—five barrels it has, London-made and loaded for bear."

Anger exploded within Morgan. Swinging his horse alongside the tail-gate, he reached through and grabbed Van Valen by the shoulder. Slamming the spurs into his mount, he jumped away from the wagon, jerking Cleve out of it and to the ground, where he hit with a thud.

"I told you I wouldn't stand for you fleecin' the people on this train, Van Valen, and by the Lord Harry—!"

Cleve rolled over and came up fast from the dust as Morgan dropped from his horse. Fury had been building in Roger Morgan for days. In his own mind he was sure it was Cleve Van Valen who stood between him and his projected marriage to Lilith.

It was true they were rarely together, or in any way seemed

to manifest any interest in each other, but he could find no other reason for Lilith's refusal. Besides, he had disliked Van Valen on sight.

Wheeling from his horse, he threw a hard right-hand punch, and more by accident than intent Cleve ducked the blow. He let go with his own right; it was a wild punch but a lucky one. The blow caught Morgan coming in, and the wagonmaster dropped as if shot.

From behind Cleve there came a wild shout, and a horseman charged by, his eyes distended, one arm outstretched toward the hills. "Indians!" he screamed. "Cheyennes!"

The wild-eyed rider raced off down the line of wagons, shouting, "Indians! Run!"

Somebody cracked a whip and a wagon started with a lunge. Grabbing Morgan from the ground, Cleve heaved him over the tailgate of the wagon, then wheeled for his own horse.

It was gone . . . stampeded by the screaming rider.

Wagons went lumbering by. He shouted at the drivers, but caught in a wave of panic, they ignored him.

Cleve drew his pistol and turned to face the charging Indians. As he turned, he fired . . . an Indian lost his grip on his lance and fell forward, sprawling on the ground, dead before he reached it.

Lilith, of whom he caught a fleeting glimpse, was firing a shotgun from her wagon seat. A few of the wagons raced by, but most of them were far too heavily loaded for any speed. The wagon train was in chaos.

One of the horses, hit by an arrow, went to his knees. The wagon tongue jabbed into the ground as the horse fell, and the wagon jackknifed and turned over. Thrown clear, the driver grabbed his rifle and, using the turned-over wagon for a breastwork, opened fire on the Indians.

Cleve, his feet firmly anchored, stood as if on a parade ground, taking his time with each shot. Within him there was bitter anguish . . . this was his fault.

The wagon train had stampeded and this opened them wide to the more mobile Indians, who could cut them to pieces wagon by wagon. To run was to invite disaster, for there was no place to run to . . . nor could the heavily loaded wagons be raised to even a trot unless going downhill. In any event, there was absolutely no chance of escaping the swift, lightly mounted Indians.

There is only one defense against mounted Indians for such a train—the wagon circle. It had proved itself time and again against any number of attacking Indians. No wagonmaster in his senses would allow a train to stampede as this one had, and had Morgan been conscious, he would have stopped the train. Had it not been for the gambling, he might have formed the wagon circle in time.

Cleve fired, then fired again. A horse stumbled and went down, throwing its rider; the second shot smashed through the chest of a charging Indian and he toppled from his horse.

Leaping for the racing horse, Cleve mounted it as it swept by him, grasping wildly for a hold and swinging astride. Yelling like a Comanche, he bore down on the head of the train. "Circle!" he shouted. *"Make a circle!"*

It was Gabe French who caught the sound of his voice and swung his wagon, forcing the one behind to turn also.

Conditioned from their many nights of making the protective circle, the others began to follow suit. Racing like a wild man, using only his grip on the horse's mane, Cleve rode from wagon to wagon, forcing the stragglers back toward the circle with shouts and yells.

One panic-stricken driver refused to turn until Cleve fired into the ground ahead of his team, causing it to swing off and turn. At least a dozen were too far out to circle. Two had overturned, another had two dying horses struggling in their harness.

Firing at an Indian with an arrow drawn to his bow, Cleve glimpsed his own horse, stopped where it had finally stepped on the bridle reins and come to a halt. He dropped from the Indian pony and caught up the reins.

For an instant he stood there, fighting for calm, taking in the surroundings. He took the moment to exchange cylinders, dropping the empty one into his coat pocket and snapping the loaded cylinder into place.

Where the two horses were struggling in their harness a man was down on the ground, his wife on her knees beside him, firing his rifle. An Indian swept down on her from behind and, long shot though it was, Cleve chanced it.

He saw the Indian jerk with the impact, and instantly the warrior swung his mount and started for Cleve. He was far down on his pony's side, and Cleve lifted his pistol to fire, but the Indian swung his horse so that only a leg was visible. In so doing, he forgot the woman he had been about to kill, and for her it was point-blank range. She fired . . . and the warrior charged on past Cleve, then let go and fell to the ground.

Mounting, Cleve rode past the woman, lifting his hand as he did so. She was momentarily free from attack, and farther out two men were making a desperate fight for their lives against half a dozen warriors.

Crouched low in the saddle, Cleve went in on a dead run, and as he closed in he chopped down with his pistol, shooting into an Indian's chest as a buffalo hunter shoots into a buffalo. His horse swept by, and turning, he brought his gun down and fired . . . missed, and fired again.

Then he was in the midst of the fight, his horse riding down one warrior who stepped back unaware; and Cleve chopped his barrel down on the head of another. He felt something tear his clothing, felt the bite of a lance, and then he was thrown from his horse, losing his grip on his pistol.

He lunged up from the ground as the Indian ran in for the kill, turning the lance with an out-flung arm. They grappled, rolling over and over in the dust, struggling and gouging. Jerking a hand free, he smashed the Indian in the face, pulping his nose.

Cleve was down on his back, and the Indian leaped astride him and reached for his knife. Cleve threw his legs up and clamped a head-scissors on the warrior, bending him far back, both of Cleve's ankles locked under his chin. Sitting up part way, bracing himself with his left hand, Cleve swung his fist against the Indian's exposed solar plexus. He struck, and struck again, then threw the warrior from him and struggled to his feet. The Indian, all his wind knocked out, was too slow getting up and Cleve kicked him under the chin.

A teamster had caught up Cleve's pistol and now he tossed it to him. He fired . . . then, having no recollection of the number of times he had fired already, he switched to his third loaded cylinder.

As suddenly as it had begun, the fight was over. The Indians were disappearing over the hill, the prairie was still. Half a mile away the wagon circle puffed with smoke as a few tried shots at the retreating Indians. The entire attack, beginning to end, had lasted not more than a few minutes.

The woman who had helped Cleve was now supporting her husband with an arm around his shoulders—he was up and walking.

One of the men in the final fight was down and badly hurt, and Cleve knelt above him, trying to stop the blood. Another driver was at work cutting a dead horse free of his harness and straightening out his team. Together, Cleve and the driver put the wounded man in the back of the wagon, and started toward the circle. Another wagon, some distance off, was also coming in.

Suddenly Cleve felt weak, and remembered his own wound. At the time he had thought it was no more than a scratch; now he was not so sure. Yet it might be he was feeling only the reaction from battle, the sudden letdown after such explosive action, such great demands upon his body. He stopped when they came abreast of his horse and got into the saddle. His side felt wet and he knew he was bleeding.

He checked the loads in his pistol, although he had re-loaded it only a few minutes before. Minutes? It might only have been seconds. He glanced at the sun . . . it was scarcely noon.

Cleve Van Valen walked his horse toward the wagons, and suddenly his whole body started to shake. He gripped the saddlehorn and clung with all his strength, fearful that he would topple to the ground. He drew rein and waited for the seizure to pass. It was not his wound, he realized now, but the nervous reaction to what he had been through.

Presently he felt better and he walked his horse around the circle, searching for the wagon. Suddenly, a slow finger of smoke mounted . . . someone had lighted a fire. With a surge of relief he stared at the smoke; there was something comforting, everlastingly normal and real about it.

So simple a thing, a lighted fire, yet it was a symbol of man's first great step toward civilization, and it was his instinctive return to reality when times of trouble came. It is his first reaction, to build a fire, to give himself the security and comfort that a fire symbolizes.

How many times had he seen women start a fire and begin to cook when the first shock of disaster was over, to offer warm food, coffee . . . how many times had it seemed as if a man, in offering fire and warm food, was saying, "See, I am a man, by these signs you shall know me, that I can make a fire, that I can cook my food."

And then he saw her standing there, outside the circle of wagons, shading her eyes toward him, shading her eyes against the sun's bright glare, standing alone and watching him come . . . not yet quite sure.

TEN

Westward the bright land lay, westward the magic names, names they had heard in story and song, the names that spelled wild country, that spelled Indians, that spelled danger and promise and hope. The Platte was such a name, Ash Hollow another.

Chimney Rock . . . Horse Creek . . . Scott's Bluffs . . . Fort Laramie . . . Bitter Creek . . . the Sweet Water, South Pass, Fort Bridger, the Humboldt River, Lawson's Meadows, Forty-Mile House . . . Day after day, sunshine or rain or wind, the wagons rolled westward, their heavy wheels rocking out a strange music from wood and weight upon the uneven ground.

Less often now did Cleve Van Valen ride the wagon. Both women could drive and he was needed to scout trail, to scout water and grass and fuel, to watch for Indians, to hunt meat. More and more Morgan had come to depend on him, forgetting his animosity for the needs of the wagon people.

High on a windy hill where the grass waved in the sun, Cleve removed his hat and wiped the sweat from the band. His hair blew around his ears, for it had grown long in the passing time. Squinting his eyes against the distance, he considered the situation and his place in it.

107

Not only had Morgan's attitude changed, but his own had altered; and not merely his attitude, but his appearance. He had tanned under the sun and wind of days of riding. He had cut wood, driven the mules, wrestled with wagon wheels stuck in the mud or sand, using his physical strength to a degree he had never used it before.

The values out here were different, too. It mattered not at all who a man might have been back in the East; here they only asked, "Can he do the job? Will he stand when trouble comes?"

Around the fire there had also been an almost imperceptible change. Now he was deferred to by Lilith as well as by Agatha.

Between Cleve and the wagonmaster there was a truce, but no more. Morgan had not referred at all to the gambling episode. Cleve had no cause to pursue the matter, and Morgan apparently was willing to let well enough alone. But Cleve had refused all invitations to play, and avoided those who gambled.

As for Lilith, he made no further attempt to ingratiate himself, and except at mealtimes they saw little of each other. It was true that he worked for them, but the needs of a wagon train must be fulfilled by its personnel, and men did what they were best suited for.

With their passing of the Great Salt Lake Desert, fear of Indians dwindled. There were Indians about, but they were apt to indulge in petty theft rather than attack. Increasingly, as they moved westward, the problem became a matter of water, grass, and fuel.

The long, winding course of the Humboldt offered little wood or water. For miles its course was marked only by low brush. Off to the south of them there were mountains, and they occasionally saw them like low gray clouds along the horizon. Some of these were capped with snow; always they were off the trail, and almost out of sight. One and all, the travelers looked for the Sierras, for the Sierras meant California, and California was where the trail ended.

Cleve still took care of the mules. He took them to water and to the corral, he harnessed and unharnessed them. And he provided the wagon with its fuel, and occasionally with fresh meat.

Naturally quick to observe and to learn, drawing upon his

memories of conversations and books he had read, Cleve Van Valen soon developed into a first-class plainsman. His eyesight was excellent, and with the revolving Colt rifle loaned him by Gabe French he was well armed. The gelding was strong, fast, and carried him far afield. Well-mounted and well-armed, he developed a liking for scouting far from their line of march, often riding on ahead to locate good camping grounds for the coming night.

Riding thus, far from the line of march, he often came upon game, and two or three times a week he returned from these forays with fresh meat. Aside from what he provided for his own wagon, he often had enough to distribute impartially among the other wagons.

"What you figurin' on?" Gabe asked him one day. "You plannin' to run for office? You're makin' a lot of friends on this train."

"All I want is to get through with a whole skin." Cleve turned his attention from the hills to Gabe French. "Gabe, when I get to California I'm going into business."

"Got any ideas?"

"No."

"Well, you give it thought. It's safer than minin', which is a chancy game any way you size it up." Gabe paused. "Might have some ideas myself."

They had camped on the Truckee, with the Sierras looming above them, when Cleve rode into camp and dropped off a quarter of elk meat at the wagon. Then he rode on, leaving a bit here, a bit there.

Agatha watched him go. "Lil," she said emphatically, "you latch onto that man, d'you hear? Ain't many men as good at providin' as him."

"He's changed," Lilith admitted.

"Maybe . . . an' maybe you just never knew him in the first place. Might be he didn't even know himself." Agatha gazed after him with a critical eye. "He's changed, all right. He's taken on some color from the sun and some beef in the shoulders. That there's quite a man."

"He's a gambler, and I never knew one really to change, did you?"

"That one might. Comes of a good family, Gabe says, who knew his folks. Got rooked out of his due and killed the man who did it."

Mountains now blocked out the western sky, and the desert lay behind them. Snow crested the peaks and ridges, and pines covered the long, steep slopes. Other wagon trains had crossed these mountains, so there must be a way, but from where the wagons now were they seemed a towering and impenetrable wall. How had the first wagons found their way through?

Three times that morning they stopped to clear small slides of rock, snow, and other debris from the narrow trail, and at best it was slow, difficult traveling. The wagons simply inched along, and Cleve scouted ahead for a camping site. When he discovered what he wanted at approximately the distance they would be able to cover, it was a pleasant meadow surrounded by tall pines where a small spring started a cascade from off the mountain.

There was good grass, plenty of fuel, and the clear, cold mountain water. After a last look around, he stripped the saddle from the gelding and rubbed it down with a handful of coarse grass.

He heard no sound but the wind among the trees, and the tumbling of the water. The gelding, he noticed, was gaunt. Even that fine, strong horse was beginning to show the effect of the miles, and even'his winter coat failed to disguise it. Suddenly Cleve was tired.

There were many miles to go before they would reach the gold fields, and more miles beyond that to San Francisco—why should he wait? Why march with the slow-moving wagons, when on his fast gelding he could be there in a fraction of the time? Why not saddle up at daybreak and ride on, and then just keep on riding, all the way to the Golden Gate?

No sooner had the thought occurred to him than he knew it was the solution. After all, what reason had he to suppose Lilith had changed, or would change? True, she was more agreeable, easier to be with, and sometimes there had seemed to be genuine liking in her manner, but he knew better than to put faith in such things.

It was true that he had no money, and a gambler needs a stake, but there might be old friends among the gambling houses who would set him up with a faro layout, and he would do the rest.

He was still considering it when the wagons rolled in, and then he became busy with the mules, the fire, the problem of fuel. But the thought remained.

Lilith was lovely. If a man had to marry for money, he certainly could do no better. She had a mind of her own, but he liked that . . . and when he came to think of it, what had gambling brought him in those wasted years? Years lost now, beyond recovery.

Yet he would be a fool to go inching along over these mountains, breaking his back with toil, when a few hours of riding would take him out of them. Why not forget Lilith? Why not leave now, tonight?

"We've not much farther to go," Lilith said suddenly beside the fire. She spoke the words and they rested there, seeming almost to ask a question.

"After we cross the mountains you won't have any use for me," he said. "It will be easy going from there on to wherever it is you're going."

"Rabbit Gulch . . . it's in the Mother Lode."

Lilith had replied almost without thinking, then as she stooped to lift the lid from a kettle the import of his remark reached her. No use for him? Did that imply that he would leave, once they crossed the Sierras?

For an instant she felt as if she had been struck. Unmoving, she stared blindly at the kettle; then she slowly put the lid on it again and straightened up.

She felt suddenly lost, empty, forsaken. What was the matter with her? After all, he was a fortune-hunter, wasn't he? A drifting, ne'er-do-well gambler? What kind of a man was that to make her feel as she did?

She started to ask about his leaving, but feared his reply. She poked sticks into the fire, then lifted the lid again and stirred the stew.

When he spoke he said what she had been dreading to hear. "I was thinking I might ride on ahead . . . we're almost there now, and I guess I'm impatient."

She forced herself to be casual. "You're going to the gold fields?"

"Frisco . . . I'm not likely to be much good at mining."

"I think you could do whatever you set out to do," she said carefully. She was struggling to order her thoughts, to say the right thing; struggling, too, against an overpowering sense of loss, or impending loss.

"Well," she said at last, "you've earned your money. You promised a day's work for a day's pay, and you have done more than your share . . . even Roger admits that."

So it was Roger now, was it? Had it gone that far? Morgan had made a habit of dropping around by the fire, and a couple of times he had seen them talking quietly, almost intimately.

What kind of a fool was he, anyway, Cleve asked himself. Morgan was a stable man, even if an unimaginative one, and he was well off, according to reports. In short, he had a good deal to offer a girl—and what did he, Cleve Van Valen, have?

He had no money, he had a reputation as a gambler, and some skill with weapons. Looked at coldly and logically, it didn't add up to much. What kind of a fool had he been to go chasing off after a girl, believing he could marry her when so many others were in the running?

The truth of the matter was, he had acted just as the kind of a man she suspected him of being would act—like an egotistical fool. All of which added up to the fact that he was wasting his time.

Agatha came to the fire and dished up their food, glancing from one to the other with a thoughtful expression. She was too worldly-wise not to understand something of what went on here, but for once she had no idea of what to do.

"He's earned it, all right," she said, "earned whatever he's to get . . . but there's things you can't pay for, believe me."

In the morning, Cleve thought, in the morning I shall go. I have played out my time, and there's always a time to quit. The thing to do was to quit when you were ahead.

"I'll be riding on in the morning," he said; "you've no need for me any longer."

She stared helplessly into the fire, her appetite gone. Finally she said, "But what will I pay you? I don't know . . . we didn't settle on anything, on any amount, I mean."

"You owe me nothing. I've had my keep."

"You've earned more than that, much more. We could never have made it through without you . . . for that matter, if it hadn't been for you when the Cheyennes attacked, we would all have been killed. You stopped that panic, you got them into a circle."

"Morgan wouldn't have let it start," he said, "and if it hadn't been for me it might never have started." He looked up. "I never told you of this before, but Morgan caught me gambling, and we had trouble. If it hadn't been for that, Morgan would have stopped that damned fool before he could go off half-cocked."

"You can't be sure of that."

He got up. "I can be sure that I distracted Morgan's attention at an important moment. I risked all your lives."

He looked around, wanting to say something more, but he could find no words. Then he said again: "I'll go in the morning. You don't need me."

Abruptly, he turned and walked away from the fire. Lilith started to speak, but did not go on . . . she just stared after him, helplessly.

"You goin' to let him get away?" Agatha asked.

"What can I do?"

"Women have known the answer to that since Eve bobbed that apple with Adam. If you don't know at your age, you ain't about to learn from me."

"I love him."

Agatha shot her a quick glance. "Bad as that, is it? I'd say latch onto him then. That's a rarely good man, take it from me. You get to my age and you'll settle for almost any kind of a man, so long as he breathes and he's warm. They're a comfort, take it from me."

"I *love* him," Lilith repeated, as if astonished by the realization. "I really do."

"Don't tell me your troubles . . . tell him."

The whole camp was bedded down, and most of them were asleep, before Cleve returned to the wagon. Lying awake, staring up at the wagon cover which was weirdly lit from the dying flames, Lilith listened to him unroll his bed and pull off his boots. She could hear every sound, and interpret it. At last he stretched out with a sigh, and after a minute she could hear his even, regular breathing.

Sleep would not come. Several times she turned over, seeking to find a more comfortable position, and then suddenly, she heard another sound.

Something—some large animal—was moving around outside the wagon. She heard a snort from Cleve's gelding and she started to reach for the rifle that lay beside her in the wagon, then she drew her hand back quickly.

The sounds continued, there was a subdued snuffling, and she could hear Cleve's horse struggling at his picket pin. "Cleve!" she whispered. *"Cleve!"*

"I hear it," he said aloud, calmly.

He lay perfectly still, listening. For an instant after he spoke there had been absolute stillness, then the snuffling began again, and a bucket rattled as something turned it over.

Suddenly the gelding started to rear and plunge, fighting the picket rope.

Grabbing his pistol, Cleve rolled out from under the wagon and started to rise to his feet, and at the same instant the animal, a huge bear, reared up, almost beside him. Angered by the plunging snorting horse, as well as by the man who suddenly appeared beside him, the bear gave an ugly growl. It was point-blank range when Cleve fired.

He shot once . . . twice . . . a third time. He fired as rapidly as he could squeeze off the shots.

Blinded by the flash of the gun, the bear lunged at him. Its paw missed a swipe that would have torn his head off, but it knocked him down with the lunge of its body.

Cleve.rolled over, but managed to cling to his pistol, and the bear brought up with a thud against the side of the wagon, then turned, snarling and fighting, tearing at the wounds in its chest. The bear sprang over him without seeing him and Cleve fired the pistol upward into its belly, then he scrambled to his feet and backed up hurriedly as the bear struggled to rear up again. Bringing the pistol level, he squeezed the trigger again and the gun clicked, missing fire.

All over the camp he heard cries and shouted questions. He stood flat-footed, amazed that the bear did not charge.

He had no extra cylinders with him. They were all in the

pockets of his coat or in his saddle pockets. Carefully, he backed away another step, straining his eyes toward the spot near the front wheel where the bear had been.

"Cleve? Cleve? Are you all right?" It was Lilith.

He waited, slowly lowering the pistol, fearful of making a sound that might provoke another charge.

Several armed men came running. "What's happened? What was it?" they called.

Cleve tossed fuel on the fire and some of the evergreen branches blazed up. The bear lay where it had fallen against the front wheel of the wagon, and the men approached it gingerly, their weapons ready.

Lilith and Agatha emerged from their wagon. Lilith ran to him, her eyes wide and frightened. "Cleve? Are you all right? Are you sure?"

Gabe French caught hold of the bear by the paw and pulled it away from the wagon wheel. It lay there, an inert mass. Three slugs had torn into the bear's chest, slightly left of center, and the three points of entry could have been covered by a man's hand.

One of the men glanced at the holes, then up at Cleve. "Man, that's shootin'!"

It was the fourth and last shot that had saved his life, for it had gone into the bear's stomach and had broken his spine. Despite the killing shots in the chest, the bear might finally have killed him had it not been for that. He had been lucky . . . very lucky indeed.

Obviously, the bear had not been looking for trouble, but had merely been rummaging among the buckets and gear around the wagon, drawn by the smell of food. The flash of Cleve's gun had blinded it, and probably it had been as eager to get away as he would have been. It was that paralyzing final shot that had kept him from a bad mauling—or worse.

He heard scraps of talk . . . "nerve" and "tackled a bear, hand-to-hand" and "shootin' like that . . . in the dark, too." But he knew he had been no hero. He had been frightened, and he had done what had to be done. Had he attempted escape, the bear might easily have turned on him. When he found the bear that close he had no alternative but to shoot.

But the story was one that would be told and retold wherever any of these men gathered.

Lilith caught his arm. "Cleve? Oh, Cleve, you can't leave now! What if that bear had come and you had not been here? What would we have done?"

He looked down at her, his hands on her arms, and something inside him made unspoken answer: "Why, you'd probably have taken that rifle of yours, drilled him dead-center, and then gone back to sleep." He said it to himself, but to her he said, "Yes, I'd better stay. I can't leave you alone."

The truth of the matter was, he decided, that he didn't want to go, anyway.

He wanted to stay here, where Lilith was. After all, he had been gambling for years, and where had it gotten him? No use cashing in his chips when he was this close to seeing what the pot held.

He would stay on to the end. After all, a girl like this, *with a gold claim?*

What kind of a fool had he been to think of leaving?

ELEVEN

Rabbit's Foot Gulch, known to all and sundry as "the Rabbit" or simply "Rabbit," was a ragged gash where the mountain seemed to have been split apart by some gigantic earth-shudder. Cleft deep into the mountain, its sides rose sheer from the creek in the bottom to the rim more than a thousand feet above.

Along the rapid, shallow creek where the canyon widened out were a few rock houses, split-log shacks, or mere dugouts where the gold-seekers huddled when not employed in panning, working their cradles, or cleaning sluice boxes.

Here and there some miner had diverted a portion of the stream to wash off the sand and gravel shoveled into the sluice box and leave the gold behind, caught in the riffles in the bottom of the sluice box.

The trail, if such it could be called, wound precariously around the huts, along the creek edge, up on the high bank, and back down to the bottom of the stream itself.

Cleve Van Valen, with Lilith beside him, rode a cautious way among the laboring men. Several times one or the other was hailed by some former acquaintance, and at their appearance work ceased for the time. Women were few at any time, and such women as Lilith were scarce at all times. Men stopped their work to stare, shielding their eyes against the sun.

It was mid-morning. Most of the miners worked with shirt sleeves rolled up, exposing their red woolen undershirts. Most of them wore clumsy, flat-heeled boots, though here and there a man wore moccasins or riding boots, or worked in bare feet. To a man, they were bearded, unshaved, mostly unbathed, and armed. Those who did not wear a gun while working had one lying close at hand.

They were a rough, tough, good-natured crowd of individualists, each one as independent as his physical strength or his gun could make him. Until a few days or weeks before, none of them had been known to any of the others, and a few weeks from now each would be off on some other creek, following the chance of gold.

One husky miner recognized Lilith. "Hey, Lil! Sing us a song!"

She waved, remembering the man from St. Louis, where he had been especially wary of the law. "We're in a hurry, boys! Next time!"

"Come on, Lil!" the bearded, hairy-chested man from St. Louis yelled cheerfully. "Tune up! Sing us a song!"

She laughed at them. "What shall I sing for him, boys? 'What Was Your Name in the States?' "

All within hearing roared with laughter, and the bearded one made believe as if to duck a blow.

Cleve turned in the saddle. "If your claim peters out, you've still got a following. You might make more singing."

The faint trail they followed turned up through the pines and away from the creek, which here filled the bottom of a canyon so narrow the sun could only strike the water at midday.

It was not much further. Cleve led the way, but he sat half turned in the saddle so as not to present his back completely to Lilith.

"I'll go to San Francisco," she said, "and I'll buy a home on Nob Hill, and I'll have my own carriage and driver. I'll have all the linen and silver and cut glass I've ever dreamed of, and I'll never sing for a crowd of men again."

After a minute or two she added, "I'll have a concert grand, and when I wish to sing I will sing for myself . . . or my friends."

"And will you sing for me, Lilith?"

"Yes, I'll sing for you whenever you like, and I'll wear fine clothes and give dinners for the people I like, and perhaps I'll go to New York, even to Paris or Vienna. Have you been to Vienna, Cleve?"

"To Vienna, to Innsbruck, Bayreuth, Weimar, Monte Carlo . . . you will like them, Lil."

The trail took a long bend, and far ahead of them they could see the widening of the canyon where lay the mining claim. They could ride abreast now, and they rode without talking. So much lay ahead of them, and soon there would be so much they could leave behind.

The trail dipped down, and they saw the scar of rubble where waste rock had been dumped from the mine tunnel. Below, a rocker stood idle upon the bank of the creek, and a small stream poured into the creek from the sluice box.

Against the mountain, under a few ragged trees, stood a flimsy lean-to; a bearded man sat on a stump near the door, smoking a pipe. A few feet away a squaw was grinding corn in a *metate*.

As they drew near, neither of the two looked around or changed their position. The man, immobile as the rocks themselves, was staring at the sunlight on the waters of the creek.

Cleve and Lilith drew up. She glanced quickly at the dark opening in the face of the mountain, then looked around her with sharp disappointment. Suddenly, she knew not where from, came a chilling fear.

"We're hunting for a Mr. Huggins," Cleve said.

"You found him."

"This is Lilith Prescott."

"So I figured. They tol' me she was a looker." He gestured with a careless hand, the nails black with grime. "It's all here, just like ol' Brooks staked it out. He must've had twenty men workin' on it at one time."

"Where are they now?" Lilith asked. "Who's digging the gold?"

"You talk about gold—you never did see such gold as this here claim produced. Just a pocket, though . . . cleared about forty-two hundred before she played out."

The fear was reality now. Cleve glanced quickly at Lilith.

Her mouth was tight against the shock, and the realization of what it would mean to Cleve.

"Mr. Brooks, he spent about three hundred before his heart give out, an' I put up a nice piece for a brass-handled casket . . . they come mighty dear, away out in the hills, like this. The rest, an' there's mighty little of it, I figure you owe me for settin' on the claim." He squinted his eyes at them. "That's only fair, ain't it?"

Cleve turned his horse. "Do you want to take his word for it, or shall I take a look? I believe him."

The bearded man moved at last. He got up from his chair. "You're welcome to look, but there's mighty little to see. Me an' the woman, we're takin' out. I mean there's nothin' here for a body, an' we favor the far-off timber. I'm a man likes to hunt."

Without a word, Lilith pointed her mount back down the trail. After a few minutes she said quietly, "It's like you said, Cleve—I can always sing. I think I'll make my start right back there . . . 'Next time,' I promised them. Well, this is our way back—back to reality."

Roger Morgan heard the sound of music before he reached the tent theatre. The first thing he saw upon entering was a long bar, behind which four bartenders worked desperately to fill the orders of men who crowded three and four deep at the bar. There were Spanish-Californians in wide-bottomed trousers and buckskin jackets, there were Chinese, Chileños, Irish, Germans, French—every race and every nationality could be found in the crowd.

He stepped to one side of the door and looked around. Several games were going, and at the far end of the tent there was a stage, empty now. Several musicians sat in chairs bunched at one side of the stage, drinking beer.

Jackass Hill was booming. One pocket of quartz was producing from a hundred to three hundred dollars a day; and another miner in just six weeks had taken ten thousand dollars out of a plot one hundred feet square. Dozens of prospect holes along the mountain had paid enough to make their owners rich—at least temporarily. They called it Jackass Hill from the braying of the jackasses in the pack trains as they passed up the hill on their way to the mines.

It was a wild, free-spending crowd. Not everybody in that crowd had struck it rich, but everybody had caught the fever, so they all acted like it, and as long as it lasted they spent money like it.

Morgan worked his way through the crowd, scanning the tables for a familiar face, and the face he half expected to see was the one he hoped not to see.

Suddenly, to the sound of an accordion and a fiddle, Lilith appeared on the stage singing "What Was Your Name in the States?"

Roger Morgan found an empty chair and dropped into it, watching her as she sang. The games had slowed, and here and there men had even ceased to drink. One and all, they watched her. There was about her none of the brassy boldness of the usual tent-theatre and gold-country performers. She looked fresh, young, and lovely. She was like a girl from home, yet with that extra something that stirred the blood of every man in the huge tent. As she went on from song to song, moving gracefully about the stage, her eyes moved from man to man throughout the crowd, making each one feel that she sang to him alone.

Finally Morgan could stand it no longer. He got up and left the tent, circling around toward the familiar prairie schooner which now served as a dressing room and living quarters. He was still waiting there when she left the tent.

"Miss Prescott?"

She started to pass by, then recognized him. "Oh, hello, Mr. Morgan. Sorry I can't invite you into the wagon. We're cramped for space."

"This ain't no life for a woman like you. I heard your mine was played out and your fancy friend had left you. Where's he now?"

"Cleve? I heard he was in Hangtown."

"You really mean that no-good went off and left you?"

"He left me, yes, but I don't agree that he's no good. Cleve is Cleve, that's all."

Morgan dug a boot toe into the earth. "You're a perplexin' woman, Miss Prescott. When a skunk needs killin' . . . if you'd left me alone I'd have run that gambler clean off the wagon train. Might have saved a lot of trouble."

"He pulled his weight, Mr. Morgan. Even you admitted that. As for running Cleve off . . . he doesn't run easily, Mr. Morgan. There are some Cheyennes who could tell you that."

"I ain't denyin' he can shoot, but he went off an' left you. What kind of a man is that?"

"All my life, Mr. Morgan, I have wanted a rich husband. Can I blame him for wanting a rich wife? We both may have been born for the poorhouse—at least I am beginning to suspect so—but we're not the kind to like it." She turned toward the wagon. "I must change."

He stepped around in front of her. "Do you believe all this? Tell me the truth?"

"Cleve and I couldn't live on love for five minutes. There's the truth for you, Mr. Morgan."

"Then you've answered the question I've been askin' for two thousand miles. So you just look here. I've got the biggest ranch you ever saw . . . you can't ride across it in a day. That land will mean money, sooner or later. You say you want a rich husband. All right, you're lookin' at him."

Lilith looked at him, but she was not seeing him, for what she saw was herself as she had once been, a wet, bedraggled girl standing on an Ohio riverbank. This was not what that girl had wanted—not this tent theatre, not what Morgan had to offer, either. She did not know exactly what it was that girl had wanted so badly, but she knew it was not this.

What Morgan offered was security, a shelter away from the wind. But when had she asked shelter of any man? Had she not always, no matter how hard the times, stood on her own two feet? Nowhere in the world was there anyone to whom she was beholden, except—a little—to Linus Rawlings.

Linus, she told herself, had understood. Even as he gave up his own free life for her sister Eve, so he had provided the means for Lilith to be free. Better than she or any of them, Linus must have known what she was facing, for in another way and another time he had faced the same himself. Freedom, Linus had known, is never bought cheaply. Linus had understood her, even as he would have understood Cleve.

"There ain't a blessed thing you'd have to do 'cept mind the kids. An' we can leave right now . . . whenever you're ready."

She smiled at him suddenly, for she had made her decision. Or had it been made long before? One never knew what it was that went to making a decision. "Not now, Roger—not ever."

"How can you say that?" He was incredulous. "You just said— Don't you believe your own words?"

"It would take too long to explain. I am sorry, truly I am."

Roger Morgan turned abruptly, angrily, and strode away. She watched him go, a little sad, but without regrets.

"Well!" Agatha appeared in the opening of the wagon. "I heard it! Why do you get the chance to make all the mistakes? Why can't I make a fool of myself for once?"

"Of course I'm a fool, but I know what I want, and I won't settle for less."

"We both should have left the train at Salt Lake. With the Mormons, you may have to share your man but at least you've got one." Agatha paused. "What are you going to do now?"

Lilith laughed suddenly. "What am I going to do? Why, I am going to do what my sister did. When she found her man she had sense enough to go after him, and she let nothing stand in her way. Well, I'm going after mine, and if he won't come to me of his own free will, I'll have to find a way to make him."

Agatha put her hands on her hips. "Now you're makin' sense for the first time since we met! I declare, I never could see you lettin' that Cleve Van Valen slip through your fingers, right when you had him, and all."

"He just wanted my money."

"You know better than that. He may have thought so, and you may have believed it, but I never saw a man look at a bank-roll the way he looked at you. Why, old as I was, I was embarrassed to see it!"

"I hope he wanted something more than *that!*"

"You do, do you? Take it from me, honey, if they want you that way, be glad of it. You can always feed them into quietness afterwards.

"No man stands hitched of his own free will. You have to bait your trap, and when they nibble at the bait, why, you just make them happy, make them comfortable, and you can tie them tighter than with chains. An' believe me, the ones you can't keep that way ain't worth keepin'.

"Make a man easy in his home life, and he won't stray, not if you have a mind to his needs. He may think about kickin' over the traces, but let him feel he can go when he likes—if you're as smart as I think you are, he'll never want to go."

The paddle-wheel steamer *Sacramento Queen* was a little smaller than the Mississippi river boats he had known, but the passengers were much the same. On the whole, though, they dressed somewhat more roughly and were somewhat more ostentatious in handling their money, of which they all seemed to have a good deal.

On the Mississippi you could tell a gentleman by the way he dressed . . . there was no such easy classification on the Sacramento. Here the best-dressed men were almost invariably the gamblers. The exceptions were a few businessmen from San Francisco or an occasional traveler from the East or from Europe. The miners, ranchmen, or farmers usually dressed in a somewhat dressed-up version of the clothes they wore every day.

Cleve Van Valen glanced at his cards. Before him was a comfortable-sized stack of gold coins, in his hand a pair of aces and a pair of deuces. His luck had rarely been good, yet he managed to be successful in a small way without it, relying on his knowledge of cards, of men, of percentages, and on his memory. His memory for cards played, as well as for how each man played the various hands, was remarkable. Months after a game had been played he could relate the exact sequence of hands; and he could estimate from past performances how each man was apt to play the various hands.

He had rarely found it necessary to aid the percentages. The average gambler was not a professional, and flattered himself that he understood cards. Moreover, the average gambler could be led to back his belief with money. Very few understood their chances of filling any particular hand. As every gambler knows, there are runs of luck that have nothing to do with percentages or even logic, and these Cleve was careful to steer clear of when they happened to others. They rarely happened to him.

Faint music came from the main salon, and unconsciously he began to hum with the sound. The song was "A Home in the Meadow." The opening bars were played, and then a girl began to sing the words and Cleve stiffened in his chair. He strained his ears to be sure of the voice, and there was no mistaking it.

He sat a little straighter. The cards seemed to have blurred a little. Another card was dealt him and almost unconsciously he added it to his hand. It was the third ace—he had a full house.

He looked at his cards, then swept the table with a quick glance. Suddenly he realized he was himself riding a streak of luck—and if a man was smart, he rode that streak hard.

Of the others at the table, there was not one whose measure he had not taken. Properly handled, there was three or four hundred dollars in that full house, and it was his for the taking.

The words of the song came to him more clearly, a song and a voice heard many times before over the open fires out upon the plains. It was Lilith, of course. Of late he had even been hearing her voice in his sleep.

A wise gambler rode his winning streaks, but which way should he ride this one?

The man in the gray vest said, "Check."

The man next to him said, "I'll listen."

And it was Cleve's turn to open. He looked again at his cards, then folded them neatly and placed them face down on the table. He got to his feet abruptly.

"What's the matter with *you?*" the gray vest asked.

"Gentlemen, my regrets. I am checking out."

Abruptly, he swept the stacks of gold coins into his hands and filled his pockets, then he started to turn away.

"Now, see here!" the gray vest began. "I—"

With his left hand Cleve turned over the hand he had laid down, turned them over in his palm, but kept the face of the cards concealed.

"Gentlemen, I am quitting, but if any of you think you have a better hand than mine—the one I am laying down—I will be glad to bet card for card that mine are better: I am laying down a hand that would have cost you gentlemen five hundred dollars, but if you doubt me—"

"No," the gray vest said, "we don't doubt you, but you've won a good bit of our money."

"So I have, and this hand would win more of it. But come on . . . card for card."

With the hand he held he was sure to win three bets and lose two, and with those odds he was prepared to gamble all day.

The man in the gray vest shrugged. "You can quit if you want to—I am not going to walk into a game when you are so willing to bet. Besides,"—and he smiled—"only one ace has showed. With three still out, there is a chance you might have one or two of them."

Cleve grinned at him. Turning his hand outward he spread the five cards open before them. "See for yourself, gentlemen. And with that, good day!"

The main salon was more than two-thirds filled with men and women seated at tables. Some were eating, others merely drinking. At one table, Agatha sat alone. Lilith, gowned beautifully, stood in the center of the stage, ending her song.

Cleve Van Valen paused, taking a cheroot from his breast pocket. Carefully, he clipped the end and lighted up. If anything, Lilith was more beautiful than when he had last seen her.

Deliberately, he stepped through the doorway and started down the length of the salon toward her. She could see him coming, and when she completed her song she turned swiftly to leave.

Lilith had seen him the instant he stepped through the door, and her knees went weak. Her heart pounding, she started off-stage, but Cleve stepped up on the stage and confronted her. "Lil, I've got to talk to you."

She was unable to reply. Somehow she seemed to have lost the faculty of speech. Her lips were dry, and when she tried to swallow she could not.

He knew that everyone was watching but he did not care. "Lily, a few minutes ago when I heard your voice I threw away a winning hand and with it a streak of luck such as I haven't had in a long time—something I did not believe I would do for any girl in the world. I threw in my hand because I hoped my winning streak would extend to you."

He took both her hands in his. "Lil . . . how would you like to hook up with a no-good gambler?"

Suddenly everything within her seemed to well up and burst in a warm, wonderful flood. The next thing she knew her arms were around him and she was ignoring the outburst of applause from the audience.

"Then we're on our way! Twelve hundred dollars I've got— right here."

"What will we do? Open a gambling house?"

"A married man should spend his evenings at home," Cleve objected. "How about a music hall? You can sing and dance, and—"

"Nothing doing," she interrupted. "A married woman should spend her evenings with her husband."

Worried, she looked up at him. "But Cleve, how long will twelve hundred dollars *last?* We can't just sit at home and—"

"Lil, have you seen, really *seen* San Francisco? It's ugly and small and full of fleas, and it burns down every five minutes, but each time they rebuild it gets bigger and finer. It's alive, Lil, alive and kicking and nothing can stop it! It makes a man want to get into the action, to build something, to start something—a steamship line, a railroad, something that will help that baby city grow—"

"On twelve hundred dollars?"

"Men have started on less. Besides, Gabe French is there— he is operating a freight line to the Nevada mines. He's always liked me, and I think I could buy a working interest.

"As a matter of fact, pa always wanted me to go into the shipping business. We could start with shipping and freight, and put our profits into real estate."

"Real estate? In California? Do you think we could make any money that way?"

"Some day somebody will. If we can just hang on long enough . . . it's possible."

PART 3

THE WAR

Before the War Between the States, the settlers trickled west by hundreds, after it, they went by thousands. It was the Union that finally opened the West, a free, united nation where all men were equal, where each had his right to his own. The open land beckoned, offered the vastest empire man could desire, providing the space and riches needed for the accomplishment of the nation's manifest destiny . . .

TWELVE

Eve Rawlings stood on the wide veranda shading her eyes to look along the road toward town. A rig was coming, but it was still too far away to make out who it was, but these days every rig stirred fear within her.

She glanced toward the field where Zeb was plowing, with Jeremiah following behind, planting corn. Her boys worked well together, and she was glad, for they were different in so many respects. Since the war began she had worried, not so much because of anything that had happened, but for fear of what might happen, and had happened in other families.

Right down the road a piece two boys had split, one going off to join the Union forces, the other south to join up with the Confederacy. Families all over Ohio, Illinois, Tennessee, and Kentucky had seen their sons and fathers go opposite ways, or brothers divide their allegiance.

The twenty years during which she and Linus had lived on the place had been happy ones. Looking at her boys plowing the field, she thought back to that terrible day when they landed after the calamity at the falls—her father and mother gone, Lilith lost somewhere upstream, and Sam wounded.

It had seemed the utmost in despair, and yet from that moment her happiness had begun. True, she had lost her parents, and it was long before she recovered from that blow, but Lilith and Zeke had showed up. She would have known that Lilith, the strongest swimmer among them, would get to shore.

And then to top it off, Linus had returned.

Now the rattle of the buggy lifted her eyes to the road again and she saw Peterson driving into the yard, wearing a uniform.

The stab of fear was very sharp, and when she glanced toward the boys they had already tied up the team and were running across the furrows toward the yard.

"Why, Mr. Peterson!" she said. "Whatever are you doing in uniform?"

"Militia's been sworn in, Mrs. Rawlings. I am Corporal Peterson now. 'Fraid this is the last time you'll see me for a spell. . . . Letter here—all the way from Californy."

"It must be from Lilith." Quickly, she ripped open the letter. "Mr. Peterson . . . Corporal . . . can you wait just a minute? I may want to answer this one right away."

"I was sort of hopin' Zeb would come with us," Peterson said. "He's about the best shot around here—most as good as his pa."

"His father went when the first bugle blew. Isn't one Rawlings enough?"

Zeb vaulted the split-rail fence and walked up to the porch, grinning at Peterson. "Say, now! You look mighty fittin' in that uniform!"

He picked up the gourd dipper and dipped it into the bucket standing in the coolness of the porch. The cold water dripped from the gourd into the bucket as he started to drink.

"Zeb," Eve said, "your Aunt Lilith says there is no war in California, and they don't believe there will be. Business is good, and there are a lot of opportunities for a young man.

"Listen to this: 'There's talk of building a railroad east, and with his business connections what they are, Cleve believes he will be in on the ground floor. We would welcome Zeb if he wishes to come—'"

"Ma," Zeb asked suspiciously, "did you write to her about me? Did you?"

"Not exactly, but—"

"Did you?"

"I only told her you didn't like farming any more than your pa did."

"Ma," Zeb said persuasively, "you've got a wrong idea about this war. It ain't goin' to be so bad. And you know pa's havin' the time of his life—"

"Mrs. Rawlings," Peterson interrupted, "I got it from the Captain himself—we won't be gone any time at all. Them easterners had trouble at Bull Run, but when us westerners hit them Johnny Rebs they'll run like rabbits."

"Why?" Eve asked coldly.

"It's simple! Them eastern soldiers are all city boys, ribbon clerks and the like. Us westerners, we cut our eyeteeth on a gun barrel. We'll give them Johnny Rebs what for, now don't you worry!"

"Ma," Zeb said, "pa left it up to you whether I joined up or not, but you know how he really felt."

"Mrs. Rawlings," Peterson argued, "there ain't much glory trompin' behind a plow. I'd sure hate to think I'd missed *my* chance. Think how it's goin' to be for the boy . . . everybody gone but him."

It was no use. From the beginning she had known it was no use. When Linus had gone she had hoped that Zeb would be willing to stay on at home, but deep in her heart she knew such hope was wasted. It was in him to go, and go he would.

She shared none of their optimism. She was nothing if not a realist, and she could see clearly, all too clearly what might lie ahead. She had listened to some of the southerners talk, and she knew their fierce pride, their certainty of victory. They were qualities not easily to be given up.

"Thank you for waiting, Corporal, I guess there is no hurry about answering this letter. Thank you again."

"You mean I can go?" Zeb asked excitedly.

"There will be things to do, Zeb. We've got to plan."

Peterson winked at Zeb. "So long, Mrs. Rawlings. Be seein' you, Zeb."

Zeb turned quickly and hurried after his mother. "Ma?"

"We'll have to get your underwear washed and your socks darned. Do they give you a uniform?"

"I reckon."

"But maybe they won't give you any shirts. Take that one off and I'll wash it. The other two are clean but they ain't ironed yet."

"Mother—"

She turned quickly, her eyes wide. "Why did you call me that? It's always been ma, before."

"I don't know," he replied seriously; "seemed all of a sudden ma wasn't enough, somehow."

"You'll be wanting to cast some bullets," she said, fighting back the tears. "You an' your pa always favored makin' your own. You'd best cast a lot of them, Zeb—I don't think those Johnny Rebs are any more inclined to run than you'd be. Don't you forget that most of them were raised just like you and Jeremiah. They'll be good boys, and they'll shoot straight."

She must keep busy. That had always been the answer. If she was busy enough she would not have time to think. After they had buried pa and ma down by the rock she had worked hard, worked so hard that Linus had to stop her a time or two, but the work proved a blessing.

She turned to the window and paused for a long minute, looking at the green hills, and up the fine meadow where the cattle grazed. Beyond it was the wood lot where the trees had never been touched. Right at the start Linus had set that piece to one side, so to speak, and would never let anybody touch a stick of it except to gather fallen branches after a storm. That was for wild game, a refuge where not even Linus himself would hunt, a full section of timberland left just as nature intended it, as wild as the first day a white man set foot on the land.

The neighbors thought him foolish, but he would have it so. "It's for the game," he would say; "they need a place in which to breed, a safe place. Besides," he would add, "the country is fillin' up with folks, and soon none of them will know how it was when we first saw it. I think we owe it to the land to keep this piece just like it was."

Had she had the right to take Linus from the wild, free life he lived? And was not her sense of guilt impelling her to let Zeb go off to the wars? Was it not that she felt she had tied one man down to the land, and so must free the other? Linus had not been unhappy, she knew that, and yet how many times had she caught him looking off into distance with that strange, longing look in his eyes? How many times had he gone off into the wilderness among the wild things? And Zeb was like him.

A time or two she had wondered if Linus would ever come back. Like the time he went after the clubfoot bear. That bear was known wherever men gathered, a great old bear, far larger than any seen around that part of the country, and mean. She heard talk of him from the first, and so had Linus. Folks of an evening would set by the fire and talk of the clubfoot bear almost like it was superhuman or something. It came and it killed . . . one winter it was their white-face calf. And the following spring it was two pigs.

He killed the Hennington boy . . . hardly a boy, for he was all of eighteen. That Hennington boy wanted the name for killing that clubfoot bear, and he took after him. It was days before they found him, and it looked plain enough there on the ground . . . he had followed the bear and the bear laid for him.

Linus had heard Indians talk of bears in the far north, up Alaska way, that would lay for a man, but in the Ohio country it didn't seem right. No Indian would hunt the clubfoot bear, and after he destroyed the Simpson hounds nobody wanted any piece of that bear.

Then he killed a colt Linus set store by, and Linus taken down his old rifle. Zeb wanted to go, but Linus would have none of it. He walked away with that springy woodsman's walk of his and it was nigh two months before he came in from the woods.

He was gaunt and rail-thin, his eyes hollow like he'd been spooked, but he was as happy as she'd ever seen him. And he took that clubfoot out of his pack and laid it on the step. That paw looked bigger than any natural bear would be likely to have, and the Indians and settlers came and stood around and stared at it like they couldn't believe their eyes. But pa had trailed the clubfoot bear, trailed him far into the deep woods and killed him. Nobody ever got all of that story from Linus, but for months he would start suddenly awake from a sound sleep and grab for his rifle, which he kept close by.

For Linus it had been a wild and strange thing, that hunt for the clubfoot bear, and toward the end it was a hunt of man for bear and bear for man, and one time he came up on that bear just a-settin' waitin' for him.

The bear set there starin' at him, lookin' right into his eyes the way no animal ever does look into a man's eye, and that bear looked into him like he wished to see what manner of man had hunted him so long and so consistent. Even the bear was ganted up, pa said, there at the end.

It was a long time later before he could put lead into him. That time the bear just looked at him, and before pa could unlimber his rifle, why that old bear taken off into the brush, just faded away.

Finally, on a sandy stretch of beach along the lake—one of those Great Lakes you hear tell of—with a raw, cold wind blowing in off the water, they met and settled it between them. That bear tried to lay for pa, but pa had been studying his tricks too long, and he was not following right down the trail, but off to one side.

He and the bear, they had seen each other at the same time, and when pa ups with his rifle, the bear came for him. That clubfoot never had seemed to slow him down none, but pa put a slug into him before the bear got to him. The slug hit hard, but it didn't slow the clubfoot bear, so pa drawed his pistol and fired into his mouth and the bear hit him a swipe that laid pa's shoulder open, then came for him, and pa got another slug into him, and that stopped the bear.

Pa out with his knife with his left hand and his tomahawk with his right, and when the bear, stopped by that last bullet, reared up and came for him, pa fetched the bear a clout with that tomahawk and then jumped away. He saw then that a bullet of his had broken the bear's shoulder, but that bear wasn't figuring to run, no more than Linus.

Linus came at him with a knife, because the bear had wound up atop of his rifle, and Linus was bleeding from that laid-open shoulder. Linus got the knife into him, though, and ripped up the bear's jugular, and then he backed off and fell down, all done up and losin' blood, and there they sat, facin' each other on that windy stretch of sand, two old wild ones.

"There at the end," Linus said, "that bear looked almost pleased it was me that done it. We understood each other, him an' me. Had he lived on, some tenderfoot might have shot him accidental, and shamed him in bear heaven."

Zeb had grown up on that story, and it was only one of many stories told about Linus Rawlings.

Eve's parents, Zebulon and Rebecca Prescott, who were buried out there in the shadow of the great rock, would have been proud of her boys. She said it to herself, and then frowned—she was wrong to call them boys, or to even think of them in that way. They were men, and did the work of men. Moreover, reluctant as she might be to see Zeb go, it was time for him to try his strength against the world.

Two days later she watched him trudge away up the road, carpetbag in hand. She had struggled to control herself while Zeb could see her, for he was having a hard time of it, without her tears. After all, Zeb had never been away from home except on short hunting trips with his father. When he at last disappeared around the bend, the tears came.

Jeremiah put his hand on her shoulder. "We'll get along, ma. I'll work hard, and I won't be lookin' over the fence all the time the way Zeb was."

There was no criticism in the remark, for the two boys had loved and respected each other. It was only the truth. Jeremiah was much like Rebecca, sturdy, hard-working, and serious-minded, although not without a touch of poetry in him, too. But his poetry was of the earth, and he loved the good soil and all he could bring from it. He was a man who treated a farm like a mistress, and the farm responded accordingly.

"You go up to the house, son, and start the fire for supper. You go on."

He turned away, knowing where she would go now, for Eve Prescott Rawlings turned always along the same path during her moments of trial. She went to stand beside the graves of her parents and the two children she had lost, for these as much as the house up yonder represented her home. They were the graves of her people.

Edith lay there, Edith who lived almost seven years and then died of pneumonia; and Samuel, who saw only one Christmas and one New Year's Day, and did not quite reach his first birthday.

Standing alone now beside the graves in the twilight of the

evening, she spoke aloud. "What else could I do, pa? He is Linus's son, and somehow he's always seemed more of Linus's blood. Maybe that's why I love him so. But you've got to help me pray, pa . . . you've got to help me pray."

Captain Linus Rawlings lay face down in the orchard studying the situation before him. The peaches were in bloom, and along the creeks there were thickets of redbud, their darkly handsome branches clustered with magenta blossoms.

It was Sunday evening, April 6th, and what he had seen that day he would like to forget, but he knew he would never forget it. Of the two armies who came together near the little church called Shiloh, eighty per cent were green troops, commanded by officers who were, for the greater part, without battle experience, and committed to the noble but foolish adage that soldiers should "stand up and fight man-fashion."

The lesson that Washington had tried to teach Braddock was still, after one hundred years, unlearned by the military. And the fault lay on both sides, and with all the commanding generals.

Sherman had informed Grant there were only twenty thousand Rebel soldiers facing him. Actually, there were forty thousand. The untrained, poorly commanded troops had walked into a slaughterhouse.

Perhaps never in the history of the world had there been so many officers assembled who knew more about the art of war and less about fighting. For there is a difference, and the difference is written in blood.

Battles are initiated by generals; they are won by company, platoon, or squad actions, and it is an Alice-in-Wonderland feature of all armies that soldiers are taught hours of meaningless maneuvers on the drill field until they move with beauty and precision . . . almost as well as a group of chorus girls. Nobody ever thinks to teach them to fight. That they must learn in the field, if they survive long enough to learn. Linus had learned and he had survived, but he had learned against the Plains Indians, perhaps the greatest fighting men the world has known.

Now he lay carefully studying the terrain before him. He

had been given a mission, and he intended to carry it out—with as little loss of life as possible.

His company lay scattered among the trees behind him, sixty-six men in all, including a few stragglers from other outfits who had survived the destruction of less ably commanded units. They liked the tall, quiet, former mountain man and they understood his way of fighting.

Throughout the long day, Linus had led his men with care, using every bit of available cover, aimed rifle-fire, and made slow but persistent advance. Occasionally they had dug in to await a more favorable moment to go forward. As a result, their casualties had been low.

His had been one of the detachments that stopped General Cleburne's advance across the cocklebur meadow when Cleburne lost a third of his brigade in the face of murderous rifle-fire. Zeb had been right in thinking, as Corporal Peterson had, that the superior marksmanship of the western boys would make the difference.

Turning on his elbow, Linus gave the arm-signal that brought up his men, and they came into position by crawling through the grass, taking no chances. Rising from the grass he led them now, for time was of the essence, in a long skirmish line across the field and into the trees. The knoll they had been directed to occupy and hold against the coming day lay just before them.

Grant was patching up his front line and the knoll was a key point. Linus moved warily. The knoll was believed to be unoccupied, but he was not one to take chances.

What led the enemy to charge, he never knew, but suddenly they came out of the trees, running fast, bayonets held low down. They didn't come yelling, but came with no sound but the swish of their feet in the grass. Had the charge come a few minutes later, with the distance much less, it could have meant complete destruction for Linus's men. As it was, there was time.

Dropping to one knee, Linus shouted, "Fire at will!" And even as his voice broke from his throat he laid his pistol on the chest of a big soldier with a shock of corn-yellow hair, and squeezed off his shot. The man toppled forward to his knees on the slope, then over on his face.

Around Linus all his men were firing up the slope into the charging men, coolly and with precision and with fearful destruction.

Then the charging ranks, ripped by the red tongues of rifle-fire, closed with his own men, and for brief minutes there was a fierce, silent, deadly struggle among the soft beauty of the peach blossoms. Men fell, shedding the bright crimson of their blood upon the grass under the trees, their bodies lying like thick gray compost upon the ground. Here and there a rudely shaken tree dropped its pink petals on the fallen men.

Above them the sky was painted scarlet and rose with the sun's last rays, and around them shadows huddled under the trees, or reached out to touch the dying men with tentative fingers.

Linus fired, then fired again. A soldier fired at him and missed, then charged with the bayonet. From somewhere off to one side a bullet struck Linus, and he felt its impact but took it standing. The soldier with the bayonet came on, and Linus fired. He saw the man's chest suddenly blossom with crimson, and as he fell, the charging soldier threw his rifle like a spear.

The hard-thrown bayonet took Linus full in the chest and went in to the guard; then the heavy butt of the rifle fell to the ground, ripping Linus's chest as it fell.

Linus caught hold of a tree branch and turned to Sergeant Kelly. "Occupy the knoll, Sergeant. Hold it until relieved."

"Captain, you . . . you . . ."

"Tell my wife . . . tell Eve . . ." His voice weakened and died, and he toppled over to one side, the bayonet still clinging to his chest by just the tip.

He could smell the warm earth, the grass, and somewhere far off he heard a voice calling, a voice like Eve's, calling him to supper.

He clutched the grass with his fingers and dug deep. Distantly, somebody seemed to say, "You're going to see the varmint, Linus. The varmint!"

Faces . . . so many faces. He felt hands turning him onto his back. A voice said, "He's hard hit."

"Bridger," his voice rang out, loud and clear, "you're a liar. I'll be up . . ." His voice trailed off into a mumble, while the sergeant crouched beside him under the redbud. "That's prime fur," Linus said, almost casually; then plaintively, "Eve? . . . Eve?"

A soldier knelt beside the sergeant. "What's he sayin'?"

"Callin' on Eve. His wife more'n likely."

"Sometimes it ain't their wives they call on," the soldier said cynically.

Linus opened his eyes and saw clearly. "Sergeant! The *hill!*" Then more calmly: "You must occupy the hill, Sergeant."

"Yes, *sir!*" Kelly sprang to his feet and started on, calling to the men.

Linus lay quietly upon the grass, fully conscious. His momentary delirium had passed. He looked up at the sky where clouds floated with the last touch of sunset upon them, and then he seemed to fall, down, down, down into a black, swirling pit, with water at the bottom.

"I've seen the varmint," he said aloud. "I've seen the varmint!"

Over him then, for a brief while, there loomed a great shadow. It might have been the shadow of a tree, but had there been eyes to see, it might have looked like a huge bear, a bear that looked down upon him with a curious understanding, for death comes to the hunter as well as the hunted.

Above him, and not two hundred yards away, Sergeant Kelly clung to the earth. He had occupied the hill. The men were arranged in a careful perimeter of defense, and each had dug a shallow trench in which to shelter himself. The sergeant was worried . . . had he done everything he could? What else might Linus have done? He was not worried about his men; he was worried about himself, for there is no burden like the burden of command.

By candle- and lantern-light in Shiloh Meeting House the surgeons worked. About them lay the wounded, the dying, and the dead, helter-skelter, on the floor, on cots, and in the pews themselves. Men cried out in the half-light that reeked of chloroform.

The surgeons worked with quiet desperation, saving a life here, seeing one pass there, saving an arm or a leg, or amputating one. It was bloody, it was awful, and it was filled with shuddering cries of pain and the anguished sobs of men who would never walk again, or see.

Litter-bearers dumped the body of Linus Rawlings upon one of the bloody tables. The surgeon lifted an eyelid and shook his head. "You wasted your time, boys."

The stretcher-bearers rolled the body from the table and immediately another was put in its place.

Throughout the night the lantern-bearers searched the field of Shiloh for the dead, sifting the chaff of ruined bodies for those who might yet live, or those whom it was possible to identify. Some lay sprawled grotesquely upon the grass, others were heaped together like debris washed upon some strange beach.

Among the dead the lantern-bearers prowled and peered, each a dark Diogenes searching with his lantern among many now honest men. Here and there they recovered valuables, letters, occasional weapons capable of further use, or other prized possessions. Some of these would be sent home to relatives, some kept by the finders.

Sometimes the searchers called out as they wandered among the human flotsam. "Anybody here from the 12th Michigan? The 36th Indiana? Who's from Birge's Sharpshooters? 16th Wisconsin, answer *here!*" Their chants became a weird litany to the dead, but one by one the lanterns vanished as the searchers grew weary of the thankless task.

Yet the voices did not go entirely unheard. Zeb Rawlings heard them, and slowly, using his one good arm, he pushed himself into a sitting position. For a moment he stared about in confusion. It was dark and cold, and something was wrong with his arm or his shoulder.

He felt for his rifle but it was missing. All he had left was his bayonet and his canteen. Catching hold of a tree, he pulled himself to his feet, watching the lantern-bearers weaving their macabre ballet among the dead. He heard their questing voices, and occasionally a faint reply. Nearby a plaintive voice cried out in the darkness: "Water! Water! Will somebody give me water?"

The voice was close by, the lanterns far off. Stumbling, Zeb went to the wounded man and knelt beside him. "Here y'are soldier. It ain't much, but you're welcome."

The man drank in eager gulps, emptying the canteen. "I

sure thank y'," he gasped hoarsely. "Hate to take your last drop, but that there was mighty fine."

"I'll send somebody," Zeb promised. He moved off across the field toward a group of men who were digging a mass grave. He could hear the sound of their shovels as he approached, and he saw two stretcher-bearers lowering the body of a man to the ground near the edge of the grave. He told them of the wounded man.

As they turned away, he started off, and the light from their lantern fell across the face of the dead man on whom Zeb had already turned his back.

It was his father. It was Linus Rawlings.

THIRTEEN

C arrying his empty canteen, Zeb Rawlings made his way through the trees. The smell of death mingled with the scent of peach blossoms and the cool dampness of night.

He almost fell over the body of a dead man and had scarcely recovered his balance when a voice near him spoke. "You tasted this water yet?"

"No."

"Try it."

Zeb cupped his hand in the pool where the spring emptied and took a tentative swallow. He heard others coming through the woods toward the spring and the creek into which it flowed.

"Taste funny?"

"It does . . . sort of."

"I seen it before sundown. It was pink, pinker'n sassafras tea."

Zeb gagged, drawing back from the water. He hung his empty canteen back on his belt, and the soldier came nearer.

"Don't seem fittin' a man should have to drink water like this. In fact, it don't seem fittin' a man should do a lot of the things we done today. Did you kill anybody?"

144

"I don't think so," Zeb said. "We had just run up when a shell exploded, and when I could see for the smoke and dirt I'd lost my gun, and then a horse soldier stuck me in the arm with a sword . . . up by the shoulder, here. The rest is all mixed up. Somebody hit me with the butt of a gun, and when I came to, the fightin' was over."

"I ain't kilt nobody neither, and I don't aim to. Where you from?"

"Below the falls of the Ohio."

"This fool war started back east. What's us westerners doin' in it, anyways?"

"It ain't like I expected. There ain't much glory in seein' men's guts hangin' out. Where you from?"

"Texas."

Zeb drew back slowly. "Say, you ain't a Reb, are you?"

"I was this mornin'. Tonight I ain't so sure."

"Seems like I oughta be shootin' at you."

"You got anything to shoot with?" the man asked mildly. "I got a pistol. Took it off'n a dead officer."

"I've got a bayonet."

"Look . . . why don't we skedaddle out of here? Leave this here war to those that want it."

Zeb hesitated. "They say there's no war in California." His thoughts returned to his mother, and he remembered her trying so desperately to make him listen, that letter from Aunt Lilith in her hand. And all the time she knew he had to go.

Together they moved away from the river. The Texan leaned closer to Zeb. "There's a spring over yonder. I seen some Yankee officers drinking there."

Once they paused to let some stretcher-bearers pass, and afterward, hearing voices, they stopped at the edge of a clearing. Two men with their backs to them were seated on a fallen log some distance away. Even in the dim light there was something familiar about them to Zeb.

"I'm planning to move Rousseau's brigade to this place. They can be situated well before dawn. Do you approve?"

"I'll approve any dispositions you want to make. If you hadn't held the flank today we'd have been whipped for fair." The speaker hesitated. "Sherman, there's something I want to say to you." He paused again. "You may find yourself in command here."

"Why?"

"I've seen some of the despatches the newspaper correspondents filed today. They're saying I was taken by surprise this morning."

"*You* weren't taken by surprise. I was."

"No matter. They're saying I was drunk again last night."

"Were you?"

"No, but a man can't fight enemies on both sides. Win or lose tomorrow, I intend to resign."

"Because of the newspapers?"

"Because," Grant replied, "of their complete lack of confidence in me."

Zeb and the Texan remained silent, listening. Zeb could see the two men in the firelight that flickered on their bodies from campfires beyond the trees. Evidently they had walked to this place, a few yards back of the camp, for a quiet talk. He had seen both men before, and even in the half-light he could recognize Grant's square figure and the battered hat he customarily wore.

"Don't you think I've felt that way?" Sherman asked. "A month ago they were saying I was crazy. Today they call me a hero. Crazy or a hero, I'm still the same man, so what difference does it make what people think? It's what *you* think, Grant."

The Texan grabbed Zeb's arm and whispered: "Y' mean that's *Grant?*"

Zeb nodded, straining his ears to hear.

"You know this war's going to be won or lost in the west," Sherman said, "and you're the one man who knows how to win it. Everything you've done proves that."

The Texan undid the flap on his holster, with great care to make no sound, then drew his pistol. Zeb, whose full attention was centered on the two men seated on the log, did not notice.

"A man has the privilege to resign only when he knows he's wrong," Sherman argued, "not when he's right."

The Texan lifted the pistol and aimed directly at the back of Grant's head, and for the first time Zeb saw the gun.

"What d' you think you're doin'?" he demanded in a hoarse whisper.

"But it's *Grant!*"

Zeb grabbed the gun with his one good hand, twisting it down and around, forcing the Texan off balance with his sudden attack, and throwing his shoulder into him. Briefly they struggled, making no sound, then Zeb drew his wounded arm from its improvised sling and reached down for the bayonet.

The Texan was wiry but less powerful, for years of farm work had built uncommon power into Zeb's muscles. It was only that superior strength that enabled him to hold the Texan long enough to draw the bayonet.

As they struggled silently, Zeb heard Grant say, "I'll think it over. You may be right."

A match flared briefly as Sherman lighted his pipe. "You know this army is better off with you than without you," he said. "There's nothing to think about."

Zeb felt his grip on the pistol slipping, but as the Texan twisted him around, the bayonet came almost naturally from its scabbard, and just as the Texan tore his gun hand free the blade went home.

The blow was a short, wicked thrust with a blade that Zeb had himself honed until the point was fine as a needle, the edge like a razor.

The Texas soldier gasped and fell back, tearing the hilt of the bayonet from Zeb's hand. The hilt pointed downward from the Texan's diaphragm. He was dead before his body touched the ground.

Stooping, Zeb took the pistol from the dead man's fingers. "Why'd you make me do it?" he asked brokenly. "Why? I'd nothing against you."

When he finished searching the dead man for pistol ammunition, Zeb got to his feet. Sherman and Grant had gone, unaware of the brief, desperate struggle that had taken place only a few yards behind them in the darkness.

Zeb's mouth was dry and his shoulder was hurting him. The Texan had said there was a spring somewhere around, and he went on through the trees, listening for the sound of water.

Finally, he heard it. A mere trickle it was, falling from a pipe somebody had thrust into the rocks to conduct the water into a basin about the size of a washtub. He knelt and filled his canteen first, not knowing what might happen to drive him from the spot; and then he drank. The water was cold and clear. He drank, and drank again, and then sat down in darkness.

He was going back to his outfit if he could find it. He had joined up to do a job and, like it or not, the job was unfinished. What would pa say if he knew his son had thought of quitting? Pa never had much use for quitters.

In after years he never quite remembered the sequence of things—the marching, the camping, the fighting, and the marching again were all lumped into one great designless mass in his memory.

He returned to his outfit to find himself the only non-commissioned officer left alive, and there was but one officer. He became a sergeant at Chickamauga, and shortly after that an officer by virtue of a battlefield commission. He became an officer not because of any feat of bravery or because of any sterling quality, but simply because he was the highest-ranking man left alive in his unit. This, he discovered, was the usual reason for battlefield commissions.

At Lookout Mountain he made first lieutenant, learning about combat the hard way . . . except for what he had learned from pa's stories, for during the long winter evenings Linus had told his boys many a tale of Indian fighting, and Zeb had learned more than he realized.

It was at Chickamauga that he learned of his father's death. There had been no mail for some time, and he first heard of it when a lean, stoop-shouldered Kentuckian came as a replacement to the company.

"It was Kelly who was with him there at the end . . . I'd gone on up the hill. We taken the hill just like he planned, 'spite of the charge they made. There as he lay dyin' your pa said somethin' mighty strange . . . somethin' about 'seein' the varmint.' Whatever that might mean."

That would have been pa, all right.

More than once pa had told Zeb and Jeremiah about going to see the varmint, and how it had nearly cost him his life, as well as ma. "Zeb," he used to say, "there'll be many a time in life when you'll be offered a chance to see the varmint. That's when you'd best stop to figure the cost before you take the next step."

Zeb Rawlings rode with Sherman on his march to the sea, and then suddenly the war was over and he was on a steamboat looking ahead for the first sight of the picturesque rock that marked the site of Rawlings Landing.

They set him ashore there with bedroll and haversack, and for a long minute as the steamboat pulled away, he stood there looking up toward the house. It was short of noon and a thin trail of smoke rose from the chimney. He could hear one of the hens cackling . . . laid an egg, most likely.

He shouldered his gear and started across the field toward the house. He walked steadily, his heart beating with great thumps, his throat tight with emotion.

Linus and ma . . . they settled this place when the country was new and wild. Linus had built the house with his own two hands, shaping the logs and laying them in place with Sam and Zeke, ma's two brothers, helping.

At the graveyard he stopped abruptly. Two new graves had been added and marked with stones, and even before he could see the names, he felt cold fear gathering in his belly. Side by side they were, as they should have been:

LINUS RAWLINGS   EVE PRESCOTT RAWLINGS
1810–1862   1820–1865

A door slammed up there at the house, and Zeb saw Jeremiah standing on the porch, shading his eyes with a hand. And then of a sudden Jeremiah dropped his wooden bucket and came running.

"Zeb! Is it really you?"

Zeb gestured blindly at his mother's grave. "I didn't know. Nobody—"

"Didn't you get my letter? She died more'n three months ago, Zeb. She was never quite the same after we heard of pa's death, and I don't think she minded goin', she missed him so.

"Only she wanted to see you again. Pa ain't really buried there, of course, but I set up the stone anyway. They'd have liked it so."

Slowly, Zeb let his eyes wander over the neatly plowed acres. There were stacks of hay, and a new barn, much better than the old one, had been built. There was a corncrib filled with yellow corn, and the stock looked fat.

"You've done well, Jeremiah, better than I ever could." He thrust out his hand. "I think I'll be movin' on."

"I need you Zeb. You stay on. With the two of us to work the place we could—"

"Only thing brought me back was ma, and she's gone. You've worked hard on this place, Jeremiah, and done a sight better than pa ever did, or me. You've a feeling for the land, and the land answers to that feeling. You could grow corn on a granite boulder if you was of a mind to. You don't need me, and the farm is all yours. That's only fittin' and right."

"I don't feel right about this, Zeb. Why should I have it all? What will you do? Where will you be off to?"

"I haven't mustered out yet, Jeremiah, and they asked me to transfer to the cavalry and go west. I think that's what I'll do."

"You sound like pa. You always was like him."

Zeb grinned, in spite of the lump in his throat. "I guess I got to see the varmint, Jeremiah."

"You'll be fighting Indians, like pa did. Do you like fightin', Jeremiah?"

"Remember pa tellin' us about the grizzly he had the fight with out west? I don't mean old Clubfoot; this was out in the Rockies. Well, I asked him did he like to fight grizzlies and he said no—he just wanted to go someplace, and the grizzly was there first."

He put out his hand again. "So long, Jeremiah."

"Well . . ." Jeremiah looked at him feeling there was something he should say, but finding no words. "Well, so long."

Zeb turned away abruptly, not wishing to look longer at his brother, nor at this place with its memories.

When he had gone several steps, Jeremiah called after him. "You keep an eye out for your Uncle Sam Prescott, Zeb! And maybe you'll see Aunt Lilith!"

Jeremiah stood there alone, his big hands empty, watching his brother go. Zeb was the last of his family, and when his family went west they never came back. Linus had come back, but that was before Jeremiah's time. None of the others ever had.

"There must be something out there," he said aloud. "There must be something out there that gets 'em."

Then, half smiling, he added, "Maybe it's the varmint!"

PART 4

THE IRON HORSE

The journey across the plains was endless, the mountains rough, the passes few, the streams treacherous and deadly. The Indian was an omnipresent threat, as unpredictable and impartial as a lightning bolt. Then came the railroad, the parallel line of steel spearing through the wilderness, the road of the mighty Iron Horse. It broke the power of the Indian, stilled forever the thunder of the bison, seeded countless towns and cities, carried the flood of farmers, cattlemen, miners and storekeepers who filled and used the West.

FOURTEEN

J ethro Stuart sat his horse for several minutes after coming upon the bodies. His eyes had immediately checked the surroundings for a possible ambush, but concealment of any kind was at least two hundred yards off and the tracks were hours old.

Obviously, the dead men were workers from the railroad, but the Indians had made an end of that, pinpointing their decision with arrows.

Jethro Stuart was a dry, laconic man who wasted little motion and less time. Getting down, he heaved the bodies to the backs of his two pack horses and lashed them there. Then he remounted, and with a last careful look around to see that he had missed nothing, he started back to the railroad.

As he rode, his eyes traced the twin lines of steel. No question about it, they were making time. Yesterday there had been bald and empty prairie where the rails now flowed westward in a shining stream.

It was progress, but Jethro Stuart was not a man who felt that progress was an unmixed blessing. When he had first come west the land still remained as it must have been for a thousand years or more, and he had seen nothing in it he wanted to change.

Now the railroad had come, brought by Mike King, and Jethro Stuart found he disliked King on general principles. But he was a man who got things done, even if he rode roughshod over everybody and everything that got in the way.

Drawing rein on the crest of the long hill, Jethro looked upon the scene below with skeptical eyes. That railroad was going to bring a lot of people west who didn't belong. When coming west was difficult, it demanded a certain type of man or woman to make the trip and to stick it, once they arrived—and they were his kind of people. If the cars got to running they would bring all sorts of riffraff west . . . all safe and secure.

"I ain't much for progress," he said to his horse. "That durned telegraph put an end to the Pony Express—never really had a chance to get goin'. Eighteen months . . . what's eighteen months?"

Officially, the Pony Express died in October of 1861, although a few packets of letters were being delivered until November. It had thrown Jethro out of work, along with many others, and it would be a long time before the country would see their like again.

Jethro had been running a stop-station for the company, and they had been good days. Why, he'd had friends all along the line, like young Bill Cody, the one they now called Buffalo Bill. Cody had started riding the mail when he was fifteen years old, and he was one of the best. "Pony Bob" Haslam and the Irishman "Happy Tom" Ranahan . . . be a long, long time before they ever got together a lot like that.

Jethro started down the long slope, glancing at the line of ties that lay ready to receive the steel rails. As he rode up to the right-of-way, men were walking back to the rail car—a flatbed drawn by a single horse. Five men on each side would take hold of a rail and draw it off the front end of the rail car, two rails being taken off at once. The foreman's voice and the other sounds moved to a regular beat, a cadence that Jethro admitted he would have liked had he not known what they were doing.

The driver's shout would begin with a "Whoa *up!*" Then the foreman shouted, "Rail," and the men would slide a rail from the car. The foreman shouted, *"Down!"* And it was dropped into place with a heavy clang.

The car would roll forward, and after it came the bolters, dropping a clamp at each rail-joint, and two spikes at each tie. Clamps were then bolted to the rails, joining them together; and then came the spikers with their heavy sledges, driving the spikes into the ties and fixing the rails into place. The wonderful rhythm of their hammers was a thing to hear.

"Whoa *up!* . . . Rail! . . . *Down!* . . . Whoa *up!* . . . Rail! . . . *Down!* . . ."

Several men glanced around as Jethro Stuart walked his pack horses up to the right-of-way, and their eyes went to the burdens the horses bore.

Slowly the pace of the workmen dwindled and came to a stop.

"Where'd you find 'em?" the foreman asked.

" 'Bout a mile over yonder."

"Know that one," one of the track-layers said, indicating the nearest of the dead men. "He was a surveyor. Met him in California. Name's Prescott . . . Sam Prescott."

The eyes of the men strayed from the bodies to look apprehensively toward the silent hills. There had been rumors of Indian trouble, but the two dead men were a fact.

Anger was never far from Mike King; it was a factor in his success and in the speed with which the railroad was moving westward. He was a hard-muscled young man with bold, hard eyes, who habitually wore a business suit. Now, seeing work halted and the men grouped around the horses, his anger blazed up. Followed by a harried young man with a briefcase, he started for the group.

The foreman looked up, startled to see King bearing down upon him, but before he could open his mouth to get the men back on the job, King pointed a stiff finger at him. "You *were* foreman here. Now you're a track-layer, or you're fired—you take your choice. And if you're fired you get back to the settlements in your own way."

Abruptly, he turned his back on the foreman, dismissing him from his mind. "You . . . !" He indicated a stocky man with hard lines graven into his face. "You're the foreman until I can find somebody better. Get these men to work!"

"Yes *sir!*" The new foreman turned sharply around. "All right, men! *Roll 'em!*" With a quick gesture he started the one horse that drew the rail car, and then yelled, "Whoa *up!* . . . Rail! . . . *Down!*"

Mike turned on Stuart. "Your name is Jethro Stuart?"

"It is."

"Stuart, you were hired to hunt buffalo to feed these men, not to stop their work. Why'd you bring those bodies down here?"

"They're railroaders. I thought somebody on the railroad might be interested."

"I am the railroad," King replied, "and I am *not* interested! You should have buried them where you found them and tracked down the Indians who did it."

"Like you said, Mr. King"—Jethro's eyes were cool—"I was hired to hunt. I wasn't hired to dig graves or fight Indians. Anyway"—he indicated the workmen—"they're mostly old soldiers. I wouldn't expect a couple of dead men to bother 'em much."

"I don't want *anything* in their thick skulls but work—you understand? Now you get rid of those bodies and start tracking down those Indians while I telegraph the army."

Abruptly, King turned away.

Jethro Stuart had not moved. Lazily, he took out a plug of tobacco and bit off a small fragment. "You keep forgettin', Mr. King, my job's to hunt game."

King wheeled in his tracks. "Your job *was* to hunt. Go to the paymaster and draw your time."

Unconcerned, Jethro turned his back on King and began to unfasten the lashings on the bodies. "Be interested to know, Mr. King—who's going to hunt your meat? You?"

The contempt in Stuart's voice infuriated King, but his anger was stifled by the realization that he could not, for the time being, replace Jethro. Without the hunter, there would be no fresh meat for the laborers; and without meat, he would soon have no crew. His anger, his feelings about Jethro, these meant nothing when in the balance against the progress of the railroad.

"All right!" He waved an impatient hand. "Forget what I said. But I want you to bring in buffalo meat, not dead men!"

Turning away, he said to his secretary, "Make a note to replace that man at the first opportunity."

Behind him something thumped upon the ground and, glancing back, King saw Stuart had dumped the two bodies right where he stood.

Anger flooded him again and he started to shout, then clamped his lips, staring after Stuart, his fury bitter in his mouth. Behind him the spikers swung their sledges in a steady rhythm . . . it had a lovely sound. Slowly, his hot burst of rage subsided.

"Mr. King," his secretary said, "those bodies—?"

"Leave 'em for the army. If they won't protect us, they can at least bury the dead."

They called it the End of the Track, and the name was about as accurate as could be. Only one might have been better—the End of the Line, and for many that was what it was.

Tonight it was here; last night it had been thirty miles away. Tomorrow night would be the last on this site, and then it would move along. If they were lucky they might spend a week in one spot . . . such times were rare with Mike King on the job. At the End of the Track there was but one law—the Railroad. And at the End of the Track, or anywhere along the six hundred miles of steel, Mike King was the Railroad.

It was a town that moved with the track, and could be taken down in less than an hour—a town without roots, populated by men without roots, and by women—with one exception—of just one kind.

A dozen large tents and fifty small ones—that was the town at the End of the Track, and nowhere in so small a space had there ever been concentrated so large a percentage of vice. You could choose your game, and your brand of whiskey. You bought rot-gut whiskey if you didn't care. If you did care, there was good whiskey; there was even champagne and expensive wine.

You could choose your kind of woman. All nationalities and colors were there, schooled in every sin, and prepared to invent a few new ones at the customer's discretion. It was rough, bawdy, brutal.

The bulk of the men who inhabited the tent city by night were the track-layers, spikers, tie-cutters, and teamsters who were building the road. But there were also the men and women who traveled to entertain and serve them. The track-layers and those who went before them were making money, and they wanted to spend it. Mike King favored the spending, because a man who was broke was a man who had to stay on the job. Labor at the End of the Track was difficult to get, and many a laborer hesitated to risk the Indians who lurked just beyond the hills. Scattered among the inhabitants of the tent city was a liberal sprinkling of blue, for the railroad would not and could not advance even a step without protection from the army. And Lieutenant Zeb Rawlings was in command.

Zeb Rawlings came out of his tent into the night and stood there with the cool wind on his face. He removed his hat and ran his fingers through his hair, and when he looked around, he looked at the hills.

He had never thought of returning East, although he contin-ued a sporadic correspondence with Jeremiah, who was pros-pering on the farm. He knew, as Jeremiah had known, that the West was for him. Here he belonged, and nowhere else.

He looked at the hills, and knew that the Indians were out there and, night or day, they were watching. How long they would be content to watch, he did not know, except that it would not be forever. A time would come, and then it would be up to him and his blue-coated soldiers.

That he would be outnumbered he took for granted. Three years of Indian fighting had taught him he could handle num-bers if he could avoid surprise. Those three years had served to impress him anew with what he had learned long ago from the tales of his father—that as a fighting man the Indian was rarely equaled.

He walked slowly along the "street" toward the gambling tents, listening to the music with only a small part of his attention. The three frontier years had left a mark upon him that was deeper than the burns of sun and wind. He had grown increasingly sparing of words, increasingly watchful. Long since, he had learned to listen with part of his mind for the night around him, to hear the slightest sound. He would never be as good at that as Linus had been, for Linus had lived longer in Indian country, and knew it better.

He entered the tent and made his way up to the bar. The tables were crowded with gamblers and spectators, and the bar was lined with men. Just as he walked up, a man stepped away and there was a place for him.

The music changed to a fanfare and a girl came on in spangles and a red dress. Zeb Rawlings watched her without interest. She had been pretty when she first reached the End of the Track, but that had been at least five hundred miles ago. She started singing "A Railroader's Bride I'll Be," and Mike King came up to the bar beside Zeb. Men moved aside for him respectfully, but warily, too.

"See those two men they killed today?" King asked.

"We buried them."

"What about the Arapahoes?"

"We tracked your men, and we found the Arapahoes, too, but the tracks didn't lead to them. It was a war party of Cheyennes down from the north who killed your men."

"The hell it was! What about those two last week?"

"Arapahoes killed them. Your men were drunk and chasing squaws. What would you do if some of those drunks started chasing your wife?"

"I haven't got a wife." He watched the girl in red without much interest. Mike King already knew all there was to know about her. "Anyway, your job is to fight Indians, not agree with 'em."

"There were two hundred Arapahoes, and I had twenty men—it seemed a good time to listen. Anyway, I'm not starting a war just to please you."

"I think I'll wire your colonel," King said irritably. "He may have different ideas as to who you're out here to please."

Without taking his eyes from the singing girl, Zeb reached into his pocket and handed a wire to King. "I reported to him," Zeb said shortly, "and as you will see, my actions pleased *him*. If you're in your right mind the last thing you'll want is Indian trouble. Start a war with the Arapahoes now and the Kiowa, Cheyenne, and Sioux will all join in."

Zeb leaned his elbows on the bar and accepted a whiskey from King to chase the milk he had been drinking. He should be sleeping off his weariness, for he was tired, dead-tired. Burying those men today had hit him hard. He had merely glanced at them, but their faces stuck in his mind. Especially one of them . . . reminded him of ma.

In his inside coat pocket was another letter from Jeremiah. He had bought another quarter section, and the letter ended: "Remember, half of everything is yours if you want to come back. Ruth and the youngsters send you their best." Jeremiah had married and had two children already.

Zeb stared at the dancing girl. "I want to see the varmint," he said aloud.

"What was that?" King asked. "Oh? You mean her? You're right . . . a varmint. All wildcat."

King turned, resting an elbow on the bar so he could face Zeb. "Did you know I'd been seeing Julie lately?"

"She told me. This is still a free country."

"You're right."

King grinned at him. "If you think those brass buttons are enough, you're wrong. I make more in a month than you do in a year."

"If you're building up to something, let's have it."

"You could be making more," King suggested mildly. "I wouldn't want to offer unfair competition. Take those men of mine—they were killed no more than a mile off the right-of-way. I want my men safe *ten* miles off the right-of-way. They're bound to drink and they will chase squaws, but I want 'em safe."

"My orders are to keep the peace. That's why I am here, and for no other reason."

"Orders are a piece of paper," King replied impatiently. "You're here to help us build this railroad. The government wants it, the people want it."

"And you want it."

"That's right. I do want it." King put down his glass. "And you're going to help me get it."

When King had left, Zeb Rawlings leaned on the bar and watched the dancers without really seeing them, nor was it the dancers of whom he was thinking. For the first time he was seriously considering a life that had nothing to do with the Army. He knew what pressure Mike King could bring to bear, and he knew that within a few days he would be hearing from his colonel, just as his colonel would have heard from the general.

The general was up for retirement and was already smoothing his way for a job in civilian life. His retirement pay would not provide adequately for the general and his family. A job with the railroad, in an executive position, would do all of that. Zeb Rawlings knew a little of this, and guessed more. Mike King used money and influence the way he used everything else to attain his ends, and without any thought of the morality involved, or the lack of it.

Zeb Rawlings had the clarity of vision of a man who had lived on the frontier and dealt with simple things. His mind was not confused with too many issues, and long ago he had sacrificed personal interest for the good of the service whenever that was required. But an agreement had been made with the Arapahoes, and if an effort was made to push them back they would fight, and that meant that innocent people having no connection with the railroad would die.

Jethro Stuart moved up to the bar beside him and accepted the glass and the bottle the bartender placed before him.

He turned toward Zeb, his position almost identical to that taken by King earlier. "Your name is Rawlings and you're from Ohio. Pa's name wouldn't be Linus, would it?"

Zeb, curiously, looked at him. "It would."

"Knew him." He thrust out a hand. "You've been seeing Julie. If you're anything like Linus, I'm glad you're seeing her."

"I've heard pa speak of you." It was odd that until now he had not connected the names. "He used to talk of you often."

"Used to?"

"He was killed at Shiloh."

Jethro filled Zeb's glass and his own. "Better'n dyin' behind a plow, and if I knew Linus he'd have wanted it thataway. I tried a plow once . . . most of a year. Took *ten* years off my life."

Jethro turned his glass in his hand. "You buried those men I brought in."

"Yes."

"Good men . . . surveyors. Had a right to be where they were. Cheyennes done it."

"You knew that?"

"I can read sign." He emptied his glass. "King will try to turn it into an excuse. Hates Indians."

Zeb Rawlings was surprised. "Hates Indians? Why?"

"They're in the way. They're no good to Mike King or his like. They belong to a way of life that King resents because it ain't his way.

"There's a kind of man who hates anything unlike himself and what he understands, and just seeing the Indians out there doing nothing that he can see, it bothers him."

"I never thought of it that way."

"King will be a big man in the country some day, but there ain't much to him. Reminds me of beaver. You put a beaver where there's water and he'll make a dam because it's his nature to make dams. Take him away from water and he's good for nothing. Same thing with Mike King. He can get things done and he will make money, and he will die never knowing there was anything else in the world.

"That's one reason he resents those Indians out there. Most ways they have it better than he does." Jethro turned away. "You drop by my place whenever you're of a mind to. Like to see you."

Zeb finished his whiskey and put down his glass. No question about it—he was tired. He walked from the tent, pausing for a moment in the open air, far removed from the tin-panny music and the rough talk within.

He wished again that he might have returned before ma died. Ma would have liked Julie.

FIFTEEN

The town at the End of the Track had a way of becoming abruptly silent. Rarely did the music, the noise, and the confusion dwindle away. They were going full blast with all the stops out, until suddenly silence descended like a dropped blanket, and then nothing remained but the night sounds—the creak of a sign in the wind, the flap of an unbuttoned tent door, the scuffing of a foot, or the sound of a man murmuring in his sleep. In the distance a lone coyote cast his woes into the starlit sky, and still further away a locomotive whistled mournfully at the unreplying stars.

Julie wrapped her cloak against the wind. She should not be out, she knew that, but after staying in the tent all evening, she desperately wanted fresh air.

Tonight when her father had come in, he glanced at her, saw she was waiting. "King?" he asked.

"No."

"That Zeb," he commented, "he's a fine lad. Reminds me of his pa."

He rolled up in his blankets and went to sleep, but Julie sat very still for a while, wondering at the comment. Jethro had never tried to influence her one way or another in her choice of friends, not since she was a little girl. They had been long apart, and somehow when they came together again he chose never to interfere. Sometimes she almost wished that he had, but he had the special western trait of letting each person go his or her own way. In this case it was something more—he trusted her.

Presently she went out to stand under the stars. She thought of the tent city in which she was a part. There were no other women at the End of the Track but those that followed the track-layers and the builders. She knew none of them, and would not. In her world and her time the two lines never crossed beyond a polite greeting.

She heard Zeb Rawlings' footsteps before she could see him, and sensed the tiredness in them. She had known he was worried, had seen the same worry in her father's face. And she knew it was worry about the Indians.

Zeb came up and stood beside her. He stood there a moment without speaking, letting the wind blow in his face and feeling the coolness.

"Zeb," she said, "what are you thinking about?"

"Haunted, I guess. One of those men we buried out there today reminded me of my mother. I don't know why, exactly . . . something in his face."

"What was she like?"

"Like? She was kind," he said, after a minute, "and she had a love for the land. She loved her family, and there was a strong vein of poetry in her thinking. Cropped out now and again. I took after pa."

"What was your father like?"

"Like me, I guess. And a good deal like your pa. It's a peculiar thing," he added thoughtfully, "you never think of your parents as much else than parents. It isn't until you get older yourself that you begin to realize they had their hopes, dreams, ambitions, and secret thoughts.

"You sort of take them for granted, and sometimes you are startled to know they were in love a time or two, or maybe carried on over something. You never stop to think of what they are really like inside until it is too late.

"Many a good father or mother is plodding away, doing the best they know how to raise a family, when their hearts are off across the horizon somewhere, hunting a dream . . . a dream that because of their family they may never find."

"I know."

"Reality has a way of raising up obstacles. Like now."

"Now?"

"I like the Army. Somehow I never could see myself away from it, not after the war. But the way things are arranging themselves, I may resign my commission."

"Is it Mike?"

If he noticed the use of the first name, he ignored it. "In a way. In another way it is something more than that. It is two kinds of life coming face to face—one a hunting, food-gathering life, the other a busy, commercial, technical life with all sorts of demands and needs. When two such peoples come face to face the one less equipped to survive must be pushed aside. It isn't right, it isn't wrong, it just is."

"And Mike wants you to push?"

"Yes."

"But if it is inevitable, why do you mind?"

"You always mind, Julie. And the pushing need not be now. Your pa thinks the Indians offend Mike . . . maybe he's right. One thing is sure. We differ, and Mike King is going to win because he can use political influence, and no Army man likes to think he's taking orders from a civilian. The president is different—he's a civilian in a sense, but he's commander-in-chief too."

Without thinking, they had begun to walk away from the tents. Zeb's hand strayed to his belt gun, assuring himself it was there. They would not go far, but he was not a man to take risks unnecessarily—only a fool did that. There were risks enough in the ordinary process of living.

"What will you do, Zeb? I mean, if you leave the Army?"

"Go west. I might start ranching. All of our family seem to want to go west, except maybe Jeremiah."

He had told her about Jeremiah, and about Aunt Lilith too. She had come to his mind when the trouble with King developed, for Aunt Lilith's husband, Cleve Van Valen, was a big man in railroading on the Pacific coast.

Not that he would ever approach his Uncle Cleve to use

influence. Zeb Rawlings was a man who fought his own battles, accepted his own defeats.

"I won't deny," he told her, "that I'd thought a time or two about ranching. There's land to be taken out west, and I've a love of the land in me. I guess I got that from ma. Only I'd stay with the Army if I could, even though there isn't much chance for a man to rise unless he's been to the Point. Promotion is slow, any time—when there's peace, that is."

They strolled, not too far from the edge of camp, then turned slowly and came back. The tent city lay still under the stars. Near a pile of ties, Rawlings saw a sentry outlined against the sky.

When they parted he almost started to ask her to go west with him, and then he thought of Mike King. King would be vice president of the Road someday, possibly even president. He would be a wealthy man. What could Zeb offer to compare with that?

After he had gone she stood a moment looking after him, reluctant to see him go and a little annoyed that he had said nothing to show he thought about her in his plans.

Would he say anything at all? She felt a sudden panic at the thought that he might not. For an instant she almost started after him, then she ducked her head and went inside.

Lieutenant Zeb Rawlings led his patrol on a long sweep around the area at the End of the Track. Wherever he rode he found the tracks of unshod ponies, some of them large parties; nowhere did he find travois trails. That meant the Indians had no families with them, and that meant they were war parties. Drawing up on the crest of a hill, he studied the country.

"Sergeant," he said, "have you seen Jethro in the last couple of days?"

"He's around. Ain't talked to him, though. Not since he brought in those dead men."

Rawlings was uneasy. The parties of Indians who had passed back and forth across the country *might* be hunting parties, for there were several good-sized villages not very far off, close enough for squaws to come and do the skinning if any game was killed. But there was little game close to the railroad, because of the noise and confusion, so hunting parties appeared to be a doubtful answer to the tracks. Of course, the Indians sometimes came to the camps to beg, or simply to watch the white man at his incomprehensible tasks.

But Rawlings was uneasy, and he was a man experienced enough to trust his intuitions.

This was open country, though less open than it appeared at first glance. The railroad moved down a wide valley, but around it were rolling hills, some of these ending in steep bluffs. The higher ridges were tree-clad, and trees grew along the few water courses. A large party of riders who knew the terrain might travel unseen for some distance by riding along the bottoms of creeks or under the trees.

Like many another soldier who served on the frontier, Zeb Rawlings had developed a sympathy for the Indian. The Indian was a good fighting man, and before the coming of the white man he had adapted himself to his surroundings to a remarkable degree.

Without horses before the white man came, the range of Indian travel had been limited. Their travois were then drawn by dogs, and with them they followed the game; and in addition to game, seeds, nuts, and berries or roots were the staples of their diet. Their greatest source of honor and pleasure came from warfare with other tribes.

The coming of the horse revolutionized their way of living, extending their range immeasurably, and giving to horses a value beyond anything the Indian had previously known. The possession of horses became the measure of status, and a good horse-thief could have the pick of the young squaws.

The Sioux, for one, had upon acquiring horses launched out on a career of conquest. Had the westward march of the white man been a little slower—say, for instance, had there been no gold rush to California, the savage horsemen of the Great Plains might have found their Genghis Khan, just as the Mongol horsemen, in a somewhat similar state of civilization, had found theirs.

Like the Mongols, the American Indians were divided into many small tribes without any sense of unity in its larger meaning. Genghis Khan had welded the free tribes of the Mongols into a great fighting unit. Tecumseh had the idea, but the menace of the white man was not sufficiently realized, and

Tecumseh came before his time. Quanah Parker had a similar idea, but he came too late.

Had such a leader appeared to lead the Indian against the white man, it is at least possible the white man would have been driven back to the sea. Certain it is that many a frontier settlement would have been wiped out of existence. In later years the white man always had the advantage of arms, for even when the Indian possessed firearms he never had sufficient ammunition for any prolonged engagement. But the Indian danger was always there.

Allowing for an occasional exception—and these were usually young officers fresh from the East—it was the Army that best understood the Indian; and had the management of Indian affairs been left to the Army it would have caused far less trouble. After the immediate subjugation of the Indians, it was in most cases some civilian appointee who stirred them again into action.

Zeb Rawlings had come in contact with Indians without bias one way or the other. He did not believe them a pack of savages to be killed off like so many mad dogs. On the other hand, he did not hold with the group—all living safely in the East—who believed the poor Indian was a much put-upon individual.

From his father Zeb had learned a lot about Indians; he understood many of their customs, their eagerness for war, their pride in courage, and what white men usually considered their treachery.

He thought of his father now as he scanned the country around. "Pa," he commented to his sergeant, "knew as much about the Indian as any man, and he was forever wary of them. The first time you try judging them as you would a white man, you're in trouble. Their standards are different."

"Jethro says the same," the sergeant commented. "What do you reckon is going on, sir?"

"Think back. How many tracks did we see last month?"

"Seen a few here and yonder."

"But mighty few. And now? How many Indians would you estimate in the parties we saw today? I mean, whose tracks we saw?"

"Could have been thirty, maybe more in that first lot, and

close on that in the next. We crossed the trails of more than a hundred Indians today." The sergeant scowled. "Seems a lot to be just perambulatin' around, sir."

"I agree." Zeb paused. "You know, Sergeant, a lot of nonsense could be kept out of reports and out of consideration if folks would just consider the problem of feeding a lot of troops. You know how much ration supply we have to figure on for our lot. Merely multiply that by ten and where are you?

"I'll tell you exactly where we are, Sergeant, and I don't like it. There are five times the Indians in this area right now than can be fed here, which means they do not expect to be here long . . . or else they expect to come into a lot of supplies they don't have at present . . . which can only mean the railroad."

At this point Zeb saw the rider come out of a coulee, and knew by the way he sat his horse that it was Jethro Stuart.

Zeb's eyes swept the surrounding hills. He was quite sure that his troop was under observation every single moment, and now the Indians would know that Jethro was joining him—it was likely they could even guess what Jethro would have to say. He thought like an Indian, and therefore he could tell them what an Indian would be likely to do.

Jethro glanced at the troop—twenty-two men, including Rawlings and the sergeant, and it wasn't enough. Not by a long sight, it wasn't. And there were not twenty more within fifty miles.

"We've been cutting a lot of sign, Jethro," Zeb said.

"The chief claims the railroad broke its agreement. They've changed their route and are cuttin' through the Arapahoe huntin' grounds."

"Is he right, Jethro?"

"He sure and certain is, Lieutenant. I tried to warn King, but he ain't willin' to listen. He's tryin' to make better time with his track-layin', so he switched routes just of his own mind. Maybe you can talk to him."

"You know Mike King," Rawlings replied dryly. "He listens to nobody."

Nevertheless, within the hour Lieutenant Rawlings rode up alongside the cars that were Mike King's office and sleeping quarters. Three flat cars stood nearby . . . the track-laying crew worked almost half a mile away, but the tent city was close by. There were stacks of ties cut from the hills not far away, and oozing pitch in the hot sun. Zeb swung down and went in, leaving Jethro to follow if he wished.

King was behind his desk, checking shipments against an order lying on his desk. At another desk at the far end of the car, his secretary worked at a telegraph key.

"King, when did you decide to change your route?" Zeb asked abruptly.

King continued to check his lists for a moment before he looked up. He had been expecting this and was ready for it, but he was quite sure he could handle this backwoods lieutenant. When he spoke impatience crept through.

"We've made no change, although we've the right to make what minor adjustments are necessary to speed construction, and speeding construction is just what we've been doing."

"You're asking for trouble. You've cut into Arapahoe hunting grounds, and the tribes are out."

"Don't be foolish, Rawlings!" King answered irritably. "Can you honestly say that what we are doing will cost them any wild game?"

"What counts is what the Arapahoes think, and Jethro says they think they're getting a raw deal."

"To hell with them, Lieutenant, and with Jethro, too. I'm not going to let the Central Pacific gain ground on me because of a few naked savages. If I wasted my time worrying about what a few miserable Indians think, I'd never get anywhere."

"Is it worth a war? A war that will cost lives?"

"What war? You say the Army is here to keep the peace, so keep it."

"And how would you suggest I do that?"

"Sell them the idea that the railroad won't do any harm. It's just two tracks and a whistle."

"They won't buy it, King. You forget these Indians have seen the railroad bring people west. It isn't the tracks themselves that worries them, it's the buffalo hunters, and the sod-busters."

Mike King chuckled suddenly, his manner changing. "Damn it, Zeb, I like you! You've got guts. I could use you in my business." He got up and walked around his desk to the sideboard. "Will you have a drink? I never lied to a man over a drink."

Zeb took the glass of whiskey. He had an idea what was coming and was braced for it. At the same time he knew the limitations of his authority, and how little his arguments would mean when they reached a peaceful headquarters miles from the scene of action, with a lot of arm-chair soldiers ready to pass judgment.

He could not stop the railroad. He could not force it to turn aside by so much as a foot. His job was to keep the peace, and he had tried. It might be that he should simply ride off in the hills on a long patrol and let King bear the consequences of his act . . . the trouble was, there were so many others who would suffer. And King had never had to bury a woman who had fallen into Indian hands, or seen the result of an outbreak.

If there was an attack the railroad could do a fair job of defending itself, for many of the track-layers were Civil War and Indian war veterans, and not a few had served in European armies before emigrating.

"Look"—King filled his own glass—"you've seen the buffalo—millions of them! Why, we had a train stopped for two days while a herd of buffalo passed, and that was only last week! How long will it take the settlers to kill off that many buffalo? Not in my lifetime nor in the lifetime of any youngsters we may have.

"I don't have any love for the noble red man, and never did. Whenever two peoples come together and one has the superior culture, the superior technical skill, the other will fold up or decline. I've heard you and Jethro say the same thing, although maybe the words were different, but it's inevitable.

"The Indian could cope with anything before the white man arrived, but now he's out of date. He's done for. Personally, I want to see all this country filled with ranches and farms. I want to see mines and mills. I want to see this country filling out and growing up, and that's the way it will do and nobody can stop it—not those fool Indians, nor you, nor anybody else. The Indian has to become a part of it, or fade from the picture.

"It isn't me who is doing this. It isn't anybody, really. It is simply that the Indian's way of life doesn't fit him to compete with a white man for land or a living. Don't blame me. I don't make the laws of nature.

"But look at the logic of it. These hunting grounds are safe for at least our lifetime and for the lifetime of the Indians you've talked to. And the sooner the Indian comes in contact with the white man and his way of life, the better his chances of surviving. The point is, however, that he has nothing to worry about. It will be fifty, maybe a hundred years before people move into this country."

Zeb Rawlings looked at the amber liquid in his glass. There was much truth in what King said, and he knew some of the older Indians felt the same way. The trouble was that he did not trust King, or any argument he might offer. Nor could he trust the young bucks who would be hunting scalps and stealing horses.

Yet why did he not trust King? Was it jealousy? Zeb scowled into his glass. He did not like to think he might be misjudging a man because of his own personal feelings.

No, it was not a matter of personal feeling; it was simply that he knew that to Mike King only one thing mattered: the railroad. To put that railroad through on schedule Mike King would ride roughshod through and over anything that got in the way. And that included Zeb Rawlings.

"All right," he said at last, "I'll see what I can do. I'll talk to them."

King went to the car door with him, his hand on Zeb's shoulder. "Don't worry about it, Rawlings. We're just crossing their land. I give you my word—nobody is going to stay."

"I'll be going."

"You seeing Julie?"

Zeb Rawlings looked up, his eyes cold and level. "Yes. Any comment?"

King smiled, that taunting smile that always seemed to be concealing so much. "No, no! You're a lucky man, that's all."

Zeb walked to his horse and paused there, making a business of tightening the cinch. He had a feeling that King had bested him, but with King one usually had that feeling, whether the issue had been lost or not.

Stepping into the saddle, he turned to Jethro, who was waiting. "Can you get me a chance to talk to the chief?"

Jethro merely nodded, turning his horse away. Together they rode into the hills.

SIXTEEN

D ay had scarcely come when they rode into the village of
Walks-His-Horses. At the first sight of it, Zeb Rawlings
felt the skin tighten on the back of his scalp. There were at
least two hundred lodges, which could mean close to five
hundred warriors.

Dogs rushed out, yapping furiously, and an Indian stepped
from one of the lodges.

"How safe are we?" Zeb asked. "Pa used to say if you came
of your own accord into an Indian village you were safe as long
as you stayed there."

"That's true . . . generally."

Jethro chewed on the idea for a minute or so. "I'd say you
are safe enough this time. Walks-His-Horses is a reasonable
man, and smart enough to figure it is better to talk than to
fight. It's his young men you have to worry about—they want
to count coups so they can stand tall among the squaws."

Walks-His-Horses was a tall, powerfully built Indian of perhaps forty years. He had a large-boned, intelligent face and
such dignity as only an Indian can have. He looked at them,
then invited them into his lodge.

When they were seated, Jethro began to speak slowly, in
Arapahoe, of which Zeb knew only a few words. However,

Jethro spoke in sign language as well, the graceful and fluent movements of his hands lending a weird touch to the moment. Slowly, other warriors began to enter the lodge.

Jethro spoke to Zeb out of the side of his mouth. "Says there's an Indian he knows who knows your pa . . . an Osage named Arrow-Going-Home. Says your pa had the name of being a great man, a great warrior and hunter."

"Heard pa speak of the Osage. They crossed the plains together back in 'forty-four or 'forty-five."

Zeb could follow some of the talk, for he knew the sign language, which was universal among the tribes, although few Indians knew any tribal tongue but their own.

The lodge filled with warriors. The air became stifling. The pipe was lighted and it went slowly around the circle. Zeb pulled on it gravely, then passed it along.

"The old man is in good temper," Jethro whispered, indicating a white-haired man of noble features who sat behind and to the right of Walks-His-Horses, "and that counts for plenty."

The talk droned on, Jethro translating from time to time items that Zeb could not grasp.

Suddenly, Walks-His-Horses began to speak. His voice was low, but filled with somber power, and as he spoke his eyes moved from one to the other.

"When I see you here in my lodge, I feel glad as do the ponies when first the green grass comes to the hills at the beginning of the year. My heart fills with joy that we can talk together as old friends, for I have no wish for trouble with my white brothers, least of all with you who speak to me here, my friend, and the son of the man known to all among Iñuaina.

"When first the white man came among us and spoke of blazing an iron trail for the Iron Horse, we were amazed and wished to see this thing, but at the same time we were frightened, for word had come to us that wherever the Iron Horse drew its wagons, there the white man came to hunt, not in dozens, but in hundreds, perhaps even thousands. These hunters we feared would kill the buffalo and leave the redman hungry, his squaws and papooses without food.

"We heard the white man killed the buffalo and took only the skin, leaving the meat to rot beneath the sun while the children of the Indian died from hunger.

"The white man promised the Iron Horse would not come close to our hunting grounds, but would take the other side of the hills. Now this has been changed and the Iron Horse and its wagons have come among us. We see the game frightened off into the far hills, where we must go with many dangers to find food.

"Now the Iron Horse has come and my young men come to me and shout their anger. They shake the arrow of war and mix paint for their faces, and they bring their war ponies in from the grass.

"We do not wish to fight the white man, but our young men are angry. They demand war. They demand the iron trail be destroyed before it brings hunters to our hunting grounds."

Zeb Rawlings was silent, choosing the words with which to reply. Why did he feel guilty before this old man? And before Walks-His-Horses? Had not Mike King given his word?

He spoke slowly, taking his time to make himself understood, and to allow for translation of those words he missed. "We look upon the Arapahoe as brothers, and your problems are our problems also. It is true the trail of the Iron Horse has been changed, for it cannot run everywhere as a pony can do. Where the trail is now the way is smooth for it, and it can run swiftly without cutting through hills or bridging streams.

"Many men will ride the Iron Horse's wagons, but they are men who go far away to the land beside the blue waters where the sun sets. They will pass over your lands but they will not stop. The man who builds the iron trail has promised me this."

The eyes of Walks-His-Horses burned into those of Zeb Rawlings. "Blue Coat, son of the man we know, I speak to you. I do not speak to the man who makes the iron trail. You sit in my lodge, you smoke the pipe, it is your voice I hear.

"I do not smoke with the man who makes the iron trail. He does not sit in my lodge, he does not hear my voice. What do *you* say? What is it *you* will promise?"

Lieutenant Zeb Rawlings hesitated, for he did not need to look around him to know his audience. The lodge was packed with warriors, many of them the young warriors who demanded war. From these he could feel bitter animosity. They were held back only by the authority of their chief . . . for how long?

When they attacked, who would die? At first it would be lonely travelers, settlers, innocent people who had done nothing to invite the red rage that would sweep the plains. Only later would they attack the railroad. Innocent people would die unless he could stop this now, unless he could stop it here.

Walks-His-Horses was an able man. He knew how fiercely the white man could retaliate, and he had come to know how ruthlessly they followed their enemies. The Indian way was to fight a great battle—one battle—and on the outcome would the decision rest. Not until the white man came did the Indian discover what a campaign meant. The Indian fought, then retired to his lodge; but the white man followed after, destroyed the Indian's corn, his meat, and his lodge. He drove off the ponies and hounded the Indian until the snow was red with his bloody tracks. The chief knew this, as did the old man who sat at his elbow. The young men did not know, or they believed they could win. They did not understand that against the white man no victory was possible.

"What I have said," Zeb Rawlings reiterated slowly, "is true. Men will ride the Iron Horse, but they go to the lands in the west where there is gold and silver. The man who makes the iron trail has given me his word. *I* give you *my* word. No one will stop. The hunting grounds of the Arapahoe will remain the hunting grounds of the Arapahoe."

The sun was setting when the two rode out again upon the hill overlooking the still distant End of the Track. As they drew rein to give their horses a chance to catch their wind, a far-off train whistle blew.

"That blamed whistle!" Jethro said irritably. "It's like the crack of doom for all that's natural."

"What's natural and what isn't? My ma came from a settling family. They believed a man should make his scratch on the land and leave it a little different. Anyway, thanks for fixing things with the chief."

"Me? I fixed nothing. You put the words in my mouth and I said what you couldn't say for yourself. That won't make 'em come true."

"I said what had to be said to keep the peace. There's a risk, I know."

"Risk? You pledged your word back there, Rawlings. Not my

word. Not Mike King's word, and not the Army's. It was *your* word they'd keep their huntin' grounds."

"I think they will."

"You got more trust in your fellow man than I have. Especially when your fellow man is Mike King." Jethro took out his tobacco, looked at it thoughtfully, and then said, "Look, son, how do you figure they aim to pay for this road? Do you think carryin' the mail and a few passengers to Californy will do it? If you do, you got another think a-comin'. They need farms and folks and towns. They need men shippin' cattle and farmers shippin' grain. Your treaty's goin' to be broken, Rawlings, and I don't want to be around when it happens. Look me up sometime when you've got a belly full."

"Where you going?"

"I'm heading back into the mountains, and it won't be Arapahoe country where I stop, neither."

"What about Julie?"

Jethro's eyes twinkled slightly. "Well, son, you just talked yourself into an Indian treaty. I reckon you will have to talk to Julie. She mightn't be no harder to convince."

The ride back was silent, each man busy with his thoughts. Zeb Rawlings did not consider, for the moment at least, the promise he had made to Walks-His-Horses. He was thinking about Julie.

No girl in her right mind would marry an Army lieutenant with plans to resign his commission, when she could marry a man like Mike King. Whatever else could be said about him, King had a future. He was a man on the way, and moving fast. With his ruthlessness and drive, he could scarcely miss having the success he wanted.

Zeb had nothing to offer but life with him, and the chance he must take, with the Army or without it. And now he had staked everything on King's word—a man whom he did not trust.

Yet what else could he have done? For the moment at least, war was averted.

After leaving Jethro, he hastily went to his quarters and bathed. Grimly, he considered the one clean uniform he had. It wasn't much, but he would wear it tonight.

Jethro Stuart had stopped at the big tent. Rowdy Jim Lowe ran the place, a powerful brute of a man, and by reputation a killer, a man who had made a business of gambling tents at the End of the Track. Leaving his mount at the hitch rail, Jethro walked through the room, weaving among the tables toward the bar.

At this hour the big tent was relatively deserted; not half a dozen tables were occupied, and only three men stood at the bar. One of them was Mike King.

Turning, King saw Jethro. "Come have a drink, Jethro," King said cheerfully. "I want to talk to you."

"What's the matter?" Jethro asked dryly. "Did the Central Pacific have a wreck? Or did you find somebody to take over my job?"

"I heard you went to the Arapahoes with young Rawlings. Well, thanks."

"I sat there and listened, mostly. I wish I believed what you promised as much as Rawlings did."

The bartender filled two shot glasses and left the bottle. "You mean you don't trust me?" King grinned knowingly, tauntingly. "You'd have done it different?"

"Been me, I'd have told 'em to raid that car of yours and hang your scalp out to dry. That'd stop your damned railroad."

Mike King chuckled. He felt good and did not intend to be disturbed. At some future date he would remember all of this, and use it.

"You've put Rawlings right in the middle, King, and you know it. And that boy has notions."

"What kind of notions?"

"Fool notions about honor. No use talkin' to you—you wouldn't understand."

King chuckled again. "Forget that talk, Jethro. Tonight's a big night." He grinned at him. "We should be friends—at least."

"What's that mean?" Jethro asked suspiciously.

"Julie and I have had a talk," King replied. "We see things eye to eye. That's quite a girl you have there, Jethro. A lady . . . every inch a lady."

"What's that mean?" Jethro asked once more.

King tossed off his drink. "We'll both tell you later. I'm seeing her tonight."

Slapping Jethro on the shoulder, he turned and walked from

the tent. Jethro glanced down at his drink with sudden distaste and turning abruptly, he left it standing and went out of the tent. Rowdy Jim watched him go, his eyes thoughtful. Jethro Stuart drank little, but it was the first time since he had worked for the railroad that he had not taken an evening drink.

Rowdy Jim recalled the expression on Jethro's face. "Something's up," he commented to the bartender, "I never saw Stuart look so mean."

"He's no gunman, is he?"

Lowe spat. "No, he ain't, but no gunfighter in his right mind would buy trouble with Jethro Stuart. One thing you learn in this country, talk soft around those old mountain men. You might kill one, but you'll have lead in you first. They die mighty hard—mighty hard, indeed!"

Stuart had been talking with King—Lowe considered that. Maybe he should drop around and see him. On the other hand, what did King ever do for anybody? To hell with him!

Jethro Stuart lifted the flap of his tent and stood there looking at Julie. She was fixing her hair in front of the mirror that used to belong to her ma. God only knew how she'd kept it in one piece all this time.

Quietly, he began gathering his things together and putting them into a pack. She watched him in the mirror without speaking. At last she turned around.

"Well, pa, this is the longest we've been together since I was a little girl. You're going off again?"

"Uh-huh."

He always went to the mountains when something went wrong, and she had been expecting it for days.

"Are you leaving me alone in this—this place? You never did that before, pa."

"You ain't goin' to be alone for long, I'm thinkin'." He straightened up and looked at her. "You made your mind up Julie? You decided?"

"Why, pa! Whatever was there to decide?" She came up to him and tugged at his mustache. She had done that when she was a little girl, and she knew he liked it.

"Now, don't you start that again." He studied her shrewdly. "You sure you're doin' the right thing?"

"Of course." Suddenly her eyes became wistful. "Don't go, pa. Not this time. I don't want you to go away again."

He felt a lump coming into his throat, and it irritated him. "Now, you stop that, I'm goin'. What you do is your own affair."

He paused. "We tried to raise you right, your ma and me. Admittin' I was gone much of the time, when I was there I tried to do the right thing . . . and I never knew any way to make a livin' but with a rifle or a gather of traps.

"Now you're a lady. No use my tryin' to live your life for you. You've got it to do." He bundled his gear together. "You sure you're doin' right?"

"Of course!" she repeated.

He went outside and let the flap fall behind him. He walked to his horse and then stopped. It was jaded, needed rest. Maybe he could make a swap with the Army.

He swung into the saddle and started away, then said aloud, "I tried, Linus. I sure enough tried."

SEVENTEEN

S pring came late to the western lands. The brown hills still
carried dark patches from the dampness left by melting
snow, while here and there in a shadowed place could still be
found a streak of snow or reluctant ice. Zeb Rawlings rode
down the hill toward Willow Springs Station, cold with anger
and despair.

The train of five cars standing at Willow Springs chilled him
even more. "There's trouble, Sergeant," he said, indicating the
train—"trouble for us. More settlers, more buffalo hunters, and
the railroad not yet out of Arapahoe country."

"We might have expected it, Lieutenant. Where people can
get, there people will go."

Of course that was true, and down deep within him Zeb had
known it very well. Why should he not know it? Had not his
own people come west by the Erie Canal and the Ohio?

Why had he allowed himself to be persuaded by King? Yet,
in the last analysis, he could blame no one but himself. He
should have let King make his own promises to Walks-His-
Horses.

Nothing Zeb could have done would have stopped the building of the railroad, nor even the changing of the route. All he
could do was protest, and report to headquarters, and it was all

too easy for some desk soldier, far from the place itself, to overrule him.

Mike King stood on the platform as the patrol rode up.

"Not in your lifetime, you said." Zeb Rawlings rested his palms on the saddle horn and looked down at King.

King grinned his tantalizing grin. "You can't stop the march of progress, Lieutenant. Anybody should have known people would come west if the railroad gave them a chance. Hell, that was why we were building the road!"

"You lied." Zeb's jaw had set hard. "You made a liar out of me. You said this could not happen in your lifetime."

"Who expected to live so long? Get down, Lieutenant, and let's have a drink. It's no skin off your nose."

"I gave them my word."

"You shame too easy, Rawlings. Did an Indian ever build a railroad? Those tracks are worth more than you, me, or all those Arapahoes put together, and they will be here when all of us are gone.

"The government gave us land along the right-of-way to sell to make the road pay; but to make it pay we need settlers— ranchers, farmers, businessmen. And there they are.

"See them? More than half came all the way from Europe, and they'll have a rough time of it, but they're tough and they will come through because they are willing to change their ways in order to survive and grow. The Arapahoes will have to change, too. If they don't, they're finished."

"That doesn't get me off the hook."

"Aw, forget it! So you gave them your word. They're just naked savages, so who cares?"

"It may surprise you, King, but *I* care. Walks-His-Horses is a gentleman, and in his way, a statesman. He has lived up to his agreement. The railroad hasn't lost a man or a horse since the day I talked to him."

Zeb Rawlings reined his horse around. "A few minutes ago, King, you were talking of these people who have come out from Europe and the East. Before the month is out some of them will die, and some of your men too. By now Walks-His-Horses knows they are coming, and we'll have a full moon the first of the week. You'd better have your men armed for trouble."

King's expression hardened. "Don't blame me for what happens! It's your job to protect them."

"You changed the route of the railroad and violated an agreement. You changed it on your own authority, without consulting anyone. In your crazy drive to get the road through, you changed the route through Arapahoe country and you had influence enough to get backing for your change, even though it was unnecessary. Furthermore"—Rawlings' tone was filled with contempt—"you failed in your object."

He wheeled his horse and led the troop away, and Mike King stared after him, his eyes ugly with anger.

"Lieutenant!" King shouted, stepping down off the platform.

Rawlings drew up. "Sergeant, take the troop on in. Get them fed and see to the horses. Get some sleep if you can, but be ready for trouble. I think all hell's going to break loose."

As Rawlings turned he loosened the flap on his holster.

King saw the movement and grew wary. Rawlings walked his horse back to him, and King's eyes lifted to meet Rawlings' eyes. Mike King was nothing if not a wise man in his own way. He was wise now.

"Sorry Lieutenant. I truly am sorry. Besides"—he held up a message—"this came for you. Came through my private wire. You're promoted to major . . . as of two weeks ago."

There was no softening in Rawlings. "You did that, King. You know and I know how hard promotions are to come by in peacetime. There's no honorable way I could get that promotion now. I know there are some officers who use political influence, even to getting special acts of Congress to put through their promotion when it won't come through the proper channels. I am not one of them. I am going to resign my commission."

"Don't be a fool!"

"You made a liar out of me, King. Oh, I know—a good deal of it was my own fault, but your road could have refused tickets. to anybody for a stop between Omaha and Salt Lake. At least for a few months.

"So Walks-His-Horses will think the Army lied to him. The only honorable thing I can do is resign, take the blame on my own shoulders, and then whoever replaces me can negotiate with him. It will be Lieutenant Rawlings who lied to him, not the Army."

"What do you care?"

"Unless the chief thinks it was my word that was broken and not the Army's, there will be a lot of people killed. I made the promise, so the blame is mine. You assured me there would be no passenger service into this area, and I believed you."

Mike King shrugged. "If you want to be foolish, go ahead. But take that uniform off and you're nothing.

"Look," King went on. "Take your promotion. Believe me, after this Indian outbreak you could even become a colonel. If you attract enough attention to yourself people are always ready to believe you have done something important, whether you have or not. One of the best friends I've got is a friend of General Sherman."

"King, the Army in this country, except for a few individuals in it, has always stayed out of politics, and it should. Whenever an army is allowed to get into politics there is soon a dictatorship. We're an instrument of the government—of Congress and the executive arm. I would accept no promotion that came to me through political channels."

"You talk like a child. Be realistic!"

"I've noticed," Zeb replied, "that whenever a man is asked to be realistic he is being asked to betray something in which he believes. It is the favorite argument of those who believe that only the end matters, not the means."

The railroad supply dump at Willow Springs served building crews to the west. The settlers had made headquarters there, a few tent stores floored with split logs had been set up, and there was the usual scattering of honky-tonks and gambling houses.

It was there that Mike King now kept his office car and living quarters. Attached to it was the cook car, and several cars for the various sections of the crew and the straw-bosses. On either side, a little back from the cars and the station platform, were long piles of ties. These formed an excellent breastwork. Several wagons, when not in use, were drawn up to fill open spaces in this breastwork.

Zeb Rawlings' troop was camped just inside this wall of ties.

Within the company area noon fires were burning and there was the low murmur of idle talk and the rattle of pans.

A quarter of a mile from the railroad were the low hills, broken in many places by gullies. Restlessly, Zeb Rawlings stirred around the troop area. His every instinct told him an attack could come at any time. Overhead the blue sky was innocent of clouds . . . a faint breeze stirred off the hills. Zeb glanced at the horses, but they were feeding quietly. In the noon stillness he heard the occasional ring of dish on dish, or a bit of laughter.

If only Julie were not here! Why, in God's name, had Jethro gone off without her? For a moment he debated rushing to her tent to bring her here, where the army was, but he had no idea what his reception would be. After that night when he had started out to call on her, planning to ask her to marry him, he had not talked with her. And weeks had gone by. He saw her occasionally, but he avoided her, and as he was usually on patrol that had not been difficult.

Bitterly, he thought back to that evening after his talk with Jethro, when he had bathed, changed his uniform, and started for Julie's tent. He had been as excited as a boy, half scared, but determined . . . and then he had met Mike King.

"Going somewhere?" King had glanced over his dress uniform with a taunting grin. "Seems to me, Rawlings, that you're all dressed up for nothing. I am calling on her tonight—and I've been invited."

Something turned cold in the pit of Zeb's stomach. "What's that mean?"

"Why, if you're callin' on Julie, you're too late. She's promised to me."

For an instant they stared at each other, and then Zeb said, "Is that the truth?"

"Gospel."

Suddenly he felt very silly in his dress blues. What must he look like to King? To the others standing around who must have guessed where he was going? Without another word, he had turned on his heel and walked away.

Now he looked toward the hills again, and saw no movement . . . nothing.

"Sergeant," he said suddenly, "get eight men with rifles to

the barrier right away. Issue fifty rounds per man. Let them eat as they stand, but they're not to take their eyes off those hills.

"As soon as the rest have finished eating, let the fire die to coals, keep the coffee on, and have every man stand to arms."

"They are tired, Lieutenant, mighty tired."

"I'd rather see them tired than dead."

He went to his weary horse and mounted. Without another word, he swung toward the settlers' camp. There he demanded: "Who is in charge here?"

A tall, lanky man with a shock of sandy hair looked up at him, grinning slowly. "This here ain't the army. We're free agents. We take orders from nobody."

Rawlings turned away from him. "Any old soldiers here? From any army at all?" he asked.

Several men spoke up. "All right. Now you men listen to me. I have no authority over you except what authority the Army has given me to protect you. There may be an Indian attack. Get your children inside the tie-wall, and stay in your-selves. Get out any firearms you have and have them ready. Appoint a commanding officer and detail some guards."

"I don't see any Indians." It was the tall, lanky man who spoke. "What you tryin' to do, Yankee? Show off that blue uniform?"

Another man sauntered from the group, slowly followed by the others who had been soldiers. The first one was a slender whip of a man with neat black mustaches and high cheek bones. There was a tautness in him that Zeb immediately liked. "Vaucelle, sir. French Foreign Legion."

"Vaucelle? I did not know there were Frenchmen in the enlisted ranks of the Legion."

The man's eyes smiled faintly. "I was an officer, sir. Will you tell us what the situation is?"

"These are Arapahoe hunting grounds. The Indians were under the impression the railroad would bring no settlers or hunters here. They will try to drive us away. I do not know their numbers, but there will be at least five hundred Indians out there—perhaps half again that many. I expect an attack soon, perhaps before sundown."

Zeb indicated the army group. "I have twenty-two men,

including myself and my sergeant. With three exceptions, they are veterans, and the exceptions are good men. But we will need all the help we can get."

"Thank you, Lieutenant, I will see what I can do."

The sandy-haired man got to his feet slowly. "I'd like to see what the Lieutenant can do. I've seen him perambulatin' around here, shinin' up to that gal lives by herself in that tent, and I—"

Zeb Rawlings swung down. "Gentlemen," he said quietly, "I hope you will excuse me."

The sandy-haired man was three inches taller and thirty pounds heavier than Zeb. He grinned a slow grin and rubbed his palms down his jeans. "Ain't had me a chanct like this here since the war, by G—!"

He closed his fingers in a big fist and threw his punch.

There was no finesse in Zeb Rawlings. He had never had an opportunity to learn there even was such a thing. Linus, on the other hand, had been victor in many a brutal fight with keelboaters and trappers, and he had demonstrated to his sons and rehearsed them in the basic elements of fighting to win.

The big sandy-haired man swung, and Zeb Rawlings went under the swing and put everything he had into a right to the ribs. The man buckled at the knees and started to fold, and Zeb Rawlings jerked up his knee to meet the falling chin. There was an ugly *clunk* and the man continued to fall. Zeb Rawlings stepped back, blowing on his skinned knuckles and looking at the man on the ground.

Then he turned. "Mr. Vaucelle, I'll appreciate what you can do. Thank you!"

Quickly, he stepped into the stirrups and turned away, and as he did so he saw Julie Stuart.

She was standing not fifty feet away, a basket in her hand, and as their eyes met, she turned sharply as if to go. He touched a spur to his horse and was beside her in a bound. "I've yet to offer my congratulations," he said stiffly.

She turned her eyes on him. "Congratulations?"

"Mike King told me he had spoken to you."

Her chin came up. "He has spoken to me many times, and what of it? I've no doubt he will speak to me again if he passes me on the way, and I shall answer, and what of that?"

"You're not—you mean you're not going to marry him?"

"Mike King? And why should a girl want to marry a railroad, I'd like to know? I've never given a thought to it."

"But he told me—I thought—"

"Do you believe everything you're told, then? Don't you know the man hasn't the truth in him? You had no reason to think anything of the sort, and if you'd been less of a fool you would have known it."

Zeb glanced toward the encampment. "Julie, you've got to get what you need and come to where the army is. We're expecting an attack."

"You change the subject very fast."

He grinned sheepishly. "It's a poor time to talk of romance and what comes after, when I have a duty to fulfill." He looked down into her eyes. "Julie, I'll be leaving the Army."

"So you told me before. If you are going to leave, you should do it soon. Wherever we settle we will want a crop in, and there's little time."

He was halfway back to the camp before the full weight of her words struck him. He rode into camp in a daze.

And then anger flooded through him. King had lied to him, made a fool of him, and he had let it happen. Wheeling his horse, he rode toward King's car just as the railroad man stepped to the door and stretched.

Zeb drew up. "You're not wearing a gun," he said. "Get one, and get it now."

Mike King lowered his arms with care. His pistol lay on his desk inside, and almost within reach was a fully loaded shotgun.

Zeb Rawlings' face was taut and white, and King, who was counted a courageous man, felt an odd sinking in the pit of his stomach. In that instant he knew he was closer to death than he had ever been. He had seen Zeb Rawlings shoot, and he knew just exactly what his chances were.

He started to speak, when a shout came from the army encampment. "Indians! *Indians!*"

A shot barked in the afternoon sun. Zeb wheeled his horse sharply around. The crest of the hill was feathered with charging Arapahoes, and even as he looked, another bunch burst from the mouth of a gully not twenty-five yards off, their horses at a dead run.

"You asked for war!" he shouted savagely at King. "Now you've got it!"

He turned his horse and raced the few yards to his own camp, where sporadic fire had already begun as his veterans picked their targets. Directly before him Zeb saw a man stagger, clutching at his throat, where blood welled between his fingers.

Glancing toward the settlers' camp, he saw Vaucelle and the ex-soldiers he had mustered lined up behind the tie-stacks, rifles poised to fire. Under their steadying influence the others were coolly prepared to fight.

Mixed among the muzzle-loaders and breech-loaders were a few of the new Henry rifles, and here and there a Spencer. You could always tell when the big Spencer hit, because the .56 or .54 caliber cartridges would lift an Indian right off his horse.

A statuesque blonde girl who might have modeled for Brunhilde was running a ramrod down a rifle barrel, loading it and passing it to a man who exchanged it for the rifle he had just fired. Another woman was bending over a wounded man, bathing a wounded arm and preparing to bandage it.

Far from their homes in a savage land, these stalwart people, many of whom had never heard a shot fired in anger, were fighting to defend their right to be here. No less than the Indians, they fought for home and family, and many would die.

King's railroaders settled down grimly. Most of them were veterans, or men who had experienced Indian battles before, and they took their positions quickly and began to fire.

The sudden fire seemed to break the onrush of Indians, for their charge suddenly split off to left and right. And then Zeb heard a sound that gripped his throat with sudden fear.

A soft, muted thunder, scarcely heard, then filling the ears with sound . . . a great dust cloud that suddenly exploded above the hill, and then the dust was split apart by a vast, rolling blackness from which came the thunder. A dark cloud of massive, woolly heads, glistening horns . . . *buffalo!*

On either side rode the Arapahoes, pointing the stampeding herd straight at the town of canvas, straight at the flimsy barricades of the settlers, many of whom were at the end of the tie-stacks.

They simply had no chance. There was scarcely time to fire and load before the charging herd was upon them. The great woolly wall of hurtling flesh came down in a gigantic herd. Many a beast among those hundreds weighed at least a ton.

And there was no stopping their insane charge. Tents flattened; women screamed. The wounded man pushed the woman aside and tried to cover her with his body; then the black mass whirled through. One instant the settlers' town was there, and then it was ground into the mud along with torn and bloody flesh. At a dugout near the railroad line Zeb saw a huge bull struggling, half through a roof, saw it plunging to escape the trap, then vanish.

And then the Arapahoes came.

They came close upon the heels of the buffalo, and leaping their ponies over fallen beasts, shot down by the desperate effort to stop the stampede or turn it, the Indians were behind the barricade, among the defenders.

King retreated swiftly toward his car, one of the few things left standing. Zeb saw his sergeant go down under the glancing blow of a tomahawk, and he fired, knocking the warrior from the saddle. A horse plunged at him and he fell aside, firing and missing.

A young warrior, his face painted with streaks of black, rushed at him, and Zeb lifted his pistol and fired. The bullet stopped the Indian in mid-stride, but then he came on and Zeb fired again. When the Indian fell three bullets were in his breast and he went down almost on top of Zeb.

Catching up a rifle, Zeb scrambled to his feet and shot at an Indian near the barricade. Then he wheeled to fire again, but the gun was empty and he charged a group of Indians, swinging the heavy Springfield like a club.

As suddenly as the attack had begun, it ended. There was only the acrid smell of gunpowder, the gasping of men exhausted by tremendous effort, and the moans or cries of the wounded. Zeb removed the empty cylinder from his pistol and replaced it with another.

Mike King got slowly to his feet from the steps of his private car, blood running down his face from a scalp wound.

"You bought it," Zeb told him savagely. "Now walk out there and look at the price!"

"Going to shoot me?" King even now smiled his taunting smile, but his eyes were wary. Both held drawn guns, and the range was close. King knew the difference then: he wanted desperately to live, and Zeb Rawlings did not care. Deep within him, King was filled with fear. He would stand and fight, but desperately did not want to die.

"Walk out there!" Zeb commanded. "I want you to see what you have done!"

Where the woman had knelt above the wounded man, now there were two bodies ground into one, their flesh churned by the flying hoofs. The blonde Brunhilde lay sprawled in ugly death, only a raw skull where the blonde hair had been. Men moaned and begged for help. Slowly the survivors collected themselves and began to move among the wounded.

The sergeant, an ugly cut upon his scalp, came to Zeb for orders. Briefly, Rawlings told him what to do. "Get eight men on the barricades as before. Turn the rest of them to collecting rifles and ammunition, and helping the wounded. We can spare only four men for the injured."

He turned on King. "How do you like it, King? You invited them here. You brought them too soon into the hell created by your broken promises. You brought them here, you killed them—now you can live with it."

"You can't make an omelette without breaking eggs," King said. "And the eggs will keep coming."

But his face was gray and sick-looking and he turned his eyes quickly away from the dead and dying. "You aren't going to kill me?" he asked.

"You? You aren't worth killing. You're dead. You've been dead for years. You're only a hammer in the hands of the directors of your road. There's nothing inside you at all."

Julie, he thought . . . where was Julie?

And then he saw her, bending over a wounded man, and he went to her.

"I'm leaving," he said. "I'm riding out."

"*Now?*" She was incredulous.

"It's best. The Arapahoes will see me go, and they blame me more than anyone else. I think you can stop any attack that will come now, but if I leave they may not attack at all."

"They will kill you."

"Maybe. I'm no martyr—once out there, I'll run for it. I'm taking the company race horse and leaving mine."

She put her hand on his sleeve. "No . . . don't go."

"I have to. If I go they'll come after me. It will be easier than attacking here again. If I make it, I'll meet you in Salt Lake."

There were no tears, no protests. They stood an instant looking into each other's eyes, and then he turned quickly away.

He walked across to where the sergeant was bringing some order into the frightful mess of the encampment. "You're in command, Sergeant. My resignation has gone in. I'm riding out. Maybe they'll want me so bad they'll leave you alone, but your position is good, their chance of surprise is gone, and the train from Omaha should be rolling in by tomorrow with more troops."

"So long, Lieutenant."

"So long, Sergeant."

"And Lieutenant—good luck."

He saddled the gray horse. It was a runner and a stayer, a horse he himself had bought but which they had kept for racing, winning a good bit of money from time to time. Now it was going to have to run.

He mounted up and walked the horse to the edge of the barricade. Vaucelle came over to him. "Over there,"—he nodded his head but did not point—"there don't seem to be any of them. You might make it."

"Thanks."

The Indians had carried off their dead, as they always did, leaving only those who had fallen within the enclosure. There were pools of blood here and there upon the grass, indication that the Arapahoes had been hard hit, too.

He started his horse trotting down the valley, giving them a chance to see him. He was heading west. That always seemed to be the answer. When things go wrong, go west.

A shot rang out. . . .

He glanced back, surprised to see the distance between himself and the fort. And then he saw the Arapahoes. There was a long line of them strung out along the ridge, and they were coming after him.

He glanced off to the north, and there was another line.

They were pointing themselves at some spot ahead where they expected to close in on him.

"All right, Jubal," he said to the gray horse, "let's see what you can do."

The long legs stretched out, the hoofs pounded the turf, the wind whipped at his face. The gray had a smooth, wonderful stride, and dearly loved to run.

Ahead of him somewhere was tomorrow—with luck. The hoofs drummed a rhythm upon the sod. He crouched lower to lessen the resistance offered to the wind.

EIGHTEEN

Gabe French paused on the corner and stared along the street. The last time he had walked on Nob Hill he had come looking for a teamster who had once worked for him, and the Hill then had been a cluster of modest wooden cottages. Now they had been replaced by ornate mansions.

He squinted his eyes against the reflection of sunlight from Jim Flood's thirty-thousand-dollar brass fence. It was all of two blocks long, and there was a man at work polishing it. Gabe had heard about that fence. In fact, come to think of it, Cleve had told him of it, and how it kept one man busy every day to keep it polished.

The gray towers of the Hopkins castle with its terraced gardens was diagonally across the street. He walked on by, ignoring the Colton, Stanford, and Crocker houses. He had never visited Cleve's home during his lifetime, and it seemed odd that he should come here now, when Cleve was dead. Yet they had been friends in the old days, and never less than friends in all the years that followed.

"One man I envied," Gabe said aloud, as he hesitated on the corner. "He had something about him . . . sort of a flair, I'd guess you'd call it."

"What was that?"

Gabe turned at the query, embarrassed to be caught talking to himself. "Asked if you knew where the Van Valen mansion is," he grumbled.

The man pointed. "Right over there. Although you can hardly call it his now. And by all accounts it won't be his widow's after today. They're selling him out, lock, stock, and barrel."

He was a prim little man with small eyes and a sour expression, and the satisfaction in his tone was obvious.

It irritated Gabe French, and he said, "They'd not do it if he was alive. Cleve Van Valen could raise millions when nobody else could lay hands on a copper penny . . . just on his name."

"I've heard that," the man said skeptically. "But I don't believe it."

Gabe felt his anger mounting. Age had brought a quick impatience to Gabe French. Heretofore he had been tolerant of fools; he was so no longer.

"A man must pay his debts," the man continued stiffly. "Van Valen always lived beyond his income."

"There was more'n a few years," Gabe replied testily, "when *nobody* could have lived beyond *his* income. Time was when one mine paid him upwards of eighty thousand a month. *Eighty thousand.* Never made that kind of money myself."

"I don't imagine you did." The stranger glanced contemptuously at Gabe's shabby clothing.

Gabe French tried to stifle his irritation and failed. A man had few pleasures when he grew old, and Gabe allowed himself his irritation at petty things. He had never been known to fret at disaster, but in these later years he found pleasure in grumbling.

He looked at the man coldly. "Not to say," he said deliberately, "that I couldn't buy and sell many a man who owns a mansion on this hill. As for Cleve Van Valen, there was never a better friend than him, or a more loyal one. Came a time—that was years back—glanders got into my horses and I had two freight contracts going, and all my stock dead or dying almost overnight.

"Somebody told Cleve, and he came over Donner Pass driving a hundred head of horses for me—and that in the late fall with snow falling. He made it through with the pass closing up behind him. Saved my bacon.

"There was another time when the two of us got ambushed by Modocs up near Klamath Lake. Our horses were killed and I had a bullet in me; and Cleve, he stood them off throughout the day, and in the night got away, carrying me on his back."

The man looked startled. "Then you— Why, you must be Gabe French!"

"That's right," Gabe said quietly, and glancing up the street, then down, he stepped off the curb and walked across.

Cleve was dead, but Lilith was alive, and by the Lord Harry, if she needed money he knew where she could get it. The trouble was that Lilith was a mighty proud woman, mighty proud.

Half a dozen rigs were standing in the street and in the short driveway leading up to the house. Gabe walked past them and went inside, pushing through a small knot of men talking by the door.

A crowd was gathered in the hall, and on the stairway stood the auctioneer.

"Two thousand dollars? Is that the last bid? Ladies and gentlemen, this trophy is solid gold and fully inscribed." He indicated letters on the side of the gold figure. " 'Mr. Cleve Van Valen. President of the San Francisco-Kansas City Railroad.' It is a treasure he held dear to his heart."

Gabe glanced around, his eyes searching for Lilith. When he saw her he was startled and momentarily dismayed. Somehow, he had never thought of Lilith as being old, yet come to think of it, she must be all of sixty now.

She sat in a chair overlooking the hall, clad in a lovely silk gown, her hair faultlessly done. Next to her was a man Gabe recognized as her attorney.

"Do I hear three thousand for this priceless possession?"

She was just near enough for him to hear her say, "Priceless, my foot! We used it as a doorstop."

The auctioneer spoke again. "Why, the gold here alone is worth three thousand—"

"Twenty-five hundred!"

"Sold!"

Gabe edged to the back of the crowd. He was only a short distance from Lilith, but to reach her he had to find his way around through a small hall. He came up behind her quietly.

"A sad day, Lilith," her attorney was saying.

"Sad? We made and spent fortunes. What's sad about that? If Cleve had lived long enough we would have made and spent another."

A clerk edged up behind her. "I beg your pardon, Mrs. Van Valen."

"What?"

"The chair. It's been sold."

"Take it." She got to her feet quickly, gracefully. "Quit apologizing and take it. Or should I say"—she smiled sweetly—" 'Take it and be damned'?"

The clerk grinned. "Sorry, ma'am."

"Get out of here," she said testily, but accompanying the words with a smile.

"If there had been any other way to pay off the debts, Lilith," the attorney said, "we would have found it."

"It doesn't matter. I have two things you can't take, my memories and my ranch in Arizona."

"I don't want to dash your hopes, but I am afraid that property is nearly worthless."

"It's there, isn't it?"

"Yes, but most of the cattle have been sold off or stolen."

"I'll get cattle. If necessary,"—she smiled—"I might even rustle a few head myself. Cleve always told me most of the big ranches were built with a running iron and a fast horse."

"You will need someone to work it, someone to manage it for you."

"I have just the man."

"Who?" the attorney asked doubtfully.

"My nephew. He's a marshal down there somewhere."

"But at your age," he protested, "in that rough country!"

"Rough? My pa and ma—they were killed going down the Ohio just looking for land. I guess I've got some Prescott blood in me after all."

Gabe French moved up quietly. "Lil?"

"Gabe!" The genuine feeling in her voice brought tears to his eyes, which he hastily excused by faking a sneeze, a very poor imitation.

"Gabe French! I might have known you would come. Let's go to the kitchen and have some coffee."

She turned on the lawyer. "You haven't sold my coffee pot, have you?"

He flushed. "Lilith . . . it was part of the set. We sold the silver, you know. A very good price, I might say."

"Oh, bother your silver! I mean the old black one."

The attorney looked relieved. "Oh, of course! No, that's still there. I am afraid we haven't had an offer for it yet."

"What he means," Lilith said to Gabe, "is that nobody would want it. That's the pot Cleve and I made coffee in all the way across the plains, and many a time after that. In fact, your wife—Agatha—it was ours together."

"Made good coffee," Gabe said. "I never drank better."

Together they went down to the kitchen, and put the pot on the fire. Then Lilith sat down and looked across the table at Gabe.

"I was sorry about Agatha, and sorry we couldn't come to the funeral. Cleve always hated funerals, and I am almost as bad. Always liked to remember folks as they were, and as I didn't see Agatha buried, she's very much around. . . . You were lucky, Gabe. You got a great woman."

"Don't I know it? I fancied her all the while, there on the wagon train, but never thought she noticed me."

He looked down at his big, square-knuckled hands. "I heard you talking up there, about the Arizona ranch. Lil, if there's anything you want . . . no matter how much, you just tell me. You know there wasn't a time Cleve wouldn't have bailed me out of trouble, and he did, many a time."

"And vice versa." Lilith put her hand over his. "Gabe, there's nothing I need. I will have enough when this is over to get to Arizona, and Zeb Rawlings is going to come down and manage the property for me. But thanks just the same."

"If I was a few years younger—"

"Forget it. Zeb can do all anybody can do. He's a marshal down there now, and he was in the Army. Civil War and Indian wars."

"I heard about him." He glanced at her thoughtfully. "Wasn't he the one who killed Floyd Gant?"

"Yes—and a good job, too."

"I knew Gant. He gave us trouble on the freight lines a few

times in Nevada. His brother Charlie was worse. Whatever became of Charlie?"

"I don't know. I didn't know Floyd had a brother."

For a while they sat silent. In the kitchen they were far from the voices above, for the kitchen was on a lower floor that opened upon another street. Just a few steps down the hill from that door and you were in Chinatown.

"They were good times, Gabe," Lilith said suddenly, "the best times. Nobody said much about it at the time, but we all had the feeling we were doing something great, that we were building something."

"I know. I was talking to a writing feller, man from Boston. He was asking me about crossing the plains and he commented on how many folks—just ordinary folks—had kept journals or diaries or something of the kind. They all seemed to have the notion they were living through something that might never happen again. He was looking around, trying to find those diaries before they were lost."

"I started a time or two. Cleve never kept one. But he believed what you're saying. I heard him say so."

She looked over at Gabe again. "I was never sorry, Gabe. I never regretted marrying Cleve. We had a good life together."

Gabe nodded without replying. He listened to the sound of the fire, and then when Lilith poured their coffee he crossed one leg carefully over the other. Certainly, he thought, nobody had ever enjoyed their money more.

"We made it big on the Mother Lode," Lilith said, "and when that was gone Cleve went off to Nevada and got in on the ground floor at the Comstock.

"I think we followed every boom there was, sometimes horseback, sometimes in a rig. I'll never forget that mine near Hamilton. Cleve took three million dollars' worth of silver out of a hole in the ground seventy by forty, by fifteen feet deep, and then a man came along and offered him another three million for the mine, and Cleve laughed at him."

"I recall."

"There wasn't three pounds of silver left in the hole. Cleve had it all. He was offered three million dollars for a hole in the ground big enough for a cellar."

Gabe shifted his position on the chair. These days if he sat too long in one position his back started bothering him.

"If I'd known about this," he said, "I'd have come sooner. You could have kept the house."

"I don't want it, Gabe. I must be practical. It's too big for me alone, and when it comes to that, I'd rattle around in it like a stone in a barrel. No, I'd rather be out there in Arizona trying to do something with that ranch. A woman in my position hasn't any business just sitting around. It won't do . . . and I wouldn't like it, anyway. I've been busy all my life, and I'm too old to change now. Besides"—she smiled at him—"I've never been in Arizona."

He finished his coffee and got up. "When you're ready, I'll take you to the station. And if ever you need me, just send word. Old Gabe will always be standing by."

He held out his hand to her. "It's a long time since I carried Cleve across that muddy street in St. Louis so he could win a bet."

She took his hand, then leaned forward and kissed him lightly on the cheek. "Thanks, Gabe. You're a real friend."

He hurried outside, afraid he would let her see his eyes watering. He was a sentimental old fool.

He glanced at the group around the other door. "Go ahead," he said aloud, "you aren't buying anything. She still has all she's ever needed."

Lilith refilled her cup. It was quiet in the kitchen, with the cook and the maid no longer around, and in many ways it was the most pleasant room in the big house. The fire felt good, for the night had been cool and dampness lingered.

From her reticule she took the photograph of Cleve that Huffman had made in Miles City, Montana, only four, or was it five, years ago.

He had been a handsome man, no question about that. "I wish Eve could have known you, Cleve," she said to herself, "and Linus."

How far, how far she had come, and how much, how much she had left behind!

PART 5

THE OUTLAWS

Some of those who went West stayed restless. Not for them the towns, the stores, the plough, the round-up. They had lived foot-loose and they would go on living that way until rope or lead put them under the sod. Lean-jawed men with snakes' eyes and rough humor, they plundered where they could, had their brief day until the Law came to the West and put them down forever . . .

NINETEEN

J ethro Stuart was too old in the mountains to ignore the feeling he now had, yet on the several occasions when he had drawn up in the thick timber to study his back trail, he had seen nobody.

But he was sure he was followed. He was followed by somebody who took great pains to keep from being seen, and it worried him.

Jethro Stuart was sixty-six years old in this spring of 1883, and forty-eight of those years he had spent in the western mountains. The place toward which he was now heading he had last seen while traveling with Osborne Russell in 1838 or thereabouts.

They had left the Rocky Mountain Fur Company to become free trappers, and following up the Stinkingwater they had found the valley.

They had been followed that time, too. Only then it was by Blackfeet, and the tribe had been pacified long since. So far as Jethro knew, there wasn't a warlike Indian in the entire country, let alone in these remote mountains near the head of the Yellowstone.

It had been a week ago today that he had seen his last human being. Unexpectedly he had come upon a Texas cabin built in a small valley. There had been corrals, a shed built of poles, and some two dozen very fine horses grazing in the meadow. He had swapped for one of those horses and was riding it now.

He had come up to the place in the late afternoon and the man had waited in the door of the cabin, a rifle across his arm, until Jethro had stopped in the ranch yard.

"All right if I come up? I'm peaceful."

"If you ain't," the man replied coolly, "I've got the means to make you thataway. But come on up."

"Last time I was through here my party was the only bunch of white men closer than Fort Hall."

"Mountain men?"

"Was. I rode with Wyeth and them."

"Get down. Company's mighty scarce hereabouts, an' when you find it, it generally ain't of the best."

Jethro got down and stripped the saddle from his mount. A tall boy came from the log cabin, rifle in the hollow of his arm. Obviously, he had been covered by more than one gun. Well, that was as it should be. It was good to know the old breed were still around. Be a sad day when a man didn't stand ready to receive company, good or bad.

"It's a far piece to be ridin' alone," the man commented. "And you're pointed into some mighty rough country."

"More than forty year in the mountains, an' more'n half that time alone. I lost my wife."

"Children?"

"Daughter . . . she married. Living down Arizona way, but it's been a time since I seen her."

"My wife passed on two year ago." The man looked at Jethro, a challenge in his eyes. "She was an Indian. A Shoshone."

"Good folks," Jethro replied calmly, and then to put the squaw man at his ease, he added, "I lived with the Nez Perce one time."

There were four at table aside from himself—the man, two boys, and a girl. She was the youngest, and maybe fourteen. The boys were tall for their years, slim but with good shoulders. All of them were excited by his coming and were filled with questions.

The food was good, he had to allow that. Tipped back in his

chair, he told them about the railroad that had been built through to the California lands. They had heard of it, but had never seen it.

"I've seen steam cars," the father said. "I'm a New York man, myself. Upper New York state. Migrated west with my family but we all went different ways, seemed like. Never did get together again."

He was a strong, powerfully built man with a strong jaw and steady eyes. The place was mighty nice, Jethro decided, mighty nice. No rawhide outfit, but kept up, and neat. There were good stacks of hay out yonder, and a field that had been planted to corn and garden truck.

Never one to miss anything he could see with his eyes, Jethro had seen nothing slipshod here. There was a dugout with a heavy door that was likely a place to store furs, and there was a grizzly hide nailed up on the barn that was the biggest he'd ever seen.

"There's bigger," the man said. "There's one old silver-tip grizzly up in these mountains I'm just a-honin' to get in my sights; but he's smart, too durned smart, and 'less a man is careful, he'll get himself bear-killed. That bear will hunt a man who starts trailin' him."

"Heard of that," Jethro agreed.

"Follered him one time, then gave up and started back. Something made me look back, and from where I stood I could see where my trail would have led. And there, all hunkered down beside that trail and a-waitin' for me was that old silver-tip. If I'd gone twenty yards further that grizzly would have tackled me head-on."

Jethro tamped the tobacco in his pipe, and noticed the look in his host's eyes.

He tossed him his tobacco sack. "He'p yourself. I came away with plenty."

"You say you were with Wyeth and them," the man said. "You ever come up against a mountain man named Linus Rawlings?"

"Trapped fur and fought redskins with him. Fact is," Jethro said, "his oldest boy married my daughter."

"Now, don't that beat all! Why, I met Linus Rawlings back

on the Ohio. Say, his wife wouldn't have been a Prescott, would she?"

"Eve was her name. I ain't sure about the last name."

"Eve! That was her! Well, now!" He turned to his children. "Remember I told you about them? And how that Eve surely set her cap for that mountain feller? I declare, she was a fine-looking girl! And that sister of hers, the singin' one. She was something to see. But pert . . . mighty pert."

Jethro studied his back trail thoughtfully, then started on. It was unlikely any of the Harveys would have followed him—not unless they had something to tell him, which wasn't likely. By the time he'd spent two days and nights at the cabin none of them had anything left to talk about.

Brutus Harvey . . . if he ever came upon Zeb again he would ask him about the name. Doubtless he'd heard his father speak it.

The rest of it he wouldn't tell him—nobody liked bad news of his family. He'd never connected Zeke Ralls with Rawlings until Harvey mentioned it. But everybody knew about Zeke . . . and he would be Zeb's uncle.

Zeb had spoken of him, although Zeb had never seen his uncle. He was the youngest of the family, and came west when Zeb's mother and father met, and after he left the Ohio River country they never heard of him again.

Harvey had met him two or three times, and had occasion to recall him.

Jethro rode on, searching for the small stream he remembered. It had flowed through a valley in a northern direction, and he believed it to be a branch of the Yellowstone. A valley he remembered . . . that was where he was heading. He had always told himself he was coming back sometime, and he certainly wouldn't do it if he waited much longer.

Not that he felt old at sixty-six. As far as he could tell by the feel, he hadn't changed any in the last twenty years, and he could hear just as well and see as far. Maybe he didn't seem to need as much sleep . . . but then he had always been a light sleeper.

As he rode he kept his eyes open for the sort of camp he

wanted. He was getting too old to care for a camp without a fire, and the sense of being followed might be an old memory of the place and the Blackfeet. What he wanted was a camp protected on three sides from approach, and in this rocky, heavily timbered country it was not too much to expect. The horse he'd swapped for from Harvey was a mountain mustang, hence better than any watchdog.

He found the place he wanted after the sun had disappeared and when there wasn't much time left in which to look. It was under the overhang of the cliff, in a place which must have once been an old stream-bed, for the cliff was undercut. There was a good patch of grass, and water nearby, and to approach the place anyone must cross an open meadow and come into a notch partly protected by the rock wall. A safe enough place, and the undercut where he would make his bed would be in the darkness just away from the fire.

He put water on for coffee and then sat back away from the fire with his Winchester to hand, chewing on jerky. It was no hardship to go without a hot meal, but his coffee he dearly loved. He fancied jerky—always had. Good for a man's teeth, too. At sixty-six he had lost only two . . . that time at Brown's Hole when he went to the grass with Hugh Glass over something.

Good man, that Glass . . . grizzly nearly killed him. Their difference had been over nothing important. Maybe a squaw, or who had the best horse. Glass had taken two of his teeth out with a boot . . . only it was a moccasin, and that was lucky, or he might have lost a fistful. Glass whopped him, and good, too, but he was young then and had a lot to learn, and he'd never seen a mountain man fight before.

The night passed without event, although about midnight the wind rose and he had to get up and throw wood on the fire.

He did that from the shadows, carefully planning it that way. He'd toss the sticks on and then sit back and watch them burn. He had rigged a little lean-to near the fire and had propped it with sticks so every once in a while a stick would burn through and let another one fall on the fire. Anybody watching wouldn't know for sure, at a distance, whether he was awake or not. When a stick fell, sometimes sparks would flare up, and after a bit the fire would burn brighter, too. It was a trick Jethro invented himself.

At daybreak he was up and taking off down through the forest before it was light. He left his fire burning behind him, but with a trench dug around so it could not spread. Nobody but a fool took chances with a fire in the forest.

He rode about fifteen miles through thick timber and emerged at last in the valley which he had been seeking. It was about seven or eight miles long, half as wide, and surrounded by high mountains, heavily timbered. A stream ran down the center in a northwestern direction, before disappearing down a tremendous canyon.

Within the valley itself the banks of the stream were low, and were skirted here and there with beautiful groves of cottonwood. Jethro crossed the stream and rode toward the point where they had camped those many years ago. At that time there had been a small party of Snake Indians living in the valley. Now as he rode he looked for sign, and found none.

Ten years or so back a lot of this country had been set aside to make a park—Yellowstone, they called it, after the river. Jethro was not sure if this valley was within the limits, but he suspected it was.

He made camp, staked out his mount and the pack horses and then scouted around a little to get the lay of the land. He found it all came back to him as he looked around. The big old pine they had used for a landmark was only half there . . . lightning-struck, some time in the past; and there was a blaze down the side of the mountain caused by a landslide that had happened in the meantime.

It pleased him to see there were beaver working, and he had made his camp with the beaver pond as protection on one side. It was a big pond, all of fifty yards across at this point, and quite a colony of beaver was working there. They were safe enough. He was through with trapping. Why had he come back, after all? Was it only because he remembered this as a place of beauty? He remembered how he and Russell had climbed the slope to look down upon it, taking in the hills around them . . . neither had ever seen anything quite so grand.

Well, he had stopped. Maybe now he would find out who was following him. Lots of thieves and renegades around, Harvey had said, but it was unlikely there would be any this far back in the mountains. And Zeke Ralls was somewhere off to the north. Whoever was out there, he didn't want it to be Zeke.

If they'd followed him, it wasn't because they'd nothing else to do, whoever they were. Chances were they wanted his outfit.

He went to his pack and got out a spare belt gun and cached it where he could put a hand on it without being suspected. Then he settled down to make camp.

He was planning to stay. This place of all others he had remembered. Here he would build a cabin, and he would settle down.

Sunlight danced on the waters of the creek, the grass out there was knee-high, and there were some fine stands of timber. He could cut logs and build a cabin and corrals here, buy some cattle from Harvey and drive them in here. . . . Or sheep. Sheep would be better in this country, and he could store up a sight of wool and pack it all out at once.

The sound of their horses came to him before he saw them, but his own horses had already warned him, for their heads had come up and they were watching closely.

When they rode into view, he saw that there were four of them.

He felt a tightness in his throat. Four was too many to watch. He was in trouble, in real trouble.

They came on, then drew up. "Hello, the fire! Can we come in?"

There was nothing he could do, so he said, "Ride in, if you're peaceful."

Only one of them was young; the others must be not very many years younger than he was himself. Their leader was a long, lanky man with a lean face, handsome in a sort of off-brand way. He wore a tied-down gun on the right side, and a gun in his left holster with the butt forward.

Jethro knew then who he was. He had heard of that fast left-hand draw Zeke Ralls could make . . . when everybody expected him to draw right-handed. It was a small advantage, but in a game that calls for split-second timing, that was enough.

It was more than enough for Jethro Stuart, who had never

been a fast man, anyway—only a dead shot with any kind of gun.

"I'm Zeke Ralls."

"Jethro Stuart."

"You came on in here like you knew where you were going."

"I've been here before, a long time back. I trapped this stream for fur."

The others were getting down. One was a big, wide-shouldered man with red hair—not tall but thick and powerful; and there was a slim older man who chewed tobacco. The young one might have been twenty-five—thin, blond, and with too narrow eyes.

They were looking around, sizing up his equipment. A knowing man, Jethro decided they were on the dodge, needed more horses, food, and probably ammunition. The chances were they dared not approach any nearby town.

"Odd thing"—Jethro spoke his calculated words carefully—"us meeting here."

"You've a lot of grub here," the young one said. "Looks like you came to stay."

"I did."

"What do you mean," Zeke asked, "an odd thing? What's odd about it?"

"We being relatives, and all."

He had their attention now. Most of all, he had Zeke's attention. Jethro had used his trump card quickly, for he had an idea there was little nonsense about them, and that they had planned to kill him quickly and take what he had.

"Relatives?"

"Zebulon Rawlings married my daughter."

"What's that mean?" the red-haired one asked. "I never heard of him."

"Shut up, Red." Zeke was all attention now. "Tell us, Stuart. Who might Zebulon Rawlings be?"

"He's a marshal down Arizona way, former United States cavalry officer. More'n that, he's the son of Linus and Eve Rawlings."

"That coffee hot?" Zeke said. "Maybe we should set up and talk."

"Why waste time, Zeke?" The young one was itching for action. "Let's get it over with."

Zeke looked around irritably. "Damn it, Kid, I want to talk. That's my family he's speaking of. Now saddle down and set up to the fire."

He squatted on his haunches and began to build a smoke. "So Linus and Eve had a family? More'n one?"

"Two . . . the other one's still farming back on the Ohio place. Zeb fought through the war, then came west."

"You know Lilith? What ever happened to her? Somebody said she was a dance-hall girl."

"An actress and singer, which is a whole sight different. She was good, too. Then she married Cleve Van Valen."

"*Who?*" Red almost shouted the word. "Why, that's the dirty—! He put a reward on us."

Jethro leaned back. His right hand was just above the hidden gun. "Well, he's your brother-in-law, Zeke. Or was."

Zeke poured a cup of coffee and Red walked back to his mount and began to unsaddle. The others followed.

Jethro was thinking back. The first time anybody heard of Zeke was when he showed up at Placerville . . . killed a man there in a saloon fight. There had been a second killing that same year at Whiskey Flat. Zeke would be about fifty-two now—close to that—with a dozen known killings behind him. And a thoroughly bad man.

"If you were here a long time back, trapping around, you must have been a mountain man."

"That's where I met Linus."

"Linus!" Zeke spat. "Eve sure cottoned to him, but I never did. He was too damned sure of himself."

The older man brought a grub sack and a frying pan to the fire. Squatting beside the fire, he began to prepare a meal.

As the talk continued, Jethro found himself almost amused. Zeke was obviously eager for news, as eager as the rest were to kill him. Jethro had a fairly good idea that he could take one of them with him, and perhaps two. The question was, which one or two? The Kid was the most anxious to get on with the killing, but which was the more determined?

Jethro knew that many an anxious one lost his ambition when the shooting started or he got a piece of lead into him.

The determined kind, they would soak up punishment and still keep shooting, and that was the man he wanted out of there first.

He found himself puzzling about Zeke. Here was a man from a pioneer family of good stock, and by all accounts the rest of them had done what had to be done in an honest, straightforward way. Zeke alone had been a bad apple.

As far as Jethro could recall, he'd never heard of Zeke Ralls doing an honest day's work in his life. He was not only a killer, but at times a particularly vicious one. A curiously lucky one, too. He had ducked out and left the gang he had worked with along the Overland stage route where he'd been raiding stations, holding up stages, and stealing horses.

He had pulled out just as Jack Slade started the clean-up that resulted in twenty-odd dead thieves, most of them men who had been running with Zeke Ralls.

He had worked out of Virginia City with Henry Plummer, and left the country just as the vigilantes started the hanging spree that resulted in twenty-six dead outlaws.

Jethro Stuart sat up and poked sticks into the fire. "Sure is nice, runnin' into you this way, Zeke," he said blandly. "Not often a man comes up against a relation in this out-of-the-way country. Lilith was living out San Francisco way the last I heard."

"Linus?"

Briefly, Jethro explained about the war and Linus, and related as much as Zeb had told him of how he died, and of Zeb returning to find his mother—that was Eve—dead.

"I'd another brother, too," Zeke said; "just older than me. His name was Sam."

"Name rings a bell. Prescott? Was that it? Sam Prescott? I'd no call to know the names of Zeb's family. He married my daughter after I pulled out. Ran into a man in Miles City told me of it."

The Kid was sitting there looking sour, and the redhead was lying on his back looking up through the leaves. No telling what that redhead was thinking . . . a tough man, too.

The wind stirred the leaves overhead, and the flames fluttered. Zeke stared moodily into the fire, and Jethro held his silence.

One of the horses snorted and Jethro started to get up, but Red was already on his feet. "You set still," he said. "I'll have a look."

After a few minutes he came back. "Mighty skittish. Must be a varmint around, or something."

"Maybe we ought to go look," Jethro said mildly. "Every man ought to see the varmint."

Zeke chuckled, then grinned at him. "You're kin, all right."

As the evening drew on, the men ate, and several times they threw glances toward Zeke which he ignored. The older man paid them no attention, nor did he have anything to say to Jethro. He minded his own affairs. This was an old outlaw, and a wise one, Jethro decided.

"You know this country?" Zeke said suddenly.

"Used to . . . it comes back to me."

"Is there a way out of here into Montana?"

"Sure . . . a knowing man could find a way out to Yellowstone Lake. From there on there's a sort of trail."

"You want to show us the way?"

"Draw you a map," Jethro said. "I'm staying right here."

"Here?"

"Always aimed to come back. This here's about the most beautiful spot I ever did see."

Jethro was listening to the night. The horses were restless. Something was moving around out there, something that frightened them. Lion, maybe. Or a bear . . . that big, old silver-tip Harvey had mentioned was some place back in this country.

The wind off the snow-covered peaks was cold. He added sticks to the fire. The older man had gone off in the shadows and bedded down for the night. He was no fool. Whatever happened, he was going to be out of it . . . more than likely that was how he came to be so old.

Jethro was tired, but he dared not sleep. Zeke nursed a cup of coffee in his hands and said nothing. Red was dozing, and the Kid finally got up and got his blankets. He threw them angrily on the ground and rolled up and appeared to sleep.

"Stay out of Arizona," Jethro suggested suddenly. "Zeb Rawlings is a marshal down there, and you'd not want to mix up with your own nephew."

"What he does is none of my business," Zeke replied. "We might be figuring on Arizona. Besides, let *him* leave *me* alone."

"He won't. He's a good man, Zeke, a very good man."

The Kid sat up suddenly. "Damn it, Zeke! What you wastin' time for? We need that outfit of his and his horses."

"You hush up!" Zeke glared at the Kid. "This man's a relative of mine." His eyes went to Jethro. "We need fresh horses and we need your grub and ammunition. You see how it is."

Something was in the brush behind them, something very big. Jethro could hear the sounds as it nosed about where his supplies had been stacked. If the others noticed, they showed no evidence of it.

"You'll have to go without," Jethro said. "I bought and paid for my outfit and came in here to stay. Riding out for fresh supplies is something I don't care to do at my age."

"That's all right, old man," the Kid said. "You won't be going back. You aren't about to need those supplies, either."

Zeke said nothing at all, but Red sat up slowly. Jethro was sure Red held a pistol under the blanket. In his place, Jethro knew he would.

It was here now, and they all knew it, and there was no dodging the issue. Jethro put more fuel on the fire. "Why buy trouble you don't need? You may get my supplies, but when I go I'll take some of you with me. As it stands you're all in one piece, but if it comes to a showdown, I'll have my say."

"You'll have nothing to say, old man," the Kid said. "You'll just die!"

"We'll go together, Kid," Jethro said, and saw the boy's eyes widen. "You always think of killing, never of being killed. Well, what happens in a showdown like this? You boys kill me, but I'm a cinch to get one of you, maybe two.

"Case like this"—he took a stick near the edge of his blanket and tossed it on the fire—"a man usually picks out who he's going to take with him. I've picked out two . . . even when a man is dyin' he can shoot, and I might get more.

"Years I've spent in the mountains makes a man tough. He soaks up injury. So you boys can figure we're going to have ourselves a ball."

That faint rustle again. The stuff he had taken from his pack horses was stacked against a big boulder, and to get at it that bear had come in close. Chances were he was within fifty feet of them right now, either his back or side toward the fire, and he would be some place in line with that big pine.

Supposing they were distracted? The idea, when it came, seemed a small hope, perhaps a foolish one, but the odds against him were such that nothing could make them worse. He could get two, he was confident of that; to get all four was out of reason—although such things had happened.

"You don't scare me," the Kid said. "You're already dead. How would you expect to even get hold of a gun with the four of us here? Seated the way you are, your gun butt canted back, you'd take too much time."

Jethro picked up a stick at the edge of his blanket. It was just a small stick, such as he had been throwing on the fire all evening.

"I could do it, all right, Kid," Jethro said. He let his eyes swing to Zeke. "You're going to let this happen?"

"You're no blood kin," Zeke said. "Sorry, but we do need that grub and what all."

"You know how it is," Red added.

"Sure," Jethro said, and picked up another stick—only it was not a stick this time, it was the gun from the folds of the blanket. He tossed a stick on the fire with his left hand, then shot the Kid through the ribs with the gun held in his right.

No sudden moves, just a repetition of what he had been doing all evening, and the thrown stick to draw their attention. If they had expected a gun it was from the holster, and when it came it was too late.

He shot the Kid through the ribs, then took a wild gamble and fired into the shadows near his stacked supplies.

A grizzly makes a big target. The distance was close, and to get at the supplies the bear had to be standing in just one spot. It was a snap shot Jethro fired; then he swung the gun back and shot at Red; but almost in that same flashing instant there was a hoarse snarl of rage, and the grizzly lunged from the woods.

Jethro's shot at Red was a clear miss, but Red lunged up from his blankets straight in the path of the grizzly.

Jethro, the only one who knew what was coming—or what he hoped was coming—rolled over and scrambled for the woods. He felt the burn of a bullet, then something else hit him and he fell, but he dragged himself on, farther into the woods. Behind him were shots and screams, and the hoarse, choking snarls of the grizzly.

He crawled on; then, getting hold of a tree trunk, he pulled himself up. He felt curiously weak, but he managed to walk out of the trees to where the horses had been picketed. They were gone. He had a sudden realization that with them had gone his last chance.

No rifle . . . The gun he held had two loads remaining; the other gun was fully loaded and he still had his cartridge belt. In all, approximately fifty rounds.

His brain felt hazy, and he knew he must have been hurt worse than he'd realized. First, he must find a place to hole up, so he stopped close against the bole of a tree where he would be almost invisible, and tried to think back.

Where could he hide?

Some of them would survive . . . or would they? He was sure he had killed the Kid—which he had coming.

Now there was no more shooting behind him, no more snarls. He walked on a little farther, and then remembered a big dead-fall he had seen earlier that day. Going to it, he crawled under it and lay down.

But he knew he couldn't stay there. He must get back, find out what had happened, and get food. And he would need to build a fire somewhere, get warm water, and wash his wound. The bullet burn was one thing, but that second shot—that had really hit him. His back felt wet as he lay there.

He must have passed out, for sometime later he opened his eyes and the sky was faintly gray. It was not yet daybreak, but was working up to it. Lying on his back had evidently helped to stop the flow of blood, but he must move with care.

Was the bullet inside him? He felt cautiously for a bullet hole where it might have come out, and found none. Then he touched a lump pushing hard against the skin . . . a broken rib? He felt again.

It was the bullet . . . he could not feel it properly and could not see it, but he was sure it was the bullet.

Cautiously, he crawled from under the dead-fall and pulled himself erect. His back was stiff, probably as much from caked blood as anything. He knelt and picked up his spare gun; then, leaning against the dead-fall, he reloaded the empty chambers.

His mind was curiously clear, but it seemed to work very slowly—too slowly.

Suddenly, through the trees, he saw his mustang feeding out on the meadow near the stream. There were several horses there together, at least one of them saddled.

He worked his way through the trees until he could get a glimpse of the campsite. Nothing stirred there. He could make out objects, though not colors. The sun would be coming up in a few minutes. He waited, keeping his eyes on the campsite.

Zeke Ralls . . . what had happened to him? It wasn't going to be a bad thing if that grizzly had got him. A grizzly at close range was nothing to trifle with—why that one looked big enough to weigh eight, nine hundred pounds.

Might save Zeb and Julie a peck of trouble, sometime, if that grizzly had gone for Zeke. He was thoroughly bad . . . would even kill kinfolk. Now, that wasn't right, even in a murdering skunk like Zeke Ralls.

Now, that old man . . . the other one. If anybody made it out of this, it would be him. He was off to one side and in the dark.

It grew lighter. Jethro's throat was dry and his head ached. He ought to be resting and treating that wound. The Shoshones, now. They had some sort of herb . . . or was it the Pimas? He couldn't remember.

He moved up to the camp, which was a shambles . . . looked like a hurricane had struck it.

Red was the first one he saw, his face torn half away by one great swipe of a taloned paw. Badly mauled, Red lay as he had fallen . . . must have died within minutes.

The Kid was dead, too. Jethro's bullet had cut right through him—right through the heart by the look of it.

Jethro held himself close to a tree and looked around slowly.

Two more . . . now, where were they? He strained his eyes into the darkness under the trees, but he could see nothing beyond the two bodies which lay where the dim light fell.

He told himself that he should care for his wound, then get on a horse and start back to Harvey's place. Yet even as he thought it, he knew he did not want to go back. He had come here to stay, and stay he would.

Slowly the light filtered through the trees. Birds were singing in the brush along the stream, and somewhere down the valley an elk bugled. There was no sign of the bear.

His packs had been tumbled down, and one had been ripped open. Then he saw his Winchester leaning against a tree and started forward.

He had almost reached it when a voice said, "I thought that would do it."

Jethro still held the spare six-shooter in his right hand. It hung down beside his leg, and there was a chance Zeke had not seen it. For it was Zeke.

"You take a horse," Jethro said, "and ride out of here. You've got no reason to kill me."

"You brought that bear down on us. You done it a-purpose."

Jethro said nothing. There was nothing that could be said, and he felt a curious lack of interest. He strained his eyes into the shadows, trying to locate Zeke Ralls.

"Sure," he said at last, wanting to make Zeke speak again, "I knew he was there. But you were fixing to kill me."

He cleared his throat. "You take a horse and ride out of here," he said once more.

Why didn't Zeke shoot, if he was going to? Jethro waited, but there was no further sound. The sun was showing above the mountaintop now, and the snow along the far ridge was bright, dazzling to the eyes.

He sat down where he was, holding the pistol across his lap. Suddenly, a shot exploded, and instantly, Jethro fired. He fired, and fired again.

Silence. . . .

That shot had had an odd sound.

Jethro got to his feet by clinging to the tree trunk, and holding the gun ready, he walked across the small opening. Zeke was sitting against a fallen log, and he was dead. The shot had been fired into the ground, probably by the final contraction of his fingers.

The grizzly had done its work well. One leg was horribly lacerated and the ground was dark with blood. Zeke's left arm was askew, obviously broken. Jethro's two bullets had both scored, but he had shot into a dead man.

He got a fire going and put on the coffee pot. He took his Winchester and placed it on the ground beside him, and he hung a blanket over his shoulders, for he felt chilled from the long night. He was going to have some coffee to set him up, and then he'd have a look at that wound. He'd get that bullet out of him and treat the wound.

He looked toward the stream. The horses had smelled the fire and were working up the slope toward him. Jethro listened to the water boiling and then he remembered to throw the coffee into the pot.

He put on more fuel. Then taking the coffee from the fire he dropped in a little cold water to settle the grounds. His hand was shaking when he filled the cup. He lifted it with both hands and tasted the coffee. Nothing ever tasted better.

The sun was over the ridge now, but it didn't seem to be warming him up much. He drank more of the coffee, and put the cup down carefully.

He looked up, searching through the mist to find the horses. Mist? . . .

It was then he knew that he was going to die. Somehow the thought did not disturb him. After all, didn't everybody, sooner or later?

He chuckled suddenly. "All the way back here," he said, "only to die."

He tried to fill the cup again, but his hand would not hold the pot and it fell on its side.

"Maybe that was why," he said aloud.

He felt the coldness in him then. He was dying; but was a man ever truly dead who left somebody behind? He was leaving Julie . . . yes, and Zeb Rawlings and their get.

"Julie?" he said loudly. "Julie . . . ?"

And then he was dead.

The old outlaw waited a few minutes longer, and then he came down out of the rocks and walked slowly up to the grove. He glanced around, picked up the coffee pot and started to fill the dead man's cup, then dropped it and hunted around for his own.

He filled his cup and stood there drinking the coffee. Thoughtfully he looked down at Jethro.

"Worth the whole passel of them," he said aloud.

He put down the cup and went around gathering up the guns. Then very carefully he went through the pockets of each of them, touching nothing but the money. He pocketed this and made a bundle of the weapons and ammunition, and then he went down on the flat and caught the saddled horse.

He led the horse back to the edge of the grove and tied the bundle of weapons, all of which represented money, behind the saddle. He rousted through the supplies and made a couple of packs. Then, riding the horse, he went down by the stream and put a loop over a couple of pack horses. Returning, he loaded them up.

There was one other thing to do. With cinch rings from a saddle, heated red-hot, he burned the names into the side of a tree:

```
JETHRO STUART  1883
ZEKE RALLS     1883
RED HART       1883
KID            1883
```

Dropping the cinch rings, he stepped into the saddle. He had found a dim trail over the rocks near where he had been hiding, and he started out.

It was noon when he stopped out on the first ridge, and he looked back. The valley lay quiet under the sun, the stream a strip of silver through the green.

"I ain't a-comin' back," he said.

TWENTY

The station was two rooms. The railroad agent was in one of them with his telegraph key and his tickets. A window opened into the waiting room itself, which had benches along the walls and a pot-bellied stove. The waiting room was twelve by fourteen feet, and much too large for the business.

Several giant cottonwood trees shaded the station and a patch of grass nearby. Their leaves rustled constantly, chafing their pale green surfaces together. Zeb Rawlings was used to the sound and he liked it.

Julie had spread a checkered cloth on the grass and was laying out their lunch. Zeb leaned against the trunk of the nearest cottonwood, half asleep.

The children kept running out and looking up the railroad track in the direction from which the train would come. Eve, who was five, helped her mother. Linus, who was seven, and Prescott, nine years old, played Indians among the trees.

"Have you ever seen the ranch?" Julie asked.

"No," Zeb answered, "but I rode through that country once. Green grass right up to your stirrups, all over that valley. You'll like it, Julie."

"I'd like it if there was no grass at all."

Prescott yelled from the tree he had climbed. "Hey, pa, look!"

Glancing around, they saw Linus hanging by one arm from a limb of the cottonwood, while with his other hand he gripped his throat, his tongue protruding to simulate a hanging man.

"Linus! You get down from there!" Julie ordered.

"He's Billy the Kid and I hung him, pa," Prescott said.

"Billy wasn't hung, Press," Zeb corrected. "Pat Garrett shot him. Two years ago come July."

"That's the only hanging tree left in the Territory," Julie said irritably. "I wish they'd cut it down."

"They might need it," Zeb commented.

"Zeb Rawlings, you know darned well that nobody ever gets lynched any more. Not even horse thieves."

"It's a beautiful tree, Julie, and it gives a lot of shade. And shade can be a mighty scarce item in this country."

"The shade of killing."

The children ran out to look up the track again, and Julie turned to Zeb. "Do you ever wonder about pa? Whatever became of him, I mean?"

"Your pa," Zeb said, "was a man who made mighty few mistakes. Whatever happened to him happened when he was doing the right thing. And whoever left those guns at the post office thought so, too."

"Zeb?"

"What?"

"Do you know anything you haven't told me?"

"Not to speak of. He left a note with those guns." Zeb drew it from his pocket. "I've been meaning to show it to you—not that it says much."

She opened the folded bit of coarse wrapping paper. On it was written: *Died game. Lamar Valley, Wyoming.*

"And nothing else?"

"Porter Clark was up early that morning, and he saw a man riding through town. He knew the man and thought I ought to know he was around."

Zeb Rawlings stared thoughtfully at the dancing heat waves in the distance. "He was an old outlaw . . . one of the wild breed who ran with Dutch Henry down in the Panhandle, fought in the Lincoln County war, the Horrell-Higgins feud, most everything."

"Did you see him? Do you think he was the one who left those guns?"

Zeb shrugged. "Who knows? Might be coincidence."

"Pa!" Prescott shouted from the tracks. "It's comin'! I can hear the train comin'!"

Zeb listened, and heard the far-off whistle. He got to his feet, then helped Julie up.

"Oh, dear, I do hope your aunt likes us, Zeb."

He smiled at her. "Julie, how you talk! Was there ever anybody who didn't like you?"

Zeb took her elbow and together they walked to the platform where a few people were waiting for the incoming train. Zeb responded to little Eve's reaching arms and lifted her up.

The boys came running up the track, and Julie called to them. "Boys! You stand back here with us. Now, do what I tell you or you can't come with us again."

Zeb looked down the platform and then very quietly put Eve down.

"Pa!" she begged.

"No, you stay there, Eve. Your pa has things to do."

Julie glanced at him quickly, but he seemed interested only in the train.

A man was talking to the station agent, another stood nearby. Both men wore belt guns, which was not surprising, since almost half the men present wore them, too.

"Do you know what she looks like, Zeb?" Julie asked.

"What?"

"Your Aunt Lilith—can you recognize her?"

Julie looked at him, and glanced around her. She saw nothing to alarm her, yet she was uneasy.

"Zeb, what's the matter?"

"Here she comes!" Zeb said, and the train pulled into the station, the big driver-wheels churning. It pulled past them, then backed up until the two passenger cars were right at the platform.

From the corner of his eye Zeb could see that the men who had been with the station agent had joined a third man not far away. All glanced his way, then looked toward the train.

The first man he had seen was a known outlaw, so there was at least a possibility the others were too. Neither of the others was familiar to him, but their manner was; and as he followed Prescott and Linus toward the cars he thought of the possibilities brought about by their presence.

Prescott and Linus brought up short at the sight of Lilith. Lilith Van Valen had always been a beautiful woman, and she had not lost that beauty with the years. Moreover, she possessed that certain distinction which comes to one from being someone . . . not in the sense of wealth, but of personality and position. Dressed in her finest, and looking still youthful and graceful, she was an elegant figure, unlike anyone either of the boys had seen before.

"Gosh!" Linus said.

"Ma'am? Ma'am, are you our Great-aunt Lilith?" Prescott asked, still not quite believing it.

"If you're Zeb's children, I am." She put her hands on their shoulders and looked into their eyes with a mock seriousness that immediately won them both. "But don't you dare call me your great-aunt in front of any young men!"

"Lilith!"

She looked at Zeb, and put out her hand. "You'll be Zeb Rawlings. I declare, you favor Linus! I'd have known you anywhere, I think."

She looked at this tall, strongly built man, with warmth and a glint of humor in his eyes. Lilith, in her time, had looked upon many men in the hard world of the frontier and, looking now at Zeb, she felt tears coming to her eyes. How proud Eve would have been to see her son now! And how pleased with her strong sense of family, she would have been to have them all together again.

"Zeb . . . Zeb Rawlings!" She felt the tears coming and fought to hold them back. "Doggone it, Zeb! I swore up and down that I wasn't going to cry!"

"You're even prettier than ma said you were. I'd like you to meet my wife Julie."

"Pleased to meet you," Julie said.

"And I'm pleased to meet you, Julie. I just can't tell you how pleased."

"You met the boys, Prescott . . . Linus. And this is Eve."

Prescott caught her hand. "Come on and meet Sam!"

"Sam?" Lilith was startled.

"He's our horse. He could pull two wagons if he wanted. You haven't come home until you know Sam."

Lilith took their hands. "Sorry," she said to Zeb. "I've got to meet Sam. I want to be sure I'm at home."

"I think this means a lot to her," Zeb said to Julie. "More than I'd have thought."

Then he glanced toward the three men, who had walked out to the cars. All three shook hands with a man who had just stepped from the train. Zeb Rawlings felt the skin tighten around his ears.

Charlie Gant . . .

At the same instant Gant, evidently warned by one of the three men, turned to look at him. Almost at once he started toward them.

A tall man with a swagger and a challenging way, Charlie Gant was a flamboyant figure even on the frontier, where flamboyance was not uncommon. Gant had always favored good clothes, and he wore them now. That he was armed went without question.

"Marshal! Don't tell me you came all the way over here just to meet me? I hardly expected it." He tipped his hat. "And the beautiful Mrs. Rawlings. What a pleasure this is!"

"Let's go, Zeb," Julie said.

"I envy you, Marshal. A well-favored, bright-eyed wife . . . as dazzling as that sun up there."

"Zeb . . ."

Zeb Rawlings smiled. "Why, Charlie! This is a surprise! I had no idea you were still in the Territory. The last time I saw you—well, I got the impression you were leaving the country."

Charlie Gant's smile remained, but his eyes turned ugly. "Having a fine family like this, Rawlings, it must make a man want to live."

Zeb Rawlings' eyes were cold. "You wanted to live, didn't you, Charlie?"

Abruptly, Gant turned and walked away; and Julie, frightened, looked after him. She caught Zeb's arm. "That was Charlie Gant, wasn't it? I thought you said he was in Montana?"

"Now stop your worrying. I'll get the luggage."

When he returned with the hand luggage, Gant and his friends were no longer there. Zeb looked around carefully before he decided they were indeed gone. With a man like Gant, you could never afford to gamble. The one certainty was that he never would—not consciously, at least.

To be a criminal, as Gant was, required certain peculiar attitudes of mind, attitudes that invariably led to failure and capture. One was contempt for people and for law; another was optimism. The criminal was invariably optimistic. He had to believe that everything was going to turn out right for him; and in addition to this he had to be enormously conceited, believing in his ability to outwit the law.

Many a time Zeb had heard a criminal sneer, "I'm smarter than any sheriff. Nobody but a fool would work for the money they get."

What they did not realize was that they were not smarter than a dozen sheriffs, or a hundred. Law was organized now. Descriptions were mailed around from office to office, and there was cooperation between sheriffs and marshals.

The very attributes that led them to become criminals were the attributes that betrayed them. Contempt, optimism, and conceit led to carelessness, and carelessness led to imprisonment or death.

Zeb shouldered the trunk and started back to the buckboard. Right now, he thought, youngsters around the country were playing they were Jesse James and his gang; and men who ought to have known better were telling about the treasure Jesse had buried.

In their sixteen years as outlaws, few of the James gang even made a decent living, and most of that time they were on the dodge, hiding out in caves, barns, and shacks, poorly fed, poorly clothed, suspicious of each other and everyone else.

Folks made a lot of the fact that Jesse had been killed by one of his own men. What most of them didn't know was that he had already murdered two of his own gang and was planning to kill others.

As for how tough they were—that bunch of farmers and businessmen up at Northfield had shot them to doll rags,

killing two of them in the gun battle. The only men the James
gang killed in Northfield were an unarmed man crossing the
street, unaware a holdup was in progress, and the banker,
beaten unconscious inside the bank, whom Jesse shot as he fled
from the building.

Several of the Jesse James outfit had been wounded, and
later, when the Youngers—Cole, Bob, and Jim—were captured Jim had five wounds, Bob two, and Cole Younger had
been shot eleven times. Charlie Pitts was dead.

Zeb turned his back to the buckboard and lowered the trunk
into place, then pushed it deeper along the bed and lashed it in
place with rope. With Julie and Lilith crowded into the seat
beside him, he drove into town and up the crowded street to
the old clapboarded hotel.

Zeb got down and tied the team. "See to the rooms, will
you, Julie?"

He turned and started up the street. Lilith caught Julie's
expression as she gazed after him. "Is anything wrong, Julie?"

"No . . . nothing."

The hotel lobby was high-ceilinged and spacious, with two
elk heads looking down from the walls, and an antelope head
over the mirror. Back of the counter, high on the wall, was a
buffalo head, huge and black.

"Ma?" Prescott caught her arm. "Can Linus and me sleep
outside? Can we, ma? In the buckboard?"

"All right," she said, "but you mustn't go running around.
You go right to sleep."

Zeb Rawlings walked up the street and into the office of the
town marshal. "Got a minute, Lou?"

"Zeb! Of course, I got a minute."

Lou Ramsey put aside a stack of papers and pushed a cigar
box toward Zeb. "Help yourself."

"No, thanks."

Ramsey bit off the tip of his cigar and spat it toward the
spittoon. "What can I do for you, Zeb? Go ahead. Name it."

Zeb pushed his hat back on his head. "Charlie Gant's in
town."

"What?"

"I saw Gant get off the train today. There were three men
waiting for him."

Lou Ramsey's face tightened a little, and he felt irritation mount within him. Why did this have to happen now? Just when he had everything going right and could relax?

"That why you came to me?"

"That's it."

"Zeb, there ain't anything we can do about Charlie Gant. He's a free citizen, and he can come and go as he likes. Furthermore," Ramsey added, "we don't want any trouble here."

Zeb made no reply, and Ramsey went on, "I know what he was, Zeb, but that's over now. It was over the day his brother got himself killed. You should have killed them both, Zeb, but you didn't, and there's nothing anybody can do about it now. All that's past—over and done with."

"Why'd he come here, Lou? Aren't you even curious?"

Ramsey stared morosely out the window. Zeb Rawlings was an old friend, and a good officer. There might be a time when he would have to ask Rawlings for help, which made it worse. His town was only sixty miles north, and Zeb handled it very well, and was known as a man who was never anxious to shoot, which was rare in old-time marshals who had grown into their jobs at a time when it was often safer to shoot first and ask the questions afterward.

Zeb was of the tradition of Bill Tilghman, Jim Gillette, and Jeff Milton—all experts with the gun, but each one prepared to give the other fellow a chance to surrender. They were good men, the best men.

Basically, there had been three types of frontier marshals. There were those like Tilghman, Gillette, Milton, and a few others, who gave a man every chance.

Then there was the type like Hickok, who gave you no second chance. If yours was the reputation as a trouble-maker, or if you came to town loaded for trouble, the first wrong move might get you shot.

And there was another sort, like Mysterious Dave Mather. If you came into their town hunting trouble they didn't wait for you; they went looking for you and shot you where they found you, and wasted no time in the process.

Wherever Zeb Rawlings carried the badge, there was law.

He enforced it quietly, surely, and without favoritism. He had even lost a few jobs because he would throw a trouble-making rancher with thousands of head of cattle into jail just as quickly as he would jail a thirty-dollar-per-month cowhand.

But this Gant affair . . . it had the look of a personal feud. Lou Ramsey did not know if that was the case, but he was afraid of it. When a man got to enforcing the law, he could not allow personalities to enter into it.

"What do you want me to do?" Ramsey said. "Run him out of town? You know I can't do that. We don't carry the law in a holster, Zeb. Not any more. Besides, what would I have to back it up? That he keeps bad company? There's no wanted posters out on him, not from anywhere."

"Charlie was always smart enough for that," Zeb replied. "He never let himself get in a bind. Charlie did the planning. It was Floyd who carried it out, Floyd who ramrodded the action."

"And Floyd's dead."

Ramsey chewed on his cigar. "Times have changed, Zeb. These aren't the old gun-fighting days." He tilted back in his chair. "The James-Younger gang was the last of them."

Zeb glanced sardonically at Ramsey. "You aren't keeping posted, Lou. Charlie Gant's still around."

"You get me a warrant, and I'll get you Charlie Gant."

The door opened and Stover, the deputy, stepped in. "Lou, they want three guards on the wagon with the gold shipment tomorrow."

"Three?"

"It's a heavy load. Over a hundred thousand dollars' worth. I'd better take Clay and Sims with me."

When Stover had gone out, Lou looked at Zeb, who was staring at the ceiling, grinning.

"What's the matter with you?" Ramsey growled. "We ship gold out of here all the time. Some of the shipments are big. So we've put on three men to guard it."

"What happens after it gets on the train?"

Lou Ramsey got to his feet. "Zeb, you've no call to make something out of this. Sure, Charlie Gant's in town . . . just about every outlaw in the country has been through here at one time or another, and we've never lost a gold shipment yet."

Rawlings got up and went to the door, but as he pushed the door open, Ramsey spoke. "Zeb?"

Rawlings turned to look back. "I don't want any trouble here," Ramsey said. "We've been friends a long time, and as a friend I'd like you to leave town."

Zeb Rawlings offered no reply, but stepped out and closed the door quietly behind him. Outside he paused on the street, thinking it through. He had Aunt Lilith to consider now as well as his own family, but to go off to the ranch with this thing hanging fire . . . he wouldn't be able to sleep nights knowing Gant was in the country. And he knew the man too well to believe he had forgotten.

Charlie Gant would never feel safe until the man who had killed his brother was dead . . . and much more important to Charlie, the man who knew that Charlie had run out on his brother when the going got rough, that he had ducked out of the fight and saved his own skin. If that ever got around, Charlie Gant would find no outlaw, let alone an honest man, who would ride with him.

Deeply concerned, Zeb Rawlings went back to the hotel, replying to an occasional greeting, but with his mind far away. He missed nothing along the street, however, but that was long practice. When a man had been a marshal for a few years he saw everything without really seeming to pay attention.

He had planned to stay inside, talking to Lilith about old times—after all, he had heard little of the family in a good many years—but the boys wanted to go up to the mine, and they had never seen a mine. Concealing his irritation, for he understood the interest the boys had, he agreed to go up to the collar of the shaft with them.

He knew he should stay inside, for one thing he had learned long since was to keep out of trouble by staying away from where it was . . . and somewhere in town would be Gant and his friends. Yet, if he was correct in his belief that they planned a train robbery, then the last thing they would want would be trouble now, in this place.

The town had one street that could be called a street. It was half a mile long, and for almost a quarter of a mile on either side it was built solid. After that it sort of tapered off, with scattered buildings and open spaces between them.

Poston Street, named for an Arizona pioneer, cut off near the end of the solidly built part and went up the slope to the mine buildings and the collar of the shaft. It ended at the mine. On one side were the mine offices, behind them the assay office, and beyond that the hoisting-engine room, which faced the collar of the shaft. There were other buildings too—a warehouse, a blacksmith shop, and a long shed for storing timber to be used in the mine.

The cage which carried the miners down into the mine was topped by a large metal bucket, or hopper, that would hold five tons of ore. As this came to the top, the bucket was tripped and the ore spilled into a huge bin from which it ran into the ore wagons below. A wagon was driven up beneath a chute, the door was lifted, and the rock ran into the wagon until it was filled. Then the metal door was dropped in place, cutting off the flow.

The hoisting-engine chugged away, shooting up a white cloud of steam. Lanterns hung about, and these had already been lighted although the evening was young.

Linus ran toward the edge of the shaft to look down, and Zeb called him back. "You stay close to me," he said sternly. "That shaft's a thousand feet deep. If you had two hundred brothers down there, each one standing on another's shoulders, they wouldn't reach the top."

"You ever work in a mine, pa?"

"Some . . . not any so good as this one, by all accounts. I worked in low-grade gold . . . a good bit of it was there, but I never saw any of it. All we miners ever saw was broken rock."

"Is this always the way they get the ore out?"

"No, for some kinds of ore they use a conveyor system, a lot of little buckets on an endless chain. But in a mine this deep that isn't practical. It's mostly used in coal mines. Men push ore cars to the edge of the shaft and dump them in a pocket, a big hole covered by steel rails, they call a 'grizzly.' The man who operates the cage fills that bucket you see on top of the cage at those pockets and hoists it on top."

As he spoke he was watching a man who came out of the assay office. It had become dark as they walked about, and he could not quite distinguish the man's face, but when he stepped into the light of a lantern, Zeb saw it was Charlie Gant. Gant saw him at the same instant, and after a moment's hesitation, he started over.

"Boys," Zeb suggested to the children, "you go in the hoisting-engine room and look at the steam engine. I'll be along in a minute."

Gant walked up to him. "Evenin', Rawlings. Marshal tells me you had a word with him. Now, would you call that friendly?"

"I never thought of us as friendly."

"I ain't lookin' for trouble," Gant said, "but if you'd like to put it on the old basis, just you an' me, that's fine."

"I've no reason to fight you, Gant, as long as you obey the law and stay out of the way. Floyd and I had differences that were strictly a matter of law. They're settled. As far as that's concerned, I've finished."

"You went to the marshal."

"Of course." Zeb tapped the badge on his chest. "I still wear it, and when you come around I'm suspicious. Other than that, I've nothing to do with it. This is Lou Ramsey's problem. I'm not asking for trouble."

"So it's peace you want, Marshal?" His tone changed. "There'll be only one peace for you, Rawlings, the kind my brother got."

"What happened to him didn't teach you much, did it?"

"Easy, Marshal." Anger burned in Gant's eyes. "I wouldn't push my luck."

"Floyd made mighty few mistakes . . . except the time he depended on you. And you were the one who got away."

Gant held himself still. Zeb Rawlings could see the anger that flared in him, but Gant controlled himself, although not without effort. For several minutes he was silent, watching the ore bucket come up, dump, and go back down the shaft again.

"I don't like you, Marshal," he said finally. "I don't like what you and your kind have done to this country, and are doin' to

it. Used to be a man felt free around here, now a man can
hardly breathe."

"I haven't noticed any honest men having trouble."

"One of these days, Rawlings, I'll pay you Rawlingses a visit.
I'll pay you a visit you'll never forget."

Turning on his heel, he strode away, and after a minute, Zeb
called to the boys, who had waited not far off. It was not until
he called them that he noticed each boy held a large chunk of
rock. Surreptitiously, they dropped them. He smiled, but made
no comment.

"What did he mean, pa?"

"Nothin' much, boys. But you know how womenfolks worry
about such things. I want you to make me a promise—a real
promise—not to say a word to ma about this. Will you, Prescott?"

"I promise."

"Linus?"

"Sure, I promise, and I bet I keep it better than Prescott!"

"Good! Now let's go back down the mountain."

They walked together down the hill, and Zeb moved along
easily, but with all his old alertness. Charlie Gant had something more important than revenge on his mind just now, but
one could never tell . . . there were times when emotion
defeated reason, and Charlie Gant was a man who knew how to
hate.

Zeb strolled along with the boys, liking the coolness of the
evening air after the heat of the day. That was one thing you
could say for the desert. It was like a man with a quick temper:
it cooled off fast once the sun went down.

The windows were lighted, and men stood along the walk,
talking and smoking. Down at the far end of the street a few
children played tag, and horses at the hitch-rail stood three-
legged . . . waiting. Inside the saloons there was a rattle of
chips, and the sounds of men at cards.

Zeb paused outside the hotel and let the boys go up by
themselves. It was a good life, he thought, and this was a part
he had always enjoyed, this business of coming out and taking
stock of a town. Yet how quickly one learned to sense trouble.
It was an instinct one acquired. Only he was not the marshal
here—that was Lou Ramsey's job.

He thought back again to the rifle and pistol left by the strange rider, and the message. If that old outlaw had left it, it was a curious mark of respect, something that went beyond the law or lawlessness.

Of course, it had been that way in the old days, and still was, in a way. The men on both sides of the law had known each other, often respected each other. Sometimes a sheriff was himself a reformed outlaw, but that made no difference. What was mutually respected was courage, fair play, ingenuity, and ability.

How many times he had sat in a ranch house and heard a rancher tell admiringly of the slick way he had been outfoxed by cow-thieves. And there were many stories about how clever Indians became at stealing horses, which was their favorite sport.

Like the time the soldier was sent out to graze the regimental race horse. He had the horse on a picket rope, but he did not even take a chance of picketing it. To be sure the horse was safe, he held one end of the rope.

It was a bright, sunny day, and the grass was good and green. The horse cropped grass and the soldier watched, and then all of a sudden he realized he was holding a rope's end and nothing more. The horse had been stolen right before his eyes.

Had he blinked? Closed his eyes for a moment, looked away without realizing? Anyway, the horse was gone, and they never saw it again.

A cowhand passed behind him. "Evenin'," he said, and Zeb answered. A tin-panny piano started down the street, and in the restaurant a dish was dropped and broke. Zeb Rawlings stood there, at peace with the night.

Old Jethro was dead, then . . . Lamar Valley. They'd have to go up that way sometime. Julie said her pa had often talked of going back up there. There was some little valley off the headwaters of the Yellowstone that he wanted to see again. And likely that was it.

Prescott came to the door. "Pa? Ma says they're going to eat supper. You want to come in?"

"Sure, son."

They were already at table, but it took him a moment to realize that the beautiful young woman with Lilith was truly his wife. She had done something to her hair, and he had never seen it more lovely. Also, she was wearing a dress he had never seen before—one of Lilith's, no doubt.

He felt a little pang, realizing he had never been able to afford such a dress for her. And likely never would. Folks expected a lot of their law officers, but they never liked to pay them for it.

He walked up to the table, keeping his eyes from Julie. "Aunt Lil, how soon will Julie be coming down? I sure want to—"

"Zeb!" Julie interrupted.

"What!" he exclaimed in mock astonishment. "Why, Julie! I'd never have known you! And I never saw you look more beautiful."

She knew he was faking his amazement, but she was pleased. "Do you really like it?"

"Of course—and thanks, Lilith. I detect your San Francisco hand in this."

"It does a woman good to change her looks once in a while—the way she does her hair . . . something . . ."

"If this is a sample, I'll accept your judgment," he said. He glanced at Lilith approvingly. "You don't need any changes, Lilith."

She looked at him thoughtfully. This nephew of hers had a quality she liked. "You're going to have a free hand with the ranch, Zeb, but we aren't going to have much capital. I came away from San Francisco with very little."

"I've never had much capital," he said quietly. "We'll get along."

"What I was thinking," Lilith said, "was that it may be necessary for you to devote all your time to the ranch."

He chuckled. "Ah! Now I see. You and Julie have had your heads together: How can we get him to stop this marshaling business and settle down?"

Zeb looked at them seriously. "I'll be glad to settle down whenever I can. Men serve as they can. I do not have the education to help make the laws—one thing I can do, is enforce them.

"Julie doesn't like me to wear a gun. I'll take it off when I can—until then it will be necessary for the men of peace to have guns, as long as men of violence do. We can't put all the force in the hands of evil."

He smiled at Julie. "You'll be glad to know—Charlie Gant is leaving town."

TWENTY-ONE

Z eb Rawlings rolled out of bed at daybreak, as had been his custom for years. The hotel room in which they had spent the night was furnished with one chair, a stand for the bowl and water pitcher, with a small mirror above it, and the bed itself—that was all.

Always a quiet man, he dressed with special care this morning, not wishing to wake Julie. In his sock feet he stepped over to the window and looked out.

At this hour the street was relatively empty, for the sun had not yet come over the mountains. But down there on the boardwalk a man was loafing, smoking a cigarette. On the ground near his feet were the butts of several cigarettes—he must have been there some time.

Lifting his eyes, Zeb looked toward the mine. There a wagon was drawn up, and men were loading it. A guard with a shotgun sat on the wagon seat, and two mounted guards were nearby.

The man in the street turned his head slightly and Zeb saw that he was one of those who had been at the station to meet Charlie Gant. It was falling into place, each neat, carefully planned piece of it. So neat, and yet so obvious.

Zeb went over to the chair, sat down, and tugged on his

boots. Taking up his hat, coat, and gun belt, he went to the door, opened it carefully, and stepped out into the hall. In the bathroom at the end of the hall he buckled on the gun belt, bathed his hands and face, and then slipped into his coat.

All these actions required time, but it was time that Zeb needed. He would first see how the boys had gotten along in their wagon, but his mind was not on them, but on Charlie Gant and the gold.

From long experience, he could almost chart the steps to be taken, just as he had been sure there would be a lookout in the street to be sure the gold shipment did pull away from the mine and was loaded on the train. The telegraph was valuable to the law; it was also a great help to outlaws.

The lobby was empty when he walked through, and when he stepped out on the boardwalk, the watcher was gone. Up the street, and some distance away, Zeb saw the gold wagon driving toward the station, which lay just outside of town. By the time it reached the station, or within a minute or two afterward, the lookout would be at the station too, or within sight of it.

Down the street in front of the Bon-Ton Restaurant a man in an apron was sweeping the boardwalk. Sunlight fell between the buildings, and at the end of the walk his broom moved in and out of the sunlight.

Linus and Prescott were just waking up and Zeb sat with them and smoked a cigar while they washed at the livery-stable pump.

Off in the distance a train whistled . . . the east-bound train which passed through only a short time before the west-bound train which would pick up the gold. Whatever was to be done about Charlie Gant had to be done now. Sitting there on the bench by the livery stable, he made up his mind about that. Not that he hadn't reached the same conclusion hours ago, but he had to study the situation for a possible alternative.

If he was let alone, Charlie would do what he had come to do, and then he would be free to locate Zeb Rawlings, and never so long as Gant lived would Zeb or any of his family live in security. There would be times when he would have to be away from the ranch, and most of the time he would be out on the range . . . his family would be alone, virtually helpless if Gant chose to strike at him through his family, and Gant was such a man.

When Zeb walked into the hotel dining room with the boys, Lou Ramsey was there, seated at the table with Aunt Lilith and Julie. He got up, his face stern.

"I had a visit from Charlie Gant last night," Ramsey said. "I don't like it, Zeb."

"Well?"

"He said he saw you. That you were looking for trouble."

"You believe that?"

Lou Ramsey looked at him angrily. "Zeb, it doesn't matter whether I believe it. You're taking your trouble to your own territory. You're not going to make trouble for me here. I won't have it, Zeb."

"There won't be any more. Gant's gone. He rode out before daylight this morning."

Ramsey hesitated, startled and displeased by the information, even though half expecting it. "Alone?"

"You know better than that. He took his outfit with him, and you know as well as I do they'll be somewhere between here and Kingman, waiting for that train."

Zeb paused, then went ahead. "Lou, if I could have three deputies . . . or even two. To get on that train with me."

"You don't fool me a bit, Rawlings. It ain't a robbery you're expecting. I know how you feel about Gant. Texas the first time—you still carry the lead where he shot you. Then it was Oklahoma, when you killed Floyd. And now . . . here."

Ramsey looked around at Julie and Lilith. "I'm sorry," he said. "You'll have to forgive me. If you can't stop him, I must, but he isn't going to make my office a part of it."

"You haven't eaten, Zeb," Julie protested. "Why don't you sit down?"

Lou Ramsey strode from the room, and Zeb seated himself. He glanced across the table at Lilith. "I'm sorry, Aunt Lil. I'm sorry all this has to happen just when you arrive."

The waitress brought coffee to the table, and then Zeb's breakfast. Slowly, the tension went out of him. He genuinely liked Ramsey, and did not want trouble with him, especially as he so clearly understood the marshal's position. He blamed Ramsey not at all for his stand; only for Zeb it was an impossible stand at the moment.

"Who is Charlie Gant?" Lilith asked.

Zeb looked at her in surprise, not that she should ask, but that he himself had never given it a thought. It might be, he told himself, extremely important to know just who Gant was.

After all, who *is* any man? Charlie Gant was a gambler. He was also an outlaw. Moreover, he was a brother to Floyd Gant, who had not only been an outlaw but a gunman.

Odd, when you came to think of it, how few gunfighters were actually outlaws. Some of them became outlaws later, often because of changes in public attitude or in the attitude of the law.

A gunfighter, or gunman, was actually no more than a man who, because of some unusual gift of dexterity, coordination, and nerve, became better with a gun than others. He was no particular type of person, other than possessing more than usual ability to face a gun in another man's hand and shoot back; nor was he of any particular profession. Most gunfighters had been officers of the law, but that was a result of their skill, rather than otherwise.

Hickok had been a stagedriver and scout for the army. Wyatt Earp, Bat Masterson, Billy Brooks, and many others had been buffalo hunters; Clay Allison, Pink Higgins, and John Slaughter had been ranchers, Ben Thompson a gambler, Doc Halliday a dentist, Temple Houston a lawyer. Billy the Kid had been a drifting cowhand and gambler, then a feudist in the Lincoln County war, and actually only an outlaw after that war ended.

Chris Madsen had been a soldier in several armies, among them the French Foreign Legion; Buckey O'Neill was a newspaper editor, probate judge, and superintendent of schools, as well as a frontier sheriff; many gunfighters had been ex-soldiers.

And who was Charlie Gant?

"Takes me back a long time when you ask that, Aunt Lil," Zeb commented, "and Lou Ramsey knows it. That's why he's edgy about this situation."

"We knew Floyd first," Julie said. "Zeb met him in the Panhandle when they were buffalo hunting."

"Not that we were ever friends," Zeb said, "but we got along all right. It was sort of nip-and-tuck between us with pistols, but with a rifle I could outshoot him.

"We had a little bet on who would get the most buffalo, and I won. Nothing was said about it at the time, but it didn't set well with Charlie. Floyd took it all right, but Charlie lost a good deal of money."

Zeb Rawlings sat back and watched his coffee cup refilled. Talking about old times brought them back, and glancing at Julie, he saw a reminiscent glow in her eyes, too.

They had been good days after he returned from the Panhandle to Kansas City, where Julie was waiting for him. He had made good money on the hunt, and they lived well. They had gone to New Orleans, and from there they took a boat to Galveston. He had bought cattle, and together they went on the drive to Kansas, where he sold at a good profit. He began to look as if he was on his way to becoming a success.

His second cattle venture was pure failure. It began with a stampede in the Nation when they lost half their cattle, and ended with a pitched battle with Kiowas in which the cattle were driven off and three men and Zeb had fought off Kiowas for three days, without water. One man died, and Zeb and another brought the third man in, half dead, across their one horse.

There had been no good news for Julie on that trip. She was in Dodge to meet him, and the little money they had was barely enough to tide them over and get them back to Texas. Zeb Rawlings went to Austin and joined the Texas Rangers. He had stayed with them two years.

He had been marshal in a small cow town in West Texas when Charlie Gant showed up again. Before Zeb took the job they told him about Gant's place . . . there had been several killings in the place, and at least two big winners at the tables had been murdered after leaving it.

Zeb Rawlings moved in, watched, listened, and conducted a careful investigation. Then a man was stabbed and left for dead out back of the saloon. He lived long enough to let Zeb know it had happened in the saloon, and at Gant's order—or at least, with his knowledge.

There wasn't evidence enough for a trial, and no court in less than a hundred miles, so Zeb walked into the saloon and up to the bar. Charlie himself came to wait upon him.

"No," Zeb said, refusing the drink. "I'm closing you up, Charlie."

Gant had merely stared at him. After a bit he said, "Don't be a fool. You can't close me up."

"As of twelve o'clock noon"—it was at that time a little after ten in the morning—"you're closed. There is a stage at two o'clock. You're to be on it."

Gant laughed, but without much humor. "You're playing the fool, Rawlings. I won't close, and you can't close me."

"If I could prove some of the murders you've committed, or had committed," Zeb replied quietly, "you would leave this town only in irons and under guard. As it is, I am giving you a chance."

Zeb Rawlings would never forget that morning. He had walked out of the saloon into the bright glare of the sun, and had no idea of how he would or could force Gant to close.

At a few minutes after eleven two of Gant's men rode into town. One of them went to the livery stable and took up his post outside. The other, after a talk with Gant, walked across the street from the marshal's office and, seating himself on the edge of the walk, rolled and lit a cigarette.

At a quarter to twelve the town's banker and several other citizens appeared at the marshal's office with shotguns and Winchesters. "We're ready if you are, Rawlings. If they want action, they can have it."

"Thanks," Zeb said, "but you just sit tight here in the office. Let me handle this."

They were disappointed, as he knew they would be, for as in most western towns the butcher, the baker, and the candlestick-maker were ex-cowhands, Indian fighters, or Civil War veterans, always aching to get back in the saddle again.

Rawlings circled out of the back door, ducked between two buildings, and got into the side door of an empty store building. From there he went to the roof.

The building had been among the first to go up when the town was built and when Comanche raids were frequent. The roof had a three-foot parapet all the way around it, with loopholes every few feet. Several of those loopholes overlooked the front of the saloon, and Rawlings had long since observed that the entire first and second floors were covered from them.

Zeb Rawlings had taken along a piece of stovepipe with one end pushed together to make a mouthpiece. Using it as a megaphone, he called out, "All right, Gant! *Five minutes!*"

The man stationed opposite the marshal's office dropped his cigarette and looked around quickly. Nervous because of the unexpected force that had gathered with shotguns and rifles, he was now really alarmed. Yet look where he might, he could see nothing. Within the saloon, Gant and two bartenders and three dealers were all armed and waiting, prepared for trouble.

The five minutes dragged.

It ended with the sudden boom of a Spencer .56 buffalo gun. Zeb had discarded his Winchester for the moment because of the psychological effect of that cannon boom from the .56.

His first shot he put into the awning post against which the watching gunman was leaning. The heavy slug struck with tremendous force, shattering the post and showering the gunman with splinters.

Instantly, Rawlings turned and, shooting through another hole, smashed the lantern above the other watcher, showering him with glass and coal oil. Both men dove for shelter, and Rawlings speeded one on his way with another boom from the Spencer, the slug smashing the wall just a jump ahead of him.

Turning his gun on the saloon, where the waiting men had yet to locate him, Rawlings began a searching fire. His first shot smashed the roulette wheel which Gant had imported at great cost; a second ripped into the bar where someone might be hiding; and a third smashed the great mirror behind the bar. The last shot clipped the window sill to the right of the door.

With seven more shells laid out, he reloaded quickly. Coolly and methodically he proceeded to rip the saloon from one end to the other with heavy .56 caliber slugs. He smashed bottles on the back bar, shot into every possible place of concealment.

When he had finished, he reloaded again, and again riddled the saloon from floor to ceiling, from wall to wall.

A shot answered him from the second floor, but he was not worried. He was moving from loophole to loophole and the adobe walls around him would turn anything but a cannon shell.

On the other hand, the flimsy walls of the rooms over the saloon would not stop any kind of a slug. A .44 or .45 would penetrate seven to nine inches of pine, and his .56 would do much better. At this range of less than sixty feet, one of those slugs would go through everything, the full length of the building unless it brought up against a timber.

Choosing all the likely spots where a man might take shelter and still see to fire back, Rawlings proceeded to search the place with rifle-fire. He had no desire to shoot anyone, but simply to demonstrate that he meant what he said.

And nobody was killed; but four of the men inside the saloon suffered minor wounds, and all were ready to leave town. Gant went, vowing to return.

Two months later, with two hired gunmen, he did return, and they timed it right to catch Zeb Rawlings emerging from the IXL Restaurant. They caught him in the door, and the first bullet turned him around, flattening him against the wall. It was that bullet that saved his life, for it was followed by the blast of a double-barreled shotgun that tore a hole in the door as large as a man's head. Though Rawlings was hit, he was not out of action. He opened fire from the doorway, then managed to get out on the street.

His first shot killed a horse, his second burned one of the hired gunmen. In the shooting that followed, both the gunmen were killed, and a bullet struck Gant in the belly, only to be deflected by a rectangular brass buckle on his belt. The buckle was large and heavy, and it saved his life.

A second bullet ripped along his ribs within inches of his heart, and Gant, thoroughly frightened, fled town. It was weeks before the bruise behind that buckle disappeared, but the scar on Charlie Gant's consciousness lasted much longer.

The following year, after Rawlings had recovered from the four wounds he had incurred in the gun battle, he was appointed a deputy United States marshal, operating in the Indian Territory.

It had been a good job. The Territory was filled with outlaws, a few of them protected by renegade Indians, but most of them objected to and disliked by the Indians. The Indians of the eastern Territory were mostly of the Five Civilized Tribes—the Cherokees, Choctaws, Chickasaws, Creeks, and Seminoles. Most of them lived like white men. A good many had education, a good many were veterans of the war, and others had ancestors who had fought with or against Jackson.

Zeb Rawlings liked them, and he liked the Osages. He enjoyed his job. A good tracker, and accustomed to long hours in the saddle, he earned the respect even of the outlaws he pursued and brought to justice.

It was one of these who gave him the warning.

Del Meggeson was a horse-thief, and a good one. He had, in the course of an eventful life, held up a few stages, rustled a few cows, fought Indians, and worked as a teamster on a freight line. He was wanted for a shooting on Cabin Creek, and Zeb Rawlings went in and got him.

Del saw the glint of light on the star, and he went for his gun. Zeb Rawlings held his fire. "*No!*" He spoke sharply, the command ringing in the hollow by the river. "Del, *I've got the drop!*"

Del Meggeson, no man's fool, froze his hand where it was. He was fair game, and knew it. He relaxed slowly. "I can't see you," he said conversationally, "and I never heard your voice before, but only one man in this part of the country would give me a break like that. You have to be Zeb Rawlings."

"Unbuckle your gun belt, Del, and let it fall."

With extreme care, Meggeson did as advised. He knew he had had the break of a lifetime.

"Come up to the fire," he said. "Coffee's on, and if you've been trailin' me, you've had a long ride."

Zeb holstered his gun, and Del saw the gesture and smiled. He liked a nervy man, and he also liked one who gave him the benefit of the doubt.

Zeb collected the guns and put them beside him. "All I've got to do is frisk you, but I'll take your word. Are you packing another gun?"

Del hesitated, then he chuckled. "You do make it hard on a man, Marshal." With his thumb and forefinger he drew a derringer from behind his belt and tossed it across the fire.

They had sat over the fire for hours, yarning about the West, exchanging stories of the country. It was over coffee the following morning that Del offered his warning.

"Zeb," he said suddenly, "I'm going to give you a little tip. Charlie Gant's in the Territory, and he's priming Floyd for you."

The story came out on the long ride east into Arkansas. The Gant brothers, after working with various bands of outlaws, had finally made a tie-up with Cad Pickett and his outfit. Charlie was the brains of the outfit, along with Cad and Floyd, but the latter had built himself a name in Texas and in the Nation. Floyd was on several wanted posters and was reputed to have killed eleven men, seven of whom could be identified.

"Floyd's fast, Zeb. He's almighty fast, and Charlie, he's been building Floyd up for a killing. Charlie will never be happy until you're dead."

"Thanks."

The showdown came sooner than he expected.

When Zeb Rawlings rode up to the store at Boggy Depot that fine sunny morning, he was not thinking of the Gants. His mission was a simple one—to find and arrest a bad Indian named Sanders who was wanted for murder.

Zeb had stopped at Fort Washita and there he was advised that he would find his man at Boggy Depot. An unknown half-breed volunteered the information.

The store was a long, low building with a shake roof, and an awning that provided shade from the sun. One man, apparently asleep, dozed in a chair near the door. There were no horses tied at the hitch rail.

Pushing open the door, Zeb stepped inside, and the instant he walked in he knew he was in trouble. The storekeeper, a stranger to him, stood behind the counter, his face white and strained.

Zeb's eyes, turning to the left, saw Floyd Gant standing at the small bar in the corner. One elbow rested on the bar, but the right hand, only inches above the gun butt, held a glass of whiskey. Another man whom Zeb immediately identified as Cad Pickett from pictures he had seen on reward posters, was at the bar with Floyd.

From the far end of the room, near the side door, Charlie Gant spoke out. "We've been waiting for you, Rawlings, and we've waited long enough."

Zeb did not stop, but walked on over to the bar, ignoring Charlie. "Hello, Floyd," he said, "I hear you've been busy lately."

Floyd Gant was not a tall man, but he was broad and powerful. His chest was deep, and his shoulders were wide and thick. The column of his muscular neck supported a square, blocky head covered with thick black curls.

"You huntin' me?" Floyd asked.

"No. As a matter of fact, I was tipped there was an Indian named Sanders around here. Know him?"

"Tipped?" Floyd's eyes searched his.

"Breed over at Fort Washita told me. Sanders is wanted for murder."

"And you don't want us?"

"I take the jobs given me," Zeb replied, "and nobody has given me a warrant on you boys."

Zeb had stopped in such a position that Charlie dared not shoot into him from behind for fear of hitting Floyd; and if Cad attempted to draw he must risk a point-blank mix-up in which anybody, and probably everybody, would get hurt. It was not a situation any of them relished, but Floyd alone appreciated Zeb's strategy.

He grinned, showing a set of beautiful strong white teeth. "You were always a smart one, Zeb," he said. "Never miss a trick, do you?"

"Uh-huh . . . I missed one this time. That tip was too pat. I should have known somebody had baited a trap."

Floyd's eyes seemed to shadow. "Now, I wouldn't say that,

Zeb. Almost anybody might miss a trick like that." He paused. "Even me," he said. "I might not guess a thing like that."

Suddenly, Zeb Rawlings realized that what Floyd said was true. He had not known. Charlie Gant had set this up on his own initiative.

Had Cad known? Zeb decided that he had, and that he was nervous now, worried about Floyd's reaction.

The only man here who knew exactly what he wanted was Charlie Gant; and Charlie, unless he moved, was out of the play. Cad would hesitate to act until Floyd did; and Floyd might not act at all, although he was the dangerous one.

"Sounds like a mistake all the way around," Zeb commented, "a mistake that could buy a lot of grief for all concerned. I think it would be a good idea to forget it, right here and now."

Charlie Gant laughed. "When we've got you boxed? Now isn't that a pretty foolish notion?"

"Right now," Zeb said, "nobody is pushing you boys. Nobody has been ordered to pick up any one of you. If anything happens here today every deputy marshal in the Territory will have one purpose—to bring you boys in for a hanging."

"So?" Charlie said. "We've been chased before."

"By Federal marshals? Who don't have to stop at state lines?"

There was no sense in talking to Charlie. Floyd was the key to this situation, and what Floyd decided to do would be done. Zeb's move was to walk right up to Floyd and face him, and throw their planning out the window. They had a bear by the tail, and Zeb could not let go. If anybody let go, it had to be them.

"I'd say, Floyd, that we're into something here that can get somebody hurt, and without anybody gaining anything from it—except Charlie, who wants me killed. I'd take it as a favor if you boys would just walk out of here and ride off."

Charlie laughed again.

Floyd was considering it—Zeb knew he was. Floyd tossed off his drink and put the glass down on the bar.

"I think that's a good idea, Zeb," he said coolly. "I think it's a very good idea."

Charlie's chair slammed back. "Floyd!" he yelled. "Are you *crazy?* We've got him! We've got him dead to rights!"

"Who wants him?" Floyd asked. "Charlie, the next time you—"

Zeb Rawlings was tight with expectation. He dared not turn his head from watching Cad and Floyd to see what Charlie was up to; but at that instant, at some signal from Charlie, Cad Pickett took a step back and Charlie yelled, "*Cad!* You declared yourself in!" And Cad Pickett drew.

Floyd started to yell, but Zeb Rawlings acted. He grabbed Floyd's arm and spun him from the bar, sending him toppling into Cad, whose gun went off harmlessly into the ceiling.

Charlie's gun exploded and a bullet fanned Zeb's ear, and then he saw Floyd was coming up with a gun. Cad Pickett jerked free, bringing his gun down, and Zeb shot, smashing a bullet into the outlaw who was immediately behind Floyd, and Floyd fired, plunging to his feet as he did so.

Zeb shot, then turned his gun and threw a quick shot at Charlie, who jumped back. Everything happened in a matter of split seconds, but Zeb would never forget the look on Charlie as that gun flared in his face.

Zeb felt the blow of a bullet, and then Floyd was on his feet and firing at him. They were scarcely ten feet apart when Zeb fired and the two heavy .44 slugs knocked Floyd back. Zeb had put two bullets right through his heart at point-blank range. He put a third shot into Floyd's skull, and then dropped the muzzle of his gun on Cad.

Pickett screamed, "No! *No!*" and Zeb wheeled to fire again at Charlie.

But Charlie Gant was gone—the side door stood open.

It ended like that. He had taken Pickett in, wounded, but glad to be alive.

Floyd was dead and, outlaw though the man was, Zeb Rawlings regretted the killing, knowing that Charlie had trapped his brother into a gun battle he had never wanted.

Charlie Gant was seen no more in the Territory, and there had been that rumor that he had gone to Montana—but that had been several years ago.

Like it or not, Zeb Rawlings knew that he was tied to Charlie Gant as long as both of them lived, tied by the hatred and the frustration that was in Charlie.

And now Charlie was back, and Zeb Rawlings was taking his family to a lonely ranch, where he himself would for a time at least be the only hand.

He could expect Charlie to know that.

TWENTY-TWO

Zeb Rawlings looked across the table at Julie, then at Lilith. "I want an end to it, Lil. I don't want my boys growing up with that hanging over their heads. There's something driving Charlie Gant that won't rest."

"What about you?" Julie demanded. "What of you, Zeb Rawlings? He's leaving you alone now, he's left town. We can leave in a matter of minutes, but you won't go."

"I have something to do first," he said quietly. "I've got to do it, Julie."

"There's been times . . . the times you've hunted someone, gone for weeks, even months. Or the times you were hurt . . . like that summer you were left for dead up on Yellow Ridge. And you would have died if someone hadn't come along.

"I never complained, Zeb. I didn't say anything. It was your job, and you knew how to do it better than anything. But not this—this isn't your town."

"Julie . . ."

"No one's asked you to face Gant. It isn't your job to hunt him down. We could leave right now, but you won't.

"We could forget all this, Zeb. We could leave it all behind. We could go down to that ranch where the boys could grow up, free and clear of all this.

"The times are changing. Look down the street, you'll see only a few men wear guns any more, where eight out of ten used to. Lou Ramsey knows.

"Think, Zeb. Is it so important that you go after Gant? Is it?"

"Yes."

"Why? Because it's an old score you've never settled? Because he shot you once? Because you think you're leaving something unfinished? Is it your pride, Zeb?"

"I'm sorry, Julie."

"Zeb! What is it? I'm your wife! I'm Julie, remember? What about the time after we were married in Salt Lake when you worked on the Comstock? Remember the fire at the Yellow Jack and Crown Point when you worked for hours helping with the rescue? Wasn't I there? Was I anywhere but at the collar of the shaft, making coffee, ready with blankets when you came out of that hole? . . . Zeb? What is it?"

"It's Charlie Gant. I made the boys promise not to tell you. He said he would hunt us down, wherever we were . . . he hinted he'd strike at me through you, maybe through the boys. He said he'd find us . . . I can't leave that hanging, Julie. I could never ride away from the ranch thinking he might come while I'm gone. He's a coward, Julie, and being a coward he would strike at me any way he could . . . but he could only get at me through you.

"I think I know what he's planning, and if I do, I'll be doing the law a service."

Turning on his heel, he walked away from them and went out of the door.

"I guess there's nothing more pig-headed than a man with a sense of honor," Lilith said. "Cleve was the same way."

She put her hand over Julie's. "But you know as well as I do that this time he's right; and believe me, it's better this way."

A buckboard rattled by in the streets, trace chains jingling.

"At least," Lilith said, "you won't be waiting alone."

Linus came in suddenly. "Where'd pa go?"

"Out . . . he had some business to attend to."

"Is something wrong?" Prescott looked at his mother. "Is it that Charlie Gant? Pa's not afraid of him!"

"You can be sure of that," Lilith said. "Do you boys know any games?"

"You mean like tag?" Linus asked.

"Or musical chairs?" Prescott suggested.

"I mean like poker," Lilith said.

"Poker?"

"Let's go up to the room. Seems to me I've a deck of cards."

"But we never . . . ma wouldn't let us play cards."

"Part of your education," Lilith said brusquely. "A man's a fool to gamble, take that from me, who was married to a gambler. But you'd best know how, because there might come a time.

"Why, later on I'll even show you how the ones gamble who don't plan to gamble—I mean the ones that want to take the gamble out of cards and make it a sure thing. Cleve was a straight gambler, but he had to know how that was done so he wouldn't be cheated. I think there's nothing to cure a person of wanting to gamble like knowing how many ways you can be cheated.

"Now, you just sit down and let your Aunt Lilith show you something about sleeve hold-outs, bugs, slick aces, shiners, readers, and second deals.

"First thing to learn is percentages. Ninety-nine men out of a hundred, Linus, who play cards or shoot craps all their lives never know the correct odds. That's what gives an honest gambler an edge. If he knows the correct chances of filling a hand or making a point, he's got something going for him."

"Aunt Lilith," Julie protested, "do you think you should?"

"I surely do. Now you hush up, Julie, and let an old lady— my heavens, did I say that?—have her way for once.

"Most things in life are a gamble. Take mining . . . we made several fortunes out of mining, and put at least two of them right back in the ground trying to get more.

"Did I ever tell you where we got the last one? It was out of the first claim we ever had . . . left to me by a man I used to talk to once in a while, cheered him up, sort of. Well, he left me this claim, and Cleve and I went out there and found it all worked out, so we left it. Years later, when we were broke, Cleve got to thinking about it, and he remembered a formation out there that was just like it was in one of the best mines on the Comstock.

"When we first got that claim everybody was looking for

gold—gold was all they could think of, and there on the Comstock this black stuff kept getting in the way. Finally, a man investigated and found out that black stuff they had been cussing and throwing out was *silver!*

"Well, Cleve remembered that rock formation and he remembered there had been black stuff on that dump, so we went back. Spent our last on beans and salt pork and a little bit of flour.

"We worked it ourselves, worked to get enough ore out to ship. Cleve, he went back there and started digging out where he saw that formation, and he found a little powder left over from the old working, and used that.

"He used to throw the ore in the wheelbarrow and I'd wheel it out. I'd wheel fifty or sixty a day, and do what cooking and washing there was too . . . but we got out a good many tons of it and shipped it out. Sure enough, it was silver, and we'd made a big strike!

"Now, Linus, you look here. You hold the cards like this for a bottom deal, and you keep the top card out a bit over the edge of the pack, drawing it back as you take off the bottom card.

"One thing you've got to remember. A clever gambler never does anything fancy with a deck—that's for show-offs. It even helps to seem a little clumsy, like this . . ."

Zeb Rawlings walked down the wide space between the two rows of stalls in the livery barn. His wagon, loaded with household gear, had been left in front of one of the stalls. Going to it, he lifted the lid on a long, narrow box tied to the side of the wagon, and from it he took his rifle scabbard. He drew the Winchester from the scabbard and began feeding shells into the magazine.

Lou Ramsey came in the door behind him, and Zeb glanced around. "I'll take that rifle, Zeb," Ramsey said.

Zeb looked at him, but made no move to hand over the rifle; he simply slipped another cartridge into the magazine.

"Your pistol, too."

"Sorry, Lou, but I can't oblige."

Lou Ramsey pushed his coat back and placed his hand on the butt of his gun. With his other hand he reached toward Zeb.

Zeb indicated the hand on the pistol. "Thought you didn't use that any more."

"I'll use it if I have to. I'd rather you didn't make me use it."

"Lou," Zeb said quietly, "I'm going out of here, and I'm taking this rifle with me."

"To kill Gant."

"Maybe . . . and maybe I'll get killed. That's your idea of this, isn't it, Lou? That it's him or me, a personal thing. Well, it could become that. If I settled down with my family and he came hunting me . . . and he *will* come—he as much as told me so.

"Unless I can stop him now, stop him red-handed in the process of breaking the law. Then it will be up to the law to put him away for good. The *law*, Lou. But I haven't much chance without your help."

Lou drew his gun slowly. "Your rifle first." Just as he seemed about to hand it over, Zeb swung the rifle barrel with a quick gesture. It caught Lou on the side of the skull and he dropped as if shot.

Quickly, Zeb turned and went out of the stable.

The train was whistling for the station, and he wasted no time.

He knew what he had to do, and he knew just how difficult it would be to do alone. He bought his ticket and boarded the train as soon as it stopped. Hurriedly he found a seat and sank into it, putting a newspaper over his face, as if asleep.

If Lou came to soon enough he would stop him, and this time he could not evade him, nor would he resist him again. He thought too much of Lou, and understood his problems too well.

He waited, his mouth dry, listening to every sound within the car and on the platform outside. Every hurried step, every surreptitious movement made him positive that he had been discovered and that the next instant the paper would be pulled from his face.

Suddenly the cars jerked, the train chugged and spat steam, and the big drivers began to turn slowly. He heard running feet upon the platform and somebody swung onto the train. Zeb remained where he was, his face covered.

The wheels began to move faster; the train chug-chugged ahead, then picked up speed, the whistle blowing.

Not until the train was rolling fast did Zeb remove the newspaper and look around, searching for Ramsey, or for any of the men who rode with Charlie Gant.

For an hour at least the train would be crossing a wide plain, with only occasional cuts through the hills, and no place where it would slow up or where thieves would be likely to bring it to a stop.

Zeb took a cigar from his pocket and lighted it. This was the one luxury he allowed himself. He sat back in the seat and thought of the railroad that lay ahead. He had been over every foot of it, and one by one he checked off the possibilities.

Yet in the last analysis it mattered very little where they stopped the train. It would be a showdown there, regardless. However, it would, more than likely, be in the mountains.

The train, as usual, consisted of a locomotive and tender, a baggage-express car, one passenger coach, two flatcars, and a caboose. One flatcar was loaded with freshly cut logs, the other with rolls of barbed wire. On the car with the barbed wire was a donkey engine.

The conductor came along to take his ticket and Zeb looked up at him. "How many men back in that caboose?"

"Just one. The brakeman."

"Is he armed?"

"No reason to be."

The conductor glanced down at the badge on Zeb's vest. "You expecting trouble?"

Zeb Rawlings sat up. "Yes, I am. You know what you're carrying?"

"Of course."

"Well, too many others know, too."

"I don't want my passengers hurt."

"Neither do I, and there's no protection for them in this car."

"Behind the seats?" the conductor suggested.

Zeb looked his disgust. "Easy to see you've never been shot

at by a forty-four. A pistol bullet would go through the backs of four or five of those seats before it stopped. Maybe more."

He got to his feet and walked slowly through the car, glancing at each man to see if he recognized any of them. Of course, Gant might be working with men Zeb had never seen, as well as with those who had appeared at the station with him. Any one of the men on board might be one of the outlaws.

Taking his rifle, he went to the front of the car and then stepped over to the express car. The door was not locked, and he went in, to face a six-shooter held in the capable hand of Marshal Lou Ramsey. There was a bandage around his head. Zeb saw Stover, Clay and Sims behind him.

"I'm sorry, Lou."

"Well," Ramsey replied irritably, "it got me here, didn't it?"

TWENTY-THREE

C harlie Gant walked back to the horses, inspecting the hoofs of each one in turn. They were excellent horses, chosen carefully for speed and bottom, but principally for speed. The first dash in their escape would be important, for the more distance they could put between themselves and the actual crime, the better.

He had planned every detail of the holdup with infinite care, and the horses had been tested at doing what they must do. First a three-mile dash at top speed, then a half-mile at a trot, a half-mile at a walk, and then a short dash. The space for the walk was through a patch of woods and they would make separate trails, all within sight of each other, then a dash across the intervening stretch into another patch of woods.

An hour after the start of their escape they would come up to the other horses. The saddles they rode during that first part were all stolen ones, and would be abandoned with the stolen horses. Mounted on other horses, they would enter a creek and ride for slightly more than a mile. The creek had a sandy bottom, and there were no obstructions about which to worry. This course would cause the pursuit to lose time in finding the point at which they emerged, and when they did emerge it would be in a sandy wash where they left only indentations in

260

the sand but no tracks that could be defined. They would leave the wash at separate points to further confuse their trail. After three hours they would change horses again, this time taking time to switch saddles.

By noon of the day following the holdup they would be eating at a ranch over a hundred miles from the scene of the crime, and in another state, where friends were prepared to swear they had never left the area.

Over much of the distance they would travel there were few water holes—some of them known only to Gant and to a few Indians long since dead. Without knowledge of those water holes any pursuit must fail. At one point, where there were no water holes for some distance, he had made an emergency cache of water to tide them over.

The plan was fool-proof.

Now, seated near the tracks, Gant took them over the route once more to be sure each man understood. The plan was to stick together; but if they could not, if one man was cut off, he was to choose an alternative hide-out equally as well hidden.

Each of the five men he had selected for the holdup was a man wanted for a killing.

"If shooting starts," he instructed them now, "shoot to kill. If any man's mask slips, everyone within seeing range is to be killed."

"What about that guard?"

"His name is Clay, and he will be alone in the car. The end of the car next to the passenger car will have the door locked, but that next the tender will also be barred. The bar bracket on the end toward the passenger car has been broken and was not repaired. A bullet will smash the lock on the door and allow us to enter.

"Remember, now, when we reach the river we will make our crossing below Pyramid Canyon; and once on the other side we will cut the ferryboat adrift and let it go on down the river. But I believe we will have lost any pursuit long before that time."

"Sounds too good to be true," Jenks said admiringly. "I never did know a job planned so thorough."

"You ride with me," Gant replied shortly, "and they will all be planned that way."

He walked out of the tiny hollow in which they waited, to look again at the track. The barricade of logs and boulders would force the train to stop, and they could board easily.

Again he went over every step in his mind, trying to find a loophole he might have overlooked. There was none.

Jenks, Indian Charlie, Gyp Wells, and Ike Fillmore had all worked with him before. Only Lund was a new man, but he had more experience than any of the others. There was nothing to worry about there. So, then—why was he worried?

Zeb Rawlings.

The man was bad luck, the worst kind of bad luck; for every time their paths crossed, things turned sour. If for no other reason than that Rawlings was becoming an obsession, he must be killed.

But first his wife and children.

Rawlings must see them die, knowing he could do nothing about it. Thoughtfully, Gant considered the men with him. Only Lund and Indian Charlie would be apt to go along with him on that.

He spat bitterly. It angered him to think of how shocked he had been at the station when he had turned and seen Zeb Rawlings. He had no idea Rawlings was even in Arizona, for after the fight at Boggy Depot Gant had left Indian Territory and gone north, and for several months he had lived quietly, holding down a railroad job in Dakota.

Gant had been in Jimtown, a small place on the Northern Pacific, when Lund came to him with the story of the gold shipments. Jenks was waiting for him in Deadwood, and they had picked up Fillmore in Cheyenne on the way south.

Carefully, they had avoided all their old haunts, coming into Arizona from California, after arranging the rendezvous at a small ranch owned by the Indian. Nobody had seen them, nobody knew who they were; and then they had to run into Rawlings, of all people.

Gant lifted his eyes from the barricade and studied the bleak desert mountains opposite. It was through those mountains they would soon be riding, for half a mile down the tracks they would cross over and head into the hills.

Rawlings! Gant would never forget that day at Boggy Depot when Rawlings had stood there so calmly, shooting as if on a target range. Gant would have sworn that *nobody*—nobody at all—could outshoot his brother. Not Hardin, Hickok, Allison, or any of them.

He glanced at his watch now. It was time.

He walked back to the campfire. "Dowse that fire and mount up."

There was no need to discuss the holdup itself, for they had been through all of that. He turned on Fillmore. "Don't forget now, Frenchy, nail that caboose. If the brakeman gives you any lip, kill him!"

Far off, the train whistled.

They stepped into their saddles, checked their gear. Charlie Gant led the way down to the point where the barricade waited.

The cut was narrow, and they had built the barricade carefully to make it look like a slide off the side of the cut. Inspecting it again, Gant doubted if any casual glance would arouse suspicion.

He felt jumpy, but there was no occasion for worry. He had planned this better than any time before, and his jobs had a way of working out. Even Floyd had admitted nobody could plan a job better.

Floyd. . . .

Why think of him now? Suppose Charlie had stayed and shot it out with Rawlings then? Could he have saved Floyd if he had opened fire? He would never know.

Just the same, he wished Floyd was here now. He was the solid one, the stayer. Floyd was one man he could always count on.

But could Floyd count on you?

The question came to his mind unbidden, and he swore and jerked on the reins so that his horse reared. He quieted it down, but his mood remained savage.

He drew his pistol and checked the action and the loads. He looked back at the others. "Ready?" he asked.

Their replies came back to him. "Ready!" . . . "Sure!" . . . "I'll say!"

They were good men. Just the same, he wished Floyd was here.

The train whistled again, and he could hear that far-off rush of wheels that reminded him so much of the wind in the pines of a great forest. It was coming up the valley now, almost to the mountains.

It might have been better had he been further from a town; but still, they must clear the track before they could go on, and that would take time. And this position gave them a straight run across the valley. A hard run but a good one, and safe enough if they made it as he had planned.

He would bring this off, disappear for a few weeks, and then he would pay a visit to that ranch Rawlings was headed for. The thought gave him a savage pleasure.

At that moment the train whistled again.

He started his horse walking forward, and the rest followed.

Only three or four minutes now . . .

TWENTY-FOUR

I t was very still in the express car, and very hot. Zeb Rawlings stood his rifle between his knees and wiped his palms on his trousers. Waiting was hell. It always made a man jumpy.

He could feel it coming now, the dry mouth, the sick, empty feeling in the belly. This time it would be for keeps. One of them would die. Charlie Gant was like a mad dog that would bite and tear at anything in his lust to destroy. Take a brave man every time, Zeb thought—I'd fear a brave man less than a coward. The coward has no scruples.

Floyd Gant . . . there was a good man. An outlaw, but a good man with it all, a solid man. You knew where you stood with Floyd Gant.

They had fought Indians together, hunted from the same stand, slept under the same buffalo robe. You took what shelter you could get when those Panhandle winds were blowing.

Without Charlie to talk him into it, Floyd might never have become an outlaw, and with him it probably started as a lark more than anything serious. In those days a good many cowhands had rustled a few head to buy drinks or to see them through a hard winter.

Out on the buffalo range Zeb had shared a fire with Floyd Gant many a time, never friendly, exactly, yet not enemies, either. There had always been that unspoken rivalry that comes between two men of almost equal ability at anything; and out on the hunt Floyd was the best hunter, except for himself.

There was no telling about that, either, when you came to think of it. There was too much luck involved. Your aim might be perfect, you might have judged the wind right—and then the buffalo might lift his head, kick at a fly, or even shift his weight. A mere shifting of the weight from one fore-leg to the other could mean the difference sometimes between a shot through the heart or lungs and a bullet glancing off a shoulder bone or breaking a leg. And a bull with a broken leg might easily excite the herd so that you'd get no more shots.

If you kept the wind in your face or blowing from them toward you, and if you took your time, you could shoot buffalo from a stand . . . and shoot for hours, sometimes. They had never learned to fear a gun, and the booming sound meant nothing to them. But the smell of blood would make them restless and they would move off. Or a wounded buffalo threshing around would start them sometimes.

Zeb looked at the others. "Hot in here," he said.

Clay nodded. "Sure is. We have to keep her locked up."

"Where do you think?" Ramsey asked suddenly.

"This side of Kingman, I feel pretty sure."

"You think they'll run for the Hualapais?"

"No."

"Indian Charlie was with them—he's part Hualapai."

"No, I don't think so. Gant will do something different. He's too smart to do the usual."

The train whistled.

"There's a cut right ahead," Ramsey said thoughtfully. "And Boulder Spring is right back in the rocks, only a few miles off."

Clay got up and went to the front of the car. The train was veering around a slight curve that gave him a view of the track up ahead.

"Barricade!" he called. "There's a barricade up ahead!"

"We're slowing down," Stover yelled.

Dropping his rifle, Zeb jumped for the door and dashed

through it, scrambling over the tender to get to the cab of the locomotive.

"Don't stop!" he yelled.

"I can't plow through *that!*"

Zeb dropped from the tender to the floor of the cab. "Open her up!" he cried. "Wide open!"

"She'll jump the tracks!"

At the edge of the brush near the tracks, Charlie Gant stared unbelieving as the locomotive seemed to gather speed. The driver-wheels churned at the track. "Why, the damn fool!" he said aloud.

The train hit the barricade with a tremendous crash and rock, logs, and debris flew in every direction. The force of the impact knocked Zeb and the engineer in a heap on the cab floor. Only a quick grab at a hand-rail kept Zeb from falling out.

But the debris had been piled on top of the logs laid across the rails, and not between them, and it was thrown wide. The locomotive stayed on the tracks, but it was slowed almost to a halt by the impact. The jolt made the engineer lose his grasp on the throttle, perhaps slowing the speed at the same time.

"All *right!*" Gant yelled. *"Take 'em!"*

Bullets smacked against the cab and one of them struck the coal, spattering the cab with tiny fragments like a sudden burst of bird shot.

Zeb took careful aim. Gant was coming up the track, and he had a clear sight on his chest. Suddenly his hand was knocked up and his bullet went wild in the air.

"Don't be a fool, Zeb!" Ramsey said. "Let him get aboard! You want Gant; now's your chance to get him in the act!"

Zeb started to make an angry reply, then he realized Ramsey was right. After all, unless Gant was actually killed on the train there might always be some who would say that he had hidden behind his badge when he killed Gant.

"Listen!" Ramsey grabbed his arm. "They're getting on behind, and they have to cross those flatcars to get here. That's when we can get them!"

Scrambling over the coal car, they started back. Stover was waiting, with Clay and Sims, inside the express car, guns ready. Zeb and Ramsey went on into the vestibule of the passenger car, and started through.

A man grabbed Zeb's arm. "What's up? What happened up there?"

"Stay where you are," Zeb replied shortly. "There's a holdup."

A woman gasped, and several men started up. "Sit down!" Ramsey commanded. "And get down on the floor!"

The Indian, Lund, and Jenks were already in the caboose. Charlie Gant came up the steps and lunged through the back door.

"Did they all get on?"

"Gyp's on the wire car. Frenchy's picking up the horses."

"Good!" He turned sharply on the brakeman who stood back, white-faced and scared. "Hit that brake!"

"No use. It would just burn out with the engine going like this."

Gant struck viciously with the barrel of his pistol and the brakeman dropped as if shot. Holstering his pistol, Gant grabbed the wheel and spun it. The wheels screeched, but the train did not slow. Smoke poured up from the caboose hotbox.

"All right, load up your guns and let's go!" He looked ahead over the weaving flatcars. "It's a long way to that gold!"

With drawn guns they started forward, scrambling over the wire and the logs.

Zeb, Ramsey, and now Clay waited inside the passenger car, while the few passengers crouched close to the floor between the seats, as far forward in the coach as they could crowd. Some had suitcases and bedrolls stacked around them. A woman with two young children sat on the floor with her back against a seat-back, and facing the open seat upon which a two-foot-high bedroll had been placed.

Gant made his way over the wire car, falling a little behind to let Lund and Indian Charlie be the first through the door. Opening it, they lunged in, and were met by a blast of gunfire.

The Indian was knocked back against the wall of the car and he went down, his face twisted into a grimace of shock, surprise, and pain. Desperately he fired, working his gun like a cornered rattlesnake, striking at everything within sight.

Lund had seen the guns an instant before the fire opened and had dropped to the floor. Shooting up, his first bullet struck Clay, turning him halfway around. Clay tried to bring his gun to bear and Lund shot again, then lunged up to his feet. He found himself staring into the eyes of Zeb Rawlings.

Riddled with bullets, he fell back against the door, which gave way behind him and he tottered back into the vestibule.

"Rawlings!" he gasped at Gant. "Rawlings is in there!"

He swayed, and grabbed at the brake wheel, but fell over the rail. For an instant he clung, his white, blood-streaked face staring up, and then his fingers began to slip.

Gant stared back at him, his muscles frozen as he looked down into that bloody, horror-filled face, and then the fingers let go and Lund fell beneath the churning wheels of the train. A scream of mortal agony sounded, and then there was only the pound of the wheels.

Only a second had passed. Wheeling, Zeb's face showed in the doorway and Gant fired wildly, desperately, and then he leaped for the car.

He grabbed for a hold, felt his fingers slip on the rough bark of the logs, then dig in. With astonishment he saw a fingernail had torn loose and his finger was raw and bloody.

Suddenly panic swept through him. *Rawlings was here!* Rawlings would kill him! Frantically, he scrambled up the logs. Astride, he turned and shot back, emptying a gun into the door, then he slid down the logs and crawled toward the barbed-wire car.

In the doorway of the caboose Gyp Wells was firing to cover his retreat, but Gant, glancing back again, saw Zeb come through the door.

In a panic, Gant fired again; and then as he moved backward, he saw where a bullet had struck the cable that bound the logs, almost cutting it in two.

Somehow, somewhere he had discarded his empty gun and drawn the second one. He could hear Zeb coming, scrambling over the logs, and as he looked up, Gyp Wells ducked back for cover in the caboose. Putting the muzzle of his pistol down against the cable, Gant fired.

The wire cable, released from its tension, snapped past him like an angry whip. He dropped to the wire car and started scrambling over the bundles. His hands were ripped, his clothing torn by the fierce barbs, but he could think only of escape.

Desperately, he looked around again. Zeb was running along the top of the logs, and even as Gant looked they started to split apart, rolling toward the down side of the car as the train rounded a small curve. Right before his eyes, Zeb disappeared between the logs, and Gant felt a wild impulse to yell. With savage delight, he kept looking back over his shoulder as he scrambled over the wire.

The logs, still held by the wire cable that bound them at the other end, had opened like a fan, one of them almost dragging on the ground beside the speeding train.

Zeb had felt himself going, and he caught wildly at the rough surfaces of the logs as they spread under his feet; then as the front wire held, the logs stopped shifting.

The butt end of the trailing log fell between two boulders as the train started to round a bigger curve. It ripped loose with a terrific wrench, almost derailing the flatcar and pulling loose the coupling pin, which had been poorly seated.

The train plowed into the curve at high speed and logs spilled off the side. Zeb felt logs falling away from him, and as he was exposed a bullet tore a deep gouge in a log at his right. Rocking with the force of the falling logs, the coupling came loose, and the locomotive, followed by the express car and coach, went rolling on around the curve.

The flatcars and caboose slowed, almost stopped, and then slowly began to roll backward down the grade.

Zeb heard a wild shout behind him, then Ramsey yelling, "Stop the train! Back her up!"

Another bullet struck within inches of Zeb's face and he crouched low beside the log, shifting his gun to his left hand to expose himself as little as possible.

Suddenly, Gant saw his chance. Zeb Rawlings was trapped on the log car. Now, if ever, he could get him. Quickly, he scrambled to cover behind the donkey-engine. Lifting his gun, he waited, watching his chance.

Zeb was crouched among the fanned-out logs, with only partial protection. Gant was out there somewhere, on the caboose or the wire car, but he dared not lift his head to look. The flatcars and caboose were rolling back down the grade, but the grade would not last forever. With Gant back there, there was at least one other outlaw whom he'd seen leap back inside the caboose.

He waited, holding his gun, ready to chance a shot.

Suddenly he heard the train whistle more loudly, and a shot struck the donkey engine with a bang.

The train . . . it was backing up. Ramsey was bringing it back to help.

Behind the donkey engine, Gant waited. Slowly, his panic left him. There was still a chance. Even if he did not get the gold, he could get Rawlings, and within minutes they would be back where Frenchy Fillmore was holding the horses.

Incongruously, the thought came into his mind: How did a man named Isaac Fillmore come to be called *Frenchy?*

A bullet struck the donkey engine, then another. Gant chuckled. Let them try. Nothing could shoot through that engine, and all he had to do was wait. He would get his shot at Rawlings . . . and then he would get to the horses, and they'd be off and away.

Ramsey would have no horses, and by the time he got some Gant would be across the Colorado and headed into the desert where no one dared follow.

In his ears sounded a *clack-clackety-clack* of the wheels of the slowing cars. Now he would get his chance. The fear had gone, the panic had gone. Zeb Rawlings was a sitting duck.

Lou Ramsey stood in the passenger car and looked out. Beside him was Stover. Clay, nursing two bullet wounds, lay, half-sitting, in a seat behind him, still holding his gun and hoping for a shot.

Ramsey pointed at the donkey engine. Four parallel lines of rope held it to the flatcar. Lifting his pistol, he took careful aim and fired. One of the ropes parted. He fired again and cut a slice in another of the ropes.

Stover lifted his rifle and settled down for careful firing. Slowly, the two sections of the train drew together. Only a few yards separated them.

Zeb Rawlings tasted blood. Somehow he had split his lip in scrambling over the logs. He saw another of the logs go and shifted his pistol to his right hand. From his belt he extracted several shells and, holding back the loading gate, shoved them into the cylinders.

The flatcars had almost ceased to roll, and as they dipped around a shallow curve, a bullet parted the last rope and the donkey engine slid over the side of the car.

Gant saw himself caught in the open as Zeb reared up from behind a log. Gant fired quickly, desperately, then dropped to the roadbed beyond the car.

Zeb jumped, his leg giving way under him as Gant fired. He came up, and for an instant they faced each other beside the track.

For an instant only they stared across their guns at each other, and then both fired simultaneously. Zeb felt the shock of a bullet, but steadied himself and fired again.

Gant seemed to jerk, and then as his eyes met Zeb's over the gun, he turned and fled, leaping into the rocks, falling, rolling over. He scrambled among the rocks, and Zeb stalked him, and when Gant came up firing, Zeb fired again. Gant went down.

Coolly, Zeb ejected shells from his pistol and loaded up, standing bare-headed under the blazing sun. He smelled the acrid smell of powder smoke, tasted the blood in his mouth, felt the terrible weakness from his wounds begin to take over as the first shock of injury left him. He was hurt, he knew, badly hurt, but he had a job to do that must be done now.

He started forward and fell. Something was wrong with his leg. He caught hold of a boulder and held himself there an instant. Gant seemed to have disappeared.

No . . . there he was, off to the left.

Zeb Rawlings turned with great effort, felt a bullet splash rock near him, lifted his gun, and squeezed the trigger. The gun leaped in his hand, and he saw Gant's shirt flower with crimson.

Zeb hobbled a step nearer, and brought the gun up again.

Gant disappeared among the rocks, not twenty feet away. Zeb started forward again, and then everything seemed to blaze with a hot bright light, and he fell forward, striking the sand with his mouth open.

He tried to close his mouth, but it was half filled with sand.

He gripped his pistol and rolled over on his back, spitting sand. The blazing sun was on his face, in his eyes.

Suddenly a figure loomed over him. It was Charlie Gant, bloody, wild, desperate . . . but on his feet.

He looked down at Rawlings, and a queer light came into his eyes.

"Bad luck," he muttered. "You always were bad luck for me. Every time . . ."

His words trailed off, and Zeb Rawlings with a tremendous effort of will brought his gunhand around as Gant started to bring his gun up.

Rawlings pointed the gun up at Gant and fired and fired, and fired again.

He felt the gun blasting in his hand, rather than heard it, for there was a fast roaring in his ears. He felt something fall against him, and then his gun was empty and a terrible weight seemed pressing him down.

"Is he dead?" He heard someone ask the question, and someone else replied:

"I don't know . . . but Charlie Gant is."

TWENTY-FIVE

The wagon and the horse were standing in front of the hotel when Zeb Rawlings came downstairs. He walked very slowly, because he still felt shaky, but it was good to step outside into the early morning sun. He stood very still, just soaking the warmth into his body.

Aunt Lilith came down with Julie, both of them elegant in traveling costumes—Aunt Lilith in her tailored gray, and Julie in one made over from one of Lilith's. Zeb watched them with admiration. Two handsomer women a man never saw.

Julie stepped aside to hold the door open for Stover, who came out with Aunt Lil's trunk on his back. He lowered it carefully into the wagon bed, and pushed it along to a good spot, then returned for the rest of her luggage. Aunt Lil might be far from a girl, but men still put themselves out to do things for her.

"Thanks, Stover," Zeb said. "Nice of you to lend a hand."

"If you'd tried to handle that trunk," Stover said, "you'd probably have opened those wounds again."

"Why we leavin' so early, pa?" Linus asked.

"We've a long way to go, Linus, but we're making the best trip a man can ever make."

"How's that?"

"Why, we're going *home!* When you've lived without one as long as I have, son, you'll know what music there is in the word."

Zeb helped Julie to the wagon seat, and then Lilith. The boys scrambled in the back with their sister, close behind the seat on a pile of hay and blankets.

Zeb hesitated just a moment before stepping up into the wagon, and Julie affected not to notice. His wounds had left him drained of strength and weaker than he liked to admit, but once on the ranch, with plenty of sunshine, fresh air, and brown beans, he'd come out of it.

Zeb spoke to the horse and turned the wagon around in the street.

Stover lifted his hat. " 'Bye, folks! Come up your way, I'll sure enough drop in."

"You do that," Julie said.

The wagon rolled down the dusty street, past the sleeping buildings, and then began the long S curve of the trail out of town.

Sam moved ahead easily, undisturbed by the wagon behind him. At the brow of the hill Zeb drew rein to let Sam catch his wind, and looked back. Smoke trailed up from a few chimneys, and in front of the hotel there seemed to be some kind of confusion. Several riders were in the street, others gathering.

"Wonder what's going on down there?" he said thoughtfully. "Now, I—"

"Whatever it is," Julie said firmly, "it's none of our business!"

Zeb glanced back once more, then spoke to Sam and the horse started on, walking with easy strides.

Suddenly from behind there was a rush of horses' hoofs and Zeb, reaching for his Winchester, turned so sharply it brought a twinge to his face.

A good two dozen riders rushed up, surrounding the wagon. "Might have told us you were pullin' out," Ramsey said, smiling at him.

"What's the matter?"

"Why, folks around town figured you'd brought the only

excitement into town in months. You've given us something to celebrate, something to shout about! You wiped out the Charlie Gant gang and we're shut of outlaws, now, for a while, anyhow—You done it!"

"Now, just a minute, Lou! I didn't—"

"Brought you a present, Zeb. Something to take along. The boys took up a collection."

He took a rifle boot from his saddle, a new, hand-tooled leather boot, and from it he drew a Winchester '76, the action engraved and inlaid with gold. On it were the words, *Compliments of the Gold City Mining Company & Citizens*.

It was a beautiful firearm. Taking it, Zeb turned it over and over in his hands, lifted the butt to his shoulder.

"Thanks, boys," he said quietly. "Many thanks."

Long after the riders had turned back, the spell of their presence remained. "Does a man good," Zeb said finally.

"You're respected," Julie replied quietly. "We may not have much, but you're a respected man."

"How much farther to the ranch, pa?" Linus asked.

"The next bend and across the valley beyond. You just keep watching for it."

Linus started to hum the tune of "A Home in the Meadow," and Lilith, caught by the memory of it, began to sing with him, and the others joined in.

> *"Come! Come!* Through a wondrous land!
> For the hopeful heart!
> For the willing hand!"

Her voice rang loud, as old Zebulon's had back at the Erie Canal.

Zeb chuckled. "You boys will have to sing louder to keep up with your Aunt Lilith."

"I sang that song a good many years ago when leaving the Erie Canal . . . or leave *on* the Erie Canal, I should say. Folks all along the canal joined in."

> "Away, away, come away with me,
> Where the grass grows wild,

Where the winds blow free.
Away, away, come away with me,
And I'll build you a home in the meadow."

"Giddap, Sam," Zeb Rawlings said. "We're goin' home."